Miss Lavigne's
LITTLE
WHITE LIE

SAMANTHA GRACE

sourcebooks
casablanca

Published by Sourcebooks Casablanca, an imprint of Sourcebooks, Inc.
P.O. Box 4410, Naperville, Illinois 60567-4410
(630) 961-3900
FAX: (630) 961-2168
www.sourcebooks.com

Printed and bound in the United States of America
VP 10 9 8 7 6 5 4 3 2 1

*For Heather, my fellow Lady Scribe and dear friend.
You say there's just one thing I like about you, but
that's untrue. Why, the list has at least three items on
it. Okay, two and a half. (You know I'm teasing.)
Thanks for the late-night brainstorming, pep talks,
and virtual head-smacks. I can't imagine this journey
without you, nor would I want to. Much love!*

One

New Orleans
June 20, 1818

GRANDMAMMA HAD ALWAYS SAID NOTHING GOOD happened under the cloak of darkness. The witching hour was ripe with men practicing their evil. Therefore, it was with much trepidation that Lisette Lavigne huddled together with her younger brother and cousin in the shadowy gardens of Passebon House, praying the night would conceal their escape from the wickedest of men, her betrothed.

The coarse language of Louis Reynaud's men carried on the sluggish air. They made no attempt to hide their presence outside the gate of her father's Vieux Carré home, and hadn't since their arrival two days earlier. The men had even followed her on a shopping excursion to Rue Royale earlier in the day, confirming her suspicions. Her betrothed sensed she no longer wished to marry him, and he had no intentions of releasing her from their agreement.

Her brother shifted and whimpered softly. Hiding

in the gardens rather than being tucked into bed at this hour would disturb any child, but to one with Rafe's temperament, a fit of temper could ensue at any moment.

Their cousin, Serafine Vistoire, placed a comforting arm around his shoulders. "There, there, sweet child," she murmured. "Look for your stars."

Rafe rocked side to side as he searched the star-splattered sky, soothing himself, at least for the time being.

The deafening trill of cicadas pierced the night, their ever-rising call tweaking Lisette's taut nerves. She forced herself to slow her breathing.

"Where are they?" Lisette whispered. "Monsieur Baptiste said midnight."

Serafine nodded. The whites of her eyes stood out in the darkness.

What if they didn't come? The wedding was in two days. This would be their only chance to flee. Lisette's fingers tightened on her bombazine skirts until her knuckles ached.

"Good evening, *messieurs*." A throaty laugh floated on the heavy air, the call of a temptress. Relief flooded through Lisette. The distraction had arrived at last.

"*Sacre bleu!*" one of the men yelped. "Are ya seeing what I see?"

"Whores. Whatta they doing here?"

"Perfect night to take exercise," one of the women purred. "Wouldn't you agree, gents?"

Her companion chuckled, her voice heavy with seductive promise. "*Oui.* Two virile *messieurs* like you must take exercise often."

Reynaud's man uttered a combination of unspeakable

words that might have impressed Lisette under different circumstances, for he excelled at the art of vulgarity. She considered herself an expert, having developed an ear for inappropriate language while visiting Papa at the waterfront.

Rafe wiggled, his control nearing the limits.

Sweet Mary. This had best work, and quickly.

"Just for a bit? *S'il vous plaît.*"

"Damn," one of the guards muttered. "I'm gonna hate myself for this, but we can't leave our posts."

Really, the man's integrity was shocking. How did one go about locating such upstanding criminals?

"May I share a secret, mister?"

"I s'ppose. What kind of secret?"

"As your friend implied, a pair of whores do not happen by on a lark. Perhaps you should think of us as a reward for a job well done."

"Reynaud sent you?"

Lisette held her breath as she waited for the woman's response.

"Shh. 'Tis a secret, remember?"

Both men chuckled as if they couldn't believe their good fortune. And anyone with sense would know better. Lisette was barely acquainted with her betrothed, and yet she understood he did nothing that benefitted anyone aside from himself.

"Ain't no harm in exercise, right?"

"Splendid. This way, sir, where we may enjoy some privacy."

"What about here? In the garden."

Lisette froze like a rabbit that had spotted the family pet. If the women led them through the gate, she and her family would be discovered. Frantic, she searched for a place to retreat among the potted flowers and garden statues.

"Flowers make me sneeze, monsieur. But I know a better spot for amorous sport."

Their voices faded as they moved away from the house.

Lisette crept from their hiding place and slung the bag of their belongings over her shoulder. "We must go quickly."

Seeing no one else outside on the walk, she pushed open the gate and captured her brother's hand. Dressed in all black to blend with the night, they headed toward the wharf.

No one spoke as they crossed Rue de Chartres. Moss draped like gauze from the gnarled limbs of the trees as they drew closer to the river.

Rafe dragged on her arm, forcing Lisette to stop. "I want to go home."

She reassuringly squeezed his hand and urged him forward. "But we have a surprise for you, remember?"

"I want to go home."

Serafine tugged his other arm. "Not now, *ma biche*. We must hurry."

Rafe had maintained excellent control up to this point, donning black clothing despite his abhorrence of the color and kneeling in the garden where dirt might soil his hands. Expecting anything more from him seemed unfair, but they required his cooperation now more than ever.

Lisette crouched at his level. "Shall I reveal the surprise now? We are sailing on a ship."

"A ship?" A twinge of interest colored his voice.

"Yes, a majestic ship called the *Cecily*. We must sleep close to the port for we cannot miss our ship."

"Cannot miss the *Cecily*." Rafe resumed his measured strides. "Baltimore flyer, clipper, frigate, Indiaman." He recited the types of ships he knew with a note of excitement.

She had handled her brother without much difficulty this time. Now if only they could enter The Abyss without drawing notice. Reynaud had nefarious connections all over New Orleans, and hiding among the derelict of the city was a risky endeavor. What manner of man must the captain of the *Cecily* be to commune with petty thieves and cutthroats?

Lisette forced her concerns to the edges of her consciousness. Captain Hillary's ship was the *only* ship departing for England and provided the sole means of protecting her brother. Nothing would deter her when it came to keeping Rafe safe.

~&~

Captain Daniel Hillary loved two simple pleasures in life: a woman's supple curves beneath his body and his Indiaman with sails unfurled, forging through the ocean waves. But damn it to hell, women and the sea didn't mix, and based upon Paulina's determined eyes staring up at him, he was in for a row.

Why she chose to make her request *before* they had taken their pleasure was beyond him. They were still wearing their clothes, for the love of God.

He rolled off his handsome mistress and flopped to his back. "I don't allow women aboard the *Cecily*. End of discussion."

Paulina lifted to her elbow and frowned down at him. Her mussed chestnut hair made her appear as if she'd already been tumbled, increasing his discomfort. "That is untrue. What of the beautiful blond woman?"

"She's my brother's intended. I can't leave her in New Orleans." He reached for Paulina, but she jerked back. "I'll leave more money this time. You will never know I'm gone."

She leaned over to nip his earlobe then trailed kisses down his neck. This was more like it. "It—is—not—the—money—I—want." She spoke between pecks, unwilling to abandon the topic after all.

Daniel sighed. Paulina resided in luxury. She would not forfeit her comfort for weeks on a bloody ship, which meant she had another objective. He lifted her chin to look at him.

"Tell me what you want, and don't insult my intelligence by claiming you only want me."

He was aware of her other gentlemen benefactors, even if she believed herself discreet. His connections kept him abreast of the happenings in New Orleans, and the reports on Paulina's indiscretions could keep him occupied for the better part of a day. If he cared to listen.

She sat back on her haunches and pushed out her bottom lip. "Don't you want to be with me all the time?"

He linked his fingers behind his head. Paulina was a talented woman who knew how to please him, but he *didn't* want to be with her all the time. He didn't wish to be with any woman all the time, not after Cecily.

"I'm content with our arrangement." He didn't bother to tread lightly with her sensibilities.

As he expected, no hurt crossed Paulina's face, only irritation. "Very well, but I *would* like some security. You spend more time in England than here now. I don't enjoy your protection as I once did. Nor do you bring me beautiful trinkets as in the beginning. I am not getting any younger, Daniel. My beauty will fade and my prospects will dwindle. I need to know I won't end up in the streets."

He cocked a brow. "This isn't your attempt at proposing marriage, I hope."

"You mock me." She crawled toward the edge of the bed.

"Wait." Grasping her around the waist, he pulled her back.

Paulina had been an accommodating mistress these last two years. He supposed he could fulfill one of her wishes, if they could get on with other matters.

"Tell me what you really want, my dear, and dispatch with the theatrics."

She turned in his embrace, victory shining in the depths of her brown eyes. "There is a house I fancy. I wish you to purchase it in my name."

"A house?"

He glanced around the exquisite boudoir with the Turkish carpet, gilded mirrors, and silk curtains, all gifts he had given her. Not to mention that horrendous ruby amulet she draped around her neck, the fruits of her last sulk. It was a wonder she didn't walk hunched over from the weight.

When he had offered his protection, her home had

required an extensive remodeling. He could ascertain no good reason to fund a different residence. "There's nothing wrong with this one."

She scooted to the far edge of the bed out of his reach and crossed her arms. "It is too small. In fact, the lack of space troubles me to the point where I fear I cannot perform my duties this evening." She tossed a sultry look over her shoulder. "A simple promise from you, however, would ease my mind."

Her petulant behavior was growing tiresome. Too tiresome. They had been through similar pouts when he'd last visited.

"Very well," he conceded, "then we shall consider our affair settled."

Paulina's eyes widened. "Pardon? Settled in what way?"

He climbed from the bed and fastened his trousers, no longer interested in satisfying his lust with her. "My man of business will complete the transaction." He shrugged on his waistcoat before grabbing his boots and jacket. "Consider the house your severance. Your services are no longer required."

Paulina gaped, frozen to the spot on the bed. "But, Daniel. You cannot—oh, Daniel, don't, please." She burst into tears, burying her face in her hands.

He stood there in awkward silence while she sobbed. *Devil take it.* What was he to do now? After all, she might genuinely hold a *tendre* for him.

Daniel took a step forward, prepared to offer a retraction, but Paulina chose that moment to peek at him.

Her dry eyes sent a flood of indignation rattling through his veins. Was there a bloody woman alive who didn't use tears to advance her agenda?

"Do give my best to Anderson and Molyneux." Plopping his hat on his head, he spun on his heel and stalked from the premises with no intentions of ever looking back.

Two

LISETTE, RAFE, AND SERAFINE REACHED THE SAFETY OF the rented room above the tavern mere moments before a sharp rap sounded at the door. Lisette's heart jumped into her throat. Ruffians wouldn't bother knocking, would they?

There was another soft rap. "Mademoiselle, I have the *blanket* ye requested. Ye must take it now."

The feminine voice eased Lisette's fears only slightly. She looked toward Serafine as her cousin tucked Rafe into bed. He turned on his side and curled into a ball.

"One moment." Lisette searched the sparse room for a makeshift weapon. Snatching up the fire poker propped against the hearth, she returned to the door. "A blanket, you say?"

"Aye, madame. The one ye *requested*."

Whatever was she talking about? It was the middle of summer. No one in her right mind asked for blankets in this suffocating heat.

"You must be mistaken." She raised the iron bar overhead, prepared to defend her family if this was a ruse, and jerked the door open.

"Lord have mercy!" The tavern wench dropped the blanket and clutched her chest.

Lisette shoved her aside and looked both ways down the corridor with the poker at the ready. There were no hulking figures lurking in the shadows as she had feared. No threats of any kind.

"Forgive me. I didn't mean to startle you." Stepping back into the room, Lisette lowered the poker and grasped the young woman's arm before she could gather her wits to flee. She held out the implement with a bashful lift of her shoulders. "Perhaps you know how to build a fire?"

The young woman shrank back, refusing to take the poker. "It's the middle of summer, ma'am."

Now she wanted to take issue with the season. "Of course, you're right. What am I thinking?" Lisette pretended to knock some sense into her head. It was better to have the wench think her dotty than dangerous. "Please, come inside."

The woman narrowed her eyes and sidestepped into the room rather than turning her back. "Ye wanted to know when Captain Hillary was back. He's below stairs, but I can't promise how long he'll be there."

Lisette glanced down at her mourning attire. She had wished to change before their meeting. Well, there was no help for it. She couldn't afford to miss him or their departure on the morrow. Monsieur Baptiste met with the captain earlier and negotiated their fare, but Lisette had received no details from the meeting. With Reynaud's men guarding her and her family, Monsieur Baptiste must have determined the risk was too high to send a messenger.

Lisette followed the young woman into the corridor. At the landing, she pressed a coin into the wench's palm, reconsidered her rash behavior in the room, and offered her two more. "For your excellent service, mademoiselle."

The woman smiled. "Thank ye, ma'am."

It was the least Lisette could do. Employment might be in her future if they were unable to locate Serafine's brother in England. But she would work herself into an early grave if need be. Rafe would never be at Reynaud's mercy as long as she was still breathing.

"You must accompany me below and point out the captain," Lisette said.

The wench led her down the staircase. "He ain't easy to mistake, ma'am. He's the most handsome of the lot."

At the bottom of the staircase, Lisette retreated to the dim edges of the room and scanned the crowded tavern in bemusement. She and the tavern wench apparently had different definitions of handsome, for Lisette would never categorize any of the filthy patrons as pleasing to the eye.

A movement from the corner of the room caught her attention, and she turned just as a striking man pushed through the assembly of riffraff, parting the crowd like Moses parted the Red Sea. His wild, dark hair stuck up at angles, and his sculpted jaw boasted a deep flush.

The wench nudged Lisette. "There he is, ma'am."

"Oh," she said on a wisp of breath.

"I best be gettin' back to my duties." The woman slipped away before Lisette could respond.

Captain Hillary swaggered across the taproom,

headed for the stairwell. His languid movements reminded her of a feral cat on the prowl, an ill-tempered beast, if she read him correctly. His shirt gapped at the collar to reveal corded muscles for the entire room to view.

Mon dieu! Lowering her gaze to the sawdust-covered floor, she swallowed hard. It would be difficult to sit through an audience with the captain without gawking. Yet Captain Hillary and the *Cecily* presented her family's best chance for survival. She must determine their time of departure, and stammering like a school girl wouldn't help.

Determined to conclude their business quickly before anyone took notice of her, she strode forward to intercept him. "Captain Hillary."

His eyebrows shot upward as his gaze traveled over her body. "Have we been introduced, luv?"

There was no time to practice proper etiquette—if there even were such codes in a hovel like The Abyss—nor was there anyone present to perform the task of making an introduction.

"I am Lisette Lavigne." She suppressed a wince. She'd meant to use a false name, but a quick look around reassured her no one was eavesdropping. "You met my representative yesterday, Monsieur Baptiste. May I speak with you a moment?"

A fierce gleam in the captain's eyes prompted her to step back. "I'm retiring to my room, madame. Would you care to accompany me?"

"Your room?" Perhaps she had been too hasty to approach the captain alone. "Couldn't we conduct our business at a table, monsieur?"

"Do we *have* business to discuss?" Despite his acerbic tone, he sauntered to a vacant table and sprawled onto a rustic chair. He swept an arm to the place across from him. "Sit. I haven't much time to indulge you."

She slid into the seat opposite him. "*Merci*, Captain. Monsieur Baptiste spoke with you yesterday about carrying my family and me to England. Unfortunately, circumstances prevented him from relaying the details of the arrangements he made on our behalf. What is the fare you agreed upon? And I must know when you expect us to board."

"I don't."

Lisette blinked, not comprehending his reply although she spoke fluent English. "Pardon? You don't what, exactly?"

"I don't expect you to board. I've refused passage to you and your family."

"Refused us? But why? We have the funds to pay you." She touched the coin purse in her pocket. Money always opened doors. "I'm willing to pay handsomely." She plunked the pouch of coins on the table between them.

"Good God, woman. Put that away before someone liberates it from you."

"But—"

"Now!" He shoved the purse back at her with a scowl.

Lisette snatched the heavy bag and tucked it back into her skirts. Her hand fluttered to her chest before she folded both in her lap. Captain Hillary's brusque manner was unexpected, but she couldn't allow him to see her flustered. Dealing with men of his caliber required a tough veneer.

"Very well, Captain. I believe I made my point. I have the means to pay, and there will be a bonus when you deliver us safely to London." The addition of a bonus was rather inspired, in her opinion.

Captain Hillary leaned back, balancing the chair on two legs. His eyes looked black in the flickering light. The eyes of a devil. "As I mentioned to your man yesterday, madame, no women sail on the *Cecily*."

Lisette uttered a small cry of outrage despite her intention to remain calm. "That is ludicrous, monsieur. A lady's money is as good as any man's."

"I have no need for additional funds."

Of course he needed money. He was simply holding out for more. "*Merde*," she mumbled.

"Pardon?" A touch of amusement lingered in his rich voice.

She met his gaze, heat inching up her face with her rising temper. "Do not pretend you care nothing for money. What percentage does the owner allow you?"

"That's none of your concern."

"I am aware of how this business operates, monsieur. You assume the risk, yet walk away with a pittance. The fruits of *your*"—she jabbed her finger against the table—"labor line the pockets of the greedy owner."

"Indeed? Well, the greedy bugger who owns the *Cecily* might be offended by having his character maligned."

She waved a hand in the air. "I shan't likely make his acquaintance."

The front legs of Captain Hillary's chair banged against the floor. "Well, madame. I wish you luck in securing passage on another ship. The *Cecily* doesn't carry women passengers."

He pushed away from the table; freedom was slipping through her fingers.

"Please, sir." She grasped his forearm. "Name your price. I'll give you anything."

He pulled from her hold and sank back into his seat, smirking. "Anything? Take care what you promise."

"I can afford any price you propose."

Resting his forearms on the table, he raked his gaze from her head to her waist and back again. "Madame, are you a widow?"

She started in response to his unexpected inquiry. Her mourning attire could be misleading. Did the captain concern himself with procuring her husband's permission to travel? Lisette hesitated only a second before nodding.

"You're no innocent then," he said.

"By the saints! The nature of my, my past is none of *your* concern."

He shrugged as he settled against the seat back. "Neither is your dilemma my concern. How splendid we should go about our evenings, neither of us concerned for the other."

This was going horribly wrong, and she had little left at her disposal. Lifting her chin, she nailed him with the evil eye as Grandmamma had been wont to do. No field hand, house servant, nor tradesman had dared to defy Grandmamma when she unleashed the evil eye.

Captain Hillary chuckled. "Is everything all right, madame? Are you suffering from apoplexy?"

"Oh, you are a beastly man." She slapped her hands against the table and bolted from the chair. "I *will* locate another ship, Captain, and may *yours* go to the bottom of the sea."

Lisette marched across the room, retreating to a far corner to nurse her wounds. She hadn't reached her destination before the weight of what she'd done hit her. Not only had she failed in her endeavor to ensure their escape, she had flung curses at the only man who could help her. What would she do now?

The captain was still lounging at the table, looking at her, his expression unreadable. When her bottom lip trembled, she clamped her mouth closed and turned away. She would sooner walk through the gates of hell than cry in front of the scoundrel.

Madame Lavigne's attempt to recover from her outburst mesmerized Daniel. Her full breasts strained against the black silk of her widow's weeds as her chest rose then fell in rapid sequence. The woman had proven arrogant, believing she could change his mind by offering more blunt, as if he were a pauper. If she had compensated her representative as well, perhaps he would have taken care to discover Daniel *was* the owner of the *Cecily*.

The only factor nearly to sway Daniel's decision had been the delicate curve of her neck and an over-whelming desire to place his lips against her bronzed skin. Her exotic beauty beckoned to him, and he wanted to pluck her like a hibiscus blossom and sample her nectar.

Daniel snorted.

He had been listening to his brother's fiancée read

from Shakespeare every night for the last few weeks. Apparently, the bard had turned him into a sap. Daniel didn't employ ridiculous analogies when it came to shagging a wench. Ever. Yet somehow, his familiar crude language felt disrespectful in relation to the widow, even if she possessed a vulgar tongue herself.

Merde, indeed.

His gaze skimmed her diminutive waist and the flare of her hips. If her pleasing figure above her skirts piqued his interest, what lay underneath begged for his exploration.

He sighed and signaled for another tankard of ale, abandoning his plan to return to his room in favor of further observation of the lady.

The serving wench placed a tankard in front of him before weaving through the tables with two more clutched in her hand. He took a draft of the bitter malt, a perfect accompaniment to his bitter mood.

Paulina was responsible for his near blunder with Madame Lavigne. Had his blasted mistress—*former* mistress—satisfied his needs as she usually did before a long journey, he wouldn't have considered proposing the stunning widow compensate him in a less than proper way, which would have saddled him with the woman and her kin. Not that he would mind sharing pleasure with the lovely widow on the journey, but the fairer gender didn't belong on his ship.

In Daniel's experience, women possessed weaker constitutions, and sea travel often translated into a death sentence for the weak. Cecily's suffering had been more than he could bear. Her glassy blue eyes and deathly pallor still haunted his nightmares. He had enough worries in regards to his brother's intended surviving the return voyage without adding Madame Lavigne to his list of burdens.

He did find the lady's mettle fascinating, though. Men had often crumpled when faced with Daniel's... *determination*, he would call it. (He was not stubborn, and he refused to even entertain the ridiculous notion.) The beguiling widow held herself together admirably.

She wandered farther into the taproom as if she might approach some of the other patrons. Unfortunately, she had gained more than Daniel's notice. Through the crowd, two ruffians approached her, circling her like prey, while the lady appeared oblivious.

The burlier one approached her head on. From the ease of the man's posture, Daniel guessed the bugger offered a smile meant to disarm her while the second ne'er-do-well eased up behind, his toothless mouth gaping in the imitation of a grin.

Bloody hell. Daniel did so enjoy relieving others of their teeth.

Three

DANIEL'S CASUAL APPROACH BELIED HIS INTENTIONS. Madame Lavigne was a foolish wench. Boasting her worth in a pit of vipers, and no escort to boot. Lucky for her he had nothing better to do than save her pretty little arse.

Grasping her wrist, Daniel hauled her to him and tucked her against his side. "There you are, my dear. Shall we take our leave?"

The man whipped around to confront Daniel, but his gaze fixed on something to Daniel's left. More precisely, one eye listed to the left while his other focused on Daniel and the widow.

His weasel-faced accomplice eased up behind him. "Ever' thing all right, Kincaid?" He was too far away to strike without warning, but Daniel remained vigilant, even as he made a show of nuzzling the widow's neck.

"I told you to wait upstairs, luv."

Madame Lavigne ground her elbow between his ribs to leverage away. "Then release me, *darling*, and I shall go straightaway."

He ignored the dull pain and slanted a lecherous grin at the men. "She's an eager lass, if you catch my drift."

"I beg your—?" A tight squeeze cut off her sentence with a grunt.

"No need to beg, sweetheart. Come along."

Kincaid blocked their path as they tried to reach the staircase. His wild eye ogled Daniel. "How'd you like a *real* man between the sheets?"

"Are you speaking to me?" Daniel asked.

"No!" The man's face flushed red. "I ain't talkin' to you."

"Splendid. You're too ugly for my tastes. Now, move aside. The lady and I have private matters to discuss."

Kincaid refused to let them pass. "She's coming with us."

Daniel dropped his arm from the young woman's shoulders with a sigh. "My apologies, luv. I had hoped the situation might play out differently, but I suppose some things cannot be altered."

Kincaid wore a triumphant sneer. He thought Daniel was surrendering her. What an arrogant prick. And stupid.

Madame Lavigne glanced up at Daniel warily. Surely, she didn't believe he would hand her over to the miscreants.

"Run," he murmured.

"Pardon?"

"Run!" Daniel shoved her out of harm's way and slammed his fist into his adversary's cheek.

Howls of approval thundered in the small taproom. Daniel followed with another right to the jaw, feeling a crack under his knuckles, and then ploughed his fist into Kincaid's doughy gut.

"Oooffff!" He collapsed to his knees, clutching his middle.

Daniel ended with a powerful hammer, and the thug crumpled to the floor, unconscious and even uglier than when he'd entered the tavern.

"Damned fast work, Captain," someone shouted from the back of the taproom. No doubt one of his crew.

Daniel shook his right hand. "Blast it all! I've bruised my knuckles on his disgusting mug." He resumed a fighting stance and nodded at the smaller man. "Come on, then. The damage has already been done."

The man's raised fists quivered. Just as Daniel had suspected, his bravado failed him without a bigger bloke to hide behind.

"Oh, bloody hell," Daniel said. "You'll have to improve your form if you wish to fare better than your friend. Off with you before I beat some sense into you."

He faked a lunge to drive home his threat. The weasel snapped from his trance and dashed for the back exit. Daniel didn't bother giving chase. The coward would cause no more trouble.

Daniel frowned at his first mate, Patch Emerson, who was exchanging blunt with another crewman at a table. "You placed a wager against me?"

Patch shrugged. "I thought he'd last longer. Four hits? Figured him for six at least."

"Indeed? That many?" Daniel's pride was pacified. "Get him out of here."

"You heard the captain," Patch said to a couple of men below him in rank.

While his crew lugged Kincaid out back, Daniel searched for the widow. Where the hell had she gone? *Damn.*

"Madame Lavigne!"

The lady was a target for every type of thief. He should have been more alert to the other dangers in the taproom. Shoving through the crowd of noisome bodies, he barreled for the front door to search the docks, but black skirts sticking out from under a table drew him up short.

He chuckled, his tension receding. The poor chit was probably suffering the vapors under there. He sauntered to the table and crouched for a better view. Round-as-the-moon eyes stared back at him, but there wasn't a tear in sight.

"Lost your handkerchief under there, did you?"

He reached out to assist her from underneath the table. His fingers curled around her hand. It fit nicely with his.

Once she had regained her feet, she pulled away and brushed off her skirts. "Do you always draw such notice in public? I daresay subtlety would have been appreciated."

"You're welcome, Madame Lavigne."

"*Please,*" she hissed. "Lower your voice." Ducking her head, she tugged the brim of her bonnet low.

Daniel's gaze narrowed as he surveyed the taproom. Everyone had returned to drinking and appeared uninterested in either of them. "Where shall I escort you, madame?"

"We have a room above stairs, but I can find my own way."

He captured her hand and led her toward the stairwell, not caring if she could find her room alone. A woman like Madame Lavigne shouldn't be staying at The Abyss, much less paying a visit to the tavern. Something was amiss with the lady, and his responsibilities as a gentleman required him to lend assistance. He would consider his duty dispatched once he delivered her safely to her room, and he'd not give her another thought.

At the landing, she tried to break away, but Daniel maintained his hold. "Which room is yours?"

She pointed toward the end of the corridor. "But I don't need assistance. You've done enough."

"You were nearly abducted, madame. Don't tell me you have no need for assistance. Where is your escort, or are you without one?"

This time she jerked free and faced him, her chin lifting a notch. "My circumstances are none of your concern. Now, good night."

Stubborn chit.

Daniel followed as she backed toward the wall and braced his hands on either side of her to prevent her escape. "What exactly *are* your circumstances, madame? Are you in trouble?"

"If an overbearing captain detaining me against my will is considered trouble, then *oui*."

Her refusal to be honest made him all the more determined to get a straight answer. "Perhaps you're no widow at all, but a runaway. Who is looking for you?"

She rolled her eyes. "Good night, Captain." When she tried to duck under his arm, he caught her around the waist. Fire flared in her green eyes. "Release me. Our business has concluded."

He let her go but regretted it when she stormed down the corridor. "Perhaps I misunderstood our conversation below stairs, madame. I was under the impression you wanted me to carry you to England."

She halted mid-march and slowly turned back to him. "Are you reconsidering?"

The only thing he knew with certainty was he wasn't ready to end their encounter. He took a step in her direction. "You're desperate to leave New Orleans. Why?"

Her laugh was forced and lacked mirth. "I'm not desperate. I'm impatient to connect with a male relation in London."

"Lack of patience on your part doesn't sway me to allow you passage. Tell me the reason you were determined to be on the *Cecily* when she sets sail instead of waiting for another ship."

"I don't know how long my cousin intends to remain at his current lodgings. He is a visitor to London."

"Does he know you're coming?"

She pressed her lips together, her silence damning.

"He isn't expecting you?" Daniel frowned. The woman lacked sense in spades. "And if your kin isn't there? What do you propose to do then?"

She closed her eyes as if trying to sort her thoughts. She looked too blasted fragile standing like that in the dim corridor. Didn't she know not to lower her guard with anyone?

"My brother is but a boy," she said at last. "He requires the protection of his guardian, and since our cousin hasn't come to us, we must go to him."

Daniel moved closer, lightly taking her hand. What the hell was he doing? He should walk away now and forget about her. She, herself, had said she didn't require his assistance. But she had also proven herself to be a harebrained twit by wandering into the tavern.

"Do you know anyone else in England?"

She shook her head. "We have a letter of introduction and funds to rent rooms for a time." When she looked up at Daniel, her expression hardened. "But we *will* find him."

Or die trying. She had no need to add the words.

Daniel understood loyalty to family. He would give his own life for his siblings. Of course, his was a worthless life, so it would hardly be a sacrifice.

She sighed. "Have you reconsidered allowing our passage, Captain? Please, I must have an answer."

A whiff of her orange blossom perfume transported him to another time. Cecily had been laughing that day, such a rare sound from her. The Caribbean breeze had whipped off her bonnet, and he'd chased it into the surf. When she'd learned of his plans to take her to England, he'd never heard her laugh again.

Madame Lavigne waited for his answer, appearing to hold her breath. Odd that he didn't feel tormented by his guilt with her near. Something about the widow eased his conscience and offered him a momentary reprieve. For a man who had known little peace for five years, the temptation was strong to keep her with him—even on ship.

Daniel rubbed his forehead. Could he allow her to risk her life so he might have comfort?

"Please, monsieur. Upon my honor, I will pay whatever price you deem necessary."

"Do you promise you're in no trouble? My ship cannot be detained for harboring a fugitive."

"I am no fugitive." The slight tremor in her hands softened his demeanor. He couldn't believe he was going to do this, but there was no telling what scrape she might find herself in next if he refused his assistance.

"Very well, madame. You have my pledge to carry you to England. Arrive just after sunrise."

"Oh, monsieur." She swept forward and placed a quick kiss on his cheek. "*Merci*."

Instinctively, he folded her into his arms. She sagged against him. Her softness and sweet scent filled him with longing.

His mistress had been right about one thing earlier. Nights on the *Cecily* became lonely after a time. How many lonesome nights had Madame Lavigne suffered since losing her husband?

His mouth grazed her ear. "Perhaps we may find comfort in one another, my dear. I can be a sensitive lover when the situation calls for it."

She drew back with a soft gasp. "You want me to be your… *lover*?" This last word was whispered.

Her surprise pleased him. She was a widow and couldn't be ignorant to the ways of men and women, but she was not wanton either.

"The journey would be more pleasant for both of us, I believe. Would you be amenable to sharing my bed on occasion?"

She stood tall, her spine rigid. "If this is your requirement, I'm in no position to argue, am I?"

She darted into her room and closed the door before he could respond.

"My *requirement*?" Well hell. They'd have to clear up that little misunderstanding as soon as possible. He liked his widows willing or not at all.

Four

LISETTE'S HEAD SPUN AS SHE SLIPPED INTO THE ROOM she shared with Serafine and Rafe. *Sweet Mary*. Had she just entered into an agreement with Captain Hillary to be his companion in exchange for passage? She paused inside the door, wavering between running after him to deliver a proper set-down for his lewd suggestion now or waiting until morning.

Serafine bolted from her seat beside the bed. "Where have you been? I've been fretting for the last half hour."

Lisette pulled the pins from her hat as she swept to the dry sink to avoid meeting her cousin's gaze. "I was engaged in negotiations with Captain Hillary."

"Didn't Monsieur Baptiste take care of everything?"

Lisette tossed the hat beside the washbasin then filled the bowl with water. "Apparently there were some final details he didn't settle with the captain. We are to arrive at the docks at dawn."

"Early is better." Serafine's hushed voice was filled with relief. "Now if we can only stay hidden from Reynaud."

Lisette grimaced before scooping water with her

hands and splashing it over her heated face. Patting her skin dry with a towel, she contemplated how much she should reveal to Serafine about her dealings with the captain. "There is a chance my presence in the tavern did not go unnoticed."

"Indeed?" Serafine fanned her face, her nutmeg skin glistening from the sticky heat.

"It's nothing." Lisette carried a wet cloth to her cousin.

"*Merci*." Serafine wiped away the perspiration then held the cloth against her neck.

Lisette and Serafine shared little in the way of family resemblance, aside from their green eyes, despite their mothers being sisters. Serafine had inherited the high cheekbones and regal bearing of their West Indies ancestors, leaving Lisette feeling less intriguing with her rounded features and *café au lait* complexion.

"I suggest we sleep while we are able," Lisette said.

Serafine crossed to the door and turned the lock, which Lisette had neglected to do in her haste to avoid questions about Captain Hillary. "I shall sleep with one eye and ear open," Serafine said.

"As will I. Together we provide a set of both." That summed up their relationship. They were a pair, and had been since Serafine had come to live at Passebon House after Rafe's birth.

They crawled into the small bed with Rafe cradled between them, under the guise of catching rest. Lisette lay in the dark a long time, assessing every creak and bump in the inn. All she could think on was her agreement with Captain Hillary, and whether she could retract her promise without jeopardizing their passage. When she did succumb to the land of dreams, images of Reynaud's rage-filled face woke her with a start.

She abandoned all pretenses of sleep when the robins outside began their wake-up chorus. She tried to memorize the sound of their carefree warbling to recall in the days to come, heaviness settling over her heart. She suffered under no delusions they would ever see Passebon House or New Orleans again. Serafine's measured breaths contrasted with Rafe's soft snores, alerting Lisette that she too was unable to sleep.

"Will we be safe with Captain Hillary?" Lisette whispered into the darkness.

"My readings are never wrong, *ma chère*. We'll live through the journey and survive in London. But you must do exactly as I tell you."

Lisette clutched the thin sheet and suppressed a sigh. Perhaps Serafine placed too much faith in her readings. She hadn't seen the captain nor did she know of his price to carry them to London.

Climbing from bed, Lisette lit a candle. Rafe didn't stir. He looked so peaceful in sleep, like any other little boy. Sometimes her love for him filled her so full, it had to escape through tears or rip her apart. She brushed the wetness from her cheeks and turned away. "I'll seek out nourishment."

No one was below stairs save the innkeeper, but he promised to send someone with food and fresh water at once. A while later, the young woman from the previous night arrived with bowls of rice, milk, and sugar. Her sleep-swollen eyes attested to the fact she had been abed still. Lisette paid her well then secured the door behind her.

While Serafine roused Rafe from sleep and helped him change his clothes, Lisette freshened up in the washbasin and donned her black mourning gown again.

Serafine wrinkled her nose. "Why are you wearing that old rag?"

"I'm afraid the captain made certain assumptions based on my attire last night. He believes I'm a widow."

"Indeed? And why didn't you correct his mistake?"

"It seemed easier than trying to explain Reynaud."

She had come to a decision while below stairs. Rafe must be kept safe, and that meant escaping New Orleans before Reynaud found them. Since her body seemed her only valuable asset with which to barter with Captain Hillary, she couldn't assume the risk of revealing the truth until they had traveled too far to turn back. She only hoped he would forgive her for deceiving him once she explained his mistake and renegotiated their terms.

❧

Daniel stared at the navigational charts and ship's log spread on his desk. He had been at his task for over an hour, but he'd accomplished little. His mind kept drifting to the beautiful Madame Lavigne.

The click of the great cabin door alerted him to the presence of an interloper. Only one person would dare to enter his quarters without knocking. His younger brother, Jake, stormed through his office door and slammed it.

Daniel smirked. Jake had a temper when riled, and usually Daniel was the one to goad him, but not today. Jake's fiancée was putting him through his paces, teasing him shamelessly. Pity Daniel's brother didn't know of the arrangements Amelia had made for their wedding on ship that evening, but she wished to surprise him. No question Jake would be pleased, and less surly if everyone was lucky.

"Where's your better half?" Daniel asked.

Jake issued a low growl as he snatched the cork from Daniel's bottle of rum sitting on the edge of his desk. "Greeting the passengers."

He didn't comment on his brother's early morning indulgence. Jake likely needed something to take the edge off.

He poured a healthy dose of alcohol into a tumbler and sipped, studying Daniel over the rim of the glass. "You've granted a lady and her child passage on the *Cecily*?"

"She's here?"

"If you refer to a female dressed in all black and a raven-haired slip of a boy at her side, then yes, they've arrived."

Madame Lavigne was earlier than Daniel had expected. Never had he met a punctual woman.

He shoved from the table and hurried to the door. "I should see the passengers to their quarters."

Jake grumbled a reply.

Daniel spied the lady at once engaged in conversation with Amelia on the main deck. His future sister-in-law was chattering nonstop and gesturing with her hands. Obviously, she had missed the company of other women on the journey to New Orleans, but based on Madame Lavigne's wary expression, Amelia might continue to suffer a lack of female companionship. Not so for Daniel. His smile grew wider.

A frail lad held the lady's hand, watching the goings-on around them with rounded eyes. When the boy moved from her side and wandered toward the railing, a willowy young woman dressed in white stepped from behind a stack of crates and followed.

Daniel's gut lurched. Madame Lavigne had mentioned nothing about traveling with another *lady*. His concerns were now tripled with three women to see safely across the sea. Not to mention a boy who could be swept away by a gust of wind.

What had Daniel been thinking last night to agree to such foolishness? He *hadn't* been thinking, and that was where his troubles lay. Madame Lavigne had a way of muddling his mind.

He headed down the steps to greet his new passengers. Madame Lavigne glanced in his direction as he approached, the corners of her pink lips curving up when she spotted him. He faltered in his step, an odd tightness in his chest making it difficult to breathe.

"Captain Hillary, I cannot thank you enough. How long does it usually take to clear the river? Will we reach the sea before nightfall?"

"You never mentioned you're traveling with another lady." His tone was sharper than he'd intended.

"Oh?" Wariness replaced her friendly expression. A breeze lifted the veil of her hat, revealing her delicate features and the elegant slant of her brows. Her golden-brown skin shimmered in the morning sunlight and an insane urge to caress her rounded cheek hit him with the force of a gale wind. Perspiration dampened his shirt as his heart raced.

"I am sorry, monsieur." Her lilting voice was too

pleasing to his ear, increasing his agitation. "I didn't think the information to be of great importance given you had already agreed to allow one lady passage."

Devil take it. Females didn't affect him this way. He didn't care for it one bit.

"I'll decide what's important," he snapped.

"Daniel." Amelia's scandalized response did nothing to stall his attack.

He jabbed a finger toward the widow. "Withhold any further information from me, and I'll toss you off my ship in a heartbeat. Do I make myself clear?"

All three women gawked at him. Madame Lavigne's cheeks flushed with color, but she nodded. "Of course, Captain. I mentioned I'm traveling with my family."

Amelia patted his arm. "Mademoiselle Serafine Vistoire is a first cousin, Daniel. She and Madame Lavigne are like sisters."

The graceful Mademoiselle Vistoire stood a foot taller than her companion, and her features seemed severe in contrast to the widow's softness. Her eyes, however, blazed with the same green intensity he'd seen in Madame Lavigne's gaze last night, verifying their claim to kinship.

"And I will not hold my tongue while you upbraid my dear Lisette." Mademoiselle Vistoire spoke with a similar Creole accent.

Bloody hell. What had come over him? Madame Lavigne would want nothing to do with him if he behaved like a brute, and he was beginning to think of nothing aside from taking her to his bed and breaking the hold she had over him.

He offered a contrite grin before sweeping a low

bow. "Please accept my apologies, ladies. I forgot myself. Perhaps you'll allow me to make amends over dinner this evening in my cabin."

He glanced to Madame Lavigne for confirmation. Her grim expression didn't alter, but she gave a sharp nod.

"Splendid." Daniel captured Mademoiselle Vistoire's hand and placed a kiss on her pristine glove. "Until then, I bid you farewell, ladies." Madame Lavigne scowled when he didn't offer her the same courtesy.

It seemed she was not indifferent to him after all, which lifted his spirits a bit. Tonight they must clear up a few matters, then he would ascertain how closely their desires aligned.

Five

A LONE GENTLEMAN SAT AT CAPTAIN HILLARY'S TABLE drinking a glass of wine when Lisette and her family entered the ship's great cabin at the dinner hour.

"Are we too early?" she asked.

"All present and accounted for, all but the captain." The man stood as she and Serafine approached with Rafe between them. "I'm Mr. Ramsey, vicar of Trinity Church in Dunstable."

Lisette returned his greeting and introduced her family.

"Madame. Mademoiselle." Mr. Ramsey snatched his wine, raised the half-empty glass in salute, and drained it.

Her gaze flicked toward the main door, hoping she had misunderstood the vicar. She had been counting on the captain's kin to provide a buffer between them this evening. "There was a young woman, Amelia, on deck earlier. Won't she be joining us?"

"My brother and his wife are dining alone this evening."

She jumped at the sound of Captain Hillary's voice and found him braced against a second doorway. His intense and stealthy observation sent a shiver along her spine. How long had he been standing there?

He nodded in greeting as he entered the cabin. Dressed in a tailored coat of black, an ivory waistcoat with gold embroidery, and fitted black trousers, he resembled a gentleman of means. He was dashing to say the least, but fancy attire couldn't disguise the edge of danger he possessed, the one she had witnessed at The Abyss. The air around him sparked with tense energy, affecting everyone around him.

Affecting *her*.

She intertwined her fingers and hugged her hands against her chest.

Captain Hillary flashed a crooked smile, one dimple piercing his left cheek. "I see everyone has made each other's acquaintance. Ladies. Master Rafe. It's a pleasure to dine with you this evening."

"Likewise, Captain." The captain's inclusion of her brother in his address pleased her, and she dropped her hands to her sides. Most people ignored her brother as the vicar had. Perhaps it was easier than confronting his peculiarities.

Rafe reached for Lisette's hand, rocking back and forth, gazing at the quarters with an unfocused stare.

Captain Hillary swept a hand toward the table. "Shall we?"

He pulled out Lisette's chair then assisted Serafine to her seat. In addition to donning proper attire, he had borrowed some manners since their earlier encounter. She could almost mistake him for a gentleman.

"Thank you," Lisette muttered.

Rounding the table, Captain Hillary assumed the

seat across from her and cocked a wary eyebrow when Monsieur Ramsey motioned for more wine. The captain refilled the vicar's glass with a slight grimace.

Monsieur Ramsey gulped half the crimson liquid, sighed, then launched into an insipid tale of his devotion to his great-uncle, who had passed away within the last month. It seemed the wine loosened his lips so much, words spilled from his mouth. "To think, I traveled all that distance from England, risking my own life, to handle his affairs. And blast it if the curmudgeon didn't bequeath every possession he had to the nuns."

A saccharine smile plastered Serafine's face. "I can only imagine how honored you must feel, for surely your selfless actions in caring for your kin inspired his charitable gift."

The vicar recoiled. "Indeed, mademoiselle? I hadn't considered that possibility." His shoulders drooped, and he stared into his goblet as he swirled his wine. "'Tis true then. No good deed shall go unpunished and all."

Captain Hillary hid a smirk with a swipe of his napkin, but amusement glimmered in his eyes when he met Lisette's gaze.

Rafe wiggled on the chair between her and Serafine, having eaten the only thing on his plate he liked, the bread. And then only the soft middle. His boiled fish and summer squash remained untouched.

Lisette exchanged his crust for her untouched piece and worried her bottom lip. Rafe was particular about what he ate. Unlike other children, he wouldn't eat just anything handed to him if he became hungry enough. He limited his consumption to four foods—bread, rice, milk, and sweets, particularly rice pudding. Yet, the accidental inclusion of a plumped-up raisin in his dish could send him into hysterics. This would not be an easy journey for any of them, she feared.

Lisette had taken rice and flour from the larder at Passebon House, but there hadn't been much room in the sack, and it had grown heavy. She didn't know how long the supplies would last. In fact, she had no idea how long the voyage would take, much less how to determine if she carried enough staples. Tomorrow she must find the galley and speak with the cook. Perhaps she could bribe him to ration the foods Rafe required for survival.

She glanced up and discovered Captain Hillary studying her brother digging his fingers into the bread. The captain frowned but held his tongue. When her brother finished eating the middle from her bread, Captain Hillary reached across the table to place his serving on Rafe's plate.

Rafe's head popped up, but he didn't look directly at anyone. "The *Cecily* is an Indiaman, a three-masted ship carrying three square sails on the fore and mainmasts. The mizzenmast has one square sail and a fore-and-aft sail."

Captain Hillary's brows lifted. "Indeed. You're observant, Master Rafe. I believe you could replace my first mate. Perhaps you can make his acquaintance on the morrow and offer your assistance."

Rafe sat on his hands, rocking, his eyes trained to his plate again. "A Baltimore flyer is a schooner. She has a narrow hull and is faster. She could overtake the *Cecily*."

Lisette and Serafine exchanged a startled look. Lisette's betrothed owned a ship. Rafe had toured the vessel once when Reynaud was courting her. She couldn't recall the ship's class, but Rafe wouldn't forget. Surely her brother didn't fear Reynaud would pursue them, not for her meager dowry or Rafe's modest inheritance. Such an undertaking would be insane.

Lisette patted her brother's knee as much to comfort herself as him. "I'm certain Captain Hillary knows all about dealing with overzealous Baltimore flyers. You needn't trouble yourself."

Rafe looked to Captain Hillary as if seeking reassurance, his large amber eyes so like their father's, minus their sire's spark of life.

The captain glanced between Lisette and her brother, his thick brows lowered. "As your sister says, Master Rafe, you needn't concern yourself. Schooners know to use caution around an armed ship."

"Thirty-two guns," Rafe supplied with a wan smile. His response to the captain was unprecedented.

"Perhaps you would accompany me on a tour of the ship on the morrow to ensure all is operating as it should."

Her brother tore off a piece of soft bread and didn't answer. His connection to the man was severed so abruptly, Lisette wondered if her imagination had fooled her.

Serafine squared her shoulders. "Rafe possesses much knowledge on constellations as well as ships, Captain. Perhaps he will discuss his interest with you." Her regal posture served as a testament to her pride. "He is a brilliant young man."

"I can see he's unlike other boys his age."

Lisette and Serafine, who had been surrogate mothers to Rafe since his birth, shot glares in the captain's direction, but he was looking at Rafe. His expression softened.

"He's more intelligent than the average boy." Captain Hillary rested his elbow on the seat back as he lounged on the unpadded chair. His relaxed demeanor chased away Lisette's fears. Rafe's differences were evident to the captain, but he wasn't passing judgment.

Rafe began to squirm before Lisette finished her meal, but there was nothing to be done for it. With the disruption to his routine and lack of adequate sleep, his restlessness could quickly transform into a tantrum unless immediate action was taken. She and Serafine stood.

"I hope you will excuse us, gentlemen," Serafine said. "It's time to put this young man to bed."

The captain pushed from the table as Lisette took her brother's hand. "It has been a long day for Master Rafe, I'm sure."

Lisette smiled. "Thank you for understanding, sir."

As they shuffled toward the cabin door, Captain Hillary cleared his throat. "Could you spare a moment, Madame Lavigne? We failed to settle your account last evening."

Lisette flinched. She had hoped to be farther away before she had to tell him she wasn't a widow and preferred another method of payment.

Serafine placed her arm around Rafe's shoulders. "I will ready him for bed while you conclude our dealings with the captain."

Lisette nodded, her heart hammering.

But then she recalled the clergyman's presence and her apprehension melted away. Captain Hillary couldn't demand his outrageous payment with a religious man bearing witness.

"Perhaps we should postpone—"

Oh, Sweet Mary.

The captain was lugging the vicar from his seat. "How nice of you to join us for dinner, Mr. Ramsey."

"But I haven't finished my wine."

Captain Hillary snatched the bottle from the table and pressed it into the vicar's hands. "Take it to your quarters. I insist."

Monsieur Ramsey's protests ceased. He accepted the gift and rushed out the door as if fearful it would hit his backside if he moved too slowly.

Alone, Captain Hillary once again resembled the scoundrel from the tavern. "This way, madame."

She hesitated before following him into a cabin located in the stern of the ship. Lisette assessed her surroundings to calm her nerves, as if taking inventory might delay the inevitable.

Merde. It was a short list. The captain was much too tidy for a man.

The only features of interest were the windows running along the back of the space, but there was nothing but blackness outside. The silence became an entity unto itself, an intolerable creature.

"Why did we stop? Won't this delay our arrival?"

"We'll raise anchor at daybreak. It's dangerous to travel the river at night."

He sank into a chair behind his desk, which was secured to the deck with ropes and two iron rings.

His furniture was as immovable as he was. Resting his elbows on the desk, he formed a steeple with his fingers and regarded her with unrelenting, dark blue eyes.

Lisette squeezed her fingers harder and broke into a light sweat. "Captain Hillary—"

"Call me Daniel. And I shall take the liberty of referring to you as Lisette."

She issued an outraged gasp. "I will *not*. It's highly improper."

How ludicrous to argue the proper forms of address after the agreement she had made with him last night, but she needed to maintain some illusion of control.

He winked. "By the end of this journey, I hope our intimacy will extend beyond a first-name basis, my dear. I endeavor to move things along. I'm sure you will forgive my impatience."

"I see." She frowned, not sure she would forgive him anything. Gripping the back of a wooden chair, she steadied herself when the ship rocked and she almost lost her footing. "May I sit?"

"No."

"I beg your pardon?" Really, the man was a complete cur.

"You neglected to tell me everything last night, madame. What ailment plagues your brother?"

She huffed. "This is absurd. I won't stand while you interrogate me." She rounded the chair and plopped on the seat, defying him to stop her.

A corner of his mouth kicked up before his expression hardened again. "Answer me, so we may commence our business before daybreak."

She didn't want to rush things along, given his

uncouth behavior, but since they hadn't cleared the great river yet, she didn't dare push him too far. It was conceivable he might leave them along the overgrown bank for the alligators.

"I'm waiting, madame."

"Raf—my brother was born different. *Special*."

"Continue."

She lifted her chin, tiring of the captain's curt manner. "He spends much time in his thoughts and keeps his own counsel. He's a brilliant young boy, as Serafine indicated. He holds vast knowledge on the constellations from perusing books he was never taught to read."

"He has had no schooling?"

"New Orleans is not England. Young boys don't leave their families to attend school. Our father hired a tutor, but Rafe never did well with formal instruction. Papa allowed him to follow his own path." She sighed and wilted against the chair; lack of sleep made her weary. "I don't know if Papa did the right thing, but Rafe was miserable. He has peculiar ways about him, and I'm uncertain how to undo his habits."

"He doesn't eat properly."

Lisette's gaze shot up, expecting to see censorship, but the captain merely stated fact. "He only eats certain foods, I'm afraid."

Captain Hillary pushed a sheet of foolscap and a pot of ink across the desk. "Create a list of what he eats. I'll do my best to make certain our supplies last. It would have been easier if you had told me everything last night, before we left port. But we'll dock in Port Albis and resupply."

She blinked, unsure of what to make of their destination. What if he planned to leave them in the Caribbean? Not everyone understood or tolerated Rafe's differences. "Do you alter your course for us?"

"You and your family are my responsibility now. I'll not have your brother starving on the voyage."

Lisette didn't know what to say, so she turned her attention to scribbling the short list of foods Rafe liked. She eased the paper across the captain's desk. "I shall pay you more for your trouble, sir."

He grinned, putting the devil to shame with the wicked gleam in his eye. "Yes, about your payment…" Crooking a finger, he motioned her to come to him.

She gripped the bottom of the chair to hide her fit of nerves.

His brows lifted as if surprised anyone would disobey him. "Come here, Lisette."

If only her welfare was at stake, she might test the limits of his patience, but she couldn't chance the captain returning them to New Orleans. Perhaps she could appease him for the moment to buy more time without compromising herself fully.

Drawing a shaky breath, she rose from the chair and walked around the desk. Captain Hillary's hands encircled her waist.

"Oh!" She jerked back and bumped the desk.

"Careful, sweetheart." He lifted her to perch on the desk in front of him. His hands rested on her hips, and he stood where she had to roll her head back to see him.

"We never discussed the price of fare to England." His warm breath wisped across her forehead and sent her heart into a mad dash. She squirmed to create distance between them, but his heat still warmed her and made her palms moist. "Twelve pounds apiece."

"Twelve pounds?"

The corners of his eyes crinkled with his smile. "This is my usual fare for passengers. Do you take issue with the amount?"

"No!" *By the saints, no.* "The price sounds reasonable, but I thought—" She snapped her mouth closed. She should be quiet and count her blessings he wasn't demanding something she was unprepared to pay.

"Yes, my dear? You have something to add?"

She shook her head. "No, twelve pounds it is. *Merci.*"

Captain Hillary's smile spread as he leaned closer. Lisette's heart couldn't beat faster if she attempted to swim across the Mississippi. "As to the matter of comforting one another on the voyage, I shall leave that up to your discretion, of course. That is all I wished to discuss. Are we in agreement?"

So he still wanted to bed her, but he would allow her to decide when. That seemed fair-minded of him, but her conscience suffered a bit. She couldn't possibly give him her innocence, so the day would never come.

His spicy scent wrapped around her, setting her thoughts awhirl. Her gaze landed on his lips colored like watermelon flesh. They looked sweet. Perhaps kissing him wouldn't be a horrible thing.

She had never kissed a man, unless she counted Reynaud's dispassionate pecks on her cheek at the conclusion of their outings. While she had endured his shows of affection, she'd never pondered what it must be like to taste him.

The tip of the captain's finger brushed the rim of her ear, sending pleasurable shudders chasing down her back. "You seem timid, luv. Could it be amorous rites were less than satisfying in your marriage?"

Lisette's body flamed. Men and women didn't discuss such topics, did they? "I didn't come here to discuss my past."

"Why are you here?"

"I'm not certain." She could have left the moment they had settled on a price, but she felt rooted to the desk. Her tongue swept across her dry lips.

Her breathing ceased when his mouth found hers. He did nothing more threatening than press his lips to hers, easing her worries that he might take more than she was willing to give. His kiss was gentle, undemanding, and shocking. Pleasantly so. Her head spun and she gripped his upper arms to steady herself, astonished by the strength beneath her fingers.

She tentatively moved her lips against his and followed with little pecks like she would place on her family's cheeks. Kissing was an unexpectedly enjoyable activity, and if Captain Hillary's churning breath was any indication, she was quite good at it. Emboldened, she applied more pressure, but she still couldn't taste him, so she touched the tip of her tongue to his top lip.

With a throaty groan, Captain Hillary hauled her against him and drew her tongue into his mouth. She stiffened in his embrace and pushed against his chest. She wasn't ready for this type of kissing, the kind that made her skittish inside and off balance. His hold loosened when she no longer returned his affection, and he released her, chuckling under his breath. He eased her from his desk.

"Come now, madame. You mustn't distract me from my work any longer." Turning her toward the door, he swatted her bottom, eliciting a scandalized squeak from her. "Run along to bed before your cousin searches for you."

She tripped over her feet but caught herself on the edge of the desk.

"Patch is waiting outside the great cabin door to escort you."

"Patch?"

Captain Hillary gathered a book from the top desk drawer and dropped it on the desk with a soft thwack. "Neither you, Mademoiselle Vistoire, or your brother are to go anywhere on this ship without Patch's escort or a man he has assigned. Are my instructions clear?"

Lisette nodded once.

Captain Hillary assumed his place behind the desk and opened the book. "I would like you for breakfast, my dear. Please be prompt on the morrow. I don't wish to come looking for my guests."

Good Lord! What could he mean by liking her for breakfast?

Lisette dashed from his quarters with her heart pounding. She didn't wish to speculate, or she wouldn't sleep a wink.

Six

DANIEL CONTEMPLATED THE BOY SITTING OPPOSITE HIM at his desk. Rafe was fiddling with the sexton and recording numbers in his journal. Daniel didn't know what he intended to accomplish by peering through the gallery windows lining the stern of the ship, but he didn't mind the lad's presence.

Rafe had begun following Daniel yesterday, and it appeared he would have the pleasure of the boy's company again today. The crewman assigned to guard the *Cecily*'s passengers had escorted Rafe to Daniel's quarters at sunrise. The lad had asked for Daniel by name. Otherwise, he'd spoken little, the conversations brief and centered upon maritime topics. In truth, Daniel found him more enjoyable than most adults.

A light knock sounded at his office door, and before he could respond, Lisette poked her head inside.

"Thank heavens!" She rushed forward to gather her brother in a hug, but he wiggled from her hold and returned to recording numbers.

Biting her bottom lip, she glanced between Daniel and Rafe. "You're not bothering Captain Hillary, are you?"

Daniel waved off her concern. "He's fine. Please, have a seat."

She remained standing. Two nights ago she'd sat when he told her to stand. It seemed her nature to do the opposite of anything commanded of her.

"I'm sorry to barge into your quarters, Captain, but I had to know if Rafe was here. It was unsettling to discover him missing. I should have heard him waking. I feel like the worst sister."

Daniel should have sent word when the boy arrived at his door and saved her this worry. "He's in no danger, Lisette."

She shot him a frown. Whether her displeasure stemmed from him using her given name or contradicting her, he didn't know.

"Either Serafine or I must stay awake to guard him," she said. "We'll take shifts."

"That won't be necessary." Daniel braced his hands against the desk and stood then stretched his arms overhead with a soft groan. Through the skylight, a cloudless sky beckoned to him.

Habit dictated Daniel take daily exercise on deck, helping his men with various tasks. His assistance was neither expected nor needed, but idleness had never sat well with him.

When he looked down again, he caught her staring at his chest. Her cheeks flushed a fetching shade of crimson, and she averted her gaze to the windows behind him.

Daniel had donned a pair of worn trousers and open-collared shirt this morning. Certain circles would consider his appearance scandalous, he supposed, but the Mississippi River was far from society and its dictates. And it was too bloody hot to concentrate when he dressed like a dandy.

Lisette cleared her throat, her lashes fluttering like dark-winged butterflies against her coffee-and-cream skin. "*Oui*, this is what we must do. We must take turns watching over Rafe."

She hurried to the gallery windows, her burdensome black skirts swishing as she moved. Sunlight flooded through the glass panes and illuminated her delicate profile as she turned to the side. A surge of desire warmed his blood as he admired the gentle sway of her back and generous curve of her bottom.

"Your quarters feature a lovely view, monsieur."

"I can't imagine anything more lovely."

"Indeed."

Lisette's shyness should have been off-putting, but instead it increased Daniel's ardor. The challenge of seducing her aroused him, more so than the prospect of tumbling a lightskirt, or even one of the less inhibited ladies of the *ton*.

Engrossed in his scribbles, Rafe likely wouldn't notice if Daniel whisked Lisette to his bed, but that seemed too debauched even for him.

He crossed his arms and leaned against his desk. "You needn't take shifts to watch over your brother. I've placed my most trusted men outside your door. Allow them to continue their watch and get your rest. Rafe has an escort when he wakes before you and wishes to leave the cabin."

Lisette twisted around, the lace of her ridiculous hat blocking her view. She batted at the offending material, finally holding the veil back with her fingers. Her arresting green eyes studied him. "That's kind of you, Captain."

"It's Daniel."

She puckered her mouth and sank to the padded bench lining the windows. "Really, Captain. Such familiarity among acquaintances is inappropriate."

She was a peculiar young woman, insisting upon propriety after their kiss last night. Perhaps she was not as amenable to becoming his lover as she'd led him to believe.

Crossing the cabin, he eased her from her seat. "Walk with me, Lisette." His hand wandered temptingly close to her bottom.

"Captain Hillary!"

She tried to scoot away, but he threaded her hand through the crook of his arm. "No need to run, dearest. I only wish to speak with you."

"Well, leave your hands out of the conversation."

He grinned. Her prudishness did nothing to diminish her appeal. "Rafe, do you wish to join us on deck?"

"No, sir."

"I'll send my man inside should you need anything."

Daniel inhaled deeply when they stepped outside. The breeze held a hint of salty sea combined with the earthy scent of the lower Delta. They would reach Balize Island by afternoon. Once the pilot guided them over the sandbars, it would take no time to enter the Gulf, and they would be free to sail for Linmead Island.

The bell clanged four times, signaling the top of the hour, as he guided Lisette to the main deck. His second mate was in charge of the starboard watch, and everything was operating as normal. His crew busied themselves with coiling ropes, sanding the deck, and wetting down planks while others served at their watch posts.

He studied Lisette from the corner of his eye. If she noticed the efficiency with which his vessel functioned, she hid her admiration well.

"Let's take a turn about the ship. I have something I would like to discuss."

"Oh?" A quiver raced down her arm. His touch unsettled her and stirred his compassion. He wished he didn't give a damn about her feelings. It would make his life less complicated, but she had that blasted effect on him. She made him question himself, to consider others' opinions of him.

She made him care what *she* thought of him.

Lisette tried to free her hand and he released her. She turned to him with a soft gasp. What had she expected? Did she think him one to seduce an unwilling partner? Clearly, she was reluctant.

Propositioning a widow in mourning had been in bad form. He was no fool, and even though he regretted his uncouth behavior, his desire for her had been honest. He could wait until she was ready, but he would appreciate a time frame. Would she be more receptive once she entered half-mourning?

A disturbing thought invaded his mind. What if her skittishness came from poor treatment at her husband's hands? He didn't want that to be the case. Her body was meant to be adored, not misused.

"How long has it been, sweetheart?"

"Uh, I…" She tipped her face up, her tongue making a quick pass over her lips. He gently grasped her chin, tempted to smooth his thumb over her shiny bottom lip, to sample her sweetness again.

Her chest rose and fell with jerky motions. "I don't know your meaning, sir. How long has it been since what?"

He dropped his hand and moved back a step. He was forgetting his purpose already: to ease her fears and determine when she would be ready to welcome him into her bed. "I don't wish to sound insensitive, but I was referring to your husband's demise."

"I beg your pardon?"

Damnation. He was unaccustomed to treading lightly and suspected he was doing a poor job of it. "Let's discuss your attire instead. Dark clothing in this climate is unwise, and I don't wish for you to succumb to heat exhaustion. How much longer do you intend to wear them?"

"I hadn't considered—"

"Because if the time to don half-mourning is near…" Now there was a clever way to determine how far along she was in her mourning.

"I have nothing for half-mourning on ship."

Daniel bit back an oath. Was she being evasive or truly naive? "There's little reason to follow senseless rules when we are far from civilization. No one stands in judgment of another on the *Cecily*. Do you understand?"

Something flickered in her eyes, something unreadable. "Perhaps."

"No doubt you've noticed I dress for comfort rather than out of an adherence to propriety."

"Indeed." Her gaze locked to the triangle of skin where his shirt fell open, and a thin brow arched. "Am I to understand that you want me to emulate you? To toss off propriety along with my mourning clothes?"

Hell yes! He would love to have her as bare as the day she was born, but he didn't care for her sarcastic tone. Scrubbing a hand over his rough jaw, he released a sigh. He wasn't getting the answers he sought, but before he could decide on a new approach, she cleared her throat.

"You make a valid point about the heat, Captain. And I'm sure Sallie would understand if I leave off mourning him."

"Sallie? Your husband's name was Sallie?"

"Uh, *oui*. After his… um, *grandfather*."

"Sallie?"

Her jaw jutted forward. "It's a man's name, too."

"No, it isn't."

"In some circles it is."

"None I've ever encountered."

She crossed her arms. "Well, I like it. It's a fine name."

He raised his hands in surrender. What did it matter? He knew what he must do now. He must earn her trust before she would come to his bed. Although he was unaccustomed to putting forth this much effort, the reward promised to be sweet.

"You're correct. Fabulous name."

"Really?" Her smile washed over him, warm and addicting. "*Merci*."

He hardly deserved thanks for refusing to quarrel with her, but he would accept it. "My pleasure."

"I should go change now."

He caught her elbow before she bounded away. "Return to my quarters after you've changed. Rafe will feel more comfortable with you there."

"Of course." She hurried toward the hatch.

"Yes. 'Tis for Rafe's peace of mind," he muttered.

⁂

Lisette bustled into the tiny cabin she shared with her brother and cousin, humming a cheerful tune. Serafine rolled over on her cot and opened one eye to peer at her.

"Good morning, mademoiselle." Lisette sang her greeting. "Wake up, wake up, oh glorious one."

Serafine groaned and pulled the thin cover over her head. "For the love of all that is holy, must you be so irritatingly jolly?"

Lisette chuckled and removed the pins from her hat before releasing the fastenings running down the front of her dress. "Do wake up, lazy bones. It's half past dawn."

The sheet rose as Serafine issued an annoyed puff a second before she threw the covers aside and bolted upright. "Where's Rafe?"

"He's fine." Lisette pulled her arms from the sleeves of her dress and shimmied the garment down her body. "Captain Hillary's man escorted him to the captain's quarters. I promised to return to watch over Rafe. I hope he doesn't make a nuisance of himself."

Serafine rubbed her eyes with her fists. "*What* are you about this morning?"

She started at her cousin's sharp tone. "I'm about watching over my brother."

"Your dress, you silly girl. Why are you changing? Did you correct Captain Hillary's mistake?"

Lisette sensed a flush engulfing her body and yanked her white cotton dress from the back of a chair. "In a manner of speaking."

"What is that to mean?"

"I didn't wish to embarrass him. It was an honest mistake. He believes I'm out of mourning now, and we shall leave it be."

Lisette had been relieved by his suggestion to change from her mourning attire. She last wore the gown after her father's death, and she didn't like the memories attached to it. Simply agreeing with the captain would have sufficed, however. Why had she felt the need to name her pretend husband? And Sallie? How ludicrous! She had no idea why she blurted a lady's name, but once it was out, she couldn't recant. Instead, she'd committed to it and must have been rather convincing for Captain Hillary to give up his argument.

She twisted around, clutching the soft dress against her. "Will you assist me, please?"

Serafine managed to look down her nose at Lisette even though her seated position placed her lower. "I'm no servant, and dressing you is beneath my station."

"I agree on principle. Practicality, however, requires me to ask for help." With no lady's maid, they must assist each other. "I promise to help you next."

Serafine rolled her eyes and climbed from the cot to help Lisette don the dress. After fastening the last button, she spun Lisette around to face her. Her fingers tightened on Lisette's shoulders, her green eyes darkening to that of the overpowering vines dripping from the trees along the riverbank.

"You're keeping something from me. What is it?"

"Nothing!" Lisette winced at the loud screech of her voice. "Nothing," she repeated in a more subdued tone. "You've always been a suspicious type."

Serafine released her, but she could still feel the imprint of her slim fingers. It was as if her cousin had branded her a liar.

Lisette swallowed hard. She had never kept anything from Serafine in all their twenty-two years together, partly due to her cousin's annoying ability to sense things and badger Lisette until she confessed any wrongdoings. But misleading Captain Hillary hadn't been wrong in the strictest sense. Her family was safe from Reynaud, and she would do it all over again. She just wished this blasted guilt was easier to bear.

Her cousin crossed her arms. "I can't fathom what you're hiding, girl, but I'll figure it out."

Not if Lisette had a say. She pasted on a smile. "I really must see to Rafe now." She rushed from the cabin before Serafine could stop her.

Seven

Captain Hillary was going to destroy everything. Serafine felt it in her bones. She could think of nothing else while her cousin and Amelia engaged in polite conversation over tea.

The uneasiness that had been plaguing her for weeks returned, this time worsened by the sense her well-laid plans were doomed.

Her brother, Xavier, had been in England when Uncle Robert died, and his condolence letter promised he would return to New Orleans immediately. That was six months ago. Her brother had been an irresponsible dolt in most matters, but not when it came to family.

She couldn't shake the feeling something bad had befallen her brother. Otherwise, he would have kept his word and returned home long ago.

Lisette, Rafe, and Serafine might be on their own now, but they would survive. While Lisette had listened to Monsieur Baptiste's counsel to seek out Xavier in England, Serafine had created a logical plan for her family's survival once they arrived.

They would take rooms at Durrants Hotel upon arrival until more permanent lodgings could be arranged. Between the two of them, Lisette and Serafine had enough money to live in modest quarters for a year and a half. Serafine, regretfully, must assume the role of Lisette's maid. A life of servitude was a bitter end to her luxurious existence in New Orleans, but her cousin would have need of at least one servant to lend her an air of respectability.

With a letter of introduction penned by Serafine's elderly neighbor to her sister, Lady Dewsbury, Lisette would be granted entrance into English society and have access to the marriage mart. A smart match would save them from the ills that befell the impoverished.

Of course none of this would come about if Captain Hillary had his way. The man all but licked his lips in anticipation of seducing Lisette every time he saw her, but Serafine's cousin would become no man's mistress. She would never make the mistake Serafine had made with Isaac. Serafine wouldn't allow it.

Amelia smiled at her. "You're quiet this afternoon. Are you woolgathering?"

"Something to that effect." Plotting Captain Hillary's unfortunate accident was more like it.

She placed her cup on the table, an idea coming to her. She could steal a peek into her cousin's future and perhaps gain some knowledge to guide Lisette away from the captain. Counting on Lisette's cooperation, however, would likely prove useless. The girl had been frustratingly evasive these past few days when caught stealing off to the captain's quarters.

Tilting her head to one side, Serafine regarded

Amelia. Perhaps her new friend could be of assistance at convincing Lisette to participate. "Have you ever had a reading, my lady? Your tea leaves, I mean."

Amelia sat up straighter. "As in having my fortune told? You give readings?"

Serafine ignored Lisette's warning look. Amelia could be trusted not to ridicule her for superstitious nonsense. She'd sensed the lady's kind heart from the first moment of their meeting, and their time together had only reinforced her impression.

Serafine smiled serenely at Lisette, daring her to say anything. "Why yes, I do perform readings. Shall I study your tea leaves?"

"What jolly fun! How do we proceed?"

"First you must switch hands," Serafine said. "You favor your right, so hold your cup with your left."

She did as instructed and blinked expectantly. "Go on."

"Now, sip your tea, being careful not to drink many of the leaves. Then close your eyes and focus inward."

The lady was an apt subject, following Serafine's directions without question, unlike her stubborn cousin who often fought against accepting Serafine's assistance in personal matters. A few seconds after Amelia closed her eyes, a wrinkle appeared between her brows.

"Try to clear your mind," Serafine urged.

Amelia's forehead smoothed, and she took a deep breath. Serafine's suggestion worked for less than a minute, just as she had anticipated. Amelia frowned.

"There's a worry intruding upon your peace."

Amelia nodded, not opening her eyes.

"*Très bon*. We shall have a personal reading today." Serafine adjusted her position and refused to meet Lisette's gaze even though she sensed it boring into her. "Think upon your concern until your cup is nearly drained."

A variety of emotions played across Amelia's face as she drank the beverage. She changed like the clouds in the sky, almost imperceptibly until the transformation was complete. Her serious expression was in vast contrast to the jovial woman she had been a moment ago.

When Amelia's cup was almost empty, she peeked at the contents then glanced up, offering the cup to Serafine.

Serafine held up a hand. "Not yet. Swirl the tea three times then gently turn your cup over on the saucer."

Again, Amelia followed her directives without question. Lisette could learn much from their new friend.

"Now take three slow breaths before turning your cup upright." Serafine leaned closer to view the interior of the cup. "Tell me what you see."

Amelia grinned. "Isn't that *your* role?"

Her smile was infectious, bringing Serafine a rush of warmth. "Yes, well, my role is to tell you what to do at the moment."

Amelia exchanged an amused look with Lisette. "How ever do you tolerate her high-handedness, my dear?"

"It's a burden I must bear," Lisette replied with exaggerated graveness.

Serafine lifted her nose and paid neither of them any mind. She wasn't high-handed in the least, not from her perspective.

Amelia studied the contents clinging to the sides of the cup. "I think I can make out an acorn."

A good symbol. Serafine had already decided she wouldn't share any bad omens with Amelia if they should arise.

"And a basket." Amelia turned the cup and tipped her head to the side to peer at it from a different angle. "Mmm, and cake."

Serafine chuckled. Amelia missed her sweets very much, as she had discovered in their short time together. The lady's appetite, however, could be attributed to the child she carried.

"I see a necklace, too," Amelia said.

"Oh?" Serafine's brows rose. "A broken circle or complete?"

Amelia looked up warily. "Complete. Is that good or bad?"

"You have no cause for concern."

Returning her attention to the leaves, Amelia twisted the cup again. "This last one looks like a lowercase *B*."

"Does the letter bring anything to mind?"

"Bibi, my dearest friend. She waits in London." She smiled sadly and passed the cup to Serafine. "I miss her terribly."

Serafine peeked at the tea leaves clinging to the sides of the cup. "The acorn represents happiness and contentment." She smiled over the gilded rim. "I hardly needed to do a reading to ascertain as much. Then there is the basket, which means being with child."

Amelia wrinkled her nose. "I thought you would tell me something I don't know."

A doubter. Very well. "Are you aware your friend, Bibi, is also with child?"

"Dear heavens, no!"

Her stricken expression sent Serafine's heart into palpitations. "This is bad?"

Amelia struggled to her feet to pace the cabin. "This is devastating news. Are you certain? Oh, this is horrible."

Serafine's shook her head, confused by Amelia's panicked reaction. "But your friend and her husband are delighted."

Amelia slid to a halt. "Her *husband*? Bibi is married?"

If Amelia knew nothing of her friend's happy marriage, her distress made perfect sense.

"The cake and necklace point in that direction."

Amelia blew out a puff of air and chuckled. "Look at me, fit to be tied over a silly drawing room game."

A silly game? Serafine's spine stiffened.

"My cousin's readings are accurate," Lisette said softly. "I'm certain your friend has been as blessed as you have been, Mrs. Hillary."

Lisette's defense of her warmed Serafine's heart. She turned to study her. Her cousin gazed back with wide eyes so innocent and pure. Perhaps Serafine's worries were for naught. No doubt Captain Hillary harbored improper thoughts about Lisette, but her cousin would never succumb to his charms. She was too intelligent to fall prey to his seduction.

Still, she would feel more comfortable if she could learn the identity of Lisette's future husband, even his initials. Then she might feel less anxious about the voyage.

"Shall I perform a reading for you also?" Serafine asked Lisette.

Lisette drained her cup. "Empty. Perhaps another time."

Amelia laughed, the hand on her belly shaking. "Oh, dear. Forgive my skepticism, mademoiselle. You *must* have a true gift, and dear Lisette doesn't wish to benefit from it. I wonder if she's hiding something."

Lisette's gaze dropped to the plank floor and her cheeks flushed with color.

Indeed. Serafine and Amelia were of like mind. Only Serafine didn't wonder. She now knew with certainty Lisette was keeping a secret.

Eight

LOUIS REYNAUD'S MAN DROPPED ONTO A CHAIR AND kicked his foot up to rest across his knee. "Searched the whole house. Ain't nothin'. No letters nowhere."

A loud buzzing sounded in Louis's ears, and his gaze bore into the ne'er-do-well lounging across the desk from him as if he hadn't a care in the world. Rising from his leather chair, Louis jammed his fists against the gleaming oak surface of his desk. A pounding started behind his eyes.

"Not only have you lost my fiancée," he said, sensing his control slipping, "you have the gall to tell me you cannot unearth a simple packet of letters?"

Wilson answered with a negligent shrug. "What yer lookin' for ain't there. Can't unearth something that ain't there."

The man was too stupid to recognize the danger of his situation, or realize nothing could save him if Louis chose to attack. Like the aggressive black mamba, the fastest of all land snakes, Louis could spring up to strike. His bite would be quick, deadly, and excruciating.

He stared at the man, debating his value. At the

moment, he could think of only one reason not to kill him. Wilson's portly form highlighted Louis's suaveness and superiority when they appeared in the same vicinity. Still, the man's failures made Louis want to snap his neck.

Louis rounded the desk. "Are you aware the black mamba isn't black at all?"

Wilson's shaggy brows pulled together. "A black mamba? Never heard of it."

"It's an African snake, a deadly creature." Louis propped himself against his desk. "My grandfather was something of a scholar. He studied animals, reptiles, amphibians, and the like. He recorded volumes upon volumes of facts in his logbooks. The bulk of his study was devoted to predators in the animal kingdom. Fascinating reading."

Louis had devoured each volume as a boy, engrossed in his grandfather's crude drawings and his own vivid imagination.

Wilson's blank expression riled Louis's temper even more.

"No one survives an encounter with a black mamba, Wilson. He is feared, revered." Louis's voice rose in volume with each sentence. "No one dares to come into his den to vex him."

"Sounds like you got yourself a snake problem, Mr. Reynaud. You want me to take care of it? 'Cause I can take care of it like that." Wilson snapped his stubby fingers. "Nothin' to it."

A low growl rumbled in Louis's chest and he jerked the man from his seat by his neck. His fingers tightened, digging into Wilson's sweaty flesh, closing off his life supply. A raspy breath hissed through the man's lips. His dirty fingernails clawed at Louis's hands as his plump face turned purple.

Louis's gaze narrowed in on a dark droplet sliding over Wilson's jawline, forging a slow path toward Louis's hand. He leaned closer. "What is that…?"

His eyes flew open and he shoved the man. Wilson smashed into the arm of the chair and crumpled to the expensive Oriental carpet.

Louis turned away and supported his weight against the desk. "You're bleeding," he accused. His head floated somewhere near the ceiling. He gulped in a deep breath to keep from going down. It wouldn't do to collapse in front of his men.

"Cut myself shaving." Wilson's raspy voice grated on the ears.

"Revolting swine." Louis's fingers tunneled through his hair. He needed to take possession of those letters. The damning words in the wrong hands would mean his death.

A fresh wave of rage flooded him and he turned back to Wilson. Drawing his boot back, Louis slammed it into the man's thigh, earning an unsatisfying howl that didn't get Louis any closer to what he desired. He wanted those letters and the sly bitch who had been evading him for days.

He wanted control of his life back.

He shot a murderous look at his other hired man cowering near the doorway. "What of the plantation? Did you find Miss Lavigne?"

Durand shrank against the wall. "No one has seen her or the boy for days."

"And what word of her cousin? Did you find Miss Vistoire for questioning?"

"She appears to be missing too, Mr. Reynaud."

Louis closed his eyes. Red flashed behind his eyelids as his blood chased through his veins. "Has no one come forward to claim the damned reward?"

Wilson hauled himself from the floor with a grunt. "That's what we come to say." His voice grated on Louis's nerves, but he resisted the urge to strike him again. Instead, he spun on his heel and stalked to the sideboard to slosh whisky into a cut crystal tumbler.

He downed the drink in one swig then refilled his glass. He shouldn't turn to spirits, not when he needed to keep his wits about him, but the soothing burn in his chest softened the sharp edge of his fury.

"Go on," he said.

Wilson backed toward the door. "Someone came forward. Says he knows Miss Lavigne's whereabouts. He's waiting in the foyer."

"Bring him in." *Imbecile.*

Durand pulled the iron ring handle and the heavy door swung inward. He motioned to someone outside Louis's office. "Mr. Reynaud will see you now."

A vile excuse of a man in threadbare attire sauntered through the doorway holding his battered hat. Louis's butler had been smart not to take the hat from him, or he would be delousing the entire house. Perhaps Louis would demand it of his servants anyway. He didn't like the looks of the mongrel.

Dusky bruises marred the man's face, adding to his ugliness, and a wild-eye swung off in any direction it saw fit.

"Mr. Reynaud." He moved toward the chair Wilson had vacated.

"Halt." Louis held up his hand. "Stay where you are."

The man came up short.

Louis leaned an elbow on the sideboard. "Say your piece and leave."

He shifted his hat from hand to hand. "There was mention of a reward."

Robert Lavigne had almost drained his coffers before Louis had discovered the identity of his blackmailer. The possibility of losing one more coin because of the damned Lavigne family inflamed his temper.

"Tell me the nature of your information, and then I will determine if it deserves a reward."

"Yer lady, Miss Lavigne, saw her at The Abyss a few nights ago. She took up with an Englishman captain."

What did the jackass mean by "took up with"?

"Heard it said," the man droned on, "her, a boy, and another wench left the next day on his ship headed to London."

Louis pictured Lisette rutting with some bloody scoundrel, and the roaring in his ears returned. He gripped the sideboard until the edge cut into his palms.

"Heard her sayin' she had to deliver somethin' important to her cousin."

"Tell me the name of the ship," Louis demanded.

"I'm thinkin' that's worthy of the reward."

Louis's fingers curled into fists. "Pay him."

Wilson scurried behind Louis's massive desk and extracted a purse from a drawer before tossing it to the man.

The nasty mongrel's errant eye landed on Louis

while his other examined the contents of the purse. Apparently satisfied, he offered a crack-toothed grin and pulled the strings to close the pouch.

"Ship's called the *Cecily*, and the cap'an's name's Hillary."

Lisette was going to pay once Louis got his hands on her. He had thought to treat her with some semblance of compassion, for he had believed her innocent of the scheme to blackmail him, and he had fancied her. But once she carried his incriminating letters to her cousin, the demands for money would begin to trickle in again. Worse, Xavier Vistoire might turn the letters over to the government, and Louis's risks would have been for naught.

Damn Lisette. His fiancée was proving to be just like her father, conniving and greedy. And soon she would be just as dead.

"Send word to Pascal to ready the *Mihos*. We sail on the morrow." But first, he had a small matter to attend to at home.

Nine

DANIEL PRETENDED TO PERUSE THE LOGBOOK ON HIS desk, but it was bloody hard to focus on anything aside from the warmth of Lisette's body beside him as she lounged against his desk. He had summoned her to his quarters under the guise of reviewing their dinner arrangements that evening, but in truth, he wished for time alone with her. That she chose to remain in his office after the conversation pleased him.

Her nails clicked against the desk, keeping time with a tune she hummed beneath her breath. Another manifestation of her nerves. So far, he had counted two such quirks inherent to Lisette: twisting her fingers together until it seemed she might wrench them free of her hands and humming to fill silence.

She had a beautiful voice.

The incessant tapping against his desk, however, was annoying. He covered her hand to stop its movement. Her humming stopped, too.

He entwined his fingers with hers to show he

wasn't upset by the interruption and smiled when she didn't flinch or try to pull away. Her shyness was fading by small degrees with each encounter, and he had been manufacturing many over the last week. It was the slowest seduction in the history of man, but as he'd rarely troubled himself to win the favor of a lady who wasn't eager for a tumble, he considered it his due.

"What was that melody, dearest?"

She blinked. "What melody?"

"The one you were humming."

"I don't know your meaning. I've remained perfectly quiet this entire time. And you are not to call me dearest."

"Hmm." He rose from his seat and leaned toward her until they were nose to nose. Still, she didn't pull away. He smiled. "I'm not to call you Lisette either, am I, my sweet?"

"You are not, *Daniel*." She spoke his name with an airiness to her voice, drawing it out and sending his pulse into a sprint. This was the first time she dared to call him by his given name.

He smoothed a finger over her cheek and across her bottom lip. Every inch of her was exquisite to the touch, like the finest Oriental silk. "And it's very improper for me to touch you, do I have that correct?"

"Funny how you know the rules and yet never follow them."

"They aren't *my* rules."

A knock sounded at the outer door.

"They're here."

He sighed when she moved away. At the threshold

of his office, she stopped to glance over her shoulder. "Thank you, Daniel. You have no idea how grateful we are for your assistance with Rafe."

He shrugged and reached for his jacket draped across the chair. "You may thank me later if our endeavor is successful."

Lisette hurried forward to play hostess to the dinner guests, which suited him since it saved him the trouble of exchanging obligatory pleasantries. Once everyone was seated, he assisted Lisette to her chair before taking the seat across from her. It was time for the performance to begin.

Daniel scooped two dollops of mashed potatoes onto his plate then rubbed his hands together.

"Sailor's Delight," he pronounced, watching Rafe's face to see if his words elicited any response.

The lad looked up from his plate of bread with what Daniel hoped was a spark of interest. Rafe's unwavering eyes fixed on his face, which was an accomplishment in itself. If Daniel could entice Rafe to add another food to his repertoire, he would consider tonight's venture successful.

Lisette reached for the serving spoon, and Daniel swatted her hand.

"Ouch!"

"None for you, madame."

She huffed. "I beg your pardon, sir?"

"This is Sailor's Delight." Daniel raised a brow. "Are *you* a sailor?"

"I'm most certainly not. In case you haven't noticed, I'm a lady."

Daniel bit back a sarcastic reply. Lisette was all

curves, softness, and graceful lines. Even a blind man wouldn't mistake her for a man. "Well, the dish is not called Lady's Delight, now, is it?"

Rafe glanced between them, a small smile lifting the corner of his mouth.

"How thoughtless of your cook," she said. "Why, hardly any of us at the table are seamen."

Jake reached for the bowl and plopped a serving on his plate. "I've been a seaman, so I shall have a serving."

Daniel's first and second mates helped themselves as well, digging into the fare with exaggerated gusto.

Rafe tilted his head to the side. "What is Sailor's Delight?"

Mademoiselle Vistoire patted his shoulder. "You heard the captain, dear child. It's food for seafaring men."

The stubborn set to the lad's jaw reminded Daniel of Lisette. "I'm a sailor too."

Daniel nodded toward Mademoiselle Vistoire. "He has worked by my side every day this week. He even took his turn at watch this afternoon. He too shall enjoy Sailor's Delight." Scooping a serving of potatoes, he placed the mound on Rafe's plate, the silver spoon clicking against the china. The lad eyed the white lump and poked it with this fork several times before he hazarded a taste.

Rafe chewed slowly, contemplated the food, and then took another bite.

Daniel met Lisette's gaze and winked. "Perhaps you should swab the decks tomorrow, madame. Then you too may enjoy Sailor's Delight for dinner."

A brush of her foot against his calf sent his heart into a gallop. The brief touch seemed intentional, affectionate, and it stirred something inside him unfamiliar but not unpleasant.

"Thank you, Captain Hillary. I shall take your suggestion under advisement."

If only she were as amenable to his more inspired suggestions.

With Rafe below deck and under the care of Monsieur Patch, Lisette settled in for the evening reading. Her spirits were still soaring after their victory this evening. She glanced at Daniel and affection swelled within her heart. He had proven himself to be the champion she had needed. Rafe was not only safe under Daniel's watch, he had blossomed.

The remaining travelers shared in her excitement, and laughter resonated in the cabin. She hadn't experienced such camaraderie since living on the plantation more than a year ago.

As a child, Lisette had spent many days loitering in the kitchen at the family's sugar farm. It had been one of her favorite places with the bustle and jesting among the staff.

In contrast, the family's quarters had remained deathly quiet. Her mother had been sickly for a long time and required rest and solitude. She often stayed abed with the curtains drawn and took her meals alone in her room. Once an entire month passed without even a glimpse of Mama, and when Lisette finally saw her, her mother's emaciated appearance had left her speechless.

Yet, everything had changed when her mother had

carried Rafe. Mama had begun to laugh again, and Lisette had her mother back for those glorious months. But whereas Rafe had given Mama new life, the good Lord had snatched it away with his birth. Lisette had buried her mother nine years ago, her father a year ago. She wouldn't lose her brother, too.

Amelia cleared her throat and began reading from Act IV of *Romeo and Juliet*.

Lisette was familiar with the tale, but she couldn't help wishing for a happier outcome each time. Why did men persist in the belief true love must end in tragedy? Tristan and Isolde. Orpheus and Eurydice. Cleopatra and Marc Antony. Surely love affairs had happy endings, too.

At the conclusion of the reading, unshed tears gathered on Amelia's lashes. "I apologize. It seems I'm prone to embarrassing emotional displays as of late."

"You've always been a tenderhearted soul," Monsieur Hillary said and helped her stand.

She entwined her arm with his and they moved toward the cabin door. "To say I'm a sentimental fool is more accurate."

Lisette, Serafine, and Monsieur Timmons followed suit while Daniel seemed oblivious to their departure. Although everyone's mood was more subdued than earlier in the evening, Daniel's demeanor raised the alarm inside her. Something dark churned within the depths of his eyes when he met her curious stare. He looked away, denying her access.

"Good night, Daniel," his brother called.

He responded with a curt nod.

She was the last to leave the cabin and paused at

the threshold. She turned to bid him good night as well and found him hunched over, resting his head in his hands. He appeared so weary, as if he'd fought whatever battle was waging inside him a thousand times and was on the verge of surrender.

A pang in her heart urged her to rush forward to offer comfort, but she held back. Perhaps he preferred time alone with his thoughts, however troubling they might be. "Good night," she said softly, closed the door, and followed her cousin.

She stopped at the hatch leading below deck.

Merde. She couldn't abandon Daniel when he clearly needed a kind word, perhaps even a confidant. He had been her champion this evening, and now it was her turn to rescue him.

"I forgot something in the captain's quarters," she said to Serafine and headed back toward his cabins.

"What did you forget?" Serafine yelled after her.

"The thing for the you know," she mumbled.

"Pardon?"

"Exactly. Just one moment, please."

When she was certain Serafine wasn't dogging her heels, she stopped outside the door to gather her wits. She knew the dangers involved with entering Daniel's cabins alone this evening, but he'd been accepting of her limits thus far. Perhaps it was time to trust him with the truth. She could at least be honest with herself. She had grown to like his attentions and might be amenable to another kiss.

Ten

DANIEL PULLED A BOTTLE OF RUM FROM THE BOOKCASE in his office. It was his best bottle, and he didn't care to waste it on the vicar. Snatching up the glass resting on his desk, he poured a generous amount and left the bottle out. He sank into the only comfortable chair in his cabin and took a drink of the numbing liquor.

Nights were the hardest, and the evening's reading brought back the worst of his memories. Cecily haunted him like an apparition. She was present everywhere in his quarters. The impractical china dishes gracing the hutch he'd had built for her. The large copper tub and hand-carved bed in his sleeping chamber. The plush rug resting along the bed where she could feel softness beneath her feet each morning. He had tried to make his ship fit for a lady of her station, the daughter of a governor, but nothing had pleased her.

He had failed before their marriage had even begun.

Daniel's gaze landed on the gashed window seat and his jaw tightened. The chipped woodwork bore testament to Cecily's fiery temper. She had launched a heavy tankard at him, missing her intended target and gouging the hand-carved scrolling instead of cracking his skull.

He couldn't recall what had set her on a tear that particular time. Probably something inconsequential; this typically had been the case. What he did recollect was her fit of rage ending with a passionate tumble that had renewed his optimism in their suitability. They had repeated this pattern several times in the first weeks of their marriage until Daniel had abandoned hope. Abandoned Cecily.

The door to the great cabin creaked, and he bit back an oath. "Go away."

He didn't wish to speak with anyone, least of all his brother.

"Daniel?" Lisette's lovely accent activated his heart, making it pound with vigor. She had come to him at last. "Lisette?"

Her slippers scuffed against the plank floor as she moved through his quarters. She appeared at the threshold of his office. "Here you are."

She twisted her hands together, making him smile. Her nervous habit drew his notice to her generous bustline, which her widow's weeds had kept hidden from view. Not so with the lower-cut gown of muslin. The pristine white contrasted with her bronzed skin.

"I'm pleased you followed my advice to don lighter attire, my dear."

"You are?" Her eyelashes fluttered as her gaze traveled the cabin, looking everywhere but at him. Her shyness was both endearing and yet irritating. She was a widow, not some innocent chit.

"Don't simply stand there. Come in." His snarl was unintended. Lisette was not the source of his ire. She was his only comfort.

"I take it Shakespeare is not to your liking." She stopped in front of him, her eyes great pools of compassion. "Would you like me to speak with Amelia about selecting something less gloomy for tomorrow's reading?"

He chuckled, the tension melting from his shoulders. So dear Lisette wished to protect him from the sappy words of romantic fools, did she? "Ask her to forgo the poetry too, will you, luv?"

"You dislike poetry?"

"Not altogether. I'm partial to a few bawdy rhymes." He winked and reached toward her, his palm up in invitation. "Come here, sweetheart."

At first, she stared, making no move to touch him. Yet she didn't retreat either. She lifted her chin a fraction before placing her gloved hand in his and allowing him to ease her onto his lap. He adjusted her so that she perched sideways on his thighs, her face level with his.

She was a tempting armful, nibbling on her full bottom lip.

"Perhaps this was a bad idea," she said, her gaze shooting toward the exit.

His arms tightened around her waist. "I have one comfortable chair in my private domain. I wouldn't ask you to sit on the floor."

She swallowed hard, two spots of pink coloring her cheeks. Lisette possessed the most beautiful skin. It glistened in the glow of the lantern light. Daniel trailed the back of his finger along her velvety jaw. Nothing

about her was severe. She was gently curving lines and
sweetness. And she was the tonic he needed to soothe
his ruffled psyche.

"Did you wish to see me about something specific?"
he asked, hoping he hadn't been mistaken about her
purpose in visiting his quarters.

"You seemed saddened by tonight's reading, more
so than I would have expected."

She waited for his response, offering him a chance
at redemption, but she couldn't give him absolution.
Only Cecily could release him from his guilt, and that
could never happen.

Daniel forced a grin. "As noted, Shakespeare isn't
my cup of tea. Neither is poetry."

"With the exception of bawdy prose," she amended,
a wry smile on her inviting lips.

He laughed. It was a true sound of merriment,
for Lisette had a way of unearthing happiness he'd
thought abandoned him long ago.

Her expression turned serious again. "I sense something is troubling you."

"You're mistaken, luv. How could I be anything
but content with a beautiful lady in my arms?"

With narrowed eyes, she shifted on his lap to face him,
her bottom making contact with his growing erection.

He grunted and readjusted her position. "Take care
not to wiggle so much, Lis."

She frowned, indicating her patience was nearing
an end. "I could move to the window seat to preserve
your comfort."

He held her in place when she tried to climb from
his lap. "Stay put. I like you where you are."

Her eyes flared and she clamped her mouth closed as if fighting the urge to take off his head. Her fire heated his blood.

"You're too surly by half this evening," she snipped. "Tell me what's stuck in your craw, and stop treating me like an imbecile. Something is bothering you. And don't blame Shakespeare for your ill temper."

She was an insistent young woman but no match for him. He had been evading his troubles for too long. He reached to delve his fingers into her silky hair, but she batted away his hand.

"Now who's surly, madame?"

"I'm unappreciative of your dismissive manner. If you don't wish to speak of your troubles, do me the honor of saying as much rather than behaving as if I haven't spoken."

"Very well. I don't wish to speak of anything but you."

Her chest rose and fell with an exasperated sigh. Regret settled over him, leaden and oppressive. Sometimes he would like to unburden himself, but shifting the load to Lisette's shoulders wasn't an option. She was his to protect and had been since that moment in The Abyss when he'd chosen to intervene on her behalf.

Besides, ladies possessed delicate sensibilities. He would likely wind up comforting her instead of the other way around. Best to distract her.

"If a man could pass through Paradise in a dream and have a flower presented to him as a pledge that his soul had really been there, and if he found that flower in his hand when he awoke—Aye, what then?"

He nuzzled her neck, but she pushed back and held

him at arm's length. A line formed between her brows. "I beg your pardon?"

"I'm reciting Coleridge." He returned to nibbling her soft skin, but she shoved away again.

"Why?"

He dropped his head back against the chair. "I'm attempting to seduce you, my dear, to make you putty in my hands."

Her brows shot up and she laughed, a joyous sound that wafted into the air, rising high before raining warmth over him. "Is that how it's done, monsieur? Perhaps you would reap better rewards with a bawdy rhyme."

"I see. Very well then. There once was a gentleman from Dover, who liked to—"

"No!" Her hand shot out to cover his mouth. "I don't want to hear—I was *teasing*."

"So was I." Her glove muffled his laugh.

The spark of amusement in her eyes faded, and her hand dropped away from his mouth. "Do you want to kiss me?"

His heart startled before taking off at a gallop and sending desire flooding through his veins. "I want to do more than kiss you, Lis."

"*Oui*, I know." She lowered her eyes. "You have been more than patient with me, but I can't fulfill our agreement. I apologize for not being honest from the start, and I pray my revelation doesn't alter your decision to carry us to England. I promise to find another means of payment."

Another means of payment? Grasping Lisette's chin, he twisted her face to meet his direct gaze. "Sharing my bed is not an obligation. I thought we cleared up our misunderstanding the first evening. Your fare is twelve pounds and only twelve pounds."

"But I thought you wished for me to… You said—" She huffed. "You *implied* I must sleep with you if I wanted passage on your ship."

"The hell I did. I asked if you would like companionship on the voyage. I'll be damned if I will coerce you." He pushed her off his lap and steadied her when she stumbled. "We'll arrive at Port Albis soon. I'll find my satisfaction elsewhere. You may go."

Her eyes rounded. "But, Daniel—"

"Go!"

He was being an unpardonable arse, but he didn't care.

Instead of dashing from his quarters as any woman with good sense would do, she crossed her arms, glared, and insulted him in French.

"I can understand you."

"*Très bon.* Now you know what I think of you." She turned on her heel and stormed from his office. The slam of the great cabin door echoed in the bare rooms.

"Hell!" Daniel would *not* run after her. The last thing he desired was another ill-advised entanglement, and Lisette's show of temper and assumptions reminded him of what he didn't need in his life. He didn't want another hysterical wife, and he didn't want to spend every moment feeling like a failure as a husband.

He bolted from his seat and snatched the bottle from his desk. He never wanted to marry again, so why would his thoughts even travel that direction?

If Daniel had ever excelled at anything in his life, it was forgetting, and he wanted to forget this night.

He raised the bottle to his lips, but the rum tasted sour now. Shoving the cork back into the bottle's mouth, he carried it to the balcony off his quarters.

He leaned his forearms against the wooden railing and stared at the moonlight reflecting off the black sea. Another image of Cecily swamped his memory, and his gut seized. His wife had once fled to the balcony and climbed atop the railing. The sinister waters had churned below, frightening him as the sea never had before. If she had slipped and plunged below the surface, she would have been lost forever.

"Cecily, please." His desperate fingers reached toward her. "Take my hand."

"I'll jump. I swear it, Daniel."

His heart hammered against his ribs even five years later. He hated remembering that moment and all the ones that refused to allow him peace.

Clutching the neck of the bottle, he lifted it into the air and drew his arm back.

"Leave me alone," he bellowed and flung the bottle. It hit the waves with a crack and disappeared.

❧

Lisette stood against the railing of the main deck with Rafe, feigning interest in the activity around her. The men chanted rhythmic songs—sea shanties—as Monsieur Patch had informed her. Their muscles rippled beneath thin shirts as they threw themselves into hoisting the sails. The first time she had observed one of the men climbing aloft to unfurl the sails, she'd been intrigued, but too many hours of watching the same activities had taken its toll.

The salty breeze off the Caribbean waters had loosened tendrils of her hair and whipped them around her face. No amount of fussing kept them in place.

For the past two days, Daniel had closed himself off from everyone. Their communal dinners had ceased, and he had refused entrance even to Rafe, which infuriated her the most.

Her brother didn't deserve to be punished when Daniel was angry with her. She would never forgive him for his ill treatment of Rafe. Fortunately, Jake Hillary had taken up Daniel's role and engaged her brother in various maritime pursuits. Under Monsieur Hillary's tutelage, her brother had steered the ship, learned to tie several different knots, and rang the bell on the half hour to signal the passage of watch. Too bad Daniel wasn't more like his brother. Amelia was fortunate to have married such a fine gentleman.

Lisette shaded her eyes from the harsh sun and gazed out at the cerulean waves. The perpetually moving entity spread outward to infinity. If Monsieur Hillary hadn't reassured her that they would arrive in Port Albis within the week, she would believe they'd never reach their first destination. Their arrival couldn't come soon enough.

When the ship docked at the island, she and her family would part company with the captain and his ship. There would be other ships bound for England, eventually. This time she could investigate and interview potential candidates before booking passage.

Lisette returned her attention to the main deck and sighed. When would Serafine relieve her? She had been supervising Rafe for the last three hours and thought she might go mad if she had to endure much more of observing the men at work.

The appearance of Monsieur Timmons, the ship's surgeon, followed by Monsieur Patch on deck sparked her interest a little. At least the two men provided something novel to watch. With purpose, the men moved toward the captain's quarters.

Lisette allowed her imagination to meander through possible scenarios that might require a surgeon's services. The arrogant captain's head swelling to such a size that he could no longer fit through the doorway. His soured disposition causing his eyes to cross permanently. Constipation caused by bad-temperedness.

Lisette chuckled. It would serve Daniel right, any or all of the ailments.

The men disappeared through the great cabin door, and Lisette lost interest.

"Rafe, let's retire below deck for a bit."

"No." His gaze didn't shift from the seaman inching along the yard above to unfurl yet another sail.

Should she insist and risk a tantrum, or wait a little longer for Serafine? As if her cousin had anticipated Lisette's desperation, she appeared on deck. Serafine looked as fresh as a newly cut flower and more rested than Lisette had felt in weeks. A knot of irritation formed in her stomach, and she bit the inside of her jaw to keep from flinging harsh words at her cousin. Lisette's foul temper wasn't Serafine's doing.

Just as Serafine reached them, the door to the great cabin swung open. Against her wishes, Lisette turned to look, her heart speeding. But she didn't discover Daniel at the door. The surgeon shook his head as if defeated and spoke to Monsieur Patch, who set off to do his bidding.

The seaman reminded Lisette of a bull. No, more like a Minotaur. His only equal in brawn was Daniel, although the captain was sleeker. Lisette frowned. Daniel's stature was not for her to contemplate.

Monsieur Patch returned posthaste with a hammer and nail then took the sheet of foolscap the surgeon held out before nailing it to the door.

"Quarantine?" Lisette hadn't been serious when she'd wished an ailment on Daniel. "Wait here," she called to her family and rushed forward to intercept the medicine man.

"Monsieur Timmons, what ails Captain Hillary?"

His strained visage made her heart skip. "I'll make the announcement to everyone in a moment. Captain Hillary has contracted the measles."

Sweet Mary. Many people died from the disease.

"The captain complained of feeling feverish two days ago and placed himself in quarantine as a precaution. Looks like he knew what he was about. With any luck, no one else will contract the illness."

Daniel had been trying to protect them by isolating himself? Now she felt even worse for wishing ill upon him.

Monsieur Timmons ran a hand over his gaunt face. Gray stubble on his jaw looked like smeared ash. Warily, he regarded her. "Have you felt feverish or discovered any spots?"

"I had measles as a child. I'm fit."

Grandmamma had sworn that once Lisette had recovered she would never contract the disease again.

After all, Grandmamma had nursed her back to health and hadn't become ill.

Monsieur Timmons glanced beyond her shoulder toward Rafe and Serafine. "And your family?"

"Neither of them have had the illness, but they are well."

"I'm sorry, madame, but I must insist all travelers exposed to Captain Hillary go into quarantine. We cannot afford an outbreak on ship."

"My brother won't take to being kept in the cabin. I swear he isn't ill. Must he go into quarantine?"

"I wish I were at liberty to allow him to roam freely, but everyone will be in jeopardy if the men cannot sail the ship. We need all hands."

She nodded slowly as the truth of his claim sank in. "I understand." Somehow they would find a way to comply with the edict. "How is the captain?"

"His situation is grave, but we won't know for a few days if he'll experience complications with his lungs."

"You will take good care of him, won't you?"

Monsieur Timmons's sighed wearily. "Now that I have been exposed, I must go into quarantine too. The captain will be at God's mercy, I'm afraid."

"But is there no one to care for him? We need him to reach our destination."

"The first mate will assume leadership in the event of his death." The surgeon's cavalier attitude inflamed her temper.

"Captain Hillary is *not* expendable. He's strong, and he can survive, but he'll need attending. How can you dismiss him as if he has no value?"

"Please understand, Mrs. Lavigne. I could request

a volunteer to sit by his bedside, but frankly, I don't know anyone who would take on the task nor have the knowledge to do the captain any good. I've done all I can for him." He grasped her arm and tried to lead her away from Daniel's door, but Lisette jerked free.

"Your efforts are not good enough." She would be damned if she allowed Daniel to die.

Eleven

A HACKING COUGH TORE THROUGH DANIEL'S QUARTERS as Lisette entered. Monsieur Timmons had told her she could find him in his bed, and after much point-less debate on the wisdom of her decision, suggested she prepare herself. He'd spoken to her as if she were some silly girl given to swooning and needless tears. Lisette understood illness after years of living with her mother, and she would not turn into a puddle of mush at the mere sight of a bed-bound man.

Jake Hillary had not been easy to convince to stay away from his brother's bedside, but he did have Amelia and his unborn child to consider. Lisette had promised to provide Daniel with the best care possible and to summon Monsieur Hillary if his brother took a turn.

Hurrying across the great room, she entered the office. Monsieur Patch would bring water to the stateroom door in a moment, but Lisette wanted to check on Daniel first.

Thank goodness Serafine had agreed with her about caring for Daniel and promised to watch after Rafe.

Neither she nor Serafine believed any man onboard could fill Daniel's boots. His crew looked to him for guidance, and he ran a tight ship. He would see them safely to Port Albis, but only if he survived.

Her stomach twisted as she neared his sleeping chamber. Lisette hadn't wanted to admit to Serafine or herself that she had other reasons for wishing for his recovery. A lump swelled within her throat, and she took a deep breath to keep her tears at bay. She wasn't one given to needless emotions, but if he died… She shook her head to rid herself of the morbid thought.

"Daniel," she called softly as she pushed open his chamber door. Two facts struck her as she entered the room: it was as dark as a tomb and sweltering. "*Sacre bleu.*"

His fever had to be burning out of control with the added heat. Why hadn't Monsieur Timmons opened a window?

"Lisette?" Daniel's voice sounded weak and scratchy. "You can't be in here."

"Nonsense. You've been trying to entice me to your bedchamber for weeks."

As her eyes adjusted to the dark interior, she was able to make out his reclined figure under the coverlet. She walked to his bed and placed her palm on his forehead, her heart racing in alarm. He burned with a fever so hot she feared his brain might scorch. She had seen it once before with a servant child. The young boy had thrashed about and uttered animal-like cries. She squeezed her eyes closed to shut out the memory.

The boy hadn't survived.

"I had measles as a child. I can't get them again."

He captured her hand and held it against his searing lips. "Are you certain?" His body quaked as a chill gripped him.

"I'm certain." She brushed aside wet tendrils of hair from his eyes. "Now do be a good patient and rest." She pulled the covers to his chin before moving to the far end of the chamber to lift and latch the window. "You need fresh air and a cool cloth for your head. I'll return with water in a moment."

She swept through Daniel's quarters to the state-room door to find a bucket half filled with water sitting outside. Looking around, she couldn't locate Monsieur Patch. No doubt the surgeon had ordered him into quarantine as well. She grasped the rope handle with both hands and tugged on the bulky bucket. Water sloshed over the side and landed on the deck with a splat.

A couple of men looked her direction, but neither moved forward to assist her. Lisette squared her shoulders. She could do this without their help. Moving slowly, she backed into the cabin and closed the door with her foot. She wobbled side to side with her burden toward Daniel's chambers, spilling a little more as she went. When she reached his room, it was already cooler.

She lowered the bucket and whisked to a small wardrobe to search for handkerchiefs. Richly woven coats and vests swayed in unison with the ship when she flung the doors open. Lisette found a drawer filled with neatly folded handkerchiefs and grabbed them all.

At Daniel's bedside, she laid her hand to his forehead

again. His scorched skin was dry to the touch. "You must drink something." She located a tin cup and dipped it into the bucket. "Can you lift your head?"

Daniel's strength had diminished a great deal, but he struggled to lift his head. Lisette slipped her hand under his neck for support and touched the cup to his lips. "Sip slowly, *mon amour*."

His lashes flickered and glassy blue eyes regarded her a brief moment before his heavy eyelids drooped again. "Thank you."

Once he had settled back on the pillow, she soaked a handkerchief in the cool water, squeezed out the excess, and gingerly laid it across his brow.

She found an upholstered chair in a corner of the chamber and dragged it to the side of his bed. The cabin was opulently draped with rich brocade linens in icy shades of blue and silver, and hand-woven carpets covered the rough planks. And it was spacious, nothing like the room she shared with Serafine and Rafe. Never did she expect to find such luxury on the *Cecily*, or any ship.

When the handkerchief on his head turned warm, she replaced it with a fresh one then curled up in the chair to wait out his fever. The clang of the bell outside signaled it was early afternoon.

Daniel slept in fits and starts throughout the rest of the day. His jagged cough often startled him from slumber, but he succumbed to exhaustion again at once. Lisette changed the handkerchief at every half hour toll of the bell, and she took her meal in his chambers for fear he would wake and need her.

When darkness descended, she lit a lantern and

fought to stay awake in order to attend to him, but her eyes felt as if someone had flung sand into them. She closed them for a moment.

"Lisette," a faraway voice called. "Lisette, I need—"

She jerked awake, recalling where she was, and moved to Daniel's side. "I'm here. What do you need?"

His cheeks were flushed red and a quick touch to his brow made her stomach plunge. "You're burning like fire." She had to cool him off before his mind became addled.

When she flipped the covers from his body and folded them at the foot of the bed, he moaned and shivered. Lisette turned to reassure him, but her voice stuck in her throat. She had forgotten Daniel was bare from his waist up.

"*Mon dieu*," she muttered.

On the occasions when he had held her close, his solid body under her palms had stirred her curiosity. She had imagined him much like the granite statue of Andrew Jackson outside the Cabildo, but more pleasing to the eye. Nothing in her limited imagination had prepared her for the actual sight of him. Not even the red patches splattered over his torso detracted from his perfection. Is this what all men looked like beneath their clothes? She trailed a tentative finger along the crevice running down the center of his abdomen toward his belly button.

"How remarkable you are."

He moaned, startling her from her reverie. "If I didn't feel like hell, I'd be pleased by your adoration."

Lisette snatched her hand back. "Forgive me, Captain. I meant only to bathe you."

She busied herself with soaking a handkerchief and wringing it out before placing the cloth across his chest.

Daniel sucked in a sharp breath. "Cold."

"I need to bring down your fever."

When she smoothed the next handkerchief along his collarbone and neck, his teeth clicked together, but he offered no more complaints.

She hummed an old song she had learned from her nurse, Alva, to distract herself as she continued her ministrations. When she stopped humming, Daniel groped for her hand.

"Sing to me."

She draped the last handkerchief over the bucket's edge and lowered the lantern flame. Lisette only sang to her brother or when she was alone. She began softly, timidly.

Daniel closed his eyes and held her hand when she returned to his side. "Your voice is soothing. Please, don't stop."

Heat rushed to her cheeks at his unexpected compliment. Climbing onto the side of the bed, she sang the rest of the melody while he drifted to sleep once more. She tested his forehead. He had cooled considerably. Her shoulders slumped as fatigue threatened to overtake her, but she couldn't move away without waking Daniel. His hand engulfed hers and refused to relinquish it.

When she couldn't sit upright any longer, she stretched out beside his lean body, soaking up the heat rolling off him in waves, and surrendered to sleep.

⤛⤜

Before he opened his eyes, Daniel sensed Lisette beside him, her unbound hair soft under his cheek. She had taken to sleeping with him the first night his spots had appeared and fever raged through his body. He'd been too weak to do anything but accept her charity, and truth be told, a few days in bed left him feeling sapped of energy even now. But this was the first morning he felt almost normal.

He savored this time to admire her while her guard was down. A long strand of ebony silk lay across Lisette's cheek and lips. In slumber, she appeared delicate as if one strong knock could shatter her, but underneath her fragile outer layer beat a heart of iron. To think she had taken care of his every need without complaint...

Humility sent a fresh wave of heat to his face.

Lisette stirred beside him and opened her eyes briefly. A breath later, they flew open. "Daniel?"

"I'm fine, Lis. Sleep some more." He placed a hand on her shoulder to ease her back to the pillow, but she resisted.

Her hand pressed to his forehead. "Your fever is gone." Tossing the covers aside, she raked her gaze over his chest and abdomen, heating his blood. "The rash has faded too."

The wonder in her voice made him smile.

"Had you hoped I might not recover?"

She issued an indignant huff. "After all the trouble I have gone to? You must be daft."

Her hair illuminated like a dark halo in the morning sunlight, and he couldn't resist smoothing the mussed strands. "I must be. Here I've had you in my bed for days without tumbling you."

She smiled smugly. "Why do you think I am in your bed? You're too weak."

"Is that so?" Daniel grasped her around the waist and rolled to haul her on top of him.

Lisette gasped. "Monsieur, put me down. You need more rest."

His breath wheezed from the minimal exertion, so he complied with her command and settled her beside him again. But he didn't release her from the circle of his arms. "Did you sleep well, luv? I didn't wake you with my coughing, did I?"

Her brow wrinkled as if searching her memory. "I don't think you woke me even once, unlike two nights ago when you kept me awake with your silly chatter. *Mon dieu*. I never knew a man could be so enamored of an inanimate object."

"What did I say?"

"Oh, nothing really," she said, adopting a teasing tone, "besides the words of a lovesick fool. You put Romeo to shame."

He laughed. "Don't tell me I spouted the stanzas of a love poem."

"Not unless someone has composed an ode to your ship."

Daniel's smile faded. He was uncertain he wanted to hear the rest.

"You kept calling out, 'Cecily, I love you' and mumbling something about being sorry. I knew you loved the sea, but that was a bit *overboard*." Lisette lifted an eyebrow in jest.

"I must have been out of my mind with the fever."

He released her and tried to turn away, but Lisette's

slender fingers closed around his shoulder. "Daniel, what is it?"

The tender concern in her voice was real. He had been the recipient of her compassionate care for too many days to fool himself into believing she feigned the emotion. He rolled to his back and trained his gaze to the ceiling of wooden planks.

Lisette rose to her elbow, her dark hair falling like a silken scarf over her shoulder. Her jewel-toned eyes roamed his face and she smiled sadly. "Cecily isn't just your ship. You named her after a woman."

He experienced a familiar tightening in his chest, as if caught in a vise that might crush him.

She caressed his cheek. The tips of her fingers grazing his skin possessed the power to ease the pain in his core, if not the pain of his conscience. "You may tell me of your love for her, if you wish."

He captured her hand and pressed a deep kiss to the palm. No longer was he certain of his love for Cecily. More and more, he felt the frustration of their encounters, her tantrums and indictments. But Cecily had been right in her accusations. If he had never bedded her, her parents wouldn't have forced them to marry.

"Daniel?"

He looked into Lisette's guileless eyes. "Cecily was my wife. She died onboard five years ago. We hadn't been married long."

"I'm sorry," she murmured. "I had no idea, or I wouldn't have teased you."

He hugged her close. "I know, Lisette. You haven't a mean bone in your body."

She snuggled her cheek against his chest and sighed. Desire stirred inside him, building as she lingered in his embrace. His hands skimmed over her back, stopping before caressing over her bottom. Lisette didn't resist him, but his pride wouldn't allow him to take her. Having relations with him now would be nothing more than an act of mercy. He had heard the pity in her voice.

He patted her bottom once and released her. "I could use some water."

"I will have one of the men bring more." She climbed from the bed and grabbed the bucket before disappearing through the doorway.

While she was gone, he sat up on the side of the bed. The instant he stood, his legs threatened to fold up on him. *Egads!* He couldn't recall ever being this unsteady, even in the days before he had acquired his sea legs.

Why had he spoken of his wife to Lisette? He had never even told his family he had married. There had been no point. Cecily had been gone for weeks by the time his ship reached London.

He donned a shirt and made his way toward the great cabin to assist Lisette with the bucket. She had been struggling with caring for him long enough. It was time for him to take his rightful place again.

She came through the outer door with her heavy burden. Closing the distance with long strides, he took the bucket.

"Thank you, Lisette. You may return to your cabin to check on the welfare of your family."

"Very well, and then I will return with nourishment."

"I can manage on my own. You needn't return."

"It's no trouble." She started for the door. "I shan't be long."

"I don't need a nursemaid."

She stopped at the threshold and eyed him. "You are right, I'm sure, but it couldn't hurt—"

"No, I don't *need* you. Now, go see to your family."

Her mouth fell open. The hurt pooling in her eyes caused a sharp pinch in his chest. She turned away, perhaps to hide her tears.

"Of course you don't need me."

Jerking the door open, she hurried from his quarters. Daniel started after her but stopped himself. Lisette might be upset with him now, but he would survive her anger. Cecily's death was his alone to bear, and so was facing his wife's parents in Port Albis. Lisette had enough to endure with her brother. Daniel couldn't expect her to be his source of strength, too. No matter how tempting it was to share his burden with her.

Twelve

LISETTE ROLLED HER MOURNING GOWN INTO A BUNDLE and shoved it into the sack that had become her luggage. Her new trunks, the ones she had purchased for her honeymoon trip before learning the truth about Reynaud, stayed behind at Passebon House.

Fury simmered inside her, unfurling in her belly. She had lost everything because of that blackguard—her exquisite gowns and her family home.

Serafine bustled around the dim cabin, gathering her belongings and interrupting Lisette's self-pity. She sighed, silently chiding herself. She hadn't lost everything, for Reynaud had been unable to take away the ones she loved. Rafe and Serafine held more value than any possession.

Serafine bumped into Lisette when she moved by her. "Cease your daydreaming." Her cousin's value depreciated a point. She ordered Lisette around worse than Daniel did, and Lisette was getting blasted tired of their imperious natures. "We'll reach Port Albis soon. Hurry up."

"I am moving fast enough. Captain Hillary won't throw us from the ship when we dock."

"I'm more concerned about him allowing us to leave. We must make our departure while he is otherwise occupied."

Lisette rolled her eyes. They were not prisoners on the *Cecily*. "He'll be glad to be rid of us."

Some of her bravado slipped as the truth of her statement sank in, and she had that dreaded urge to cry. Daniel had been all too eager to toss her from his cabins.

Serafine wiggled past her with a pair of Rafe's pants in hand, placed them on the cot, and turned. "We must search out another ship to carry us to England the moment we arrive."

"Why so soon?" Lisette was tired of bland fare, never-ending waves, and hours of tedium. A few days on soil would be a welcome respite.

Her cousin pursed her lips. "We are leaving before you change your mind. It's clear you have fallen in love with Captain Hillary."

Lisette fumbled with the sack. "I have not."

Serafine snatched the nightrail Amelia had given her from Lisette's fingers. "Yes, you have."

"You're mad." She turned her back to her cousin. "I'm grateful to Captain Hillary for helping us escape and for taking an interest in Rafe, but I have no love for the scoundrel."

"Lisette." Serafine spoke at her ear, causing her to jump.

"Sweet Mary! Keep to your side of the room."

Serafine grabbed her shoulders and pushed her down to sit on the cot. "Banish these childish longings. The captain will never want anything more from you than a moment between the sheets."

Lisette flinched. The harsh words ripped through her heart.

Merde. It was true. She had been having second thoughts. How could she deny her feelings when every moment she thought of leaving Daniel made her throat thick with unshed tears?

"You deserve a better life, Lisette."

She nodded and fiercely swiped at the traitorous tears welling in her eyes. Daniel behaved as if nothing of significance had passed between them during his quarantine, and nothing had except in her fanciful imagination. While she had grown fond of him during his convalescence, he felt nothing for her in return. He had made it clear he had no need for her when he had tossed her from his quarters, and he hadn't sought her out since that moment.

She met Serafine's gaze, defiance radiating from her. "I *don't* love him."

"*Très bon*, because he is not meant for you."

Lisette shot to her feet and brushed past her cousin. "How would you know who is meant for me?"

"There is a gentleman in your future, an Englishman, and an obscenely rich one at that. You will marry *him*, and he will provide the security we seek."

"I suppose your tea leaves told you as much."

"It's simply my hope." She paused. "Lisette, I should have told you before we left, but I'm afraid something bad has happened to Xavier."

She slowly swiveled around to face Serafine. "What are you saying? Why would you believe something has happened to your brother?"

Her cousin's expression clouded over. "Xavier

promised to return at once, but we've received no word from him in months. He wouldn't abandon Rafe. You know he cares for the boy."

Lisette gripped the sheer fabric of her extra chemise, her irritation melding into anxiety, but now wasn't the time to dwell on what they might find in England. They had more pressing matters to attend to in Port Albis. "We shall deal with the situation if it comes to pass. Your nerves are getting the better of you."

She resumed packing.

"Perhaps," Serafine said, "but if my fears are realized, our survival depends on you marrying well."

"You are as likely to capture a gentleman's attention as I am."

Serafine was silent for so long, Lisette began to think she had won an argument for once. The soft clearing of her cousin's throat stripped her of that notion. "You're mistaken. No gentleman will have me."

Lisette turned to deliver a retort but held her tongue. Tears streaked down the beautiful planes of Serafine's face. Lisette dropped the garment she held and gathered her cousin in a hug. "*Ma chère*, why do you speak such foolishness? What gentleman wouldn't want you?"

Serafine shook her head and held on tighter, smothering her sob against Lisette's shoulder. Her cousin had always been proud. For her to have said this much about her insecurities was miraculous but troubling. Serafine and Lisette may not be pale beauties with pure European blood coursing through their veins, but they were exactly what many superior, gently bred men needed.

They carried decent dowries, and they would bear sons imbued with the strength of their ancestors who had survived the wilderness of Louisiana when weaker men and women died before ever reaching their destination. Any man would be a fool to overlook either of them.

"If we don't locate your brother in London, we will both make smart matches if we must. Never doubt it." Lisette eased from Serafine's hold.

Her cousin offered a tentative smile and looked away.

"Serafine, what is it?"

She shook her head. "It's unimportant. Perhaps when we have more time…"

Serafine's slumped shoulders and defeated sigh made Lisette's heart ache. "You will confide in me later? You must realize you may tell me anything."

Serafine sniffled. "I know."

Lisette chose not to further her inquiry. When her cousin was ready, she would share her burden. At least, she had always trusted Lisette in the past.

There. That was one more thing Reynaud couldn't take from her, the trust her kin placed in her. Why, the blasted cur had hardly taken a thing, now that she thought about it.

❦

Lisette kept Rafe close as the *Cecily* neared Port Albis. The placid waters sparkled like a star-filled sky as sunlight bounced along the surface of the bay.

Serafine stood on Lisette's other side, their arms linked. "It's beautiful."

"*Oui.*"

Dotting the bay, the unadorned masts of slumbering ships jutted into the air while their flags of allegiance flapped in the breeze. Most flew the British colors, but as Daniel had explained to Rafe that morning over breakfast, Linmead Island was an English colony.

In the distance, a massive curved wall of stone hovered on a hill overlooking the waters, the fortress's black cannons peering over the barrier. Stark white Palladian houses sprawled across the knoll. Their porticos and domes reminded her of the artists' renditions of ancient Greece displayed in the gallery at Passebon House.

As the *Cecily* neared shore, men scurried along the docks, preparing for their arrival. Port Albis proved a larger metropolis than she had thought. In her imagination, the Caribbean islands had been barely one step above uncivilized. How uninformed she had been.

Anxious flutters began in her stomach. Not only must she locate shelter, she needed to book passage on another ship. The prospect felt daunting now. She had hoped Daniel might offer his assistance in finding an inn, but he hadn't spoken directly to her since she'd stormed from his cabins.

He stood near the helm with Monsieur Patch. Daniel's wide stance drew her attention to his sturdy thighs, and his linen shirt strained across his muscled chest, highlighting his strength. His authoritative voice carried on the air, commanding all those around him. To see him now, one would never guess how helpless he had been a few days earlier.

Bon. Daniel no longer needed her, just as he had said. He glanced in her direction but turned back to

Monsieur Patch when he discovered her watching him. Would he truly allow her to walk away without a word after their time together?

She rubbed the back of her wrist across her nose to ease the annoying tickle that signaled impending tears. Squaring her shoulders, she reminded herself Daniel held no significance to her. Her family's continued survival was the only thing of importance.

Rafe pointed toward an approaching entourage on shore. An open-topped carriage with four white horses and a liveried driver at the reins rolled down the hill toward the docks. Four men wearing British-red uniforms rode on horseback and escorted the conveyance.

"It's the governor-general," Rafe announced.

"How could you know such a thing?" Serafine asked.

"Captain Hillary said he would greet us."

Lisette shaded her eyes as she located Daniel again. He was frowning in the official's direction and a frisson of apprehension coiled in her chest.

"*Mon dieu*," she murmured to Serafine. "I hope there's to be no trouble."

The appearance of his father-in-law at the docks didn't surprise Daniel, but he had hoped to delay their reunion. Cecily's parents treated him with kindness he didn't deserve.

He had killed their daughter.

If not by his own hand, then by his insistence that she abandon her home. Cecily had never wanted to leave Port Albis, but his need to prove his wife wrong overrode her desires. Daniel was not a poor tradesman. He was the son of a gentleman and an heir to his maternal grandfather's mercantile shipping company, one of the largest in the world, second only to the East India Company.

He would have showered Cecily with every luxury her mind could imagine once they reached home. She would have had a large household to manage, any number of staff she required, and her obsession for pretty things indulged to no end.

A sharp pang of shame pierced underneath his ribs. The foolishness of his youthful pride had cost Cecily her life, and he must live with this knowledge forever. Perhaps he was no wiser now, allowing Lisette and her family onboard, but they had held up well. He would see them safely to England as if his own life depended on it.

Lisette stood near the railing twisting her hands together as if wrestling with whether to approach him. Her distress added to his guilt. He should have prepared her for the ship's arrival in Port Albis. She likely worried about where her family would stay, but Daniel would see her and her kin settled.

He swaggered toward the gangplank where she stood. Upon meeting her gaze, a trill of anticipation raced down his limbs, and he quickened his step. *Hellfire.* He had missed her over the last couple of days, but only now did he realize to what extent. He should have sent for her before their arrival instead of keeping his distance, but he hadn't trusted himself to safeguard her from his troubles when she had enough of her own.

"Lis," he greeted softly.

She extended her hand as if she were a man sealing an agreement with another. "Captain Hillary, thank you for your fine service. My family is grateful to you."

Daniel captured her hand and tucked it into the crook of his arm. "Stay close, luv. I don't want to lose you in the crush."

"Captain Hillary." She tried to tug free of his hold, but he refused to relinquish her as he led her toward the gangplank.

"I'm afraid I must subject you to an introduction to my wife's parents."

She stumbled, but he steadied her descent. "Daniel. Why didn't you say something earlier?"

The pomp and circumstance surrounding the governor and first lady's arrival to greet him was embarrassing. Cecily's father climbed from the carriage before assisting his wife then escorting her to wait at the bottom of the gangplank. Someone must have identified the *Cecily* early, because the governor and first lady had had time to dress in their best.

"I fear they will insist we stay as their guests," he said to Lisette. "They don't look kindly upon a refusal to partake of their hospitality."

"No, not *us*. We'll locate an inn."

Daniel smiled when Cecily's mother waved. "You don't want to miss the ball they are sure to throw. Besides, I promised to protect you, and protect you I will."

If he were honest with himself, he would allow that he wanted Lisette close to shield him from the overwhelming guilt that plagued him each time he stepped foot in the governor's home. He needed her more than he liked to admit.

Thirteen

LISETTE SETTLED AGAINST THE CARRIAGE SEAT AND narrowed her eyes at Daniel. Serafine stared out the window, not even bothering to make eye contact with anyone, while Amelia fidgeted with her reticule.

It had been two days, a full forty-eight hours, since their arrival at the Governor's House, and Daniel hadn't allowed Lisette out of his sight except when she excused herself to her chambers. His unexpected attentiveness made it impossible for her to slip away to find another ship traveling to England.

And he'd been pleasant, which riled her to no end. She barely recognized him as the cold, dispassionate captain he had been before their arrival to Linmead Island. Nevertheless, she wouldn't allow herself to forget what he was *underneath* his fancy waistcoat and brilliant white cravat.

He was unequivocally marvelous—*monstrous*!

Memories of his spectacular bare chest invaded her thoughts, sending hot tingles all over her body. She shifted on the seat and trained her gaze out the window, pretending interest in the passing landscape.

Pondering anything lying beneath Daniel's waistcoat served no purpose except to remind her of the reason she had to end their association.

Captain Daniel Hillary was her Achilles' heel.

His chuckle broke the somber silence. "Such glum faces all around. I've never seen ladies so opposed to shopping for a ball. I should have insisted Jake accompany you instead."

Amelia wrinkled her nose. "My attendance is hardly appropriate given my condition. I have no inkling as to why the first lady is insisting upon my participation."

"This isn't London," he said. "Societal rules are more lax. Try to enjoy yourself."

Serafine sniffed. "Lisette and I hold no place in society. We shouldn't be attending high-ranking officials' balls or wasting money on frivolous dresses we will never need again."

A mischievous twinkle lit Daniel's eyes. "Feel at liberty to discuss the situation with Her Excellency, ladies. I learned years ago to follow the first lady's directives without question. It requires less energy than debate."

"It's difficult to believe anyone could direct you in anything," Lisette said.

"Madame has a point." Amelia sent a soft smile across the carriage for Serafine. "If I must attend this affair in *my* state, I'll require someone to stand in front of me to block the view. Please say you will attend."

Serafine offered a begrudging grin. "Only for *you*. I refuse to enjoy myself upon Captain Hillary's suggestion."

Daniel drummed his fingers on the hat resting on his lap. "Mademoiselle Vistoire, I have the distinct impression you don't care for me."

Serafine was spared from having to answer his accusation when the carriage rolled to a stop in front of a rustic shop with oyster shells set into the foundation. A tidy sign announcing their arrival at Madame Morel's Boutique swayed in the ocean breeze.

She paused on the walkway to savor the sweet scent wafting on the air. Port Albis was a different world compared to home, and they hadn't yet traveled a quarter of the journey. How displaced would she feel once they reached London?

For a brief moment, she considered abandoning her search for a new captain. Daniel had given his word to deliver them to England and had kept them alive this far. Perhaps it was unwise to entrust their livelihood to an unknown entity.

Lisette shook the notion from her mind. As she and Serafine had discussed at length, surviving the journey was just the first step. If any of them hoped to stay alive for any time in London, Lisette must find a husband. And in order to secure passage on another ship, she would need to find someone willing to assist with the task of locating a Britain-bound vessel. Although Daniel wouldn't allow her to venture into the town alone, he couldn't stop her from seeking assistance from one of the governor's guests at the ball.

Bamboo chimes clanked as Lisette and Serafine entered the establishment.

"Oh," Lisette said on an outpouring of breath. A rainbow of exquisite bolts of silks lined the back wall from ceiling to floor. A shimmering plum caught her eye, and she crossed the room to glide her fingers over the sheer fabric.

"*Si belle*," she murmured.

"A divine choice, mademoiselle."

Lisette snatched her hand back and glanced at the dressmaker who had slipped up beside her. "Oh, no. I couldn't…" She had no business donning such bold colors, but she couldn't tear her eyes away from the elegant cloth. "Perhaps a dress of pale yellow or ivory would make a better choice."

"Pale yellow? Nonsense." The woman wrestled the bolt of fabric from the display and held a corner to Lisette's cheek. "The plum enhances your dark coloring to perfection. You should listen to Madame Morel. I am the most sought after modiste on Linmead Island."

Considering the small geographic area, Lisette wasn't certain this was any great accomplishment, but she had to admit her choice in cloth was divine.

Madame Morel guided her toward an oval looking glass and draped a corner of the silk over Lisette's shoulder. "See for yourself. Madame Morel is never wrong."

"*Oui*. It is nice."

Daniel sidled up beside the shop's proprietor and tipped his head to the side, studying Lisette's reflection. "I must agree with Madame Morel. It's perfect." He smiled at the modiste. "Madame Lavigne requires a gown for the Governor's Ball. Show me your sketches."

The woman twittered like a young girl when he offered his arm and led her away.

"Captain Hillary," Lisette called, but he didn't pay her any mind. *By the saints.* She would not leave the style of her gown up to a man. She made to follow, but Serafine detained her.

"You'll not allow him to dress you like his mistress," she hissed. "And he cannot purchase either of our gowns. I won't stand for it."

Lisette's gaze darted toward Amelia, appalled that she might have overheard Serafine's outrageous assumptions. If she had, she was polite enough to pretend to be engrossed in comparing bolts of lace.

Lisette pried her arm from her cousin's grasp. "I'm sure Madame Morel would not steer me in the wrong direction. Now if you will excuse me."

"Lisette, *please*," she whispered.

Serafine's commanding manner was wearing Lisette's patience thin. In fact, if her fortitude were a cloak, it would boast gaping holes. She swept by Serafine. "'Tis only a ball gown."

As she reached the table where Madame Morel and Daniel pored over the pages of a sketchbook, he stood and offered his chair before pointing to the current drawing. "That's the one. Can you have it ready in time?"

"*I* will decide which gown suits me best," Lisette snipped and hauled the book across the table for a better look.

She suppressed a sigh of pleasure as she sank onto the chair. Daniel's choice was divine with a daring neckline and ethereal skirts that would sway with each step so she would appear to be walking on a cloud.

Merde. She couldn't agree with him now. She flipped through several sketches, all adequate, but... *Oh, why must he have seen the fashion plate first?*

She studied the other drawings and debated between making a different selection to spite Daniel and following her wishes. In the end, she turned the page to his favorite gown.

"This one is quite nice," she mumbled.

Daniel smirked. "Excellent choice, madame. I couldn't have chosen better myself."

How she wanted to tell him to take a plunge off a tall cliff, but instead she tossed her head and ignored him, earning an infuriating chuckle.

"This way, madame." The modiste ushered her through a set of crimson velvet curtains trimmed in gold fringe and urged her to stand on a platform. With speed that marked her as an experienced seamstress, she took Lisette's measurements.

"I shall have your gown ready in plenty of time before the ball."

"*Merci*, madame."

Lisette commissioned Madame Morel to create three more looks then wandered to the front of the shop and stood with her back to the shop window to wait for Serafine and Amelia.

With time to think upon her ball gown, uncertainty buzzed around in her head like a persistent housefly. Perhaps she should have solicited her cousin's advice before choosing the style. Serafine, her senior by two years, had enjoyed a season in New Orleans society. She knew about societal expectations and judgments whereas Lisette wallowed in ignorance.

Her social interactions had been limited to attending the cathedral every Sabbath, which hadn't prepared her to don daring gowns or dance within the circle of a man's arms. Lisette's heart tripped and tumbled end over end.

Lord, have mercy. Balls involved dancing. Why hadn't this dawned on her earlier? She would look like a fool at the Governor's Ball. How was she to charm a gentleman into assisting her and her family if she moved like a one-legged hen on the dance floor?

She clasped her hands at her chest and took a slow, deep breath to calm her riotous belly. She needn't panic, not yet. Surely she could figure out something before the Governor's Ball so no one would realize she didn't know a minuet from a—a—*another* dance.

She could name only the minuet? How could that be?

Daniel approached her as Serafine disappeared through the curtains for her fitting. "You're anxious again."

"I am not."

He raised a brow and nodded toward her entwined hands. The tips of her fingers glowed red while her knuckles had turned white.

"I hadn't realized I was—" Lisette dropped her hands to her sides and cleared her throat. "It's simply a habit."

"A nervous habit."

She shot him a warning glower when a witty retort refused to come to her.

He touched her elbow. His blue eyes radiated concern. "What's the matter, Lisette? Perhaps I can help. Is it the gown?"

"The gown is exquisite."

"Then what troubles you?"

She sighed with resignation. What did it matter if he knew her education as a lady had been neglected? "Papa—he never allowed me to receive instruction in dance. He thought it was a frivolous pursuit."

"I see." His cocky grin returned. "Well, luv, you're in luck because I'm an excellent dancer."

He teased her again.

"Why do I bother confiding in you?" She spun on her heel and marched from the boutique with Daniel following behind. "Is there anything to which you do not claim to be an expert?"

"Wait a minute, madame, what are you implying?"

She stopped on the walkway outside the shop, derailed by the glorious scent wafting on the breeze. "What is that delightful aroma?" She threw a censorious look at Daniel as he reached her side. "And do not claim it's *you*."

He laughed. He had a hearty, pleasant laugh that embraced her heart and increased her frustration and worries. "Whatever is that to mean? Does my scent offend you, madame?"

Only in the sense that his unique blending of salty air and masculinity appealed to her more than she cared to admit. "Yes. *No!*" She tried to wave away the fog confusing her mind. "Please, I don't wish to have this conversation now."

"Come with me." He grasped her elbow and led her around the side of the building where a vine of white, waxy flowers weaved through a weathered trellis. "It's jasmine."

She walked closer and plucked a blossom to savor the sweetness. "Oh, I never knew anything could be this... *perfect*."

"It's no more perfect than the perfume you wear."

"Well, I prefer the jasmine." She smiled, the barrier between them crumbling a little. "I apologize for my outburst, Captain. I'm allowing my concerns to color my behavior. I'll find a quiet place at the ball and observe."

Could she truly enlist a gentleman's help from the sidelines?

He took the jasmine blossom from her fingers and tucked it into her hair, trailing his thumb along her cheek then over her lips. "You are to call me Daniel, remember? I should be the one to apologize for my behavior on ship. I never thanked you for taking care of me."

She knew she should pull away, but she longed to feel his touch, to remember the warmth of his fingers on her cheek when she needed comfort in the long days ahead.

"I didn't mean to come across as arrogant about my skill on the dance floor either," he said. "I had lessons as a young man. If you follow my lead, I won't allow you to look like a fool. I promise."

The heavenly fragrance from the jasmine vine and Daniel's nearness made her head spin. "But that will not help me when I dance with another partner."

"I don't wish for you to have another partner." He traced a circle on her chin then urged her forward to meet his mouth.

Sweet Mary and Joseph. Her willpower was weak.

Daniel's kiss was gentle, just as it had been the first time. Encouraging, almost pleading, but not demanding as he was in every other instance. This side of him caught her off balance, and she leaned in to him, encircled by his protective arms. Reaching around his neck, she urged him closer, parting her lips when his tongue brushed against them. A moan sounded deep within his throat, flowing into her and rattling her senses. She answered his call with a soft murmur and hugged him tighter.

He broke the kiss but didn't release her as he nibbled down her neck, sending tremors everywhere.

"*Mon dieu, mon amour,*" she said on a wispy breath. "You're making me shake uncontrollably now."

Daniel ceased his lovely assault and smiled down at her, keeping her within the circle of his arms. "I believe that might have been praise, but I'm never certain with you, Lis."

"You may consider it high accolades."

His brow lifted with an arrogant slant. "Expert status, would you say?"

She was too enchanted by him to find fault this time. "I'm willing to concede that you are in fact very good at kissing."

"I'm also an excellent dancer, as you will learn this afternoon when I give you your first lesson."

Louis Reynaud studied the pennant on the masthead. A strong wind from the northwest whipped the flag into a frenzy. "Two points on the larboard bow then dead ahead."

The helmsman nodded sharply and followed his command, turning the wheel to the left.

From Louis's calculations, he and his crew would dock at Port Albis in five days. The *Mihos* skimmed the mighty waves, unbound by gravity. His ship was everything he was, sleek, stealthy, and unstoppable.

Wind blasted his unbound hair from his face, filling him with feral aggression. *He* was the lion god, and no one stole what belonged to him.

After careful consideration, he'd decided to spare his fiancée's life. Lisette would have a long time to make amends for her disobedient actions, and he'd see that she was repentant.

Louis smiled and turned his attention to what, or rather who, waited for him in his quarters. The man had proven useful in accessing the *Cecily*'s manifest. Now his presence would ensure Lisette's return, along with Louis's letters, once they caught up to Captain Hillary's ship. Entering his cabin, Louis's gaze landed on the man still sitting at the table where he had left him. He regarded Louis with caution. His quarry was wise but weak, which pleased and disappointed Louis at the same time.

"Mr. Baptiste, I'm surprised by how accommodating you have been. I expected more trouble from you."

Fourteen

"STEP BACK, SIDE, TOGETHER, SHIFT WEIGHT. Now back, to the right—" Daniel tightened his grip on Lisette's hand and tugged her to the right when she slid to the left.

Again.

"Right! Right! Damnation, woman. How do you not know your right from left?"

"Stop barking at me. I thought you meant *your* right."

Daniel threw his hands in the air with a frustrated growl.

Lisette's green eyes sparked with irritation as they stood toe to toe in the deserted ballroom. "*You* are the one going the wrong direction."

The stubborn tip of her chin made him grin in spite of himself. He liked a spirited lady and Lisette showed more courage than most when faced with his displeasure.

Daniel rolled his shoulders and took a deep breath. He'd conquered more difficult challenges than teaching a lady with no sense of direction to waltz. He could master Lisette too.

"I can't be going the wrong way, my dear. I'm leading."

"Hence, the problem." With an exaggerated huff, she pulled herself up tall. "Shall we try again?"

"As you wish, madame. On three. One, two, three." He and Lisette stepped forward at the same time, the toe of her slipper slamming into his shin.

"For the love of—" Daniel bit back a string of oaths and wrestled for control of his temper. It wouldn't do to blister the ears of a defenseless young lady.

"*Sacre bleu.*" Lisette held her head with both hands. "Just stick me in a corner with the wallflowers. I'll never learn to waltz."

Her bottom lip trembled and her eyes grew misty. This was the closest he'd even seen her come to shedding a tear. It was just a dance. He saw no need for her to be so critical of herself.

"Of course you will learn, Lis. Come here."

She hesitated a second before stepping into his outstretched arms. He hugged her, resting his chin atop her silky hair. She wrapped her arms around his waist and buried her face into his cravat. If they were onboard his ship, he wouldn't be wearing the blasted thing, and he'd feel her cheek against his bare skin. His lower belly tightened with regret.

What a pair they would make in London, a gentleman who abhorred the privileges afforded him and a lady who couldn't dance and bubbled forth French curses like a hot spring. He cared nothing for what the *ton* thought of him, but the fools would massacre his dear Lisette.

Daniel loosened his hold and kissed her cheek. He'd do everything he could to prepare her for her first encounter with the ravenous beasts, leaving no one a reason to find fault with her.

"I have an idea." His hand spanned her waist and he lifted.

She gasped and clung to him. "What are you doing?"

"Kick off your slippers and place your feet atop mine."

"I will not! Don't be ridiculous."

"We're alone, luv. Besides, it's only feet. I won't even notice them while I'm gazing at your tempting lips."

"Daniel." A crimson flush claimed her cheeks, making her even more alluring than usual. She nibbled her bottom lip as her wary gaze lifted to his. "Will this *truly* help me to learn?"

He nodded. Hell if he knew, but he didn't care at this point. All he wanted was to hold her close. Perhaps he would never let her go. More and more he was loath to have her away from him. If he could go back and reenact their last encounter in his cabins, he never would have made her leave. "You do wish to learn, don't you?"

"Yes," she conceded at last. Although her voice rang with doubt, Lisette's slippers dropped to the wooden floor, and her small feet landed on top of his boots. She wobbled until she adjusted her balance then stood stiffly while gripping his hand. "I'm ready. I think."

"Don't think. That is your first lesson. Close your eyes and *feel* the dance."

Lisette's black lashes lay against her skin, and he was tempted to kiss each eyelid before sampling all the other places he wished to place his lips. But he would never teach her the waltz in time if he allowed his desires to rule.

"Ready?" Daniel swayed at first to allow her to grow accustomed to the motion. Her movements were wooden and unnatural, so he slipped his hand down to her hip to direct her; his fingers curled gently into her flesh. "Like this, sweetheart. Match my rhythm."

Her luminous eyes flew open and held him entranced. "Should I hold you there, too?" Her hand lowered to his waist, easing toward his hip. Her fingers rested against his buttocks.

Daniel's throat felt as if it had shrunk, and he swallowed hard. "That's perfect."

She pressed her body closer to his and rested her head on his shoulder, duplicating his easy undulations. With each sway, she melted against him further.

"Are you certain I'm doing everything correctly?" Her cool breath whispered across his ear, sending chills racing down his back.

"Yes. You are marvelous, luv," he murmured, his voice thick with yearning. "You're ready."

He stepped slowly forward so as not to startle her, but Lisette gripped him tighter anyway. "I'm going to fall."

"I won't let you." His mouth grazed her temple and his arm tightened around her back while his other cradled her bottom. The sweet scent of orange blossoms emanated from her. His breaths came harder, faster, and matched hers. "Let's move again."

He eased to the side, pausing until she regained her balance. "Now back to the start."

He shifted their weight to the other foot and repeated the steps. The more they danced, the more harmonious their movements became. Lisette's added weight made him feel clumsy, but this was the first time he'd ever truly enjoyed a waltz.

Eventually, she no longer anticipated the direction, flowing from one step to the other without hesitation. She hummed a sweet tune, her voice washing over him and flooding him with the feverish memory of her singing while she had lovingly bathed him. His head spun and his chest grew tight. He wanted to make love to her.

Here.

Now.

Lisette's eyes flew open and a smile lit her face. "I'm feeling it, Daniel."

His heart lodged in his throat. He was feeling it too, this thing that bound them together. The novel sensation swirled around him, a combination of loyalty, passion, and eager anticipation. He had lusted after women many times, slaked his desire, and then went his merry way. It had been the same every time. But he didn't want to walk away from Lisette. He almost thought what he felt might be love. Yet, he'd been in love before, hadn't he? What he shared with Lisette felt different than anything he had ever experienced with Cecily.

Thoughts of his wife acted as a dousing with cold water, and he set Lisette away. "Nicely done. That concludes our lesson for today."

She beamed. "I did it, didn't I? I can't thank you enough, Daniel." Such a small gesture on his part, and yet she was as happy as if he'd bestowed diamonds upon her.

She lifted to her toes and placed a kiss on his cheek before retrieving her slippers. "I must hurry to my chambers before Serafine and Rafe return from their stroll with Monsieur Patch."

Lisette had insisted they keep her lessons a secret from everyone.

She stopped at the threshold and glanced over her shoulder. "Same time tomorrow?"

Daniel nodded, forcing himself to stay put when she breezed from the ballroom rather than giving chase as he wanted. Blinking the room into focus, he was struck by the magnitude of his depravity.

Here he stood in Cecily's home and more than anything, he longed for Lisette.

"Damnation." Daniel stalked into the stone corridor and headed toward the south gallery. He wanted to see his wife again, to remind himself of how she once looked.

During his first stay at the governor's house, Cecily had guided him to the south gallery to admire the portraits. She'd been flirtatious even with her maid present, batting her lashes and pursing her lips. Daniel had been flattered by her attempts to charm him, but he hadn't responded in kind. Dallying with the governor's daughter, no matter how fair of face, would have been unwise for business. His grandfather had cultivated a friendship with the governor that benefited Daniel. Remaining in the official's good graces meant he and his crew would continue to receive a warm welcome in Port Albis.

Cecily, however, hadn't appreciated Daniel's aloof manner and had voiced her displeasure at every

opportunity. And she had orchestrated *many* opportunities to cross paths with him during his stay.

Daniel arrived at the gallery and paused as he tried
to recall the location of Cecily's portrait. His gaze
landed on her youthful face, and he moved closer.
In the painting, Cecily sat prettily on a scarlet chair
with her hands folded in her lap. Her virginal white
gown covered most of her porcelain skin. Her smile
was innocent. Now he could see it though, a flare of
defiance in her pale blue-gray eyes.

Cecily had arranged a dance with him at a party
hosted by her parents the evening following the tour
of the gallery. She'd stood closer than was proper,
holding his gaze.

*"Simon painted my portrait more than once, Captain
Hillary."*

*"Indeed, Miss Bristow? I would have thought you too
impatient to sit still for two portraits."*

*"You underestimate me, sir. I fear it will be your undoing.
Do you wish to hear of my experience?"*

"As you wish." He was being polite. Daniel found her
childish prattle banal.

*"Every afternoon after posing in the morning for the
portrait in the gallery, I stole away to Simon's house. It
was a pitiful sea shanty. Nothing to recommend it. Simon
lived as a pauper, but he was passionate about his art. And
his subject."* She plastered her body against Daniel's as
they twirled the ballroom. He drew back to reestablish the
appropriate space between them.

"I unfastened my dress," she whispered, *"and allowed
him to capture my bare breast on canvas."*

Daniel hid his shock. Her behavior was scandalous and

undeniably arousing. "Why would you do such a thing? Have you no sense of the consequences?"

She tossed her head. "Because I could, Captain Hillary. Have you never done anything simply for the joy of doing what you shouldn't?"

"Not when I was a child." He held her gaze a long time until she looked away. Red rushed into her cheeks, leaving dark splotches on her neck and chest.

"He made me feel beautiful," she murmured. "And I am a woman, not a child."

Daniel shook himself from the past and scrubbed his hand over his jaw. Cecily had needed him, desperately. He hadn't realized his calling at that moment, but later as they had faced her parents, he'd known his purpose: to save Cecily from herself. But there had been no one to save her from him.

᭱

Lisette's buoyant mood carried her into the glittering ballroom with her cousin at her side. Golden light from the chandeliers spilled over the guests gathered for the affair, filling the room with good cheer. Surely among the gentlemen present, there would be one willing to assist her. "Let the search begin," she whispered to Serafine.

Several soldiers clad in red uniforms with yellow fringe and shining buttons ceased their conversation and looked at Serafine and Lisette as they approached. Their avid attention gave Lisette pause, and a slight shudder passed through her. What if every gentleman she appealed to for assistance requested the same arrangement Daniel had posed in New Orleans?

She forced down her anxieties. Shyness would not serve her family. Lisette tried to hang on to the confidence she'd experienced when looking at her reflection in the mirror moments earlier. Never had she felt more beautiful than she did in her glorious gown of plum with matching slippers.

Her coiffure had been styled to perfection with tiny braids looping around her head like a crown and curls spilling down her back. This was the first evening she and Serafine hadn't needed to play lady's maid to each other, thanks to Her Excellency's generosity. The luxury of an assistant was welcomed and much appreciated.

As she scanned the crowd, her newly acquired scent drifted on the air. She smiled reluctantly. Daniel had presented her with an elegantly wrapped gift at the end of her last dance lesson that morning to congratulate her on her progress. Inside the box lay a delicate bottle of jasmine oil tucked into a crimson velvet pouch. It was silly for her to feel sentimental over his gift, and she should have refused to accept his offering. Yet, his thoughtfulness had touched her and filled her with regret that they would be parting soon. She wanted something by which to remember Daniel.

Serafine pointed with her fan. "I've located Amelia and Monsieur Hillary."

Their friend was a vision in a gown of emerald that disguised her expanding belly better than any of them had expected. As Lisette and Serafine wound through the crowd to reach Amelia and her husband, a prickling sensation rippled along the back of her neck. She looked over her shoulder and came to a sudden stop.

Her breathing ceased as she turned toward the source of her disquiet.

Daniel was ambling toward her. His dimple appeared when their gazes met; his blue eyes flared like the spark of touch-paper caught in a tinderbox. How she wanted to touch her finger to the small dip in his cheek.

His black tailcoat embraced his broad shoulders and skimmed his tapered waist, while his ivory trousers clung to his muscular legs. My, he was a dashing man when dressed properly.

"Mademoiselle. Madame," Daniel greeted. "How lovely you look this evening." He swept a long leg in front of him and bowed low, triggering a mesmerizing shifting of muscles in his thigh. He was as covered as she'd ever seen him, but his attire left nothing to the imagination. Not that she needed to imagine anything.

Sweet Mary. Lisette snapped her fan open and waved it briskly to create a breeze. "Good evening, Captain. Goodness, it's stifling in the ballroom, is it not?"

Serafine raised her brows. "I'm comfortable."

Daniel's grin widened as he offered his arm. "Perhaps madame would like to take refreshment. Please, allow me to act as your escort."

Lisette hesitated, not at all certain contact with him would ease her discomfort. It certainly wouldn't further her goal of locating assistance from another gentleman. Still, she looped her arm with his.

Serafine looked between Lisette and Amelia, worried creases appearing on her forehead. "I promised to shield Mrs. Hillary from curious stares. Perhaps you would retrieve a glass for me, too?"

"My pleasure, Mademoiselle Vistoire."

Daniel guided Lisette along the outer edges of the gathering toward the refreshment room off the great hall. When they joined the crush milling about the smaller room, he drew her closer to his side. "I can see the table ahead."

Many a polite gentleman smiled as they waited in line, easing much of her concern that she would be unable to find someone willing to help her.

Daniel's forearm began to twitch with each gesture of friendliness. "Once we return to the ballroom, I wish to sign your dance card before the other gentlemen approach you."

"I would be honored to grant your request." She patted his arm. If not for Daniel, she would be hiding in a corner this evening. Perhaps he would claim a waltz. "I never thanked you for instructing me. I believe I can follow well enough now, but looking at this crowd, I'm no longer worried about a misstep. The gentlemen seem benevolent. I'm sure they will overlook my mistakes."

"Indeed," he mumbled.

The sea of bodies parted as Daniel delivered her to the refreshment table. He ladled yellow punch into two cut glasses then handed one to her. "It's pineapple."

Lisette sniffed the concoction before tasting it. She closed her eyes, swept up in the ecstasy of the sweet drink. "It's delicious."

"I prefer brandy myself."

She smiled and returned the greeting of a passing gentleman who looked kindly upon her.

Capturing her free arm, Daniel hurried her toward

the ballroom. "No time to dally. Mademoiselle Vistoire is likely parched by now."

"Slow down." Lisette planted her feet, but her protest was for naught. He possessed the strength of five men. Holding her glass away from her so as not to soil her gown, she trotted beside him.

Daniel released her when they reached Serafine, Amelia, and Monsieur Hillary. The three huddled together wearing distressed looks while two matronly women gushed over the joys of childbirth.

"Fascinating accounting. Your descriptions are so vivid." Monsieur Hillary hooked a finger between his neck and cravat and yanked. "If you will excuse us, ladies, I promised to escort my wife to the refreshment room."

Amelia sent a grateful look toward her husband. Her complexion was paler than usual. "Yes, thank you, sir."

Monsieur Hillary backed up a step and bumped into Daniel. The glass of pineapple punch in Daniel's hand sloshed down Monsieur Hillary's pants leg.

"Dear heavens, Mr. Hillary," one of the ladies cried.

The elderly women whipped out handkerchiefs— one from her reticule and the other from between her bosom—and blotted Jake Hillary's breeches in a flurry of activity and chorus of "*oh my*."

"Please." He attempted to deflect their hands while the women struck with the precision of copperhead snakes. "Do not trouble yourselves on my account."

A peacock feather jutting from the taller woman's hat jabbed poor Monsieur Hillary in the eye. He knocked it aside, bending the feather to hang at an awkward angle.

"I really don't require any assistance."

"There, there, sir. We will set you to rights in no time."

The ladies were enthusiastic in their ministrations, wiping places clearly not doused with punch. With exasperated eyes, Monsieur Hillary sought out his brother, who hadn't stopped laughing. "Daniel, a little assistance, please?"

Daniel handed Lisette the empty glass and stepped forward to pull Monsieur Hillary from the melee. "Thank you, ladies. How kind you are. My brother is set to rights now."

"Oh, yes," the plumper one agreed. Clutching her handkerchief to her chest, she appeared the picture of a child disappointed to have her fun interrupted. "Happy to have been of service, sir."

"Yes, thank you," Monsieur Hillary grumbled.

The ladies smiled once more then moved on to speak with another guest.

"Good *Lord*, this isn't London," Monsieur Hillary said.

Amelia came to his side. "Are you all right?"

"I feel I must bathe again."

She patted his hand. "My poor darling, go upstairs and do what you must. Mademoiselle Vistoire and I will find our way to the refreshment room."

Monsieur Hillary left the ballroom to change while Amelia and Serafine sought out refreshment.

"Your brother was practically mauled," Lisette whispered. "How humiliating."

"He has survived worse." Daniel held out his hand. "Your dance card, madame."

"Certainly, monsieur." Lisette's smile soon began

to fade as Daniel scribbled his name to a second dance. And then a third and a fourth. "What are you doing?"

"I made it clear at Madame Morel's that I have no desire for you to dance with other gentlemen."

"Return my card." She tried to snatch it from him, but he turned his back. "Give it to me at once, monsieur."

Daniel finally passed the card back. He had claimed every dance.

"What about *my* wishes? Are your desires more important?"

His stern hand on the small of her back made her jump. He propelled her forward and outside through the glass doors lining the veranda, into the darkness, before she realized his intentions.

"*Non.*"

"Just one moment alone, darling. That's all I ask."

The constant breeze off the sea lifted the curls cascading down her back, and the scent of jasmine surrounded her, reminding her of his earlier generosity. She stopped resisting and followed him to a hidden corner of the sprawling terrace.

"Well, *are* your wishes more important?" Lisette's voice lacked the conviction it had possessed a moment ago.

Daniel faced her. The moonlight darkened his eyes to shining pools of black. "Tell me you want to dance with other gentlemen, Lis." Her body quivered as his arms captured her around the waist. "If that is your true desire, I won't interfere. But I must hear you say it."

No part of her desired anyone other than Daniel, but her longings wouldn't provide the safety her family required.

She backed out of his embrace. "I must go."

"Must you?"

Lisette bit down on her lip. He was dangerous to her welfare and that of her family. She should go at once, but her feet refused to obey.

Daniel brushed a loose strand of hair behind her ear, his fingers lingering on her skin. She shivered.

"Answer me, luv. Do you wish to dance with other men?"

Non. "*Oui.* But I shall save a place on my card for you. A waltz? Minuet? What is it you want?"

"You," he whispered, wrapping his fingers around the nape of her neck. "You, *ma chère.*" His breath caressed her cheek, so warm and exciting.

Their lips drifted closer together.

"I should resist you."

He chuckled under his breath. "Please don't."

"Lisette!" Serafine called out from the dark, startling them apart. "Are you out here?"

Lisette suppressed a sigh. Would her cousin ever trust her to do what was best for them all?

Fifteen

Daniel gritted his teeth. Lisette's bothersome cousin was spoiling his pleasure yet again. He would need to do something with the wench when they set sail. Too bad tossing her overboard was out of the question.

He guided Lisette away from her approaching relative, not wishing to place her in the position of needing to defend herself against her cousin's judgments. "Use the south doors. I'll intercept her."

Lisette hurried toward the light spilling from another set of glass doors then disappeared inside the governor's mansion. Daniel pulled the cheroot his father-in-law had given him from his jacket, lit it using the flame of the closest torch, and waited for Mademoiselle Vistoire to discover him.

"Lisette," she hissed. "Where are you, you incorrigible girl?"

Daniel almost felt sorry for Mademoiselle Vistoire. The role of Lisette's keeper couldn't be easy, but it seemed a self-appointed position and unnecessary given Lisette's widowhood.

The lady's footsteps pattered in his direction. As she emerged from the shadows, the torchlight made her black tresses gleam.

"Out and about with no chaperone, mademoiselle? A risky venture for an innocent. Who knows what unsavory characters you might run across on a dark night?"

Her lip lifted with derision. "Such as yourself, Captain Hillary?"

"Perhaps." A plume of smoke rose from the tip of the cheroot, swirling into the air. "What brings you outside, my dear?"

"Where is my cousin?"

"I imagine she's in the ballroom, where you belong."

Mademoiselle Vistoire's hands landed on her hips. "She is not. I searched the entire hall."

Daniel raised a brow. "I question the accuracy of your claim, but it matters little to me. As you can see, Madame Lavigne is not in my company. Do you suspect someone else has captured her fancy?"

She marched across the remaining space and looked up with hardened eyes. "Take *me*."

Daniel fumbled his cheroot but recovered it before it slipped from his fingers. He hoped he misunderstood her. "Take you? Take you where?"

She scowled. "To your bed, imbecile."

"Egads!" He tossed the cheroot to the ground and crushed the burning tip with his boot. "You are out of line, mademoiselle."

"Am I?"

She attempted to throw her arms around his neck, but he captured her wrists. She jerked against his hold, but he refused to release her for fear she'd further disgrace herself.

"We both know you practice no discernment when bedding a woman," she spat. "I'm familiar with men like you. You have your way with the fools then fling them aside for the next pleasure."

His jaw dropped and his hold loosened. Her gall was beyond the pale.

Mademoiselle Vistoire extracted her arms from his grip and rubbed her wrists. "Let's be reasonable, Captain. Lisette's prospects for securing a proper match once we reach England are better than my own. Rafe and I need her to marry well, perhaps to a titled gentleman. She cannot catch a husband if you ruin her."

"Ruin her?" The lady was a complete noddy. "Your cousin is a widow. The only thing she's likely to catch in London is a rake at her back door."

His fingers curled into a fist. The idea of the black-guards misusing Lisette made him want to pound them.

Mademoiselle Vistoire crossed her arms. "I haven't the slightest idea as to your meaning."

He wouldn't like to explain his meaning either. Daniel rolled his shoulders to lessen the tension between his shoulder blades. He must recall he was in the presence of a lady, even though she behaved with less than ladylike manners.

"There is no denying Madame Lavigne is a beauty without compare. I'm certain she will turn a few heads. But she is a widow with no issue. Her fertility will come into question, and these illustrious *noblemen* you seek require an heir."

"Lisette is plenty young enough to produce offspring," she argued.

"Irrelevant point, my dear. The *ton* makes judgments quickly. So unless your cousin has significant financial assets to bring to the union, she has no chance of marrying, and even then her prospects are limited to men in dire need of funds."

Serafine scoffed. "You have an interesting perspective, sir, but you are mistaken. My cousin is not a widow."

"Of course she is. Lisette said as much in our first meeting."

"She allowed you to believe her to be a widow, because that seemed the best course at the time."

Uneasiness swirled in his stomach. Mademoiselle Vistoire was annoying and interfering, but she didn't strike him as a liar. "But she wore widow's weeds."

Her severe brows arched over her mocking gaze. "Her mourning clothes were made to grieve her father."

If Lisette wasn't a widow, he had already overstepped his bounds. Did her cousin expect him to offer for Lisette? "What are you implying, mademoiselle?"

The willowy young woman stepped forward, all aggression dissipating. She grasped Daniel's hands. "*She* is an innocent, Captain, but I am not. Please, if you must take one of us to your bed, choose me."

The weary slant of her eyes and downturn of her mouth conveyed no desire for him, simply resignation. Mademoiselle Vistoire considered herself a necessary casualty in the quest to save her family and preserve their future.

"Mademoiselle, I'm at a loss as to how to respond. Thank you for the kind offer, but I must decline."

"I see." Tears pooled in her eyes. She released her death grip on his hands and turned away, furiously swiping away the evidence of her distress. "Of course you must decline. Forgive me. I wasn't thinking."

Daniel felt like a cur. He hadn't meant to injure her sensibilities, but how was he to explain his desire was only for Lisette? "You needn't apologize," he called to Mademoiselle Vistoire as she walked away.

She lifted her skirts and dashed for the terrace stairs. "Mademoiselle, wait."

She kept running and disappeared into the moonlit gardens.

Damnation. The last thing he wanted was to chase the wench, but she left him little choice. Lisette would be beside herself if harm came to her cousin. He glanced back at the house, hoping to catch a glimpse of Lisette so he might enlist her assistance, but instead found Mr. Ramsey had stumbled out the door.

The perpetually foxed vicar could drink his weight in burgundy, rum, or brandy. Perhaps all three at once. He wouldn't be the best candidate to assist Daniel, but he was all that was available.

Daniel stalked across the terrace, his boots striking the stone. "Come with me." Grabbing the clergyman's upper arm, he dragged the man toward the gardens.

Mr. Ramsey's shrill scream sounded like a lady. "Don't hurt me. I'll give you anything you want."

"Silence. I have no cause to harm you."

The vicar released a loud sigh.

"*Yet,*" Daniel added for good measure, earning a pathetic whimper. "When we find Mademoiselle Vistoire, you must escort her inside where she'll be safe. Her reputation will be less damaged if she is discovered with you. Now, help me locate her."

Together, they infiltrated the gardens. Daniel called her name quietly. Mr. Ramsey attempted to call to her as well, but his mouth issued a series of slurs before he tripped over a flagstone.

Daniel caught him before he fell. "Perhaps you should lay off the spirits, sir."

"I only had one drink. Maybe two, but the glass was half empty each time."

Daniel didn't care to argue the point. "Try to be of assistance," he snapped and released the vicar.

If Daniel were smart, he would leave the man in Port Albis. He wouldn't, of course, not after he had given his word to carry the man to England in exchange for performing the marriage ceremony for his brother.

They scoured the gardens until Daniel was ready to give up, but a rustle in the bushes brought him up short. A soft mewling sound came from the other side of the hedge. He put his finger to his lips to signal for the vicar to remain quiet. Easing around the hedge, Daniel discovered Mademoiselle Vistoire sitting on the ground with her knees hugged to her chest. Her head rested on her arms folded across her knees, and her lithe frame shook with suppressed sobs. Light from one of the garden torches cast her in shadow.

"Mademoiselle, please don't cry."

She looked up, but Daniel's request had the opposite effect of what he intended. The woman dropped her head back down and wept in earnest.

"What the bloody hell?" Mr. Ramsey rounded

the hedge in haste and careened into a rose bush. "Damnation! What the devil has me?" A thorn had snagged the man's coat, and he thrashed like a fish in a net. When the connection was severed, he stumbled forward and plopped to his knees. Another round of curse words not fit for anyone's ears, much less a lady's, flew from the vicar's mouth with amazing clarity given his drunken state.

Mademoiselle Vistoire's tears had ceased, and she stared at the vicar with wide eyes. "Gracious, Father. Perhaps you should ask for forgiveness as long as you are on your knees."

Daniel met her gaze. A soft giggle escaped her, soon followed by a full belly laugh. Her reaction caught him by surprise, but laughter was an improvement over her tears.

Mr. Ramsey fixed his blurry eyes on her and frowned. "Father? I'm your father? How could that be? I've always been so bloody cautious."

Mademoiselle Vistoire hooted, doubling over and holding her stomach. Her laughter was so intense she tipped over to lie on the grass.

The corners of Mr. Ramsey's mouth inched upward. "What's so bloody funny?" He chuckled. His expression brightened, and he chuckled once more. Mademoiselle Vistoire's laughter proved to be contagious, and soon the vicar issued hearty guffaws despite having no clue *he* was the joke.

For Pete's sake. They both were insane. And Daniel must have been deranged himself to expect any help from the vicar. Hooking the man under his arms, Daniel hauled him to his feet.

"Mademoiselle, would you lend your assistance? Mr. Ramsey is three sheets to the wind."

She wiped the tears from her cheeks before pushing to her feet and dusting off her gown. "What will you do with him?"

Daniel clamped an arm around the man's waist and urged him back toward the house. "Deliver him to his chambers where he may sleep off his fog."

"How shall I provide assistance?"

He glanced at her over his shoulder. "If you follow us inside, I need not be concerned for your safety."

She nodded sagely. "I see." Falling in place, she walked back to the house behind Daniel and the vicar. They passed through a back door and ascended the servants' staircase. She waited outside Mr. Ramsey's chamber door while Daniel tucked him into bed.

When Daniel rejoined her in the corridor, her gaze dropped, reminding him of Lisette. A rush of affection softened his attitude toward her cousin.

"I'm mortified by my earlier behavior, sir. I hope you do not think ill of me."

He lifted her chin so she must look him in the eye. "I consider you brave beyond your years, mademoiselle, and your family loyalty is to be commended. I'll do nothing to bring harm to you, Lisette, or Rafe. On my honor, I shall protect you with my life. You needn't trouble yourself over your cousin either. I promise not to take advantage of her."

She blinked back more tears and inhaled a shaky breath. "I shall hold you to your word, Captain."

"I have full confidence that you will, mademoiselle." He offered his arm. "Shall we return to the ball?"

"I prefer to retire, if it is all the same to you. I'll send a message to Lisette so she won't worry."

"As you wish." Daniel escorted her to her chamber door then returned to the ballroom. The quartet was playing a minuet. He searched the sidelines for Lisette, but a swirl of plum skirts on the ballroom floor demanded his attention. She was dancing with a gentleman who ogled her like a dog eyeing a juicy steak, probably thinking her widowhood marked her as an easy conquest.

Daniel had thought the same of her when they first met, as would every man making her acquaintance. Widows were fair game in the art of seduction.

Fire streaked through his veins when her dance partner's hand missed hers and brushed the side of her breast. The man was too conveniently clumsy for Daniel's liking.

Lisette flushed, her lashes fluttering as she seemed to be working out if the man's action was intentional or a true accident. Daniel held his breath, hoping she would trust her intuition, but she continued the dance, offering a polite smile to her partner.

Damn Lisette for lying. She had risked her virtue by boarding the *Cecily* and pretending to be a widow. Even now, her reputation would be destroyed if word of her traveling without a chaperone reached London. For the love of God, she had slept in his bed. Touched his bare chest. Reverently. Admiringly. The memory aroused him to no end.

The only honorable response was to offer marriage.

Daniel's fingers curled into fists when the bloody gent's hand slipped again and grazed her arse. Lisette needed to be saved from herself. Unfortunately for her partner, nothing would save him from a sound beating.

Sixteen

LISETTE ALLOWED MONSIEUR ETHELBERT TO PARADE her around the perimeter of the ballroom floor at the end of the dance, following a long line of other couples. Daniel had failed to mention anything about a promenade in his lessons. She would take him to task for his omission later. She would have felt foolish had she left Monsieur Ethelbert alone on the ballroom floor, especially after he had pledged to make arrangements on her behalf to travel aboard the *Lena Mae*.

She had been observing a quadrille when Monsieur Ethelbert discovered her hiding in an alcove and requested her dance card. Too embarrassed to hand him her card allotting every dance to Daniel, she had slipped it into a potted fern, linked arms with Monsieur Ethelbert, and led him toward the dance floor. Her bold acceptance had the poor man turning two shades of red, but she hadn't wanted him to discover her card in the plant. Fortunately, he seemed unaffected by her lack of decorum in the long term and what he lacked in grace while performing the minuet, he made up for it in eagerness to help solve her dilemma.

When they rounded the corner of the dance floor, Daniel moved into their path. A scowl darkened his handsome face.

"Egads," Monsieur Ethelbert mumbled, coming up short and dragging Lisette to a stop.

She ignored Daniel's menacing presence and turned her back on him. "Thank you for the turn about the floor, monsieur. You will keep your promise to call on me tomorrow, will you not?"

"My pleasure, madame." Monsieur Ethelbert lifted her hand to place a kiss on her knuckles but flinched and dropped her hand as if contact might sear his lips.

Monsieur Ethelbert shot another look beyond her shoulder where Daniel lurked. She had known he was there. She felt his eyes burning holes into her back.

"Nice to have made your acquaintance, madame. Until tomorrow." Monsieur Ethelbert was still uttering his good-bye as he scooted away.

Lisette swung back toward her self-appointed protector. She too had been wary in their first encounter, but the captain possessed a soft heart underneath his hard exterior. Yet, when he behaved like Attila the Hun, his ability to be kind was over-shadowed. Daniel had best not have frightened the man away for good or she would box his ears.

She could overlook his boorishness for the moment, however. After all, they would part ways soon, and she wouldn't attempt to fool herself into believing she wouldn't miss him.

Offering a grin in greeting, she approached him. When he didn't return her smile or give evidence of meeting her in the middle, a sense of foreboding settled on her shoulders. She searched the faces around her. Serafine was nowhere in the vicinity.

Quickly closing the distance between her and Daniel, Lisette drew in a shaky breath. "Where's Serafine? Is something wrong?"

"She has retired for the evening." His expression gave away nothing.

"Is she ill? Perhaps I should go to her."

"Your cousin is fine. Dance with me." Grasping her upper arm, he led her onto the floor without waiting for her consent.

She jerked her arm from his grip. "You needn't manhandle me, monsieur."

"Well, pardon me, madame." Daniel took her hand with exaggerated care, mocking her, as they assumed position for the waltz. She narrowed her eyes. If he insisted on being unpleasant, Lisette could match him deed for deed. They locked gazes as the interlude between sets stretched out. She refused to look away first.

"Don't try my patience any more than you already have, Lisette."

"Do not try *mine*."

The viola's smooth voice lifted on the air and soon swept over her, dulling the edge of her irritation. When the cello's deep wail took lead and high-pitched violins wove in and out in the background, she set aside her desire to do battle with Daniel, at least while they waltzed. Afterward, his ears would receive a blistering.

She loved twirling the floor in his arms. He danced like a gentleman and made her forget for a moment what a scoundrel he was. Daniel's gracefulness made her feel beautiful and skillful. With the lightest of touches to her upper back, he guided her around the floor, gazing down at her the entire time, his eyes burning with something she didn't recognize. Her stomach began to make loops to rival the most experienced of couples on the dance floor.

Daniel shook his head. "It's baffling how I couldn't see the truth until this moment."

"I fear I missed a vital part of this conversation. Please enlighten me as to the topic."

"You're untouched, an innocent."

Lisette stumbled over his boot but recovered her footing thanks to his quick assistance. "How absurd. You are well aware I'm a wi—" Her voice cracked. She cleared her throat, but her protest to his accusation refused to dislodge.

"Look at me." Daniel's tone discouraged argument, and she met his heated blue gaze for a moment before looking away. Why did it seem he could see inside her?

"Tell me I am mistaken, Lis."

"I'm sorry. I cannot."

A grim smile softened his features. "I'm relieved to see lies don't come easily to you. Explain yourself."

"I believe you already know the details. You wish to test me."

"I want to know the reason you misrepresented yourself," he said with uncharacteristic calm. "Your actions were reckless and foolish. I demand an explanation. You slept in my bed, Lis."

"You were ill," she murmured. A light perspiration dampened her brow.

Daniel's placid expression while he chastised her rankled, and she didn't appreciate his candor in a public venue. She would not defend her actions here with onlookers.

"I don't wish to discuss my circumstances, monsieur. Upon our first meeting, you said my troubles are not your concern. We agreed on that point."

The music ended moments later, and Lisette stalked from the floor. Daniel matched her stride and linked arms.

"You'll not escape easily, mademoiselle."

His iron hold kept her in place as they performed the promenade in strained silence. Instead of releasing her at the end of the parade as she expected, he directed her toward the exit.

"Where are we going?"

"Somewhere private. We have a matter of great importance to discuss."

Lisette clenched her teeth. "You have *no* authority over me, monsieur."

"That's to change."

She tried to break his grip. "Release me at once."

"No." He didn't slow his pace or loosen his grasp on her arm.

The governor's wife emerged from the crowd and moved into their path. "Captain Hillary, *there* you are."

He slid to a stop, jerking Lisette back when she didn't anticipate his sudden halt.

"Your Excellency." Daniel bowed stiffly but kept a firm hold on Lisette.

Cecily's mother swept her assessing gaze over her then turned a grave look on Daniel. "You aren't leaving, are you, Captain? I had hoped we might share a dance."

Lisette seized the opportunity to rid herself of his boorish company. "Captain Hillary was escorting me to the door. I am retiring for the evening."

"So soon, madame?" she asked. "I do hope you aren't feeling under the weather."

"I'm fit, Your Excellency, but unaccustomed to this amount of activity. The evening has been delightful, but I pray you will excuse me."

Cecily's mother tipped her head. Gray streaked through her golden tresses and fine lines etched the corners of her nearly translucent blue eyes, but the bloom of her youthful beauty remained. Had Cecily resembled her mother? If so, she'd been lovely. It was no wonder Daniel couldn't forget her.

A pain throbbed in Lisette's chest, but she forced a polite smile for Daniel so as not to alert the first lady to their troubles. "Please, dance with Her Excellency, Captain Hillary. I'm capable of finding the door."

His jaw twitched, and Lisette held her breath, steeling herself for an argument. Slowly, his fingers uncurled from her forearm, and he offered his hand to Cecily's mother.

"Indeed, madame." His pointed stare communicated that their conversation was not over. "Your Excellency, shall we?"

"Splendid." Cecily's mother accepted his hand and moved toward the dance floor. "Good evening, Madame Lavigne," she said without looking back.

The first lady's dismissal stung, but not as much as Daniel's low opinion of her. Surely, he thought her a trollop after their kisses and presence in his bedchamber. And maybe he was correct. Maybe she was a wicked young woman, because Mary help her, she couldn't trust herself in his presence.

❧

Daniel's gaze strayed to the ballroom entrance for signs of Lisette returning. His teeth ground together as he ruminated on their situation. Her recklessness left him no choice but to offer for her. At his core, he remained a gentleman, and compromising an innocent was not to be tolerated.

Damnation. A rush of frustration made him shake. He'd had no choice in his first marriage either, and he hated being the casualty of a young woman's carelessness again.

Yet, this had never been a game for Lisette as it had been for Cecily. In the corridor at The Abyss, Lisette had pleaded with him through her eyes. She had denied any danger, but he'd recognized the truth and ignored his misgivings. Daniel wanted answers now. He wanted to know what had made her so desperate to leave New Orleans.

"What do you think you are doing in regards to Madame Lavigne, Daniel?"

His mother-in-law's cutting tone snatched him back to the present. He hadn't been the recipient of her stern frown since the morning he'd stood before Cecily's father and accepted responsibility for compromising their daughter. Cecily's mother had stared at him that day, shaking her head as if she couldn't comprehend his gall, much like now.

Did she realize his intentions with Lisette? He hadn't considered how Cecily's parents would look upon him taking another wife.

"You misunderstand, Your Excellency."

Her brows migrated together, displaying her increasing disapproval.

"I promised to deliver Madame Lavigne and her family to England," he rushed to explain. "Our association is impersonal, or it has been."

"Balderdash. I saw you whisking the young woman to the terrace, and I suspect your intentions were less than honorable." Her eyes narrowed. "I've been aware of your *appetites* for some time, sir. There are no secrets in Port Albis, no matter how discreet one might think he is."

Daniel hadn't blushed since he was an untried youth, yet he burned with the intensity of a flame doused with oil.

"Enough of this foolishness. It is past time we spoke of Cecily and set things to rights. I shall summon you on the morrow. Be ready."

She walked away before the music ended, leaving him alone to face the curious stares of the other guests.

Seventeen

DANIEL PACED THE GALLERY AS HE WAITED FOR Cecily's parents. He stopped to check his watch. Was this part of their punishment? To build up his dread until he wanted to climb the walls? He started to put his watch away, but checked it once more to reassure himself he hadn't read it wrong.

Blast and damn. Cecily's parents had kept him waiting for twenty minutes. He shoved the watch deep into his pocket and jerked on his waistcoat to adjust it. He just wanted to get the whole damned affair settled once and for all. For five years, he had been waiting for this confrontation. Waiting for Cecily's parents to level accusations at him. Waiting for someone to acknowledge what he had done.

Daniel reached the end of the gallery and stopped to gaze at the azure waters on the horizon. Calm settled over him like an early morning mist blanketing the seas he loved. Finally, he could speak the truth and maybe free himself from the prison Cecily's death had built around his heart.

He returned to stand before the paintings on the

wall. Cecily's translucent blue eyes stared out from her portrait, her smile mocking. He hated that bloody portrait. It marked the moment the sweet child her parents had spoken of in past encounters had transformed into a coldhearted creature and, in turn, altered him.

Daniel abhorred the man he had become since Cecily's death. No, that was untrue. He hated himself the moment he didn't toss her from his chambers. And he'd hated the husband he had been to her, becoming distant like his father when she had turned him away.

A swish of skirts wrenched him from his self-recriminations. Cecily's mother glided across the polished marble floor. "I apologize for keeping you waiting. Shall we take a turn about the gardens?"

He looked past her shoulder for signs of the governor. "Will His Excellency be joining us?"

She twined her arm with his and guided him toward the glass doors at the far end of the gallery. "My husband must never know of our conversation," she whispered as they walked outside into the sunlight.

Daniel's heart sped up a beat. "Why?"

"Promise me, Daniel."

He nodded, unsure if he was wise or foolish to give his consent, but unable to deny his need to hear her out. "I give my word."

In silence, they retreated deep into the gardens. The ocean glittered in the distance and a faint breeze cooled his forehead.

"I cannot allow this to go on any longer." The lady's voice wavered. "I've caused you undue suffering, and this knowledge destroys me inside."

"You have caused *me* suffering?" Her words made no sense.

"Yes, I have done this to you. I've allowed you to blame yourself for my daughter's death when I am the one at fault."

Never once had he stopped to consider that Cecily's mother might blame herself. "You had nothing to do with Cecily dying."

She laced her fingers as if praying and pinched her eyes closed. "I did," she murmured. "I didn't intend to, but because of me, my daughter is dead."

This was madness, the aftermath of sorrow. Grief could play strange tricks on one's mind. Reaching out, Daniel patted her shoulder. The gesture seemed inadequate, a halfhearted attempt at comforting her, so he gathered her in a hug. Part of him wished he could hand over the burden of his guilt to Cecily's mother, but he never would. "Your only mistake was in surrendering your daughter to my care. I failed her, not you. I never should have insisted she leave Port Albis."

When she pulled away, her eyes were flooded with tears. "Cecily's rightful place was by your side. She was your wife, Daniel. She made her choice when she stole into your bed while you slept."

"How did you—?" He bit back his reply. It didn't matter any longer. Cecily was gone, and he wouldn't add to her mother's suffering by tainting her memory.

The first lady shook her head, a rueful smile in place. "I knew my daughter well. Your silence does not protect her. I loved her dearly, but I was never blind to Cecily's failings. Not like her father was."

Her intense pale gaze held Daniel in place. "I realized the circumstances that led to my daughter's presence in your chambers as soon as I learned of the incident. Cecily didn't require enticement, and I'm certain she orchestrated her discovery."

Daniel frowned. The poor woman had weaved a twisted tale in her mind. Cecily wouldn't have planned her ruin, not with him. Her disdain still felt like a punch to the gut.

"Your daughter never wished to marry me. She wouldn't have arranged to be found."

Cecily's mother shrugged and sank down onto a stone bench nestled among a bed of herbs. "I can only speculate on what went through her mind. She was a complicated creature."

That seemed a kind word to describe his wife, but he agreed that there had been nothing easy about Cecily.

Her mother stared into the distance. "She was unhappy with some of her father's decisions. Perhaps she protested through her actions or thought to change his mind. I cannot fathom that she believed her father would force her into marriage, especially if the union would take her from home. He spoiled her beyond what was correct, but what was he to do under those circumstances? She shouldn't have tested him."

Daniel joined Cecily's mother on the bench and inhaled the pungent scent rising from the herbs. Cecily was a mystery he'd been trying to puzzle out for years. To hear her mother hadn't understood her any better eased his conscience.

What he *had* comprehended about his wife was her distaste for marriage and despair at leaving Port Albis.

Even after their passionate interludes aboard ship, she would beg to return home. He had sensed she used those moments when he sought a connection with her to bend him to her will, but he had been powerless in the beginning to resist her.

He had wanted to love Cecily, to be an adequate husband when he'd taken his vows, to save her from whatever lingered behind those expressionless eyes. But in the end, he had hardened his heart toward her. It had seemed the only means of his survival.

When Cecily had complained of feeling ill, Daniel had discounted it as another attempt at manipulation. It wasn't until she was too sick to recover that he'd realized his folly in not alerting the ship's surgeon. She succumbed to illness two days later, having refused to hear his apologies.

His hand found her mother's and wrapped around her slender fingers. "Indulgence didn't cause your daughter's death."

Her gaze swept over his face, a groove etched into her brow. "Please, tell me what happened. You mentioned before that she became ill."

"A stomach ailment."

She nodded. "I see."

He looked away, focusing on the purple flowers against the green of the herb. He didn't wish to see her expression when he told her the rest. "If I had acted sooner—I should have called for the surgeon. Perhaps something could have been done to save her."

Her tears fell on their joined hands. "She still would have succumbed to the illness. The damage had been done before you took her away."

Daniel sighed and offered her a handkerchief. This conversation was accomplishing nothing. He began to suspect Cecily's mother saw herself in competition with him for most vile creature on earth, and it was his title to defend. "If I may be blunt…"

"When are you not, dear boy?"

Fair enough. "I think this entire affair has rendered you a bit touched in the head."

She jerked the handkerchief from his grasp to dab at her cheeks. "I'm in full possession of my faculties, sir."

He suppressed a smile. His comment hit its mark and elicited the response he desired. Perhaps he was being selfish, but he preferred her irritation to her consuming sorrow.

"Everything started a year before your marriage," she said. "I intercepted a message meant for the governor. It was from the blackguard we had hired to paint Cecily's portrait."

Daniel's fingers curled into fists. Any involvement with that devil didn't bode well.

"He claimed Cecily had posed for a risqué portrait, and he threatened to display it for public viewing unless we paid the price he demanded. All I had in my possession was my pin money, but I promised to pay him over time. It took me months, but after I paid the last installment, he released her portrait. I still can't believe Cecily degraded herself in such a manner. I couldn't possibly have allowed her father to learn the truth."

She folded the cotton square embroidered with Daniel's initial and picked at the threads. "His Excellency worshiped our daughter. Cecily was his most prized possession. I decided no one could ever see her like that. The knowledge would have destroyed my husband.

"When I confronted her with the evidence, she admitted to her wrongdoing. She swore she loved the deplorable man and wished to marry him." The first lady's face flooded with color. "She said he had compromised her, but claimed they had used precautions. Good heavens. She shouldn't have known anything of such a nature."

"I'll kill him," he muttered.

"I am afraid someone else has already done the honor in Nassau."

The slow burning fury inside him wasn't squelched. Somehow, it didn't seem good enough that the man met with an early demise, not after the suffering he had caused Cecily's mother.

She sniffled. "Almost a month before your ship docked, Cecily came to me in confidence. She carried the artist's child, and she was despondent. He didn't want children, and she feared he would toss her aside if he learned of her condition. When I refused to assist her with ending the pregnancy, she threatened to end her life." Her mother grasped his hand and leaned toward him. "Daniel, the look in her eyes…"

"I understand, Your Excellency." He had innocently speculated on how many sons Cecily might bear him the night she had perched on the balcony railing and threatened to throw herself into the sea. She had been like a cornered, wild animal.

Her mother wiped her eyes. "Given the choices, I procured an herbal remedy to assist her, but I demanded she end her association with the man. Her father would never allow her to marry him. He had already denied his suit. All the man wished to know was the amount of Cecily's dowry." She sighed and all life seemed to drain from her. "Cecily promised to ingest only the small amount as directed. I should have known not to trust her. It wasn't until she prepared for your departure to England that I learned what she had done. She requested more for the journey because she had ingested the entire jar in three days. She reasoned that she hadn't seen results as quickly as she had wished and therefore needed to take more."

"And you believe this killed her many weeks later?" He shook his head and stood. It was time to put an end to this conversation. He couldn't allow her mother to carry his burden, no matter how badly he wished to hoist it on someone else. "Cecily died from tainted food and my neglect to summon the surgeon soon enough."

The first lady tipped her head to the side and looked up at him. "Did any of your crew suffer from the same effects? Did any of them die?"

"No, but they were all men. We're stronger. We don't easily succumb to ailments." He offered his hand. "We should return now."

She accepted his assistance and rose from the bench. They moved arm in arm toward the mansion. "Comfrey is a dangerous herb. I had to know what might happen to her after I learned what she had done. My source told me ingesting too much brings on a liver ailment, symptoms that appear to be a stomach illness."

Daniel stopped and looked into her troubled eyes.
Good God. She wasn't grasping at loose threads after
all, was she? She spoke with sincerity and a quiet pain
that comes with knowing the awful truth.

"Please, I must know if I'm correct. Would you
describe her pallor as having been yellowish?"

His mouth felt dry and he tried to swallow. Cecily's
complexion had been disconcerting, an unnatural
pallor that still made him shudder. Was there nothing
he could have done to save her? "Aye, she bore a
yellowish tinge."

"The comfrey—dear heavens, her death *is* my fault.
I killed her." She choked on a sob.

Placing a comforting arm around her shoulders,
Daniel supported her weight. To feel responsible for
another's death was a special torment he didn't wish
upon her.

After a while, she hugged him close and patted his
back in an affectionate gesture mothers reserved for
their sons. "I hope someday you may find it in your
heart to forgive me for keeping this horrible secret."

Daniel might have mustered the energy for indignation, but for the first time in years, the dark cloud
casting his life in shadow had lifted a little. All he
felt was gratitude to her for opening his eyes to the
possibility he might be blameless. "There is nothing to
forgive, Your Excellency."

He offered his arm and began escorting her back to
the house.

"Daniel, may I offer a word of advice?"

He nodded.

"You have mourned my daughter long enough.

It's not right for you to stop living just because Cecily is gone." She stopped and turned to face him. Her intense ice blue eyes bore into him, making him squirm inside. "You mustn't mask your sorrow with rum and whores any longer."

Damnation. He really wished the lady possessed less boldness, not to mention fewer spies around Port Albis.

"Please, release my daughter's memory to me. I will keep it safe in my heart always." She squeezed his hand, fresh tears in her eyes. "It's time to love again, my boy, and I think that young lady, Lisette, deserves more than you've been willing to offer her."

Daniel snapped his mouth closed. He didn't wish to discuss Lisette. She was his concern alone, and he would do right by her. He certainly didn't require anyone to hold his feet to the fire to encourage him to offer for her.

❧

Louis reclined in his chair and sipped his brandy. "Would you care for a drink first, Monsieur Baptiste?"

The gentleman's expression remained blank. What was going through his mind? Louis might attempt to draw it from him, but he suspected nothing but air resided between the man's two ears.

Eventually, Baptiste gave a sharp nod.

Pascal hurried to the decanter when Louis glanced his way. From his vantage point behind his desk, Louis studied Charles Baptiste's appearance with a disdainful sniff. His jacket sported worn elbows and a button dangled from his waistcoat.

It was hard to believe Lisette could care one whit about Baptiste.

"I'm unconvinced you will be of any service to me. Perhaps I should toss you overboard to reserve our rations." Louis leered over the rim of his glass when Baptiste recoiled. "Convince me you have influence with my fiancée, and I shall spare your life."

Pascal plunked a tumbler of brandy on the table in front of Baptiste. The man tested the glass with his fingertips before closing his hand around the container and taking a sip.

"Miss Lavigne listens to me on most occasions," he said in a raspy voice. "I'm like a father to her."

"Let's hope you are correct. If you fail to produce the desired response from Miss Lavigne, you are no use to me. The sharks, however, will consider you a tasty morsel."

Baptiste frowned and grabbed the glass from the table.

Louis held his empty tumbler out for Pascal to refill. "Robert Lavigne was your business partner. What did you know of his dealings?"

Baptiste's glass halted halfway to his lips. "I kept his books. He ran a profitable sugar plantation. This is all I know of his business."

"You were more than his bookkeeper, Monsieur Baptiste. I had you investigated."

His eyebrows lifted. "Investigated? For what purpose?"

"I'm a careful man. I probe into the backgrounds of all my associates."

Baptiste grunted and took a gulp of his drink. "We are hardly associates, sir."

"Yet you will help me bring my fiancée back to New Orleans where she belongs, will you not?"

"If the *Cecily* has already departed when we reach Port Albis, will you abandon your chase?"

"No." Louis shrugged one shoulder. "We shall catch her in open sea. She is too clumsy to escape the *Mihos*. Where we catch her makes no difference to me. I will return with my property, every piece of it."

"And what, pray tell, will you do with Miss Lavigne?"

"I will wed her, of course. And then she will learn to become an obedient wife, even if I must deliver a stern lesson every day of our marriage."

"And the boy?"

Louis sneered. "What concern is it of yours what becomes of the idiot? He pleases my future wife, so I suspect he will be useful in convincing her to bend to my will."

Baptiste frowned but refrained from speaking, which demonstrated wise judgment in Louis's estimation.

❧

Serafine threw her belongings in the new trunk she had purchased in town. Captain Hillary had sent word midmorning the *Cecily* would depart within the hour and anything not on the ship at the appointed time would be left behind.

Her family would not be one of those things stranded in Port Albis.

The captain's change in plans had caught everyone off guard, but Serafine didn't mind leaving her humiliation behind on the island.

Gracious. What a fool she had made of herself by offering to sleep with the captain. She had known the risks involved, but she hadn't prepared herself for his rejection. Even Isaac had deigned to *bed* her. She hadn't been good enough to marry, but she made for an adequate partner between the sheets.

For three months she had been his mistress and fooled herself into believing Isaac Tucker loved her. When it was time to take a wife, she had felt certain he would offer for her. Never mind that young white men never married outside of their culture. She had believed Isaac was different.

The room blurred as tears filled her eyes. Why did she hurt after all this time? Isaac left for the Continent weeks ago, and she had received no word from him, not that she'd anticipated she would. She had hoped for a letter begging for her forgiveness and proclaiming his love, but she had never expected it.

Their last encounter should have extinguished any optimism that he might realize his mistake in leaving her. As he had said, his parents demanded he marry a lady of good breeding, and her Creole lineage didn't fit with their dreams of upward mobility. Isaac had always been too quick to heed his mother's wishes. Serafine was better off without him.

A light knock shattered her musings. Lisette wandered into the chamber with a sly smile.

"Are you packed already?" Serafine asked, reverting to French.

"No." Her cousin strolled to the window seat. "I have been otherwise occupied with a caller."

"Then return to your chambers at once and finish the task. What about Rafe's belongings?" Serafine tossed the last of her things in the trunk and closed the lid. "Come along. I can assist."

"There's no need." Lisette picked up the book Serafine had borrowed from the governor's library. Serafine must remember to return it.

"Of course there is a need unless you plan to leave everything behind. Now, let's go before we run out of time."

She started for the door, expecting Lisette to follow.

"We are not leaving with Captain Hillary," Lisette said, still perusing the book. "I just spoke with Monsieur Ethelbert. He booked passage on the *Lena Mae* on our behalf. We will depart for England in three days."

Marmalade. Why must her cousin heed her advice now when for the first time in her life Serafine was wrong? "Do you think that is wise? At least we know Captain Hillary."

Lisette slammed the book closed. "You were the one who demanded we part ways with the scoundrel."

"Perhaps I was mistaken," she muttered.

"Pardon? Speak up, please. Because surely I misheard. You? Wrong?"

"I said *perhaps*."

"No, you were correct. I realized to what extent last night." She ignored Serafine's raised brows. "The deed is done. We no longer require Captain Hillary's services. If I never lay eyes on the man again, it will be too soon."

Serafine suppressed a sigh. This was a bit of a problem, because after last night, she knew Captain Hillary was the only man she trusted to carry them safely to their destination. "Very well. Allow me to speak with the captain on our behalf. Then you mustn't see him again."

Lisette started. "Never again?"

Just as Serafine suspected. Deep down, her cousin didn't wish to be rid of Captain Hillary, but her stubbornness would never allow her to admit it. "I only wish to save you the hassle, dear. I shall go to him straight away." She left before Lisette could protest.

Eighteen

LISETTE PAUSED OUTSIDE THE DOORS OF THE GOVERNOR'S mansion and took a deep breath to quell her anxiety. Everything would be fine. They didn't need Daniel to reach London. Captain Olsen, the *Lena Mae*'s shipmaster, seemed capable and trustworthy enough from all accounts.

A carriage sat at the bottom of the long marble staircase outside the doors, waiting to carry Lisette and her family to the Black Dog Inn at the wharf. They couldn't impose on the governor and first lady any longer now that Daniel was gone. She rubbed her hand across her nose and blinked to hold back her silly tears.

Rafe leaned out the carriage window and waved. His responsiveness wasn't as surprising as it would have been two weeks earlier, but it gave her pause.

Under Daniel's care and Monsieur Patch's patient attention, her brother had blossomed. His problems might never go away completely, but he had made strides. Perhaps her decision to part company with the *Cecily*'s captain and his crew had been unwise.

The governor and his wife stood with Serafine beside the carriage, wishing them *bon voyage* when Lisette reached the drive.

"Madame Lavigne and Mademoiselle Vistoire, what a pleasure to have had you as our guests. We do hope you will honor us with your presence again."

Lisette blinked, confused by the first lady's rush of warmth. "*Merci*, Your Excellency. We would be honored if we ever find ourselves in Port Albis again."

Cecily's mother swept Lisette into a hug and kissed both of her cheeks. "Take good care of him," she murmured.

"I will." She slowly extracted herself from the lady's embrace. Her Excellency had spent hardly any time in Rafe's company, not enough to warrant this level of concern for his welfare. The woman had grown dotty overnight.

Lisette thanked their hosts again, climbed into the carriage, and balked. "Monsieur Ramsey?"

The vicar slumped on the seat next to Rafe, shading his eyes from the sunlight. "Madame, please lower your voice. And pull the curtain before my head splits in two."

Lisette frowned but did as he requested. Daniel had abandoned the vicar. Monsieur Ramsey had ingested a ridiculous amount of rum on the journey to Port Albis. Surely, he had drunk his fare and then some on that leg of the trip alone. From all appearances, he'd done significant damage to the governor's supply last night as well. She couldn't fault Daniel's choice, but she didn't wish to be saddled with the man either.

Serafine climbed into the carriage after Lisette and

assumed the spot beside her as the door closed. She, too, pulled the curtain closed on her side and settled back against the seat with a contented smile.

When the carriage lurched, Lisette steadied herself against the side. The carriage wheels clicked on the cobbles as it moved downhill toward the wharf. Lisette lifted the curtain to take in the sights she would never see again, but the drive was quick and soon the carriage rolled to a stop on the docks.

"Our lodgings are down the way." Irritation laced her tone. "It's too far to carry the trunks. What is the driver thinking?"

The carriage door jerked open, and Lisette opened her mouth to issue orders to the footman.

Daniel stuck his head inside and nailed Lisette with a glare. "Jiminy. Does the phrase ready yourself to depart within the hour mean nothing to you?"

Serafine tossed a smile in Lisette's direction and shrugged before accepting his hand to climb from the carriage.

"Traitor," Lisette mumbled.

Serafine's smile widened. "I fear my cousin has no sense of time, Captain. I tried to hurry her along, but she can be quite impossible at times."

Lisette bristled. "But we are not—Captain Olsen is expecting us."

"He was kind enough to return your fare, made-moiselle." Daniel lifted her brother from his seat and swung him down to the dock. "Patch will take you aboard, Rafe."

Her brother's running footsteps echoed on the wooden slats.

"Come along, Ramsey."

The vicar groaned as he lumbered from the carriage.

Daniel offered his hand to Lisette. "Did you believe I would allow you to travel aboard another ship, my dear?"

She scowled as she climbed from the carriage. The reason she wished to cut ties with Daniel came back with perfect clarity. He was always taking charge of her life.

"It's not your decision to make," she said with an imperious lift of her head. It was the same stance Serafine assumed with her to express her displeasure. Lisette wasn't certain she had perfected it, but she didn't care at the moment. "You have no authority over any of us. I demand you return the fare to Captain Olsen and deliver our belongings to the Black Dog Inn."

Daniel linked arms and held her in place. "No."

"*No?* You cannot say no to me."

His lips twitched. "No." He drew out the word, setting her teeth on edge.

"Stop telling me no." Lisette struggled to break free of his hold without making leeway. She quivered with rage. "Release me, you jackass."

Movement ceased on the dock as the men stared in their direction. She must sound like a vulgar street urchin, but Daniel's overbearing behavior was making her damned furious. Lisette took a steadying breath, collected herself, and walked arm in arm with him toward the gangplank, careful not to meet anyone's gaze. She would settle the matter without prying eyes to witness their battle of wills.

"Your quarters, *now*," she said through clenched teeth as they walked up the gangplank. She and her family were not staying aboard Daniel's ship, no matter what her cousin had said to him.

Inside his quarters, she pointed at him. "*You* don't decide anything for me. I don't need you to reach London. And if you tell me 'no' once more, I will scream like... like..."

"Like you are now?" His crooked grin fueled her temper.

"Move. You are barring my way." She attempted to shove him away from the door, but he didn't budge. "Remove yourself now, monsieur."

"*Non.*"

Lisette shoved her fists down to her sides and drew in a giant breath to scream.

Daniel's hand clamped over her mouth. "Egads, Lis. I'm teasing. Don't scream."

Her shriek stuck in her chest, but anger still blazed from her eyes.

"I do believe you are telling me to go to hell with that look, mademoiselle." He removed his hand from her mouth. "Please, come to my office where two civilized adults may speak without anyone outside overhearing."

"Do you *have* another civilized adult waiting in your office to speak with me?" She stomped through the open doorway.

Daniel chuckled as he trailed behind her. "Mademoiselle, you are reeking of animosity today."

"I reek of nothing." Really, the man needled her at every opportunity.

"Your father was Robert Lavigne, the sugar farmer, was he not?"

Some of the fight drained out of her. Keeping her secrets had become tiresome, and it mattered little now if he knew the truth. They were far from the danger Reynaud presented.

"He wasn't the proprietor of just any sugar plantation. It's the largest in the area, Lavigne Manor. And some day it will belong to Rafe, but not if he is sent to an asylum to rot."

Daniel's face darkened. "Who wishes to send him to an asylum? Your cousin?"

"Of course not." She threw up her hands in frustration. Talking to him was like talking to a tree stump. "Why would I seek out Xavier if he meant to bring harm to Rafe?"

"Then who?"

Lisette's thoughts went to Reynaud and she shuddered inside. "I don't like to speak of him. Listen, I must gather Serafine and Rafe. We appreciate all you have done for us, but I think it's best if we part ways now."

He closed the distance between them and placed a finger under her chin to tip up her face. "Give me one good reason. I've promised to deliver you safely to England. You have no reason to doubt my word."

She looked into his earnest eyes, and her heart plummeted. Her mouth felt dry with him so close.

"Just one reason, Lis. Say it."

I cannot trust myself around you. "I don't want to see Rafe hurt."

"Neither do I, luv. I promise he'll be safe on the *Cecily*."

"He can be hurt in other ways, Daniel. What about when we reach London? You treat Rafe as if he's something more to you than a passenger." *As if I am something more.*

"And I'll never see him again, is that it? You plan to marry a duke, associate with a different caliber of society, and forget all about me?"

Lisette burst out laughing. His response was that unexpected. She stepped out of his grasp. "A duke? *Mon dieu*, where do you get such ridiculous notions?" *A duke indeed*. Folding her arms, she sighed. Perhaps if she were frank, he would allow her to leave.

"I will count myself fortunate if I marry a man of trade, an honest and kind man who will accept Rafe as he is. That is all I seek from a match."

His gaze held her captive, the heat in his blue eyes scorching her.

Her clothing clung to her damp skin, and she fidgeted with the neckline of her dress. "Please, stop looking at me in that way. This is the reason I can't stay with you. No one will offer for me if I'm ruined. I fear you will be my downfall, that I will fail my family. I can't do that to them."

"I see." His eyes twinkled and a dimple pierced his cheek. "Then I'm sorry."

Lisette gave a small shake of her head. "Sorry? For what?"

Sweet Mary. Were they moving? The ship jerked as the sails caught the wind. The unexpected movement knocked her off balance, but Daniel captured her around the waist.

"Daniel, no." She broke free of his hold and

dashed to the gallery windows. Port Albis loomed in the distance, shrinking by the second. "You've abducted us."

He came up behind her. "You're the only one who doesn't wish to be onboard." His arms circled her waist, and he hauled her back against his chest. "Only we both know you want to be here, Lis."

He turned her in his embrace and lowered his mouth to hers. Lisette's good sense wrestled with her shameless yearning. How she had wished for another kiss from Daniel since that day outside Madame Morel's dress shop. Her jasmine perfume mixed with his subtle, spicy scent and overwhelmed her senses.

"Daniel," she pleaded, "my family needs me. Please, don't use my weakness for you against me."

He brushed his thumb across her lower lip, setting her nerves ablaze. "What if I need you, too?"

A warm feeling expanded in her chest. Did he return her feelings? She rolled the words around in her mind. He *needed* her. The word couldn't mean the same to him.

Lisette snapped out of her trance and shoved against his chest to break free of his arms. What an imbecile she had become. "*Your* needs can be met by anyone, you selfish scoundrel. My family's survival depends on me."

Shaking, Lisette dashed from his office and out the great cabin door before he tried to detain her again.

❧

"Bloody hell," Daniel mumbled when the door to the great cabin slammed. That hadn't gone as he had hoped. He hadn't approached the business of offering for her hand in the typical manner, but he was not a typical gentleman. Most would say he was no gentleman at all. Although he knew how to play the part and his father's position granted him membership into the *ton*, he had been shunning society for years.

If England's elite couldn't accept his grandfather, a man who had given Daniel everything—a love for the sea, a purpose for his life, a means of following his passion—then he had no time for the elite. His grandfather had loved Daniel and his siblings in a manner the *ton* was incapable of understanding, and his generosity was unparalleled. Upon Grandfather's demise, he had willed his fortune to Daniel and two of Daniel's brothers, providing the younger sons with a means to be independent from their father.

Daniel could take care of Lisette and her family, but she would be deemed bad *ton*. While the designation didn't bother him, perhaps it would her. Lisette alone would face the snide comments and cuts direct most of the season while he was at sea.

He moved to his desk and pulled the logbook from the top drawer, but he couldn't focus on his work. Burrowing his fingers through his hair, he blew out a noisy breath.

Damnation.

He could salvage her reputation if he asked his sister-in-law to assume chaperone duties, and Mr. Ramsey's silence could be bought. Lisette could still make a decent match. Daniel knew which merchants had sons of marriageable age. Perhaps he could broker a union on her behalf.

The great cabin door creaked as someone entered, and he bolted from his chair. "Lisette?"

When he reached the entrance of his office, his shoulders drooped. Rafe had strolled in as he had every day before their stop in Port Albis.

"Ahoy, mate," Daniel called in the most jovial voice he could muster.

Rafe smiled coyly as if the act embarrassed the hell out of him, but it was a response. Daniel couldn't help but puff up with pride. The boy was making great strides onboard the *Cecily*. This was the reason Lisette and her family belonged with him instead of Captain Olsen. Rafe needed more than for his sister to make a good marital match. He needed people who understood him.

Rafe hugged his journal to his chest and wandered into the office to take up sentry in his usual spot. As he jotted notes and made drawings in his book, Daniel opened the logbook on his desk to review the last recordings before they had docked in Port Albis.

Several minutes later, he'd read the same entry at least five times and still had no idea as to the content. All he could think on was the coming evening and seeing Lisette again. He must issue an apology and offer his assistance in helping her make a match if that was her wish. He didn't want to do so with an audience, but she might refuse to speak with him alone.

Hellfire. He didn't want to see her married to someone else, but she had accused him of caring only about his desires. At the very least, he had to offer her a choice. He blew out another ragged breath.

Rafe glanced up from his drawings. His forehead

wrinkled as his brows merged. "You breathe heavily." His tone was conversational, as always. Daniel appreciated that the boy never spoke with censorship.

"Yes, I suppose I do." *Especially when I think of your sister.*

Rafe returned his attention to marking impressively straight, parallel lines. Was that the decking of a ship?

He closed his weathered book with nary a sound and glanced up. "I need to practice my knots."

Daniel checked his watch lying on the desk. Three o'clock. It was eerie how Rafe knew the time without ever asking or consulting a clock. At this same time every day, he practiced tying knots with different lengths of rope as Daniel had taught him. Much like Daniel, the boy was a creature of habit.

"Retrieve them from the great cabin and lay them out on the table."

Unlike him, Rafe showed no impatience or need to rush. Daniel could learn a lot from the lad.

He rubbed his eyes and sighed again before attempting to return to his work, but Rafe's sketchbook drew his attention. Opening to the middle of the book, he blinked in surprise at the meticulous drawings of the *Cecily*. The wheel, capstan, and mizzenmast. Rafe exhibited great talent for a young boy. Paging backward, Daniel discovered drawing after drawing of his ship, but toward the beginning, he unearthed a different ship. It was a detailed drawing of a Baltimore Flyer.

Daniel stood with the book in hand and walked into the great cabin where Rafe concentrated on perfecting a square knot. "Did you sketch this from another book?"

Rafe didn't look up until he finished the knot.

"Nice work, seaman." Daniel tapped the drawing again. "Did you copy this from a book?"

"It's the *Mihos*. Monsieur Reynaud said I couldn't touch anything."

"Who is Reynaud?"

"The *Mihos* is his ship." Rafe picked up two untied lengths of rope. "I didn't like hiding from the men in the garden. I don't like the dark."

Daniel's eyes narrowed. "Hiding from what men? Were you playing a game?"

"No, it was no fun. They didn't want me to come on the *Cecily*."

"What the devil?" Daniel frowned, his jaw tightening.

Rafe looked up at him with large, golden-brown eyes. "Don't worry, Captain. Lisette is smart. She tricked them so I could be on a ship like I always wanted."

Apparently, Lisette had neglected to reveal key information to him when he had agreed to provide passage to England. Tonight he would question her. It was high time Daniel learned the full story of Lisette Lavigne and her flight from her home.

Nineteen

As Lisette and Serafine rose from the dinner table, Daniel stood. "Ladies, if I may have a word with you in my office?"

Lisette's insides knotted. "Now?"

He smiled. "This will only take a moment. If you please."

If you please. He almost made his request sound as if she could refuse it, but politeness required her to accommodate him.

Monsieur Hillary scooted back from the table and assisted Amelia to her feet. "We should be going now. Good evening, madame and mademoiselle."

Amelia stifled a yawn. "Yes, please excuse our early departure, but I fear I might collapse in my bowl of mush if we stay much longer."

"Be grateful for the mush," Daniel warned, but a soft smile played on his lips.

Monsieur Ramsey followed suit. He looked a great deal sadder this evening than he had at the Governor's Ball. Lisette felt a twinge of sympathy for him.

Serafine put an arm around Rafe's shoulders. "I'm

afraid it's time to escort this young man to bed, Captain. Perhaps my cousin can assist you with whatever it is you need."

Lisette shot a venomous look at her cousin. If she didn't know better, she would swear Serafine was teasing her, but she hadn't mentioned anything of her earlier encounter with Daniel.

"Splendid." He swept an arm toward his office. "Shall we, Mademoiselle Lavigne?"

"This can wait until tomorrow. It has been a tiring day." She made to follow Serafine and Rafe, but Daniel captured her arm and pulled her farther into his cabins. He released her once they stepped inside his office. Closing the door, he held up his hands.

"I promise your virtue is safe. I mulled over my actions from this morning and realized I was indeed behaving in a selfish manner. I offer my apologies."

Lisette narrowed her eyes. He would not lure her in easily this time. Holding herself rigid, she moved to the upholstered chair and sat. "Please, get on with it so we may conclude our business."

A tic at his jaw was the only indication she'd ruffled his calm control. "Not until you acknowledge my apology, my dear."

"Really, Daniel. Must you play games with me? If you're sincerely sorry, which I doubt, then I accept. That doesn't change the fact I don't trust you."

His strong brows, like thick slashes above his aqua eyes, lowered dangerously. She'd seen this look the moment before he'd slammed his fist into the ruffian's jaw at The Abyss. A tremor coursed through her.

"Perhaps we should work on building more trust

between us. You may start by telling me about Reynaud," he said.

Lisette's hand covered her gasp. "How do you know of him?"

Daniel crossed his arms and leaned against his desk. "Rafe. He said Reynaud had men who didn't want you on my ship."

"He said that?" Lisette had no idea Rafe knew anything about her fiancé. She had tried her best to keep her concerns to herself for fear of upsetting her brother. Had she and Serafine exchanged words about Reynaud within Rafe's presence?

"Rafe said you had to hide from these men, and I have a feeling your brother didn't reference a game of hide-and-seek." Daniel's expression lost its hard edge. "Is this man the reason you were desperate to leave New Orleans?"

Tears clogged her throat. She hadn't stopped to remember the fear she had felt crouched in the garden until this moment. She forced back her emotions and willed her pulse to slow. Swallowing, she nodded.

"*He* threatened to lock up Rafe."

"Yes. My own fiancé wished to lock him up." Her voice rasped.

Daniel pushed from the desk and stood before her. "Lisette." He spoke her name like a tender caress and held out his hand. "You needn't carry this burden alone. Please, may I offer you consolation?" How easy it would be to surrender to his comforting embrace, but she couldn't.

She shook her head and looked away. "I'm all right

now. We are safely away from him. I have no cause to be upset any longer."

Daniel knelt at her feet and met her gaze. "He has driven you from your home, Lis. You have every reason to be upset."

The cabin blurred. For weeks, she'd held back her sorrow. Why must she shed tears now? She was weak, a pathetic excuse of a woman. She was as weak as her mother who had languished in bed all those years, growing frail and useless, wetting her pillow with her tears. But Lisette couldn't stop the swell of emotion. Everything was compounded: her father's death, Reynaud's betrayal, her foolishness.

"He's a monster. I couldn't—"

Daniel wrapped her in his arms. "You will never see him again, my love."

Several tears slipped past her lashes as Lisette squeezed her eyes tightly. She would be damned if she'd cry for that man. Reynaud had made her think he would provide for her and her brother. He'd claimed to be their answer. He'd lied. Everything he promised was a lie.

"I want to forget him."

Daniel drew back and swiped a tear from her cheek with the pad of his thumb. "What does he have to gain with you gone?"

"Nothing. He has lost access to my dowry. And I think he hoped to gain control over Rafe's inheritance." She leaned into Daniel's palm as he feathered his fingers along her jawline. What a naive little goat she had been. "Xavier, Rafe's guardian, has been gone for over a year. Reynaud offered to speak with his connections about seeking guardianship over Rafe after we married. Thank the Lord, I learned of his true intentions before the wedding. I couldn't allow him to commit Rafe to an asylum. He would die in confinement."

"That's the last place Rafe belongs." There was fire in his words.

She cradled Daniel's face and searched his gaze. "You mean it, don't you?"

"Of course I mean it. Rafe is a brilliant lad. The world is fortunate to have him be part of it."

Daniel would make an amazing father some day. He was so patient and kind to her brother. *I love you.* The sentiment reverberated in her heart. Daniel was exasperating, overbearing, and arrogant. And his heart still belonged to Cecily. Perhaps it always would. But Lisette loved him all the same.

He smiled and captured her hands to pull them away from his face, but he didn't release them from his warm grasp. "If you keep looking at me that way, I won't be able to keep my promise to you."

She started and removed her hands from his hold before leaning against the seat back. Daniel moved to the chair behind his desk and leaned his elbows on the surface, waiting for her to speak again.

She licked her lips. "I didn't know what Reynaud was like when he offered for my hand. He seemed kind and I was so tired. Our father had been dead for three weeks, and I was lost. I didn't know what to do, how to settle Papa's accounts or make wise decisions regarding the operating of the farm. Serafine was no more informed than I was, and Monsieur Baptiste was in Boston. Reynaud stepped in and made the decisions I could not."

"You weren't a fool. You were grieving."

"I was weak. My father wasn't in the crypt more than a month when I accepted Reynaud's offer of marriage." She glanced down at her hands twined together. Guilt sat heavily in her gut. "When Monsieur Baptiste returned to New Orleans, he was livid. He demanded I end the engagement and chastised me for not observing the proper mourning period. My father's dearest friend was ashamed of me. I'm ashamed of myself."

"Then your father's friend is a fool. No woman can be expected to step into her father's shoes. She needs someone to offer proper counsel."

"No, Monsieur Baptiste was right, at least about Reynaud. Two weeks before we were to wed, I called on my betrothed at his home. I aimed to talk him into allowing Rafe to accompany us on our honeymoon. We had discussed it the evening prior, and I felt certain with a little more persuasion, Reynaud would consent. He appeared to like Rafe well enough." How could she have mistaken Reynaud's cool regard for her brother for fondness?

"A maid showed me to the parlor, but I was kept waiting a long time. Eventually, I decided the timing of my visit was inconvenient, so I went to let myself out. When I opened the parlor door, I heard him speaking with another man. His guest made a rude comment about Rafe, and I expected Reynaud to defend him, but he didn't. Instead, he laughed."

His cruel ridicule still left her shaking. "He said

once we married, the *idiot* could be placed where he belonged, at Rivercrest Lunatic Asylum."

"What an arse. Is that when you decided to run away?"

"Not immediately. I didn't know what to do, so I confided in Monsieur Baptiste. He promised to help us somehow, but his ability to provide protection is limited. He's advanced in age, and he lacks the funds to do more than to live modestly. The only solution he could think of was to search for Xavier in London. He assisted us with locating a ship leaving New Orleans before the wedding."

Daniel pressed his lips together. "And I refused his request."

"But you changed your mind."

"*You* changed my mind, Lis." A smile softened his features again. "It's an annoying ability you possess, making me question myself."

"Have I only one annoying habit?"

"The others are hardly worth mentioning." He winked to show he teased, but his merriment soon dissolved into thoughtful silence. "You could have been killed if Reynaud's men had caught you that evening."

"I knew they wouldn't."

"How could you be sure?"

"Serafine read my tea leaves. She said we would escape undetected."

"And you placed your faith in tea leaves? What other predictions has she made?"

She shrugged, her body heating under his incredulous stare. "What other choice did I have? And she was right. We did escape."

He nodded slowly, the hint of a dimple in his

cheek. "I suppose I can't argue with the logic of consulting Mother Earth when you have indeed escaped unharmed. What else did her ladyship reveal?"

"Nothing."

"You're twisting your fingers again. There's something else, isn't there? What did Serafine tell you, Lis?"

She forced her hands to her sides. Her body burned even hotter. She would like to pretend she didn't hear him and change the topic, but the stubborn set to his jaw indicated how futile the attempt would be. Her gaze skittered around the cabin before resting on Daniel again.

"She said I am destined to marry an obscenely rich Englishman." She winced, expecting him to laugh, but he didn't.

"That rich, eh? Narrows down your prospects a bit."

❦

"Serafine." The voice called her name softly. Its pleasant tone rolled over her tenderly and familiarly. "Serafine, wake up, my child."

Grandmamma?

"Serafine, they're coming. Wake up!"

Serafine woke with a jump, kicking her leg over the side of the cot where it dangled. She stared into the darkness, trying to get her bearings. Lisette's and Rafe's even breathing filled the space, and slowly it dawned on her where she was. They were on the ship.

She sat up on the side of the cot. A cold sweat drenched her nightrail and her throat felt caked with grit. She hated these late-night awakenings when her heart raced, and she felt like she might toss up her accounts. This was the third night in a row, and just like the other times, she was overcome with an evasive sense of dread.

There was no explanation for her distress. They were safe on the *Cecily*. And Captain Hillary had been true to his word. He treated Lisette with the greatest respect. Serafine no longer worried about her cousin. Soon they would arrive in London, and she felt certain the captain would assist them with finding rooms to let if she asked. And still, her uneasiness clung to her.

The bell tolled four times topside. She needed a drink.

Feeling around the floor with her foot, she bumped against her slippers, donned them, and then snatched the wrapper lying across the cot.

She glided out the cabin door and closed it with care before following the narrow passageway, touching her hand along the wooden sides of the ship to guide her, and headed toward the galley.

The ship creaked as it rocked gently on the waves. She had grown accustomed to the ship's nighttime sounds—the swish of water against the bow, the peal of the bell, footfalls of the watchmen on deck.

As she neared the galley, a cloud of warm air poured from the room and surrounded her when she entered. Dim embers smoldered in the stone oven, reduced to almost nothing.

She felt around for a cup, her thirst driving her.

Strong hands seized her from behind. She screamed.

"Lordy, it's a miss!" Poor Cook sounded as frightened as she was.

"It is I, Mademoiselle Vistoire."

Cook released her and lit a candle from the embers. Shadows cast the craggy lines of his face in relief. They appeared as canyons. He grinned and the light reflected off his gold tooth as he lit the lantern sitting on a small table. "You the one been raiding the larder? I thought I be catching Mr. Timmons, or better yet, the uppity Mrs. Hillary."

"It's not me, good sir. And Mrs. Hillary is not uppity." She felt compelled to defend her friend. "I'm sorry to have frightened you, but I was looking for a drink."

Cook set the candle in a holder and reached for a cup sitting on the shelf. "I made some lemonade before closing the galley. You want some?" He poured her a cup before waiting for an answer.

"Thank you." The drink was lukewarm, but it eased the scratchiness in her throat.

"You have trouble sleeping, miss?"

"I would pay for a full night's sleep. This is the third time this week."

Cook poured himself a glass of lemonade, too. "Something troubling ya?"

"No—" She stopped to reconsider. "Well, there is something, but I don't know what it is. I think I had a dream."

"What about?"

"I can't recall, but I woke with this dreadful feeling that doesn't want to go away." She sipped her drink, studying the cook. He'd had fifteen years at sea. Maybe this type of thing was common for a first-time sea traveler. "Is this normal for someone like me?"

Cook cocked his head. "I don't know, miss. Is it?"

It was a silly question, she supposed. Serafine drained her cup then handed it back to the man and pulled her wrapper tighter around her. "Maybe it's normal for me. Thank you for the lemonade, Cook. I'm sorry I disturbed you."

He held out the candle. "Take this with you so you can see the way. Just don't forget to put it out."

Twenty

DANIEL'S FIRST MATE STUCK HIS HEAD THROUGH THE opening to his office. "Captain, there's something you might want to see."

"A ship?"

"Aye, and she's moving at a fast clip."

Daniel shoved away from his desk and hurried outside to the quarter deck, where his man, Leon, peered through the spyglass.

"Can you tell what class she is?" Daniel asked.

Leon handed the spyglass to him. "She's too far away to tell, but with her speed, I'd venture she's a clipper or a flyer."

Daniel held the glass up to his eye. On the horizon, a small speck bobbed in the distance, growing larger by the second. Whatever she was, speed was on her side.

"Change course," he barked to the wheelman. "Three points on the starboard bow. Unfurl every sail. Let's see if we're being followed."

He slapped a hand on Leon's shoulder. "Good eye, man. Keep me informed."

Daniel's muscles tensed as he headed below deck to

seek out Jake. The other ship could be harmless, but he had been sailing long enough to know encounters with other ships rarely occurred by chance.

When Cook, an uneducated man with superstitious beliefs, had reported his encounter with Mademoiselle Vistoire in the galley and warned him ladies were often the first to sense danger, Daniel had thanked and dismissed him. He hadn't been able to dismiss his sense of foreboding when Cook had returned to the galley, however. It stayed with him throughout the evening meal and hadn't gone away by the conclusion of Amelia's nightly reading.

Daniel had doubled the watch at once.

He rapped on Jake's door and a short time later, it swung open.

"Shh, Amelia's sleeping." Jake stepped into the corridor and closed the door behind him.

"I may need your assistance. Come with me."

Jake followed him topside and into Daniel's quarters.

"There's a possibility we are being followed," Daniel said as soon as the door latched.

Jake's brows formed a vee. "Pirates? Seems unlikely."

"No, a man called Reynaud. Lisette's fiancé." Daniel stalked to the sideboard, tugged open a drawer, and withdrew a bottle of rum. His brother might need a drink once Daniel told him everything.

"Fiancé? But she's a widow. When would she—?"

"Please, have a seat." Daniel waved to a chair then retrieved a tumbler from the hutch and poured a generous amount of liquor into it. "It appears Lisette and her family hold a few secrets."

"Not unlike you," Jake grumbled as Daniel plunked

the drink in front of him. "I still can't believe you never told any of us about your marriage to Cecily. For five years, you've kept this to yourself."

"Cecily is in the past. It hardly matters at the moment." Daniel assumed the seat adjacent to his brother. "Right now I'm concerned with our immediate future."

"Tell me the risks."

He repeated the story Lisette had told him about Reynaud, as well as revealing his suspicions that the man might be responsible for her father's death. "It seems damned convenient he arrived to rescue Lisette less than a fortnight after her father's throat was sliced from ear to ear. Not to mention, Reynaud made promises to Lisette that leave me with the impression he intended to gain control of Rafe's inheritance. He wouldn't be the first blackguard to live off the estate of his ward."

Jake frowned as he sipped his drink. "But why pursue the lady? Isn't it obvious she has cried off? Why not find another lady to take her place?"

"Excellent question." Daniel drummed his fingers against the tabletop. "I suspect his pride has been damaged, which is more important to many men than financial gain."

"When he catches us, will you turn her over to him?"

Hell no. Fierce protectiveness reared inside Daniel, but he couldn't allow his emotions to rule his decisions. He rammed his fingers through his hair. "Reynaud may well be a monster. I don't want to let her go with him."

"Then don't. We have the firepower to fight."

"But what about Amelia and your child? Should I endanger them and my men for Lisette?"

His brother's bluster died down. "I understand the situation is not to be taken lightly, but…"

A pain gnawed at Daniel's gut. Jake and his growing family meant everything to him. He had given his brother hell as long as he could remember, but Jake had been too trusting. He'd needed someone to toughen him up before the world knocked him on his arse. Daniel wouldn't do anything to bring actual harm to him.

"I can't make the choice for you, Daniel, but if you feel anything for Lisette even close to what I feel for Amelia, you can't let her go." Jake held his gaze without wavering. "I'll stand by your decision, whatever it may be."

"I know you will. You are loyal to a fault."

"Says the pot to the kettle." Jake moved to Daniel's side and slapped his back affectionately. "The way I figure it, we all benefit from the lady's continued presence. You're less of a jackass with Lisette onboard."

Daniel chuckled. "I'm not certain she would agree."

"No, I don't suppose she would." Jake flashed a sardonic grin and snatched the tumbler from the table to drain it.

By late afternoon, there was no longer any question the other ship was following them. Their pursuer would overtake the ship in approximately two hours, if all variables stayed the same. The *Cecily* was too large to outrun the smaller vessel, but she could blast her to the devil.

Daniel could just make out the lettering on the bow. *Mihos*. The Egyptian lion god, also known as the

Lord of Slaughter. He would be damned if Reynaud got his paws on Lisette or those she loved.

The trouble was making certain she didn't override Daniel's decision. As she had told him on more than one occasion, he had no authority over her. Likely, she wouldn't go with Reynaud of her own accord, unless the arrogant bugger coerced her. Daniel wouldn't assume that risk, and thanks to Amelia's initiative, he had a perfect solution.

Patch accepted the spyglass from Daniel and peered through it.

"Gather all the passengers in my quarters in ten minutes," he commanded his first mate then turned on his heel. He must speak with one passenger before they all gathered around his table.

                           *

Lisette huddled at the long table in the great room along with the usual dinner guests, minus Rafe and Daniel's men. Daniel stood at one end of the table, commanding all eyes on him. Her pulse jumped as he met her gaze. There was no amusement there today. Something was gravely wrong.

"A situation has arisen over the last few hours. It has come to my attention we are being followed by another ship."

Serafine grasped Lisette's hand under the table and squeezed. Lisette held on tightly.

"Who is it?" Her voice was barely a whisper.

Daniel walked around the table and knelt by her side. "It appears to be Reynaud."

"No," she and Serafine said in unison.

Lisette's heart slammed against her ribs. It couldn't be Reynaud. "He wouldn't pursue us across the ocean. That would be insane."

Daniel's hand brushed her shoulder. "I'm sorry, luv. I realize the insanity of the situation, but it is Reynaud, and he's coming for you."

"Well, send him away," Amelia said. "She obviously wants nothing to do with him, or she wouldn't have fled in the first place."

Lisette ducked her head. Did everyone know of her lies now?

"I have no authority over Mademoiselle Lavigne," Daniel said, "but I would like to offer my protection all the same."

Lisette met his gaze and her heart filled to bursting. "You would protect us from Reynaud? I don't know how to thank you, Captain."

"There are a few details we need to work out between us, but I believe this would be better done in privacy." He stood and offered his hand. "May I speak with you in my office, mademoiselle?"

Her stomach plunged. She felt sick. What would he demand for his protection?

Serafine nudged her. "Go," she whispered.

Lisette pushed back the wave of nausea rolling over her and rose from her chair without taking his hand.

"Please wait for us here," he said to everyone gathered at the table. "We'll have need of you in a moment."

Lisette preceded Daniel into the office and moved to the windows along the stern. All she could see was blue, nothing sinister outside. "How far away is he?"

He came up behind her and placed his hands on

her waist, drawing her against him. "He will overtake us before nightfall, but we can defeat him in a fight. I'll refuse to hand you over, as I'm certain he will demand. I expect a confrontation to ensue, but I swear I won't give you up, Lisette." His breath lifted the tendrils of hair that had fallen from her coiffure and sent a cold shiver down her back.

She couldn't look at him. He knew how much her family and their survival meant to her. Would he dangle his protection like a carrot to get what he wanted? "What is it you wish in return?"

"Nothing." Daniel sounded genuinely appalled and released her.

She turned toward him. "You want nothing from me in exchange?"

"A small amount of gratitude might be nice."

Heat licked up her neck. He had done nothing to break his vow of protecting her virtue since they had departed from Port Albis. "My apologies, Captain. I'm grateful for your assistance. I simply do not expect your protection without some price attached. It would be unfair of me to ask it of you."

A corner of his lip lifted. "Yes, there is much I'll have to bear as your protector, but I believe I'm up for the task." He gathered her hands in his and urged her closer. "Lisette, the most effective means available to me to protect you is to make you my wife. Mr. Ramsey has agreed to wed us now."

"Your *wife*?" She felt as if a piece of the sky had broken off and landed on her.

"I know your aspirations are aimed higher, but I can adequately support you and your family."

"But that's untrue. In reference to my aspirations, I mean," she added in response to his glower. "I would be fortunate to be your wife. In fact, I could do much worse."

He chuckled, the lively spark returning to his eyes as he slid his arms around her waist. "Thank you, luv. That's high praise coming from you."

"You know my meaning," she said and swatted his shoulder. "Are you certain this is the only way?"

"Absolutely." He nuzzled her neck, sending flutters of excitement to the tips of her fingers and toes. "But you must say yes first."

Marriage to Daniel seemed the easy way out of her troubles. She wouldn't be forced to hunt for a husband in London, he would provide for them well on the *Cecily*, and he would keep them safe from Reynaud. The only drawback was Daniel loved someone else while her heart belonged to him. This gave her no small amount of anxiety. Yet she would be mad to turn down his offer when he would keep Rafe from Reynaud's grasp.

"No more hesitating. Give me an answer, wench."

"Wench?"

His dimple appeared. "So sorry. I meant to say my darling."

"That's more like it," she said with a smile, but her jocularity faded. If he would make this sacrifice for her, she must offer him something in return, even if his acceptance would bring her pain. "But, Daniel, once we reach England, if you wish to annul—"

His hearty laugh drowned out her words. "Impossible. There will be no grounds, I can assure you. Everything is in excellent working order."

She blinked. Whatever did he mean? Her eyes widened as understanding flooded over her. He intended to make her his *wife*, not simply give her his name.

Her legs trembled and she leaned against him for support. "I see. But if you wish to live apart once we arrive—"

"Be quiet, Lis." Her argument was swallowed up by his kiss. His soft lips moved with possessiveness over hers, and he pulled her snug against him. Her fingers splayed over his chest.

Sweet Mary and Joseph. She could explore Daniel's hardened body without any cause for shame once they spoke their vows. And he could explore her too. Her stomach somersaulted. The thought of baring herself to his eyes made her tremble even more.

He broke their embrace and captured her hand to lead her to the great room where everyone waited.

"If I may have your attention," Daniel called, and every eye looked their way. "Mademoiselle Lavigne has accepted my offer of marriage. We shall marry today."

Cries of delight and applause erupted around the table, even from Serafine. Her cousin bounced from her seat and across the cabin to fling her arms around Lisette. "This is the right thing to do," she murmured in her ear. "Don't doubt yourself."

Why the change of heart?

"Let's go below deck. Amelia has the perfect dress for the occasion."

"Did everyone know his intentions except me?"

Amelia linked arms and whisked Lisette out the great cabin door. "Mr. Ramsey folded under pressure. He didn't stand a chance at maintaining Daniel's confidence."

Serafine and Amelia giggled like young girls as they assisted Lisette with preparing for her nuptials.

"I've grown fond of Daniel over the last several months," Amelia said. "I believe he will make an excellent husband. Perhaps a bit overbearing at times, but from what I've seen, he'll not get away with riding roughshod over you, mademoiselle."

Lisette bit the inside of her cheek. "Do you think he truly wishes to marry me?"

"Of course." Amelia repositioned a hairpin and stepped back to admire her creation. "You look lovely. Perhaps I'll no longer require a lady's maid once we arrive home. I've gotten quite good at arranging hair."

"You employ a lady's maid?" Lisette hadn't given much thought to Amelia's station in England.

Her friend laughed, her bluest-of-blue eyes sparkling. "What a silly question. No lady goes without one. You must begin interviews the moment we arrive in London."

"Oh no, I wouldn't expect a lady's maid to travel onboard with us. Besides, I'm not certain I should burden my groom with the expense."

"Dear girl, do you really have no idea whom you are marrying? Daniel Hillary is one of the wealthiest gentlemen in England. Your future husband not only owns the *Cecily*, he is part owner of the second largest shipping company in the world. Daniel, Jake, and their older brother inherited their grandfather's fortune. You have no cause to worry about burdening him."

Merde. Lisette wanted to crawl under her chair. At The Abyss, she had called the owner of the *Cecily* greedy. She buried her face in her hands. "I am a complete fool."

Amelia hugged her. "You're nothing of the sort, dearest. And you are good for Daniel. Now, I'll leave you so you may have some time with Serafine before the vows are spoken."

She bustled out the door, leaving a stunned silence in her wake.

Lisette glanced up at her cousin. "Did you know about Daniel's wealth?"

"Amelia hadn't said a word."

"He's my Englishman. We'll have no more worries once we reach London."

"Heavens above, how could that be?" Tears welled in Serafine's eyes. "I'm sorry I misled you."

Lisette grabbed her hand and squeezed. "I wouldn't have believed you if you'd claimed his intentions honorable."

A knock at the door startled them. "Enter."

One of Daniel's men poked his head inside. "The captain ordered me to bring yer things to his quarters, miss."

"So soon?"

Serafine nodded toward Lisette's trunk. "At the end of the far cot."

The man completed his duties with efficiency, tossing the trunk on his shoulder. At the door, he stopped. "Congratulations on yer upcoming nuptials, miss. The captain'll take good care of ye."

Once the man disappeared, Serafine sat on the

edge of her cot and leaned forward. "About the wedding night…"

"Stop!" Lisette held up both hands. "Must we discuss such things *now*? Don't worry. Someday I'll enlighten you on what transpires between a husband and wife." Such as the day the devil donned a ball gown and danced a country jig.

Serafine's mouth dropped open; her cousin was finally at a loss for words.

Another knock sounded at the door. "Miss, the captain is waiting for you."

Twenty-one

THE WIND-SWOLLEN SAILS OF THE *MIHOS* CARRIED HER over the waves, and her flags whipped from the mast. Frothy white water parted for her bow. Daniel's newfound enemy would be upon them soon.

He handed Lisette the spyglass. She gazed through it then passed the glass back to Daniel. "It's him. I recognize the flag."

The *Mihos*'s personal flag displayed a red lion standing erect with claws bared against a white background.

Daniel hugged Lisette to him and kissed her temple. "Take Rafe, Serafine, and Amelia below deck. Stay out of sight no matter what transpires on deck. Have I made myself clear?"

Lisette's emerald gaze narrowed and her jaw jutted forward. He returned her glare without blinking. She may dislike him ordering her about like one of his men, but he was in charge.

She turned to her entourage. "You heard the captain. We are to cower below deck."

"Now, that's a good wife," he said. To annoy her

further, he popped her on the bottom, eliciting an outraged squeal.

"Monsieur!"

Several of his crew chuckled, and she turned crimson, slaying Daniel with one dirty look. *Good*. He preferred her angry with him than frightened by the coming confrontation.

"Run along." He made shooing motions with his hands and grinned in the face of her displeasure.

She snatched Rafe's hand in hers and marched to the hatch with him in tow. Serafine hurried behind, throwing a wary glance over her shoulder before disappearing below deck.

Jake shook his head and offered his arm to Amelia. "You're hopeless. I'll be back in a moment. Don't start the fun without me."

Amelia looked paler than normal. "Jake, you will be careful, won't you?"

"Of course, sweetheart. There's no cause for concern."

Daniel felt a twinge of apprehension as his brother escorted his pregnant wife below deck. What if Daniel had underestimated Reynaud and was placing everyone in danger? Perhaps he should have tried outrunning the other ship. He shook off his uncertainty and squared his shoulders. There was no turning back now.

Daniel gazed through the spyglass again. The *Mihos* had dropped half her sails and was slowing.

"Heave to," he said to Patch.

His first mate called out his command. "Heave to."

They would hold their position, readying for battle if they must. The *Mihos* was still out of range of the guns, but Daniel refused to shed blood if he could avoid it. Putting the fear of God into the *Mihos*'s crew was another story.

"Fire a warning shot in case she is contemplating unfriendliness."

His order echoed along the deck. "Fire once across the bow."

The thunderous boom of the cannon vibrated in Daniel's chest, and the deck under his feet quivered. The ball crashed through the surface of the sea, shooting water into the air approximately thirty feet from the approaching ship. Her remaining sails dropped amid distant shouts from the seamen on the *Mihos*.

Daniel had their attention.

He counted on most of the crew from the other ship having no experience in battle. Not so on the *Cecily*. After the war, the Royal Navy no longer required the services of as many sailors and released them from their duties without pensions. Daniel had employed several of these men, paid them well, and provided the best conditions possible on ship. In return, the *Cecily* possessed a loyal crew ready to fight for her.

The *Mihos* raised her white flag, the first victory for Daniel and his men.

"Let's see what she wants."

The crew on the other ship bustled on deck, readying a rowboat. None of the men appeared to be the captain.

Jake met Daniel on the main deck. "The firing of the gun has the women on edge. I hope this matter can be resolved quickly."

"Me too," he said. "This jackass is interfering with my amorous rites."

"Only you would think on such things at a time like this."

"Are there more pleasing subjects to contemplate than bedding one's wife?"

His brother grinned. "You pose a valid argument."

A rowboat carrying a crewman from the *Mihos* headed their direction. Each dip of the oars into the waves carried the vessel closer and increased the tightness in Daniel's shoulders. Reynaud must be mad to chase Lisette this distance. His mental state didn't bode well for negotiations.

He glanced at Jake's hardened profile. "You will watch out for her if I'm unable."

"There will be no need."

A few moments later, the rowboat bumped against the ship's hull. Miguel, the *Cecily*'s most skilled marksman, crouched on the mast-top platform and trained a rifle on Reynaud's man while Patch pointed a pistol over the side.

"Captain Reynaud wants no trouble, sir," the man called. "Permission to come aboard?"

Daniel gave a sharp nod to lower the rope and withdrew his flintlock from the holster as Jake raised his firearm.

A moment later, Reynaud's man climbed over the railing, eyeing the weapons with caution. "I want no trouble either, Captain Hillary."

Daniel flicked a hand in the man's direction. "Check him."

His first mate patted down Reynaud's crewman,

found a pistol in his waistband, and disarmed him. Stepping back, Patch pointed the man's own firearm at his chest.

"State your captain's business," Daniel said.

The man's drawn face was unshaven and dark circles marred the skin under his eyes. He hadn't slept for some time if appearances were any indication. Perhaps Reynaud had pushed his men to the point of exhaustion, making a tense situation potentially volatile.

"Captain Reynaud seeks his lost property. He asks that you return it, and we shall leave the way we came."

"Your captain is mistaken," Daniel said. "I'm in possession of nothing belonging to him. Everything onboard the *Cecily* is mine."

"'Tis not goods, sir. He searches for his betrothed. She is a passenger on your ship."

Daniel smirked. "Sounds as if your captain's betrothed has cried off. Perhaps she doesn't wish to go with him."

"Nothing more than a lovers' quarrel. Surely, Captain Reynaud and the lady could work out their differences if you allow them to speak privately."

What methods did Reynaud wish to employ to convince Lisette to return to him? A dark storm stirred within Daniel's chest, and his fingers curled around the smooth handle of the gun.

"Perhaps I could allow a meeting *if* your captain's betrothed was onboard, but I assure you, she is not."

"The young lady travels with her brother and another female, Mademoiselle Serafine Vistoire."

Daniel schooled his features to give nothing away. "As I said, your captain is mistaken."

"Captain Reynaud spotted her by your side, sir. He knows his betrothed is on your ship."

"Damnation. Are you implying my *wife* was betrothed to your captain?"

"Wife, sir?" The poor man's complexion paled to that of a powdered wig. "You married the lady?"

"This is a pickle," Jake interjected, speaking directly to Daniel while keeping his firearm pointed at the man. "But I suppose a marriage renders a betrothal null and void. Nothing to be done for it, I fear."

Daniel wasn't convinced Reynaud would give up easily after coming this far. "Indeed. Quite unfair to the gent, though. He is likely out a lot of blunt." He offered a conciliatory smile. "Tell your captain I will make reparations double the amount of my wife's dowry."

Reynaud's man cleared his throat. "My captain has requested to speak with you, sir, if he is not allowed an audience with Miss Lavigne. Can we arrange a meeting aboard the *Cecily*?"

Daniel gritted his teeth. *Bloody hell. Take the money and get the hell out of here.* "Your captain inconveniences me. I shall not be as generous in further negotiations."

Dread clouded the other man's already dull mud pie eyes. "Understood, sir."

Daniel stated the terms for allowing Captain Reynaud and four crewmen onboard. "He has fifteen minutes to arrive."

With Daniel's finest marksmen surrounding him and Jake, they waited on the main deck for their unwanted guests. In the time Daniel had allotted, a rowboat holding five men headed toward the *Cecily*. Reynaud was easy to identify with his rich coat and beaver hat. Sunlight glinted off the ornamentation on his hands. The arrogant dandy had donned rings on every finger this morning.

Two men tugged on the oars while Reynaud and two other men took position in the bow. Curiously, the middle crewman looked frail and was slumped over on his seat. He wouldn't be much assistance in a tussle.

When the boat reached his ship, Daniel gave permission to board. The first man up the ladder and over the rail turned to reach for something below. Every man with a firearm tensed and steadied his aim. In a moment, Reynaud's man heaved a body over the side and dumped it on the deck. A painful groan rose from the crumpled heap.

"What the devil is this?" Daniel nudged the lump with the toe of his boot, and the man rolled over to his back. His face bore the faded yellow bruising from a previous beating as well as a fresh cut to his lip and a purple, bulbous eyelid. Something familiar about the man tickled the back of Daniel's memory.

A jolt of recognition passed through him, but he stilled his features as if he were fashioned of stone. Reynaud intended to manipulate Lisette's sentiments and coerce her into leaving with him. He was a damned fool.

"I have a present for Miss Lavigne," a crisp voice answered.

Daniel looked up to see the gentleman he had

guessed to be Reynaud swing a slender leg over the railing. Once over the obstacle, he flicked imaginary dust from his tailored jacket and wrinkled his nose when he glanced down at the injured man. Reynaud's boxy head and heavy, dark brows left him teetering on the edge between handsome and grotesque.

"There is no longer a Miss Lavigne," Daniel said. "I've married the lady. And she has no need for a broken-down old man."

Reynaud's nostrils flared, reminding Daniel of a bull. "If you knew your *wife* better, you would realize you are mistaken."

Daniel didn't like the turn this encounter was taking. "This meeting is finished. Take that bag of bones with you and get the hell off my ship."

A shriek from behind ripped through him like a bolt of lightning, freezing his blood in his veins. *Blast and damn, Lisette.*

"Monsieur Baptiste," she cried in anguish, rushing forward.

Jake swung around and intercepted her a few steps from the hatch.

"I told you to stay below," Daniel barked.

She struggled to break free of Jake's hold. "What have you done to him, you monster?" Her eyes glimmered wildly, landing on Reynaud and earning a derisive lifting of the blackguard's thin lip.

Daniel aimed his pistol at Reynaud when he made to advance. "Hold your position."

The man sported a full-out sneer. "Come with me, Lisette, and I shall release your beloved Mr. Baptiste unharmed."

"Go to hell." Daniel jammed the barrel of the firearm against Reynaud's chest.

In a flash of movement, Daniel was staring into the gaping holes of four pistols while his men aimed their firearms at Reynaud's men.

"Drop your weapons," Patch snarled. "Now or you all die."

Reynaud laughed. "But not before your captain takes several lead balls to his person."

Lisette's jagged sob made Daniel forget himself, but he quickly trained his pistol on Reynaud again when the man tried to move forward.

"Take her below deck."

"Daniel, no. *Please*. I can reason with him." Her strident protests continued even as Jake toted her down the hatch.

Daniel's palms slicked with perspiration, and his blood pounded in his ears, but he forced a calm outer appearance, raising an eyebrow as if the situation were humorous. "I'm beginning to believe you came out on the winning side, sir. My wife is proving to be a difficult wench."

Reynaud's square jaw twitched. "She's in need of harsh discipline."

Rage flew through Daniel and his finger squeezed against the trigger. He wanted to kill the bloody black-guard and rid the world of him, but to do so would mean his own death and possibly that of his men.

"Be that as it may, I'm not turning the task over to you. If you and I must die today, then so be it."

Reynaud's dead eyes met Daniel's glower. Daniel planted his feet and tensed in preparation for a fight.

The air crackled with aggressive currents. The only sounds came from Mother Nature—the wash of waves against the sides of the *Cecily*, the whoosh of wind—as Daniel and Reynaud locked in a battle of intimidation.

Daniel hardened inside. He would take a bullet if it meant ending Reynaud's life.

A spark lit his opponent's eyes. "A worthy foe at last." The muscles in his jaw shifted under his pasty skin. "Let's discuss payment, Captain Hillary."

Daniel signaled his men to lower their firearms. It was a risky move, but the only viable option. "Shall we retire to my office to discuss the terms?"

Not for one moment did he judge Reynaud's cooperativeness as a concession. The desperate hunger in his gaze betrayed him. He wasn't surrendering anything, but he sure as hell wasn't leaving with Lisette.

❦

Lisette rammed her shoulder against the cabin door, but the wooden slats didn't give.

"Stop it." Serafine grabbed her from behind, her arms linking around Lisette's waist. "This is madness."

"He locked it." She broke free of her cousin's hold and kicked the door then cursed under her breath.

"You promised you wouldn't go on deck. You were only going to take a peek," Serafine said.

"I need your help." Whipping around, Lisette threw her arms wide, prepared to scream her fury. She faintly registered that Amelia was in the background perusing a constellations book with Rafe. Her posture was stiff and her hand quivered. The fight in Lisette ebbed.

She stepped closer to Serafine and lowered her voice to a harsh whisper. "Why aren't you helping me?"

"Trust your husband to deal with the situation."

Lisette's throat constricted as if some unseen force wrapped its chilled fingers around her neck. *Mon dieu.* Reynaud's men held guns on Daniel. They were going to kill him. She gulped in a lungful of air, her head spinning.

"No. I cannot leave this in his hands." Lisette stumbled back to the door and banged her fists against the rough surface. "Release me. For the love of God, please let me out." She screamed until her voice grew hoarse and her hands were on fire. "Let me out. Let me out."

When she could no longer shout, she increased the intensity of her pounding. The blows jarred her bones, and pain shot down to her elbows with each hit, but she wouldn't stop until someone unlocked the door or she broke through the wood.

The slide of the lock caught her notice a second before the door flung open. Daniel loomed in the doorway, his blue-black eyes aflame. Lisette scurried backward, but he snagged her. His fingers sank into the soft flesh of her upper arm. His grip was firm, but not painful.

"All is well." He spoke with deceptive tranquility as he threw a glance at her companions. "Please adjourn to the great cabin where tea and biscuits await you."

Lisette swallowed hard. Daniel was angry, but thank the heavens, he intended to set aside his temper, at least for the moment. She made to follow the ladies and Rafe, but Daniel held firm. "Not you, darling."

His humorless smile sent a trill to her fingertips and her stomach pitched. Once they were alone, he closed the door and released her. "What the hell were you thinking?"

Her legs quaked with the effort of standing. She walked backward, groping behind her for the ladder-back chair, and collapsed on it before she crumpled to the floor.

Daniel advanced, taking his time as if he had nothing on his mind aside from a leisurely stroll. He didn't fool her.

She lifted her chin and met his gaze. Just as she would face a fierce canine, she hid her fear. "Everything was taking longer than it should."

He braced his hand on the seat back and leaned over her. With one finger under her chin, he tipped her face up. Turmoil swirled behind his eyes.

"You could have been killed."

His voice rattled and scraped, abrading her heart. A yawning hole opened wide inside her, sucking her into the dark cavern. *Daniel* could have been killed. She bit down on her trembling bottom lip. He could have been lost to her forever.

His image flickered as single tears filled her eyes and overflowed to slide down her hot cheeks. His brown locks fell forward on his face as he leaned lower. She hesitantly swept his hair aside, behind his ears. Her finger skimmed the rim of one ear. Daniel shuddered and turned into her hand with his eyes closed. His lips touched her palm, his warm breath feathered outward over her wrist.

Wonder flooded her senses. Daniel was hers now.

He was safe and he belonged to her. No one could ever take him away. No one.

Loosely twining his fingers with hers, he drew her hand to his mouth and placed a kiss on the bruised edge of her fist. She flinched.

"What's the matter?" He rocked back, his brows angled together, and twisted her hand to view the raw flesh. "What did you do? Is that from pounding the door?"

"I wanted out," she murmured, struck by how childish she sounded.

He frowned. "Monsieur Baptiste means that much to you?"

Daniel meant that much to her, but she couldn't bring herself to say it. She knew she would never have his heart, not like Cecily did. She must be content with his protection and not burden him with her tender feelings.

"I have known him all my life," she answered.

He sighed, a long and weary breath. "Come with me to Mr. Timmons's cabin."

"I don't require a surgeon. My hands are a little bruised only. Nothing serious."

Daniel urged her from the chair. "Come anyway."

Twenty-two

"REALLY, DANIEL, I DON'T NEED TO SEE MONSIEUR Timmons. It's only a scrape." Lisette regarded her hand in the dim lantern light as her husband escorted her to the infirmary. The lights swung from hooks, casting moving shadows across the plank floor and sides of the ship.

"Just do as I say for once without argument."

She thought it best to hold her tongue. After all, her earlier actions could have gotten him killed. He no longer seemed as angry, but she was unhappy with herself now that she had had time to consider her actions.

Reaching out, she touched his arm and drew to a halt. An ache throbbed in her chest. How had she grown to love him like this?

"If anything had happened to you…" Her voice quivered with emotion. "I'm sorry."

Daniel pressed his lips together. After a long pause, he nodded. "Very well. Now, stop stalling our progress."

His dismissal of her feelings stung, but what had she expected? He viewed her as another responsibility, and his honor would see her safely delivered to London along with her family. What would become of them after that time, she didn't want to contemplate. She had no fear he would leave them with unmet needs, unless she counted the need for him to love her in return.

"Here we are." One of Daniel's men stood outside the infirmary as if keeping watch. Daniel placed his hand on the small of her back, yanked the curtain aside, and propelled her forward.

"Monsieur Baptiste," she cried.

Her father's dearest friend smiled then winced. "Gads, that hurts."

She swept to the side of his cot and knelt while the ship's surgeon retreated to a corner.

"Monsieur, I am sorry to have gotten you involved," she said. "I never meant for any of this to happen to you."

"You're not at fault, dear girl." Monsieur Baptiste's one-eyed gaze shot beyond her to Daniel. His left eye was discolored and swollen shut. "It is fortunate you found a protector in Captain Hillary."

She glanced over her shoulder. Daniel stood with his arms crossed, his expression neutral.

She turned back to Monsieur Baptiste. "Yes, he has been a Godsend. How did you come to be on the *Cecily*? I thought…"

She had heard Daniel demand Reynaud's men take him back to his ship.

"Your husband purchased my release."

She peered over her shoulder once again to find Daniel frowning.

"Consider this a wedding gift, Mrs. Hillary." His

chilly tone communicated his displeasure. Monsieur Baptiste was another mouth to feed. Another responsibility for her husband.

"*Merci*," she mumbled.

Monsieur Timmons stepped forward. "My patient needs his rest now."

Daniel gently grabbed her arm to assist her to her feet. "Examine her hands before we go."

Lisette's face flushed. "I've told him it's nothing."

The surgeon rounded the cot and captured her wrist, turning it to the side. "A minor abrasion. Clean it with soap twice a day until it heals."

She frowned. Lye would burn, no doubt. But she would follow his directives if that would satisfy Daniel and keep him from dragging her back to the infirmary.

They said their good-byes and left Monsieur Baptiste to rest. On deck, the watch remained doubled.

A splinter of fear worked its way into her heart. "Do you think Reynaud will still pursue us?"

Daniel took her under his arm, snug against his side. "It's a precaution, luv. No need to worry." His warmth spread through her, easing her tremors if not her concerns.

"What happened today? I thought he was going to kill you."

"I'm too stubborn to die, my dear."

Lisette stopped outside the cabin door. She wouldn't allow him to brush aside her questions. "I want to know how it is we're all in one piece and Reynaud is gone."

He sighed. "We reached a monetary settlement. I made certain it was an amount he couldn't refuse."

She tipped her head to look up at him. "How much did Monsieur Baptiste cost? I can reimburse you."

"Let me take care of you, Lis, and stop making the task so blasted complicated."

She clamped her mouth shut then preceded him into the great cabin to find her family enjoying tea with Amelia and Monsieur Hillary.

Serafine poured her a cup. Lisette sank onto the seat next to her cousin and accepted the offering with her thanks.

Daniel sent a pointed look Lisette's direction. "Fill your cousin in on the latest happenings." He disappeared through his office entrance and closed the door.

Lisette shared the news of Monsieur Baptiste's abduction and rescue.

Serafine huffed. "I always thought the man brainless, but I never realized how dense he truly is."

Monsieur Hillary and Amelia leaned forward, clearly interested in their exchange.

"Serafine, don't insult Monsieur Baptiste. He was Papa's closest friend."

"Which illustrates my point perfectly. Why didn't he anticipate Reynaud would come to him? Reynaud had to realize you had received assistance in fleeing. If Monsieur Baptiste had gone into hiding for several days, Reynaud never would have found us."

"You can't blame Monsieur Baptiste. Reynaud is crafty."

Serafine shrugged. "It doesn't require a crafty man to capture a dolt."

Daniel returned to the great cabin in time to overhear this last statement. He had removed his jacket, waistcoat, and cravat. He moved to the sideboard and poured himself a drink. "Tell me, mademoiselle, what do you think I should do with the dolt in my infirmary?"

"I wouldn't give him any job too mentally taxing, if that is your meaning."

"I thought to send him back to New Orleans. Perhaps we'll dock next in Lisbon."

"No." Lisette jumped from her seat. "He can't go back. What if Reynaud kills him?"

Daniel raised a brow and sipped his drink. "I hope you aren't suggesting he reside with us in London."

So, the added responsibility of Monsieur Baptiste did vex her husband. "No, I don't wish him to reside with us, but…"

Daniel sighed. Loudly. As if she was more trouble than she was worth. "Very well. He may stay as a guest for a short time. A very short time." He downed his drink then set it on the table with a clunk. "As you must recall, this is our wedding day. I'll thank everyone to leave us alone now. Dinner shall be served in your own cabins this evening."

Lisette's mouth dropped open. She wasn't certain what bothered her more, his rudeness to their guests or implications they intended to engage in intimacy.

Once they were alone, Daniel stretched his arms overhead. His shirt gapped open at the neck once his arms fell to his side. "Tiring day."

She had grown accustomed to seeing him without the usual articles of clothing favored by gentlemen. He was less intimidating than when he dressed in proper attire, but the thought of him without a stitch of clothing on made her heart sprint.

"You've never mentioned your grandfather," she said as a way of stalling.

Daniel pulled out a chair and dropped onto it. "Why would I? Is he relevant?"

Lisette turned the fine bone china cup on the saucer. Delicate pink blossoms decorated the edge. "I wouldn't know his relevance to you. Only you can answer that question."

"You weren't referring to his worth then? I had assumed my inheritance made me a more desirable husband of a sudden. No need for an annulment or residing apart now?"

Why must he goad her? "I found you desirable long before I discovered the worth of your accounts."

His dimple pierced his cheek. "What a lovely thing to say, Mrs. Hillary. I suspect you might have a *tendre* for me."

"And how unfortunate for me," she snapped. His mockery hurt.

Daniel reached across the table with his palm up. "Lis, I didn't mean to upset you. I am touchy when it comes to my worth, and I'm pleased to know your regard for me is genuine." He captured her hand when she didn't place it in his. His fingers traced each knuckle. His light touch sent delicious currents racing through her. "Your fondness for me pleases me, and I return it in kind."

Fondness. How despairing the word. She examined the porcelain cup as she circled it on the saucer. "This is beautiful, but out of place here. Why do you have such delicate pieces onboard?"

When she met his gaze, the teasing light was gone.

"The dishes belonged to Cecily. The set was a wedding gift from her mother."

Lisette's mouth formed a silent "oh." An oppressive weight pressed on her chest. Cecily would always be between them, Lisette's opposition even in death.

Daniel searched her face and then frowned. Snatching the cup and saucer from her, he pushed to his feet. "Follow me." He stalked to his office without waiting for her.

"What are you doing?" Lisette scrambled from her seat to run after him. He had reached the balcony by the time she entered. He'd gone mad, *corkbrained*, to borrow a phrase from the English crewmen.

Drawing his arm back, he hurled the cup into the churning waters.

"Daniel!" She rushed forward to stop him.

He looked over his shoulder, smiled, and then flung the saucer like a discus. It sailed through the air and shattered as it hit the surface. "My Lord, that felt amazing. Bring me the rest." Laughter rang in his voice.

"But you're breaking the dishes."

"I'm ridding us of them, yes. Now hurry. I need your help."

Hope sprouted inside her. Daniel was throwing away a piece of Cecily. Lisette dashed to the great cabin and ripped the larger plates from their home. With a stack in hand, she hurried back to the balcony.

Daniel grabbed a plate, tossed it, and then took the stack from her. "You throw one too."

She shoved her hands behind her and backed away. "I shouldn't."

Shifting the load to one arm, he held out a plate. "Cecily has no place between us, luv. Toss it."

She smiled tentatively. "If you are certain…" He thrust the plate at her. "Very well. I *will*." Lisette cast the dish into the sea as far as she could and then grabbed another. Together, they dispatched the dinner plates and rushed to gather the remaining dishes. Daniel dumped an armload over the railing, and she followed his example. One more trip saw the last of Cecily's china tossed overboard.

Her breathing was heavy from exertion and exhilaration. Maybe their marriage stood a chance after all, although they would dine on wooden saucers for the remainder of the voyage.

Daniel gathered her in his arms. A joyful smile lit his face. "What else shall we toss overboard?"

Lisette laughed and hugged him. "That's enough." And it was. His actions spoke of optimism and new beginnings. She didn't require anything more.

"I should toss you over my shoulder and carry you to bed," he said.

A muffled knock sounded at the great cabin door.

"Damnation." He kissed her cheek and released her from his embrace. "That will be water for your bath."

A bath sounded divine. She hadn't enjoyed such luxury since their stay in Port Albis.

He led her from the balcony. "One last gift for my bride."

"I have nothing to give you."

"I'm content with what you have to give me, my sweet." Her insides flipped again as he lifted her hand and placed a gentle kiss on her fingers. His gaze held her frozen in place. "You have given me a taste of freedom."

Lisette had no idea as to his meaning, but the intensity with which he spoke these words filled her with love.

Twenty-three

Daniel hesitated outside the chamber door. Lisette's splashing had ceased several minutes earlier, but he didn't know if she had finished dressing. He suspected his sudden entrance might increase her apprehension, and frankly, her obvious fear of consummating their marriage frayed his nerves to a degree. He had never bedded an innocent, but he'd heard horrid tales of wedding nights ending in swooning or hysterical crying.

"Bloody hell," he groaned under his breath and rapped on the door. He wouldn't allow such ludicrous notions to run amok in his brain. He damned well knew what he was doing.

"Yes?" Her voice didn't waver, which seemed a good omen.

"Dinner has arrived."

"Oh." She sounded confused by his announcement, prompting him to ease open the door.

Lisette perched on the side of the bed, pulling a brush through her silky hair. She had donned a light cotton nightrail, a demure ensemble trimmed in lace with a white satin bow enclosure at the neck. Her attire was more suitable for a young girl than a woman, but there was no mistaking Lisette for a girl. She adjusted her position on the bed and her full breasts swayed, the faint rose color of her nipples showing through the insubstantial material.

Daniel's pulse quickened. "You have dressed for bed."

A pink flush colored her cheeks. "I thought we…" She trailed off and lowered her gaze but then peeked at him from underneath the dark fringe of her lashes. If he didn't know any better, he would think her an experienced coquette.

"And what a brilliant thought, my dear. Dinner can wait." He crossed to the bed in two strides and sat beside her, taking the brush from her hand. "May I?"

Her solemn green eyes lifted to meet his direct stare. "Yes," she whispered before turning her back to him.

He drew the bristles through her midnight locks. Rarely had he seen hair so black it assumed a blue reflection in the light. The pale ladies of Mayfair seemed dull in comparison to his alluring bride. Upon smoothing his free hand over her hair in the wake of the brush, fine strands twined around his fingers as if they possessed a will of their own. He luxuriated in her softness.

Setting the brush aside, he lifted the heavy curtain of hair cascading down her back to bare her neck. His fingers curled around her shoulder as he placed his lips against her supple skin and inhaled. *Jasmine.* The enchanting fragrance would forever remind him of his sweet Lisette.

He sprinkled light kisses upon her neck, savoring her scent. A shiver shook her from head to hip, and he felt the tremors against his thigh.

"Are you frightened?" he asked.

She glanced over her shoulder; her rose-petal lips parted. "No."

Turning toward him, she kissed him as if to prove her claim. Passion flared in his core. He wanted to toss her back on the mattress and make her his. His muscles twitched with the effort of denying himself.

"Are *you* frightened, monsieur?" Her breath fanned his cheeks, the scent of tooth powder making him smile.

"I was apprehensive at first."

Lisette pulled back. A tiny crease formed between her arched brows. "Why?"

"Our marriage was sudden, and I wasn't certain if you would be ready for this."

She nibbled her bottom lip. "I don't know what to expect, is all, but I am ready. I want you here."

Daniel's lungs filled on a deep inhale. He'd been holding his breath without realizing. "I want you, too, Lis."

When he reached for the bow at her neckline, her hand covered his and halted his fingers. Her searching gaze bore into him. "Are we truly married?"

Was this the source of her hesitation? She feared they were not legally wed? Of course. Lisette wouldn't know the laws governing his homeland. "I assure you we are bound forever in matrimony. Nothing can challenge the validity of our union."

Her hand cupped his cheek. "But it's not too late to undo the vows, correct?"

It bloody well was too late. She couldn't willy-nilly decide to toss him over and escape her promise. She had married him without any coercion, and she was of sound mind. Lisette was good and married whether she liked it or not.

He checked his ire and forced himself to speak in a patient tone. "I've not changed my mind since I offered for you this morning. Am I to assume you are suffering from regret?"

"No…"

Daniel's gut roiled. There was so much meaning behind that one word, an unspoken question. What was it she needed from him?

He buried his fingers in her hair and urged her forward. "Lisette Hillary, I desire you above all women. I'm pleased you are my wife, and I will endeavor to make you happy to have married me."

Her dark lashes fluttered and lay against her cheeks. She released her breath on a broken sigh. "But will you ever love me like you loved Cecily?"

God, no. Cecily was an illness, a plague upon him. She had possessed his mind and wrecked his peace. Lisette was everything his first wife was not.

"I will love you better," he promised, believing it in his heart.

The crease between her brows eased, and her eyes rose to meet his gaze again. The soft glow there warmed him inside. "Then I'm already happy I married you."

Their mouths brushed together, hers moist and plump, and a jolt struck his lower abdomen. He had experienced the same thrill every time she'd allowed him to kiss her. And, as with every other time, he forced himself to hold back for fear of overwhelming her.

Her kiss seemed cautious as she tested the waters. He invited her exploration by allowing her to initiate each touch—chaste pecks then firmer kisses and finally the tip of her tongue tentatively touching his lips. Each loving caress heated his blood.

He cradled the nape of her neck and swept his tongue into her hot mouth. Lisette stiffened for one moment but soon opened to him. By the second sweep, she melted against him then followed his lead. Her actions were bolder with each pass of her tongue, and she wrapped her arms around his neck, pressing her curves against him.

He grinned. This was more of what he had expected from his wife. Lisette was anything but meek. Her courage had impressed him from the moment he'd met her in The Abyss, and she didn't disappoint him now.

His fingers found the end of her bow and tugged, untying the top of her nightrail. A small triangle of luminous skin peeked through the opening, and he placed a kiss there, marking her as his. A rapid pulse beat at her collarbone. The pounding repetition mesmerized him.

He placed his lips against the spot and savored her essence. Her breath grew heavy as he nibbled her elegant neck. A couple of licks and her head rolled back. His kisses followed a path to the delicate place behind her ear before he captured her earlobe. Her soft moan nearly broke him.

Lisette's heart thundered in her chest. Had Daniel

truly promised to love her better? His reverent adoration of her body went a long way in convincing her of his sincerity.

Grasping the hem of her nightrail, he tugged it over her head in one swift movement, leaving no time for trepidation. His gaze roved over her bare breasts, his eyes blazing. Lisette fought the urge to cover herself. She had never felt as vulnerable as she did with all her flaws uncovered. Heavy breasts, full hips, and rounded thighs. There was nothing delicate about her appearance.

Daniel slid a finger along the side of her breast. "You're beautiful." Heat unfurled in her belly when his fingers caressed the tip of her breast. "Lie back on the pillow."

She hesitated, uncertain what he wished of her. Was she to climb under the covers?

His hand pressed gently against her chest. "Just lie back, darling."

She scooted toward the middle of the bed and eased back; her head sank into the pillow. Her breasts tingled as his hungry gaze roamed over her.

"Amazingly perfect," he murmured. "I underestimated your charms."

How completely embarrassing, and yet thrilling, to be devoured by a look. When she began to fidget, Daniel ripped his shirt over his head then bent over to remove his boots. Taut muscles rolled under his tanned skin. A strong tug between her legs made her gasp.

He glanced back over his shoulder. "Are you all right?"

She nodded. "Yes."

His smile scattered her nerves. *Mon dieu.* Would she always feel this anxious when he visited her bed?

Daniel climbed on the mattress and stretched out beside her. She rolled toward him into his arms and their lips met. Kissing was the most amazing activity ever. Nothing could ever compare. She felt certain of this.

His fingers closed on her nipple. She jumped and Daniel released her. The sensation had been like a pleasurable tickle, teetering on the edge of annoying, but also delightful. She wanted to feel it again. Thrusting her breast forward a little, she hoped he would touch her again, but instead, he rolled her to her back.

"Daniel."

He chuckled. "You think you might like more? Let's see, shall we?" Lowering his head, he licked her nipple, one long brush of his velvety tongue that made her hips buck. He stroked her again, and her hips rose from the bed. Splaying his hand across her abdomen, Daniel held her in place and closed his mouth around her hardened bud.

His tongue drew circles on her breast and suckled until a violent storm stirred down low. With each lick and graze of teeth, it was harder to swallow her moans or stop her hips from writhing. She ached between her legs like nothing she had ever known. It was excruciating.

"I can't take it anymore," she said with a whimper. "I hurt."

Daniel lifted his head and placed a gentle kiss on her cheek. "Forgive me, darling. I quite forgot myself. I'll ease your ache." The hand on her stomach inched into her curls before caressing her sensitive flesh.

"Oh," she said on a gasp. "Oh!" Her mind turned to bread pudding and all she could utter was a single letter of the alphabet.

Mon dieu. She had been wrong. This was much nicer than kissing. Daniel's mouth sought her breast again while his finger eased inside her then out again to glide over her heated skin. She felt wicked with him touching her down there, and damnation, she took to wickedness straight away. His moist digit continued to stroke her.

Her eyes flew open. She couldn't have—*Sweet Mary, Mother of God.* "Am I *wet*?" Her voice squeaked in alarm.

"Very wet," Daniel confirmed; his blue eyes twinkled with amusement. "Just as you're supposed to be. Now, do be quiet and calm yourself. I'm trying to make love to you."

Lisette rested her head back on the pillow and closed her eyes. How was she to relax when her body behaved with complete unpredictability? Who knew what embarrassing thing might happen next? But her concerns vanished when he dipped his finger in and out of her again then circled this incredible spot down there she hadn't known existed.

"*Oui,*" she said on a sigh.

His continued caresses between her legs and his hot breath on her breast triggered a vibration in her lower belly. Her body tensed and quaked. She gasped and held her breath as the pleasing sensation grew in strength with each pass over her special place and draw on her nipple.

The vibrations shook her, narrowing her awareness to the building pressure inside her. She panted. She was going to explode. She gripped Daniel's wrist, thinking to stop him, but abandoned the idea. She had never felt so alive. The pleasure grew in intensity, and her hips bucked as she surrendered to whatever power overtook her. Another stroke of Daniel's hand and a cry burst from her, then another and another. Her wits fragmented and scattered to the unknown while pinpricks of colored lights flashed behind her closed eyes.

Mon dieu. Mon dieu.

Whatever had gripped her let her go to float back to earth. Her heavy limbs sank into the mattress.

Daniel rolled her onto her side and gathered her to him. Her cheek rested against his bare chest, her breath slowly evening out. The contrast to their bodies tweaked her curiosity. His muscles were tense whereas she had never felt so fluid.

"What just happened to me?"

"You came." He snuggled her and kissed the top of her head. "Promise you'll remember this feeling later."

Lisette smiled lazily. "It will be impossible to forget."

His hand cupped her bottom and pulled her closer. A hard ridge pressed into her belly. "I fear you may have some discomfort the first time we couple."

She sucked on her bottom lip instead of asking what the devil he meant. Now that the fuzzy feeling had begun to recede, her modesty reappeared. Lisette crossed her arms over her breasts and cuddled close to hide his view of her.

"You've seen all of me," she said, "and yet you still wear trousers."

"Fair enough." He released her and rolled from the bed.

"Wait." She snatched her crumpled nightrail and clutched it to her chest.

Daniel grinned and unfastened the waistband of his pants. She averted her gaze when they fell to the floor, but soon her curiosity demanded satisfaction. One quick peek didn't quench her curiosity, so she had to look again.

By the saints. She had never guessed men could hide anything of such consequence inside their trousers. "It appears a bit unwieldy."

Daniel grinned as he climbed on the bed and advanced toward her. "I've learned to manage it well enough."

Lisette scooted backward until she came up against the headboard. Her eyes rounded. Daniel grasped her hips and tugged, stretching her out beneath him, then snatched her nightrail and tossed it on the floor.

"Do you wish to come again?"

Again? A thrill shot through her at the same time her cheeks flushed with heat. He saved her the humiliation of answering and kissed her with more force than the first time.

Lisette's body responded with eagerness, arching into him when his mouth nibbled a trail down her neck. He stopped to lick the hollow of her collarbone before returning to her breasts. Her fingers burrowed into his wavy hair while he stroked her bud with his tongue. The familiar twinges started between her legs again.

"Touch me again... down there," she whispered.

Daniel met her gaze. "You want me to touch your quim."

"Oh." No one had ever mentioned a specific name for down there. Of course, it wasn't like an elbow. Not everyone possessed one, only ladies. Odd a man should know the name and not her.

Daniel waited for her response while his fingers tweaked her nipple and sent waves of pleasure to her toes.

"Will you touch my... quim, please?"

He winked. "With pleasure."

But instead of using his fingers to relieve her ache, he kissed his way down her abdomen and settled between her thighs. He caressed her legs, eased them apart then kissed her down there. Lisette gasped. His tongue passed over her special spot and she gasped again.

Tension coiled in her belly, tighter and tighter until she writhed underneath his lips. It was happening again. She was about to unravel any moment, but he ceased his decadent attentions before she hurtled over the edge.

"Not yet," he chided as he crawled up her body and kissed her cheek.

His bulky member touched her, startling her.

"Shh, everything is all right." His deep blue eyes stared into hers and radiated with warmth. His member brushed against the place where he had put his fingers. "I'll go slowly."

Now Lisette understood what he meant to do, and her heart thumped violently. She gritted her teeth in preparation for what could only be an abysmal idea. Her spine stiffened as he surged inside her, but no pain flooded her senses, overwhelming her as she had expected.

Her eyes popped open wide. "Why, I barely feel anything at all."

Daniel issued a strained chuckle. The cords in his neck stood out as he braced his weight with his forearms. "You do know how to prick a man's pride."

"I don't under—oh!"

Her breath hitched when he pushed deeper, receded, and then seated himself fully. He stilled. The position seemed awkward and the full sensation strange, but not unduly painful.

He kissed her temple. "Are you all right?"

"*Oui.*" She wiggled her hips to find a more comfortable position.

Daniel sucked in a sharp breath. His eyes closed and ecstasy swept across his handsome features. Her pulse sped, and she shifted her hips again.

He stared down at her with passion darkening his eyes. "You're the best thing ever to happen to me, Lis."

She beamed with his compliment. Daniel began moving with caution, whispering endearments in her ear and kissing her as he slid in and out of her. Each movement began to feel more and more natural. She rocked her hips in rhythm with his, just as they had done when dancing.

"Yes, sweetheart, just like that."

His hand cradled her bottom and tilted her hips to sink even deeper into her. Lisette lifted her face, and he ceased movements to kiss her with tenderness.

He brushed the hair from her eyes. "So perfect," he murmured.

Her heart doubled in size, she was so filled with love for him.

Daniel shifted his weight to his knees and pulled her down the bed to bury himself within her again. His thumb brushed her spot and pleasure shot through her limbs, making her fingers and toes tingle. With each slow thrust, he stroked, bringing her closer and closer to coming.

Another sweep and thrust sent her soaring high over the summit, springing into the clouds with a joyful cry.

Daniel hugged her tight against his chest, twined his fingers with her hair, and pumped harder and faster. His vigorous movements were possessive and thrilling. She smiled and licked her lips.

"Ah, Lis, yes."

He issued a strangled call with his head tossed back. A moment later, he rolled to his back, pulling her with him, and collapsed into the mattress. Lisette laid her cheek against his chest and listened to his solid and strong heartbeat. She placed a kiss over his heart. Some day it would belong to her. She wouldn't have it any other way.

Twenty-four

SERAFINE GLANCED WISTFULLY AS AMELIA'S HAND clutched her rounded belly. "I declare, this child is a natural-born pugilist like his father," her friend said, a blissful smile softening her expression.

"Is he kicking again?"

"He has enlisted the aid of his elbows and knees this time. My gullet will be black and blue before he is birthed."

They were ensconced in Amelia's quarters, embroidering dressing gowns for the child. Serafine had grown to care for her companion over the past weeks, and with Lisette favoring the company of her husband, Serafine and Amelia had become each other's confidants.

Serafine didn't begrudge Lisette her happiness with Captain Hillary. Quite the opposite. She rejoiced in seeing her younger cousin settled into an advantageous union. Serafine no longer worried for any of their futures. Regretting she would never have the same opportunity as Lisette wasn't the same as envy, was it?

Jabbing the needle through the simple frock, she

frowned. Serafine would never know the honor of being a wife or the joy of motherhood. She had thrown away her aspirations four months prior, gambling on a man who had later broken her heart. She was a fool.

"You're fortunate to be loved," Serafine said. "To have your whole life ahead of you with a child on the way."

Amelia glanced up from her task. "Don't allow the lack of eligible gentlemen aboard the *Cecily* to discourage you, dearest. We will arrive in England any day."

"I don't expect my prospects will improve in London."

Her friend nibbled her bottom lip as she concentrated on making a perfect stitch. "It's true it's late in the season, but I am certain a few good men have held out for someone more to their liking. We'll call on Bibi the moment we arrive. My dear friend will have the latest *on dit* concerning the marriage mart."

Serafine inwardly shuddered. She could never enter the marriage market given her state of impurity. Deception at any stage of marriage seemed a recipe for doom. There was no sense in engaging in pretense with Amelia either.

Serafine cleared her throat and focused on the delicate white fabric and light blue stitching. "I won't be entering the marriage market."

"Why ever not? I thought you wished to wed and have children."

"I do, but just because a fish wishes to be a bird and sprout wings doesn't make it possible."

Amelia clucked her tongue. "I hardly think of you

as one given to nonsense. A fish with wings? Stop speaking as if you're an anomaly. You are a lovely, engaging young lady, and there will be a gentleman to fall for you. You will see."

Serafine abandoned the tiny garment on her lap. "Even if that were so, and I doubt the validity of your claim, I couldn't possibly marry."

Tossing her embroidery on the table, Amelia huffed. "I take umbrage, mademoiselle. Have I ever been known to tell a falsehood? And why can't you marry?"

Serafine's cheeks heated when confronted by her friend's aggrieved glower. "You couldn't possibly understand. Look at you." She flung her hand up and down from Amelia's head to toes. "You're exquisite with your flaxen hair and ivory complexion. You're the epitome of a lady." Her voice cracked and tears welled in her eyes.

She covered her sob with her palm and turned away in mortification. Never had she shed tears in another person's company, aside from Lisette.

Amelia's chair legs scraped against the planks as she staggered to her feet. "Serafine."

Her compassionate tone ripped open the wound in Serafine's heart she had thought almost healed.

Amelia patted her shoulder then rounded the chair to hug her. "Dear girl, you cannot think poorly of yourself based on your coloring."

Resentment surged within Serafine's chest, making it tight and her shoulders stiff. "And why not? Others take no issue with devaluing me based on my outer appearance."

"Tell me who," Amelia demanded. "Daniel will have him quartered and fed to the fish."

Serafine recoiled. "Blessed be! No one on ship. The captain wouldn't really do such a horrible thing, would he?"

Amelia's lips twitched. "I have never known him to dole out such severe punishments. But it sounds frightening, no? He should add it to his repertoire of threats."

Serafine released a breathy chuckle and wilted on her chair. Her head dropped forward, and she contemplated the mess that had become her life.

Amelia dragged her seat closer and sat. Their knees almost touched. "I can see your heart is breaking. Won't you share what makes you suffer so?"

Having never spoken of her shame to anyone, Serafine's secrets weighed on her. Her leaden limbs sagged, and her chest felt crushed under the heavy burden. She looked into Amelia's caring face, and all she wanted to do was release her painful past.

"His name was Isaac Tucker."

Amelia nodded, her expression one of graveness. "There is always one who breaks a poor lady's heart."

Her friend was too kind, and a consummate liar. "You have never suffered a broken heart."

"I have *too* had my heart broken. By my husband, of all gentlemen. His rejection devastated me, and I suffered for nearly a year."

Serafine gulped. Heavens, if Amelia could suffer heartache, anyone was at risk.

"But as you can see, even hopeless situations have a way of correcting themselves," Amelia said with a soft smile. "You may or may not have a future with your Mr. Tucker, but you cannot give up on love."

Serafine lifted one shoulder, willing to give lip service only to her friend's declaration. "I'm sure you are correct."

Amelia's arched brows lifted. "Mr. Tucker is from New Orleans, I take it?"

"*Oui.*" Serafine had never traveled farther than two miles outside of the city.

"I see. And does he show a fondness for architecture?"

Serafine's eyes narrowed. Had he returned to America without her knowledge? "You've met Mr. Tucker?"

Amelia pursed her lips and screwed them to the side then back again as she seemed to mull over her response. She took a deep breath and released it slowly. "We met in London a few days before the *Cecily* departed for New Orleans. If memory serves, the gentleman was traveling to Edinburgh next, but I wouldn't be surprised if he has returned to Town. He seemed quite enamored of the architecture."

Isaac had been in England? But he was to be on the Continent. Her stomach churned as her imagination ran wild with possibilities. *Mon dieu, Serafine. Have you learned nothing?*

She picked up her embroidery again and sniffed. "With any luck, our paths shall never cross."

❧

Daniel leaned back in his chair and kicked his boots up on the desk with a contented sigh. He was supposed to be reviewing the logbook and finalizing documents for their arrival, but his wife proved as distracting in the other cabin as she was when in his office.

Lisette's sweet voice lifted in song and drifted through the open doorway. He could close the door and mute the disruption to some degree, but he enjoyed listening to her. She was singing a French folk song, but a moment ago, she had belted out a gospel hymn that had his toe tapping.

With a low growl of frustration, he eyed his ledger. He must complete his work now, or he would be up half the night when he would prefer to retire with Lisette. Twirling the quill between his fingers, he conjured an image of his wife dressed in her maidenly cotton nightrail and smiled. She had proven herself a pleasing bed partner in many ways, and her innocent eagerness to learn aroused him more than the most experienced of courtesans ever could.

He had happily indulged her curiosity by teaching her common terminology for body parts and the acts of copulation itself. When her full lips had formed the word "cock" the first time, it had sounded both sweet and vulgar. Daniel had employed every bit of willpower not to urge the lesson in a completely inappropriate direction.

Devil take it! She was his wife, good and proper. He would do well to remember the fact and treat her as such.

Daniel swung his legs from the desk and leapt from his chair to close the door, but he halted at the threshold. Lisette sat at the table with Rafe, concentrating on the pieces of ropes in her hands. She had taken to practicing knots with her brother every day, encouraging him to demonstrate the square knot, figure eight, and thumb knot while she imitated his movements. Lisette's patience seemed endless as she attended to her brother's strict routines without complaint, and her devotion was reaping marked results.

Rafe leaned his head against her shoulder. "Right over left. Left over right," he recited.

Lisette tied a passable square knot then held it out for Rafe's inspection. The lad lifted his face and smiled at his sister. "Splendid work, Lisette."

Daniel suppressed a chuckle as Rafe parroted his sister's words of praise usually reserved for him.

She wrapped an arm around his bony shoulders and planted a kiss atop his head. "You are kind, monsieur."

Rafe didn't shy away from her embrace, as he tended to do at the start of their journey.

Daniel's gut contracted and the smile fell from his face. Lisette would make an excellent mother. She already was the perfect mother figure to Rafe. They hadn't discussed children, but Daniel had taken no precautions. What if she opposed the idea as vehemently as Cecily had?

He gave himself a mental shake. Lisette was reasonable, loving, and thoughtful. She didn't possess an ounce of vanity. She would welcome his issue when the time came.

Daniel leaned against the doorjamb to observe Lisette and Rafe further. Neither one looked up from their tasks. This was his family, the ones he cared for most. They were his to protect, and each day they drew closer to England lessened his fears that they might not survive the journey. And once he had them back on solid ground, he would never allow either of them to step foot on the *Cecily* again.

The boards creaked as he shifted his weight and Lisette's head swung around. Her rose-colored lips curved into a charming smile, and his pulse launched into a frenzied rush of desire.

"The air is cooler as we approach England," she said. "I fear I might catch my death in London before we set sail for warmer climes again."

Daniel pushed from his slouch and wandered to the table to place his hands on her shoulders. She lifted her face, and he kissed the tip of her nose. "I shall endeavor to find ways to shelter you from the chill, luv."

"Will we be long in London?"

He slid into the hard wooden seat beside her and scooped up her ropes, turning the knot to inspect it. "Not bad."

She beamed as if he had paid her a real compliment, such as bestowing upon her the designation of an Incomparable, which she was to him at least. He had never known a woman like her, and he possessed no desire to seek out another to test his hypothesis.

"Perhaps my newfound skills will be of benefit on our next voyage," she teased. "I could assume the position of first mate."

He whispered in her ear, "You may assume any position you desire."

Lisette playfully swatted his arm. "You're impossible."

Not wishing to reveal his plans to ensconce his wife safely in England rather than dragging her around the world, he changed the subject. "Did you visit Mr. Baptiste today?"

"*Oui*. Monsieur Timmons thinks his ribs have almost healed. Either way, Monsieur Baptiste offers no complaints, not that he ever has."

Perhaps not within his wife's hearing, but Daniel thought the man whined more than a colicky infant. He disparaged his lodgings, despite the fact the infirmary on the *Cecily* had to be far superior to the brink on Reynaud's ship. And he criticized the food, which set Daniel's teeth on edge. For a man surviving as a direct result of Daniel's generosity, Mr. Baptiste possessed a giant set of brass ballocks.

He'd even lamented his lack of freedom to wander the decks at will, but no one who had spent days confined on his enemy's vessel would be granted any freedoms on Daniel's ship. It meant nothing to him that the man was a prisoner and the victim of atrocious abuse. Mr. Baptiste was not to be trusted without proving himself worthy of such an honor.

Lisette trailed her fingers along Daniel's forearm. Her touch sent tingles along his skin. "I think Monsieur Baptiste is well enough to join us for dinner this evening."

Daniel withheld his opinion of the man's company. He'd not take pleasure in extending an invitation to his table, but Lisette did harbor affection for the old codger.

"If it pleases you, then I will ask him to join us."

She stood and slipped behind his chair before wrapping her arms around his neck. Her heated cheek grazed his ear. "I would be well pleased." Her lips touched his temple, marking him with a kiss.

Daniel squeezed her hand then reluctantly extracted

himself from her embrace. If he was to speak with Mr. Baptiste, he should do it now before he changed his mind and instead carried his wife back to their bedchamber.

"Then by all means, allow me to extend a personal invitation." If the man's ribs no longer pained him, laudanum wouldn't addle his mind any longer, and Daniel might be able to gather more information on his enemy.

He sauntered out of the great cabin into the bright sunlight and shaded his eyes with his hand. His crew continued with their duties, paying him no mind. The cooler air washed over his exposed skin as he strolled along the deck. It was a welcome reprieve from the Caribbean heat.

The season would be ending soon, but perhaps they would arrive in time to attend a ball or two. Daniel had never cared much for the tedious affairs, but he was eager to present his wife to society. Perhaps Lisette would form associations and acquire invitations to the country to keep her occupied while he returned to sea. He could always encourage his sister's friendship with Lisette, and she would have Amelia and Serafine for companionship too.

A pang vibrated in his chest. If Lisette had companionship, he wouldn't worry about her suffering the same loneliness he would experience being parted from her.

He ducked his head as he went below deck, blinded for a moment when he moved from the brilliant light into the dim bowels of the ship. When his eyes adjusted, he stalked to the infirmary to find Mr.

Baptiste and gather whatever reconnaissance he could on Reynaud.

Although there had been no more sightings of the *Mihos*, Daniel had read the blackguard's determination in his expression. Reynaud hadn't abandoned his original objective.

Daniel flung aside the curtain and barged into the infirmary. Mr. Baptiste fumbled the book he held, dropping the tome on the floor with a resounding smack. Daniel nodded to Timmons, who glanced up from his game of Patience then returned his attention to the cards.

"My wife informs me you are healing, sir."

Baptiste eyed Daniel as he retrieved the book from the floor. *The Iliad*, from Amelia's collection. She had read every page aloud after dinner on the voyage to Port Albis. He would place a bet that Lisette had provided the man with this source of entertainment.

Baptiste coughed into his fist and winced. "I'm still sore, but my injuries no longer pain me when I breathe."

Daniel grabbed a vacant wooden chair, swung it around, and plopped down. Resting his forearms on the seat back, he slouched to give the appearance of not having a care in the world. "And yet it's often preferable to the alternative."

The gentleman cocked his head. "The alternative, sir?"

"A cessation of breath versus a little pain upon inhalation to remind you that you are indeed still alive."

Baptiste hadn't relaxed his posture since Daniel entered the space. His knuckles flashed white where he gripped the book's spine. "I suppose it's all in one's perspective, and you make a compelling case."

Daniel rapped lightly against the seat back twice as if their meeting neared the end. "Very well. You seem fit enough to attend dinner in the great cabin. I'll expect you this evening."

"Wait," Baptiste blurted as Daniel stood. "What about my own quarters?"

"I have no other lodgings available." Daniel's voice came out steady and low, daring the other man to challenge him. "And if you'll recall, you didn't pay a fare."

Baptiste's eyes darkened. "Indeed, you've bought and paid for me. I suppose I'm at your mercy."

"That you are, sir, and I ask so little in return. Tell me what you know of Reynaud."

The older man shrugged. Without bruises distorting his face, he looked distinguished. Perhaps he was someone's father, brother, or uncle.

"Reynaud is a criminal. That's all I know of him."

"Tell me of his criminal tendencies then."

Baptiste scoffed. "It's not as if I'm a member of his group of thugs. What information do you expect me to provide?"

"Something to convince me you are indeed friend rather than foe. Then I might be willing to locate a cabin for you."

"I see." Mr. Baptiste's shoulders drooped, and his defeated gaze dropped to the floor. "Ask me what you wish to know, and I'll try to answer to the best of my ability. But as I have already stated, Captain, I know very little about Louis Reynaud."

"You didn't want Lisette to marry him. You must have had some reason to oppose the match."

Baptiste's dirt-brown eyes sought out Daniel. "The girl deserved better. Reynaud wanted to get his hands on her dowry and then to live off Master Rafe's inheritance."

Daniel sank back to the chair. "How would he have accomplished the feat when Rafe has a guardian in England?"

"Xavier Vistoire has sent no word from England for a long time. No one believes he intends to return to America or fulfill his guardianship duties. Reynaud has associates in prestigious governing positions. He intended to use his connections to push through his petition for guardianship of the boy."

Baptiste hadn't told him anything Daniel didn't already know. "Is there still a chance of him gaining control of the Lavigne estate through his government associations?"

"I don't see how that would be possible unless..." Baptiste shook his head.

"Unless what? Finish your thought."

"Unless Reynaud is able to convince everyone he did indeed marry Miss Lavigne. Couldn't he have an entry in his log stating he had married her? He could pay witnesses to support his claim, and who would oppose him?"

"Would he be believed with no bride?"

Baptiste shrugged. "People die at sea all the time, Captain Hillary. Who is to say Miss Lavigne and Master Rafe didn't succumb to illness on the journey?"

Indeed. "Then the property should revert to the next of kin."

"There is no other next of kin. If Reynaud married Lisette, he would be the only family she has left.

Reynaud associates with the type of men who can forge Mr. Vistoire's death certificate, then he would face no opposition. And if Mr. Vistoire ever returned to New Orleans, he would indeed be a dead man."

With a sigh, Baptiste placed the book beside him on the cot and reclined, showing the first signs of dropping his guard. "Captain, if I may be so bold as to offer my advice, forget about Reynaud. Allow him to have Master Rafe's properties and money. Your wife and her brother will have a full life with you in England."

It would be a bloody cold day in Hades before Daniel allowed Reynaud to steal from his family.

He bounded from the chair. "Thank you for your cooperation." Now he could better develop a countermove before he returned to America to deal with the blackguard.

Twenty-five

LISETTE, RAFE, SERAFINE, AND MONSIEUR BAPTISTE hugged the ship's railing as the *Cecily* maneuvered along the Thames. All except Rafe wore matching expressions of awe. The river traffic was obscene in comparison to the Mississippi, where they had gone days without seeing another ship. Nearing London, Lisette feared they might collide with another vessel.

Every size imaginable clogged the waterway. Rafe called out each ship or boat class as they passed as if he had observed the scene a thousand times and grown bored of it all.

Carriages raced across the bridges spanning the murky water, making Lisette's head whirl. A dank fog hovered over the crowded buildings as far as she could see, and the soured stench of the vast city offended her sensibilities. It was true New Orleans almost rivaled London in unpleasant smells, but she missed the fresh air at sea. Hopefully, they wouldn't be long in London.

Monsieur Baptiste clucked his tongue. "I've heard the fog is so dense at times pedestrians stumble into the river and lose their lives."

"Monsieur," Serafine scolded, "remember your audience."

He shot a look at Rafe then smiled apologetically. "Indeed. My apologies, ladies."

She stopped listening to the banal talk of buildings and weather when Daniel emerged from his quarters, distracted by the defined edge of his jaw and the way his hair had begun to curl at his nape. Surely, her husband had grown more handsome over the last two weeks for it couldn't be her imagination.

Her heart skipped when he offered a dimpled grin before taking up position beside the helmsman on the quarterdeck.

"Home at last," Amelia called out.

Lisette peered over her shoulder to discover Amelia and her husband approaching arm in arm with a downtrodden Monsieur Ramsey trailing behind them.

Monsieur Hillary's tense expression caught her by surprise. He had struck Lisette as perpetually light of heart during their time onboard. "We should call on my parents as soon as we arrive," he said to Amelia. "I fear the change in our status will be a shock to Mother, however pleasant our tidings." He smiled kindly in Lisette's direction. "Perhaps you could encourage Daniel to call on our parents soon. Our mother has a tendency to worry herself into a state if she doesn't hear from him upon his return."

She nodded. "Of course."

Her own mother had never shown much awareness of her existence as a child, so the concept of worry over one's issue, even as a grown man, made her heart warm toward Daniel's mother.

"You have a sister in London too, do you not?" she asked.

Monsieur Hillary's face softened just as Daniel's had when he had spoken of the young woman. "Our younger sister, Lana. She will be thrilled to welcome you into the fold."

The prospect of becoming part of a larger family lifted Lisette's spirits. Perhaps her time in London would be tolerable after all.

Monsieur Ramsey assumed the vacant spot beside her. He stooped over, resting his hands on the railing. "Home at last. I should reach the parish before nightfall, a failure."

His heavy sigh and despairing frown engendered pity from Lisette. As Daniel had explained to her a few days ago, any son not of first-born status had few options in England. Monsieur Ramsey likely had a choice between the church and life in the military, which seemed no choice at all. She didn't think him suited for either profession.

"I had hoped to return home a rich man," he mumbled. "Ah, well. What is there to do?"

Lisette patted his hand. "It's odd how fate has its own plans, monsieur. I wish you good fortune in your homeland."

He offered a sad smile. "*Merci*."

Leaving Rafe in Serafine's care, Lisette returned to the great cabin for one more glance around to reassure herself she wasn't leaving anything onboard. She would miss their time in these small cabins and looked forward to the day she, Daniel, and Rafe set sail again.

The grinding of the windlass signaled the dropping

of the anchor, and the men's heavy steps echoed on the deck as they went about their last duties.

The cabin door flew open and Daniel stuck his head inside. "Come along, luv. I sent Patch to secure a hack. It's time to see your new home."

She smiled with a shy lift of one shoulder. "I'll miss our home onboard."

He moved inside the cabin, closing the door behind him, and then came to gather her in his arms. "But I have an adequate town house with plenty of room for everyone, including your Mr. Baptiste."

She chuckled when he spat the other man's name and touched her palm to his cheek. "You are a kind and generous provider. Thank you for allowing him to stay as our guest. It needn't be long, just until we figure out where he may go."

As Daniel led her from the great cabin and down the gangplank to the waiting conveyance, Lisette viewed the filthy wharf with interest. Funny how any place felt right with her husband by her side. She would reside in an oversized trunk if he wished it, as long as they remained together.

"Your brother plans to call on your parents today," she said. "Perhaps we should pay our respects as well."

Daniel drew her close. "Don't fret, my dear. We will soon receive an invitation for dinner. Mother always hosts a party when the ship docks. I can only imagine how quickly one will come once she learns I've arrived with a wife."

"You've sent her notice already?"

He chuckled. "You have much to learn about London. The ship's manifest lists you as my wife.

Word should reach Mother before we arrive to Curzon Street."

"I'm uncertain if that is a fortuitous system or not."

"Generally not." Daniel halted several steps from the carriage and turned her to face him. A worry line appeared on his forehead. "Lis, you must realize I had a life before I met you. Some aspects of my former life don't make me proud. If you hear rumors…"

She squeezed his hands. "As long as everything stays in the past, I shan't pay any notice to gossip."

"My entertainments in London are forever confined to the past. You have my word."

"Excellent," she said with a cheeky grin. "I'm greedy when it comes to entertainments. I prefer to stay center stage."

❧

London's rapid communication system did not disappoint. A mere two hours after their arrival at the town house, Daniel's mother and sister descended upon them. Lana had grown even larger with child in the weeks he'd been gone. Her venture across Town to procure an introduction to his wife would raise eyebrows among the elite, not that he agreed with their censorship.

The current thinking a lady should lie in wait was nonsense. Women all over the world gave birth to healthy issue without taking to their beds for weeks. Some even birthed while toiling in a field. Of course, he wouldn't go so far as to suggest rigorous exercise, but paying calls exerted nothing more than one's patience.

"You'll not drop your child on the Aubusson, I hope." His teasing tone matched his welcoming grin as he gathered his little sister in a hug.

"Daniel, really." His mother huffed and turned three shades of red.

Lana returned his embrace with verve, planting a loud, smacking kiss upon his freshly shaved cheek. "I wish it were time. I have two months of misery left to endure. I welcome a respite in the country."

Once he released his sister, his mother didn't step forward to initiate or receive any contact, not even a courteous kiss on her knuckles. Theirs had never been an affectionate relationship, and he had come to accept her way of expressing fondness involved lavish parties thrown in one's honor. Her gaze darted around the drawing room. "Where is she?"

"Please, have a seat. I've ordered tea and biscuits." Daniel directed both women to the settee. "Lisette will join us in a moment."

Mother bustled to the small sofa and smoothed her skirts several times before sitting. She leaned forward with a grave expression. "I didn't dare believe the rumors, but it appears you have truly arrived with a wife. Wherever did you find her?"

He couldn't hold back a smile. "On the top shelf of the quaintest shop. I went in for a hat and came out with a wife."

"A milliner's shop?"

Lana giggled. "He's jesting, Mama. You spoke of his bride as if she were an object to be found."

"I did not. I simply wondered how it is my incorrigible bachelor son arrived in London *leg-shackled*, to use a term he has often employed to describe the state of matrimony."

"Lisette booked passage on the *Cecily*, I fell madly in love with her, and had to have her as my wife. Satisfied?"

A noise at the doorway interrupted their conversation. They turned at once to discover Lisette standing at the threshold. A becoming flush pinked her cheeks.

Daniel rose to greet her. "There you are, luv. Do come in so Mother can put her fears to rest."

His mother groaned. "Daniel."

Lana wiggled to the edge of the settee and pushed herself to her feet. She approached Lisette, but before Daniel could make introductions, she tossed her arms around Lisette's neck. "What a pleasure to meet the lady who has captured Daniel's heart at last. Welcome to the family. I'm Lana."

Lisette's eyes widened a brief moment, but she returned his sister's enthusiastic greeting with kindness. "*Merci*. Your brothers have spoken highly of you. It's a pleasure to make your acquaintance."

Mother smiled, her features softening for the first time since she had arrived. "It seems my youngest son has also arrived with a wife." She reserved her loving expressions for Jake. He had always been her favored child, and she'd been orchestrating opportunities for Jake to win Amelia's heart for over a year. "Now if only Benjamin will make a match, I shall know peace."

His mother stood, glided across the room to gather Lisette's hands in hers, and placed kisses on her cheeks.

"What a darling girl you are," Mother cooed. "Jake and Amelia told me all about the changes you have wrought in my wayward son. Do come and join me on the settee."

A tic started at Daniel's brow, and he placed his fingers against the spot to cease the annoying sensation. Would he ever win his mother's approval? Not bloody likely. Why he should care now when he had flaunted his vices in front of her for years, he couldn't say. Perhaps he didn't wish to see the light of admiration in Lisette's eyes fade when she looked at him.

Serafine and Rafe arrived holding hands as the tea cart appeared, and Daniel facilitated the introductions. He could have kissed his family for their warm acceptance of Lisette's kin. His wife beamed and turned a loving gaze on him. His worries about losing her admiration had been for naught.

His mother sat and assumed the role of hostess, pouring tea for everyone and offering chocolate biscuits. "We have much planning to do today if I'm to throw the most glorious ball of the season to celebrate your nuptials. Of course, we haven't much time until everyone returns to the country." She handed a cup and saucer to Serafine then poured one for Lisette. "Jake and Amelia's opportunity has passed, I'm afraid, although I am thrilled with the prospect of another grandchild."

Daniel made to sit, but one sharp look from his mother halted his descent to the chair.

"We have much to discuss, Daniel. We must discuss a visit to Madame Chastain, and then there are the choices for flowers in addition to the menu. We cannot be disturbed with sighs of boredom from your side of the room."

In the past, his mother's words would have offended him, but today they brought a smile to his face. "Very well, Mother. Please assist both ladies with setting up accounts with Madame Chastain and any other shop-keeper you see fit. I know they are in good hands."

He turned to Rafe. "I thought to make a return trip to the docks to finish some business. Would you like to accompany me?"

The lad's eyes lit. "Back to the ship?"

"Indeed, and if any of the fleet is docked, perhaps we can tour the other ships."

"I need my sketchbook."

"Let's retrieve it then." He bowed to the feminine gathering in his drawing room. "Good day, ladies."

A few minutes later, he left the town house with a spring to his step. The females in his family would keep Lisette so busy, she likely wouldn't even realize when he left for America or notice his return. He would speak with Jake and Lana later to request an invitation for Lisette and her family to join one of them in the country as soon as the season ended. His siblings would ensure Lisette was well cared for in his absence.

Twenty-six

LISETTE'S HEAD SPUN BY EVENING. AFTER SETTING A date for the ball, Daniel's mother had insisted she and Serafine visit the modiste that very afternoon. Lisette had been exhausted from their voyage, but unwilling to disappoint Daniel's mother. She had hated to see Lana excluded from the outing, but as the young woman had explained, a lady in her state couldn't be gallivanting about Town. Then she had frowned and mumbled the words "blast it all," endearing her to Lisette even more.

Now in the comfort of her new chambers, Lisette removed her half boots and rubbed her sore toes. She wasn't made for the life of a lady of leisure if her entire day consisted of nothing but shopping. Pulling the pins from her hat, she dropped them on the dressing table before tossing her hat on a nearby chair. She had just released her hair when Daniel entered.

"Splendid. You've returned." He came up behind her and placed his hands on her shoulders, kneading her tensed muscles. Each press of his strong fingers loosened the knots that had been forming all day. "How did you fare with Mother?"

"*Très bien*. It is clear she will be an asset in navigating these next few weeks." Lisette touched his hands to still their movements then met his gaze in the looking glass. "Thank you for today."

"Of course. You and Serafine may set up accounts wherever you like."

She turned on the bench to face him. "I meant for lying to your mother this morning, about the circumstances of our marriage."

Daniel lowered to a knee so they were eye level and slipped his hand under her hair to cradle her neck. "I don't know what you mean."

"I overheard you telling your family you have fallen in love with me."

"*Madly* in love," he clarified with a cheeky wink.

Her body flushed with heated pleasure. "*Oui*. I thought perhaps you had exaggerated too much, but your mother and sister took you at your word."

Daniel's fingers twined with the strands of hair at her nape and sent tremors along her spine. The spicy scent of his cologne infused her with longing as he leaned toward her. His mouth hovered a breath away from hers.

"Was I lying?"

Her throat clogged with emotion and tears pricked her eyes. Did she dare hope her husband loved her? "I'm grateful you didn't mention Reynaud. I imagine your family's opinion wouldn't be as positive if they knew you took your vows to save me from my *fiancé*."

"Former fiancé." His thumb stroked her jaw. "Lis, I would have protected you from him no matter what. I married you because I wanted you."

She swallowed against her disappointment. He desired her, which wasn't the same as love. Yet, it was something. Weeks of travel and the near endless afternoon of shopping caught up to her. Lisette slumped forward, resting her head against his shoulder.

His arms wrapped around her, and he placed a kiss on top of her hair. "I'm pleased you find Mother and Lana amiable. My family is like yours, loyal. I'll have no worries with them looking after you while I'm gone."

Lisette's insides convulsed and she drew back. "Gone? Where are you going?"

"I'm a seaman, my dear. I can't stay in London forever if you are to have new gowns and all the fine things ladies require."

"Then I don't want any of those things. I wish to be with you."

His brows lowered as they always did when she displeased him. Before he could speak, she rushed on with her argument. "Rafe loves being onboard the *Cecily* and so do I. Life at sea—"

"Is no place for a family." Daniel pushed to his feet and gazed down on her. "Our journey was easy this time, but the dangers are too great. I won't risk your safety or that of Rafe."

"If sailing is too dangerous, I don't want you at sea either." Lisette jumped up and captured his arms. The magnitude of strength under her fingertips stole her breath. He appeared invincible, but he was as vulnerable as anyone was. And living without him would tear her apart. "You could have died if not for me playing nursemaid. It's clear you need me to take care of you as much as I benefit from your protection."

Daniel smiled in a placating manner that riled her temper. His hands slid behind her head and his fingers linked. "I never properly thanked you. I shall have to make up for my oversight."

The instant his lips touched hers, she thought to shove him away, to confront him on using his sexual prowess to disarm her. Instead, she softened in his embrace, her body siding with him rather than what she knew to be true. Daniel needed her as much as she needed him. And somehow, she had to convince him before he tried to abandon her in England.

Louis Reynaud found The Peregrine a damned disappointment. Nothing about the East End tavern reflected the supremacy of the real-life hunter, a formidable predator that attacked its prey from above, swooping down at an ungodly speed. The falcon had might and the element of surprise to his advantage. No warning of danger. No chance for his victim to escape before he sank his razor talons into his quarry's soft body.

Louis regarded the repulsive patrons of the dim establishment and sneered. No surprise attacks would come from these carnival curiosities. Their stench would set off the alarm long before they reached striking distance. Slumped over the wooden-slat tables, coal dust under their fingernails, they appeared to be wearing grotesque masks in the distorting flicker of the lanterns.

"Yer quite the toff." The serving wench's husky voice invaded his musings.

His gaze raked over her from scuffed boots to ratty hair. *Another unworthy one.*

She flashed her decaying teeth, the tip of her tongue poking through the jagged hole. "Ye stick out like me man's Thomas after months at sea. Bring ye an ale?"

Louis directed his attention to the tavern entrance. "Go away." When she didn't move, he turned a glare on her. "*Now*, while you still have legs to carry you." She scrambled back several steps and bumped into another table.

He hadn't raised his voice. There was no need. The woman sensed danger and reacted as any self-preserving creature. She fled.

"Not as stupid as you appear," he mumbled.

A gust of wind plundered the tavern when the door opened, blowing the stench of unwashed bodies in his face.

He scowled at the newcomer as he weaved through the tables. "What the devil took you so long?"

His man hesitated in his step and eyed Louis as one would a rattlesnake, with caution and respect. The corners of Louis's mouth inched upward. "Have a seat."

"The maid kept me waiting," Wilson explained. "She couldn't carry word to me until the household departed for the evening. There's some kind of sawray they're attending."

Louis blinked. "A sawray?"

"Aye. A celebration on account of Miss Lavigne marryin'."

"Do you mean a soiree?"

"Exactly." Wilson snapped his fingers and pointed

at Louis. "A *sawray*. Damned English. Why don't they just call it a party and be done with it?"

Reynaud's teeth scraped together. "Soiree is a French word, you buffoon."

Wilson shrugged and signaled for the serving wench. "And this ain't France, so my point stands."

"Quiet!" Louis didn't wish to speak of his former fiancée or her foolish choice to marry Captain Hillary. In truth, he'd prefer to cut out his companion's over-used tongue than listen to his discourse on *any* topic. Yet, that would be a messy endeavor.

Queasiness churned in his gut as he imagined the scene in too much detail. He gripped the edge of the table when he pitched to the side, but his fingers slipped from the oiled wood.

Wilson bolted from his chair and caught him before he tumbled to the floor. "Mr. Reynaud, are you all right?"

Louis's head swam a moment before everything began to right itself. His sight homed in on Wilson's meaty hands on his pristine coat. "Unhand me." He jerked from his hold and glowered.

His man released him and slunk back to his seat.

Louis scrubbed a hand over his face. *Hellfire*. When would he shake this horrible illness that plagued him every time he thought about——? A shudder passed through him and he sucked in a deep breath to settle his stomach. He was better off thinking about Lisette.

His former fiancée had been nothing if not trans-parent, just as one would expect of a guileless female. He had never had any trouble reading her every emotion when they were together. She'd been able to deceive him only because she had feigned illness the night she fled. He knew the true mastermind behind her escape. It was her devious cousin, Serafine Vistoire.

In a world filled with born killers, Lisette would always be the victim, but not Mademoiselle Vistoire. A paragon of strength and willfulness, she had confronted Louis in the study the night of his engagement dinner. The bitch had stared into his eyes, hers full of fire and condemnation, and berated him for taking advantage of her cousin's grief.

Lisette would never have the courage to blackmail him, but Serafine Vistoire would. Too bad a woman finally worthy of him would die for her efforts.

"Did the maid search her belongings?" Louis asked.

"She didn't find anything out of the ordinary."

"What did you learn of her brother, Xavier Vistoire's whereabouts?"

A bleak expression darkened Wilson's countenance. "I asked around but no one's seen him in months. His landlady said he left in the middle of the night without paying his rent."

Mademoiselle Vistoire would try to deliver the letters to her brother at his new location. The danger to Louis wouldn't end until he had possession of his property again, and his blackmailers were dead. He would gleefully slit their throats as soon as the opportunity arose.

"Egads." His hand clutched his roiling stomach. He would just have to close his eyes. "Perhaps she keeps them on her person. What's the location of the celebration?"

Serafine stood on the outskirts of the dance floor, attempting to blend in with her surroundings. Never had she felt more conspicuous than now, dressed in lily-white, standing among the pale, cherub-faced innocents. She didn't belong in the London ballrooms, and as sure as the sun would rise on the morrow, she had no business shopping for a husband.

Not that she was in the market, but Daniel's mother insisted there was still time left in the season to make a match. The tenacious Madame Hillary had dragged Serafine into this ridiculous charade while tuning out her protests.

Serafine had never met anyone with more devotion to marrying off every unattached person of marriageable age within a fifty-mile radius. She couldn't decide if the woman wished others happiness or desired company to share in her misery.

She suspected the latter.

Madame Hillary had an overwhelming aura of sadness about her Serafine understood all too well. Serafine believed herself skillful at hiding her feelings, but she too carried sorrow deep inside her heart. Perhaps this was the reason she had acquiesced to dressing up like a porcelain doll and smiling throughout the endless line of potential suitors Madame Hillary introduced her to this evening.

Tired of flashing her teeth and her jaws aching, she found a chair half-hidden by a folding screen and two potted ferns and slipped into it. She just needed five minutes to herself. On the other side of the room, she caught a glimpse of Lisette in her scarlet gown gliding around the floor with her husband.

Serafine smiled. Lisette was the family jewel and appeared as suited for the ballroom as the other ladies in attendance.

Two young girls stepped in front of Serafine with their backs to her. She sat up straighter, intending to ask them to move so she might enjoy the view of the other dancers.

"The newest Mrs. Hillary is fetching." The taller of the girls, all angles and bony prominences, lifted her fan to speak quietly to her companion. "But did you see her American cousin? The elder Mrs. Hillary must be as batty as rumors suggest, sponsoring the likes of *her*."

Serafine's request stuck in her throat; a small hiss of air passed between her lips.

"I haven't the faintest idea what Mrs. Hillary is thinking, Pru. What would any gentleman want with the American?"

"A hefty acquisition, I imagine." Pru's sardonic chuckle grated on Serafine. "That's what most desperate gentleman want."

Pru's friend laughed. Round as she was tall, the lumps of flesh oozing over the top of her corset jiggled like the aspic served at dinner. "But her dowry would require tripling to gain any gentleman's notice."

The noxious pair cackled, thinking their insults clever, but Serafine had heard worse said about her in New Orleans. Malicious whispers had followed her and Isaac wherever they went.

Pru flicked her fan as if the exertion of laughing couldn't be borne. "She's as common as they come, Maddie. One would swear she has been strolling in the sun without a hat for forty days and nights in preparation for this evening."

Serafine rolled her eyes, rose from her seat, and tapped the awkward girl on the shoulder. They both turned and gasped. Maddie at least had the decency to blush.

Serafine smiled sweetly and unleashed a flurry of words she knew they wouldn't understand just to illustrate who the common ones at this gathering really were.

Pru huffed. "I beg your pardon?"

The girls parted as Serafine pushed between them. She didn't bother translating. They were not worth her time.

"What did she say?" Maddie hissed.

A deep chuckle halted Serafine's retreat, and she looked over her shoulder to locate the source. A dark-haired prince—at least he appeared regal in her eyes—regarded her with the most striking blue gaze. Wry amusement twinkled in the depths of his eyes. "I believe the lady said only the dumbest cow would think the sun appears at night, but my French isn't what it used to be."

"A cow?" Pru shrieked.

That wasn't exactly what Serafine had said, but she liked the gentleman's translation.

The statuesque woman on the gentleman's arm lifted her champagne flute in salute. "Well spoken, mademoiselle. You are an excellent judge of character."

Pru and Maddie bumped into each other as they curtsied to the pair. "My lord, Miss Truax, we didn't see you standing there."

Miss Truax's frosty demeanor sent a shiver through Serafine. "Nor does his lordship wish to see either of you now." She flicked an elegant finger, pointing as if ordering about canines. "Off with you, Misses Flaherty and Channing, or you will find your names omitted from every prestigious party list for the next two seasons."

Blood drained from their already pale faces. The girls clutched each other's arms and fled to the side of the room where several chaperones appeared to be partaking of their own gossip, speaking behind raised palms, sometimes gasping over what must be a juicy tidbit of scandal.

"Those two ninnies have rubbed me the wrong way all season," Miss Truax said. "I hope you won't allow their horrendous lack of manners to spoil your evening, Mademoiselle Vistoire."

"You know my name?"

The lady tossed her chestnut hair and smiled. "Of course, mademoiselle. I make it my priority to learn the identities of all new persons. Heaven knows the usual suspects are terribly boring."

Her gentleman companion chuckled. "Why, thank you for your generous commentary on my company, Miss Truax."

"I wasn't referring to you, Westin." She squeezed his arm and leaned into him. "You and Lord Andrew are the only ones to ever make these tedious affairs entertaining, and your brother had to spoil my fun by taking a wife."

"How selfish of him." A glorious smile lit his eyes. As a servant passed, Lord Westin took the lady's empty glass and placed hers and his on the sterling tray.

Serafine wasn't sure how to interpret their easy banter. Were they lovers? Her cheeks heated at the thought. It seemed an unkind speculation to make about the duo who had come to her rescue.

"I see I am at a disadvantage," she said. "You know me, yet we haven't been introduced."

Miss Truax dropped the gentleman's arm and stepped forward "How thoughtless of me. And here I reviled those harebrained chits for crude manners. I'm Johanna Truax. And if I may, please allow me to present Lord Westin, the heir apparent to the Duke of Foxhaven. He is quite the perfect catch and in the market for a wife." She had a droll quality to her voice, as if teasing him.

Lord Westin ignored her baiting and gathered Serafine's hand to place a kiss on her gloved knuckles. "It's a pleasure to make your acquaintance, mademoiselle. You would do well to pay no mind to anything Miss Truax says. Her impertinence knows no bounds."

"His father is demanding he make a match this season, or else," Miss Truax said in a stage whisper.

Lord Westin's jaw twitched, but aside from this fleeting sign of irritation, Serafine wouldn't have known he felt anything untoward. His neutral expression fascinated her. So much hidden behind the cool formality required of his station.

"If it is any consolation," Serafine offered, "I fear I suffer a similar fate. Madame Susan Hillary has taken it upon herself to see me settled in marriage before the year-end. I believe I have become her charitable cause. She has no idea her endeavor falls under the category of lost causes."

The sparkle returned to Lord Westin's deep, blue eyes. When he smiled, comforting warmth wrapped around her like a fatherly embrace. *Fatherly. Ha!* The gentleman was much too young and dashing to be her father. Perhaps brotherly would be a more apt description, and she sensed this was the nature of his association with Miss Truax, too.

"You have my sympathies, Mademoiselle Vistoire," he said. "Once Mrs. Hillary has her mind set…"

Serafine groaned. "My intuition mustn't always be correct."

"A woman's intuition is nothing to ignore."

"Thank you both for coming to my aid this evening." She flashed a rare smile at Lord Westin. "I enjoyed your translation, but I didn't call either miss a cow."

"Because you don't know them well enough," Miss Truax interjected.

Lord Westin nodded. "It is always my pleasure to come to the aid of a lady." He lowered his voice. "I have a bit of Gypsy blood running through my veins myself. If anyone knew…"

Miss Truax tapped her fan against his shoulder. "As if no one knows, Westin. Your wanderlust and mysterious dark looks practically scream out your heritage."

"Your flattery is never-ending this evening, my lady."

Miss Truax clapped her hands as fiddle music filled the air. "It's a quadrille."

Lord Westin bowed to Serafine. "If you will excuse us, mademoiselle, I'll have no peace if I renege on my promise of one dance with Miss Truax. The quadrille," he said with a shake of his head. "She takes pleasure in bringing a sweat to my brow."

As would many ladies. Sweet marmalade. What a depraved thought to have in her head. She should be ashamed.

"Thank you again for your aid, my lord." Serafine excused herself on the pretense of retreating to the ladies' retiring room. Out of the couple's sight, she loitered at the perimeter of the room, mortified by her unbecoming thoughts. No one would ever mistake her for an innocent if he or she could see inside her mind.

She quashed a sigh. How she missed Isaac's touch. And how she hated herself for wanting him still. Why had everything gone so wrong between them? Isaac had promised to love her until death the night they had made love under the stars, but here she was with heart still beating and Isaac was nowhere to be found.

The heat of too many bodies jammed together threatened to overcome her. Nausea rose in her throat and she hurried through the opened veranda door for fear of casting up her accounts on the fine marble floor. The tepid air provided little relief, but a slight wind cooled her enough to ease her sickness. She moved into the darkness and away from the spotlights created by the candlelight spilling through the soaring windows. If she did become ill, she wouldn't like to be on display for the guests inside.

She wandered to the stone balustrade, leaned against it with eyes closed, and inhaled. As the breath flowed from her lungs, she repeated her deepest wish.

Home.

All she had ever wanted was a place to call home, a family to care for, and a husband to love. She'd thought Isaac had been the answer to her dreams, but instead, she'd allowed him to steal them away. Because of her stupidity, she'd ruined her chance for a home of her own.

A swift wind whipped along the veranda, lifting tendrils of her hair at her nape, and an icy chill swept down her spine. A scrape of a boot sounded behind her.

"Greetings, Serafine."

Twenty-seven

DANIEL LED HIS WIFE INSIDE THE GREENHOUSE. THE sounds of the party were muffled as he pulled the door closed and created a sanctuary from a world in which he'd never wanted to be included. The glass walls had trapped the heat of the summer day, and a warm mist hovered on the air. His fancy attire clung to him and his cravat became confining. Placing the lantern he'd stolen from the terrace on a shelf, he shrugged out of his jacket and loosened the knot at his neck.

Lisette faced him, a tantalizing grin curving her full lips. "You are much too cross for a ball thrown in our honor. Are you regretting becoming leg-shackled already?"

Given he had admitted during the waltz he wanted nothing more than to find a vacant room and shag her silly, he knew she was teasing him. Her assessment of his demeanor, however, was accurate. But not for the reason she cited.

Daniel had been alert to the stir she had caused among the ne'er-do-wells in attendance this evening. Lisette's marital status wouldn't make her any less desirable a conquest to the bloody rakes about Town, but Daniel's presence at her side and menacing glares had held them at bay.

Resentment turned his stomach. How dare any man think to possess anything belonging to him, much less his wife? To make a cuckold of him would be a grievous mistake.

He must see Lisette bound for the countryside before he returned to New Orleans. Yet, even the sanctuary of the country wouldn't guarantee her safety, and it was the urge to caution her against the vipers that had led him to whisk her from the ballroom.

He shook his head slightly. That wasn't entirely true. He wanted her to know she was *his*, but short of beating his chest and making a fool of himself, he wasn't certain how to assert his claim.

Lisette reached out to smooth a hand along his upper arm; her fingers tightened around his muscle. "What is troubling you, *mon amour*?"

"I abhor how those lecherous hounds are devouring you with their looks. You're not a jam tartlet."

"I hadn't noticed." She stepped into his embrace and tipped her head up. Her eyes sparkled in the lamp light, her sooty lashes like a black velvet frame to accent precious jewels. "And my *tartlet* belongs to you."

Daniel chuckled, his tension uncoiling with her near. "You're incorrigible, Lisette Hillary."

Damn if he didn't want to abandon the entire venture to New Orleans and stay with her, but he must make this last voyage. Inquiries had turned up nothing on Mademoiselle Vistoire's brother, which left Rafe's future too uncertain.

Once Daniel arrived in America, he intended to petition for guardianship of the lad. He had already engaged a solicitor to pursue the matter. To see Lisette truly happy, he must secure Rafe's inheritance and see that the lad could never be taken from them.

Daniel had yet to share his intentions with Lisette, but now was not the time. This evening was special, and he didn't want to spoil it for her. If not for the turmoil churning inside him at the thought of another man having her, he wouldn't have taken her away from the merriment. He'd never seen her smile as brightly as when he'd led her into the waltz. She had referred to it as their dance.

He drew her closer and caressed the silky skin at her nape. She shivered and snuggled into him, laying her cheek against his chest.

"Promise me you'll be cautious around the gentlemen," he said. "Many are not above using anything at their disposal to make a conquest."

She laughed softly, her warm breath tickling his neck. "They would have a devil of a time prying me from your arms." Lifting to her toes, she kissed him.

He held her in place and seized her mouth. She dissolved against him, parting her lips and inviting his exploration. Her tongue swept against his, intertwining with it in an erotic dance of sorts.

His breath tore from him in a harsh pant. Knowing he couldn't touch her, revel in her fingers upon him, taste the sweetness of her mouth for many months, left him desperate to fill the emptiness expanding inside him. He pushed the sleeves of her satin gown from her shoulders and down her arms to reveal the lacy edge of her corset and the swells of her generous breasts.

He traced the weave of scarlet ribbon trimming her undergarment. "I want to lay you bare, darling, and make you come amongst the orchids."

"Now, now." She smiled up at him, one side of her mouth lifting higher than the other. "There's no need for pretty words. Just tell me what you *really* want."

He chuckled and shook his head, chagrined by his clumsy attempt at wooing her. "Forgive me. I sometimes forget to behave as a gentleman with you."

Wrapping her arms around his neck, she drew him to her. Her eyes darkened, blazing with barely controlled passion. "If a gentleman cannot pleasure me as you do, I have no need for one."

Her kiss was hard and demanding, her tongue seeking his. Her fingers tightened on his waistcoat. She tried to tow him closer. When he didn't budge, she gravitated to him instead, molding her body to his.

He grabbed her hips and spun her away. She issued a small cry of protest before his arm circled her waist and pulled her snugly to him again. Her bottom pressed against his thighs as his lips sought out her neck. He licked the curve where her shoulder and neck met, drawing his tongue slowly across the spot. A shuddering sigh passed through her. Releasing his hold, he worked the fastenings at the back of her gown and shoved the garment down to her waist before tugging her corset laces. The red satin slid past her hips and fell in a heap around her feet. Her corset and petticoats soon joined her gown.

When she tried to turn in his arms, he held her in

place, his hands seeking out her breasts. His thumbs brushed her nipples, firm beneath her chemise. Lisette melted against him, her breath changing to ragged sighs.

She made another attempt to wriggle around to face him, but he hugged her tightly.

"Stay. I want you like this."

She surrendered to his ministrations, but not before verbalizing her exasperation with a short huff. He stole into her chemise and cupped her bare breasts while he showered her temple, neck, and shoulders with soft kisses.

Reaching behind and working her hand between their bodies, she curved her fingers around his cock and gently squeezed. Daniel closed his eyes and leaned into her touch. Not since their wedding night had she allowed him to take sole command of their love-making, and he was more hers because of it.

He fisted the skirts of her chemise and eased them up over her hips. His knuckles grazed the smooth skin of her buttocks.

Loosening the fastenings of his breeches, she slipped her hand inside and wrapped him in warmth. He sucked in a sharp breath, urged her forward, stepping clear of her garments, and placed her hands against the ledge of a shelf. He circled his palm over her full bottom then slid his hand between her legs. His fingers played over her heated flesh, finding and circling her pleasurable place. Lisette sighed and arched into his caress. His shaft brushed against her, his yearning to claim her powerful. Easing her legs wider, he was poised to slide inside her.

He curved his body against hers and placed a tender kiss behind her ear. "My beautiful Lissie," he whispered.

Her breath came out in soft gasps, her heart thumped heavily against his chest. When he entered her, she sighed and pushed back against him until she surrounded him. His fingers curled around her soft hip as his hand splayed across her taut stomach. She met his thrusts as she always did, moving in time to music only they could sense.

Yet, no matter how exquisite it was to be immersed in her, having her accept him, something was lacking. He couldn't see her expression. Watching his wife as she reached her completion did something strange to him. It created a fullness that settled in his chest, warm and bursting like rays of sunshine through darkened clouds.

He withdrew then gently turned her to stand in front of him. Dark wisps of hair had loosened from her coiffure and fallen around her face. He tucked a strand behind her ear, lifting her chin to place a reverent kiss on her lips. His heart beat in his throat. He couldn't speak.

I love you. He loved her beyond a doubt. And only her.

Coaxing her to a bench tucked among the foliage, he sat and pulled her atop him. They joined again and this time he could watch every nuance of her expressions. The softening of the line between her brows. Her lips parting on a sigh. The shadow of passion in her gaze.

Observing her increased his desire and lured him closer to release. She rocked her hips, his hands cradling her bottom. Her neck arched back, her breath quickened, and then a quiet cry burst from her again and again and again as she surrendered. Daniel moved her against him, pursuing his own completion with her tightly surrounding him. It was just out of reach, but he chased it with fervent determination until he seized his release, or it seized him. Currents of pleasure coursed through his limbs and left him shaking.

Hugging her close, he rested his head against her breasts and listened as their breath slowed until it evened out again. She kissed his forehead.

"My lady's maid would be in hysterics if she could see my state of dishabille."

He nuzzled her breasts and kissed the valley between them. "But your husband is pleased."

She laughed, a low husky sound, as he nibbled up her neck. "Then perhaps my husband can act in place of my lady's maid. It's too early to leave, and I can't return to the party in my chemise."

"My pleasure." He would be damned if anyone caught a glimpse of her without every inch covered. The hounds would never stay away otherwise.

Daniel eased her from his lap, retrieved her garments, and began to help set her back to rights. Her hair was worse for the experience, but she could hie off to the retiring room before they returned to the ballroom.

With lantern in hand, he led his wife through the gardens toward the veranda. Serafine's low voice carried on the air as they neared.

"Isaac, let me go."

"You heard Mademoiselle Vistoire," a gentleman snapped. "Step aside."

Daniel released Lisette and rushed up the stairs to thrash whatever scoundrel was accosting Lisette's cousin.

Luke Forest, the Marquess of Westin, stood in front of her, blocking her from the other man. "Don't touch her again." Westin's warning hit its mark and the stranger staggered back a step.

"Serafine, *please*." His accent identified him as a bloody American.

Lisette reached Daniel's side. "Monsieur Tucker, what are you doing in London?"

"He's harassing a *lady*." Westin's emphasis on the word lady left Daniel wondering what part of the conversation they had missed.

Lisette hurried to Serafine's side and wrapped her arm around her shoulders. "Monsieur Tucker is a fellow resident of New Orleans. We are well acquainted with his family. I'm certain he didn't intend to harass my cousin."

Daniel's fist tightened. "Acquaintance or no, no one gave you leave to touch Mademoiselle Vistoire."

"I didn't mean—" Mr. Tucker's wild gaze flew to Serafine. "Tell him I didn't hurt you."

Her steely eyes grew moist. "But you did, Isaac. And it cannot be undone."

Daniel nodded to Westin, communicating silently with his Oxford alumni.

The marquess offered his handkerchief to Serafine. "Please allow me to escort you inside, ladies."

Once Westin had the women out of sight, Daniel advanced, snatching Tucker by the waistcoat. "What is it that cannot be undone?"

Tucker yanked free of his grip and squared his shoulders. "If you wish to deliver a sound beating, I'll accept it as a man. I deserve any ill treatment I receive." His valor caught Daniel by surprise. "If only I could win her heart again, I would subject myself to worse than a thrashing."

Daniel lowered his fists. The gent's expression would rival a wounded hound. He had never seen such pitiful eyes on a man. "Whatever you did to her, I expect you to make amends. Call on her tomorrow at 17 Curzon Street. Do not disappoint me."

A glut of fresh heat swept over Daniel, and his muscles tensed. In Port Albis, Serafine had made claim to being no innocent. And he'd bet his fortune this scoundrel was responsible.

"Come prepared to make things right, or else." Daniel spun on his heel and stalked back inside Hillary House.

Westin loitered at the entrance. His eyes lit with enthusiasm. "Do you require a second?"

Daniel came up short. The marquess courted death at every opportunity. It was a damned shame too, because Westin would make a fine duke one day, if he lived long enough.

"The matter is settled," Daniel said. "Tucker will call on the lady tomorrow."

"I see." Westin rubbed his chin, a wicked smile on his face. "Splendid."

Daniel didn't ask what scheme the marquess was hatching. He had enough worries without adding the adventure-seeking nobleman to his list.

Another massive bouquet of flowers obscured Lisette's view of the servant carrying them into the drawing room. Gardenias this time. "From Lord Westin again?"

"Aye, mistress. 'Tis the sixth to arrive for Miss Vistoire. Where shall I place 'em?"

Lisette bit her lip as she contemplated the area. They were running out of surfaces to hold the lovely arrangements. She hurried to the sideboard and scooped up a figurine. "Here will be fine."

The maid lifted the bouquet with a small groan and settled it on top. She took the figurine from Lisette's hands. "'Pears Laird Westin is smitten with the lass."

Lisette smiled, bemused by the woman's bizarre accent, which was unlike any other in the household. "An interesting development to be certain. My cousin is expecting another gentleman caller today."

The maid's eyebrows shot up, but she made no comment.

Daniel passed the maid on her way out. "What the devil is going on here? The drawing room resembles the garden."

"I'm uncertain. Arrangements have been arriving for Serafine every half hour. Six in total so far. And all from Lord Westin."

Her husband chuckled. "I believe the marquess is sending a message to Mr. Tucker."

"Oh, dear. You don't think Lord Westin intends to court Serafine? My dear cousin is angry with Monsieur Tucker, but I believe her heart already belongs to him."

"Among other things," he grumbled then snatched a gardenia from the vase and tucked it behind Lisette's ear. A tender smile softened his furrowed brow. "Perfect. Just what the bloom needed."

Lisette stepped into his embrace, but a gentleman clearing his throat at the drawing room threshold halted their kiss.

Daniel's grumpy demeanor reappeared, and he didn't look behind him. "What do you want, Baptiste?"

"We had an appointment ten minutes prior, Captain. I've been waiting in your study."

Daniel looked up at the ceiling and issued a heavy sigh.

"We could reschedule if you prefer," Monsieur Baptiste offered.

"Oh, no. This interruption serves as the perfect illustration as to the necessity of our meeting." Daniel leaned down to whisper in her ear, "Later, my dear," then he placed a chaste kiss on her cheek.

Lisette's face flushed. Husbands might be entitled to kiss their wives at will, but they didn't do so in the presence of others. Monsieur Baptiste was like a father to her. Even a kiss on her cheek felt scandalous.

She hurried to the nearest flower arrangement and fussed with it. "Please, conduct your business with Monsieur Baptiste. I expect Serafine's gentleman caller will arrive soon, and I have my chaperone duties to fulfill."

The men excused themselves, leaving her to await Monsieur Tucker's arrival. She hoped Monsieur Baptiste appreciated Daniel's offer to stay in the rented rooms her husband kept. She too had grown a bit tired of the gentleman's company after two weeks, but she still wouldn't ask him to return to New Orleans as

Daniel had suggested. If not for Monsieur Baptiste, she never would have met her husband, and her life wouldn't be as perfect as it was now.

A light knock sounded at the door. "Enter."

Daniel's butler carried in a small dish holding Monsieur Tucker's calling card. "Please inform Mademoiselle Vistoire she has a visitor," she said.

"Yes, ma'am."

Lisette smoothed her skirts and wiped the moisture from her palms. She hoped today's meeting went well, because in reality one thing kept life from being as good as it could be: Serafine's happiness. If Daniel's conclusion was correct and Monsieur Tucker had compromised her dear cousin, he best be prepared to make things right. Otherwise, her husband would have to race her to the dueling pistols.

Twenty-eight

Daniel sauntered into his study with Baptiste trailing behind. He nodded toward the empty chair across from his desk. "Have a seat."

Rounding the mahogany piece, he sank into the leather seat and propped his elbows on the padded armrests.

Baptiste offered a terse grin, as if the action caused him discomfort, and then sat. "Before we begin, I have a matter of import to discuss." He reached into his jacket and extracted an envelope. "This arrived in the morning post."

He nudged the letter across Daniel's desk. Paulina's rudimentary script stood out against the starkness of the folded foolscap. Even travel across the ocean hadn't eliminated the scent of rose àttar. His former mistress had drenched the letter. It was a wonder the ink hadn't streaked and become illegible.

"The missive was inadvertently mixed in with your wife's correspondence. I noticed the New Orleans address when I offered to carry the mail to Mrs. Hillary. Naturally, a letter from home captured my interest." Baptiste shifted on the chair. "I didn't wish Madame to receive a shock."

Daniel snatched up the letter. "I no longer have an association with this woman. I don't know why she would write."

"It's not my place to judge your actions, sir. You have generously provided safe haven for me. I simply wish to protect the girl from further heartache. I hope you understand."

Bloody hell. He never would have considered he and his burdensome guest might have something in common. "Lisette is to know nothing of this letter."

"Indeed, which is the reason I brought this matter to your attention. Will you respond and insist Miss Fanchon cease correspondence?"

That was one option, or Daniel could ignore Paulina's letter. She would come to understand his decision to end their association remained firm.

"I will handle the situation." Daniel's brusque tone resulted in a sliver of remorse. Mr. Baptiste was trying to be of assistance. The man cared for Lisette, or he wouldn't have saved her the embarrassment of discovering Paulina's letter. "I appreciate your discretion."

"I realize you wished to speak with me, but there is another matter I would like to discuss first, if it pleases you."

Daniel's shoulders stiffened. The man's demeanor hinted that he wished to request a favor, and Daniel had extended all the courtesy he could offer. When he had married Lisette, he hadn't consented to accepting responsibility for the welfare of a grown man.

"Say your piece, Baptiste."

"I have become a burden to you and Mrs. Hillary. It doesn't sit right with me." He cleared his throat and adjusted his waistcoat. "Mrs. Hillary has made her wishes for me to remain in London known, and I do not wish to plague her with fears for my safety. I'm certain she is correct to assume Reynaud would bring harm to me if I was ever unfortunate enough to cross paths with him. Nevertheless, I cannot remain in this household or continue as a recipient of your charity."

Daniel leaned back in his chair. "What solution do you suggest?"

"I've a good head for business, having worked alongside Monsieur Lavigne the last seventeen years. And I've been responsible for the plantation's continued success since his death. Neither your wife nor Master Rafe were suited to manage the mill." Mr. Baptiste leaned forward, a gleam of excitement in his eyes. "I know I could use my talents to earn my keep. I would make an excellent man of business."

"I have a man of business already."

"I'm aware, sir. But perhaps you have connections that might help me secure a position. A letter of reference would open doors for me. And once I've secured employment, I could rent a room and provide for myself."

The idea had merit. In fact, it was bloody brilliant and eliminated the need for Daniel's speech tossing Baptiste out on his arse.

Daniel yanked open a drawer, dropped Paulina's letter inside to deal with later, and extracted a sheet of foolscap along with a key. "I keep rented rooms in Piccadilly. Since I no longer have use for them, you

are free to reside in the space until you are able to find
employment and your own lodgings. I'll arrange for
your move today."

Dipping his quill in ink, Daniel scrawled the
address on the sheet. "As for your letter of recom-
mendation, I will have it completed in a couple of
days. I have more pressing matters requiring my
attention at the moment."

Such as issuing a challenge to Mr. Tucker if he
didn't make amends to Lisette's cousin.

Serafine maintained her rigid posture as Isaac was
ushered into the drawing room. A small bouquet of
white daisies was cradled in the crook of his arm.
His gaze darted around the room at the mammoth
arrangements perched on the sideboard and tables
before lowering to his own offering. A ruddy flush
colored his cheeks, giving him the freshly scrubbed
appearance of a boy after his bath she used to
find dear.

Lisette rose with a smile. "Monsieur Tucker, how
nice of you to call."

Isaac was here for one reason only. Captain Hillary
had threatened him.

He bowed first to Lisette and then to her. "Good
day, Madame Hillary. Mademoiselle Vistoire, it's
lovely to see you again."

"I see you've brought flowers for Serafine."

His cheeks darkened considerably, and he hugged
the bouquet to his chest, crinkling the black and white
paper wrapped around the stems.

Lisette wrinkled her brow. "Is that *The Morning Herald*, monsieur?"

"Oh, well, yes. I had thought to read it later, but then the stems were wet and dripping on my jacket. I didn't want to soil my..." He glanced down at his smudged glove then shoved his fist behind his back. How like Isaac to act first without thinking.

Lisette swept forward and relieved him of the daisies. "Indeed. I will take these to the housekeeper to place in a vase." She worried her bottom lip as she looked around the room. "Heavens, where shall we place them? Lord Westin's arrangements do take up a lot of space. It seems Serafine made quite an impression on the marquess last night."

Serafine's face heated and she shifted on the settee. Lisette's attempts to needle Isaac were too transparent. He would likely consider himself fortunate to push Serafine onto another gentleman and flee.

Isaac's pallor took on a greenish hue in the drawing room light. "Mademoiselle Vistoire is indeed impressive."

"*Oui*. I know no one more remarkable. Any gentleman would be lucky to have her for his wife. Please, have a seat, monsieur. I shall return in a moment with the flowers and refreshments."

Lisette swept from the room. When her lively energy no longer charged the air, Serafine and Isaac stared at one another. She held her breath, frozen, unsure, and irate. Serafine had been proud and strong when she had met Isaac in New Orleans. His rejection wouldn't reduce her to a mousey shadow of herself.

He rose from the chair and came to sit beside her on the settee. Her heart bolted in her chest and blood thundered in her ears. His presence flustered her mind and senses.

His wide eyes swept over her. "I can't believe you are in London."

"I thought you were in Edinburgh, Monsieur Tucker." She tried to hide his effect on her behind icy indifference.

"I've been in Town several days pursuing a certain enterprise." A lock of shaggy blond hair fell into his eyes as he leaned forward to grasp her hand. He needed a haircut, and based on his haggard appearance, a good night's sleep might do him good as well.

She pulled out of his grasp. "How goes your enterprise? Have you made an arrangement with one of the twittering debutantes I saw at the ball last night?"

A scowl marred his face. "My endeavors have nothing to do with seeking a wife. You know it is you I love."

She crossed her arms, hugging her body to cease her insides from quivering. "Yet, you could not marry me because your papa wouldn't allow it."

"My parents didn't approve. I knew as much from the start of our association. I should have warned you to be more discreet."

Serafine sneered. "Did not approve? How mild it sounds when you say it now. I believe your words were they did not want descendants with tainted blood."

He fidgeted with the brass button on his waistcoat. "They—my parents want to keep everything pure, no foreign influence."

"Foreign? My ancestors settled in New Orleans a decade before yours." She jabbed a finger in his direction. "If anyone is a foreigner, it is you and your kin. How can you defend them?"

"I'm not defending them. I'm trying to explain."

"There's nothing to explain, Monsieur Tucker. You may go." She tried to bolt from the settee, but Isaac captured her arm. His touch disturbed her equilibrium and sent her thoughts spinning.

"Amelia Hillary thought we should speak," he said.

"Amelia confided in you about me?" Her friend's betrayal was like a hard slap in the face.

"She procured an invitation for me last night, nothing more. Once I learned you were on the same ship with her, I called on her. She's the only person I know with connections, at least the only one who would help me." He leaned closer as if he breathed her in. "I had to see you, Sera."

Lifting her chin, she glared. "I thought you brave at one time, but now I see how cowardly you really are."

Isaac flinched.

"First you kowtow to your parents, and now you buckle under Captain Hillary's threats."

His eyes darkened. "I'm not here because of Captain Hillary, and my parents are as good as dead to me. I'm here for you."

He scooted across the settee, sending Serafine jerking back against the tufted cushion, and captured her hands. "Sera, I can see I'm too late. But I can't leave everything as it has been between us. I can't allow you to believe you are not good enough."

Her heart slammed against her ribs. His touch left her dizzy. "Release me, Monsieur Tucker. Have you gone mad?"

"I can't let you go if you are going to run from me again. Not until you hear me out."

"*I* was not the one to run away." She shoved against his shoulders and he released her. Storming to her feet, she marched several paces away and whirled on him. "*You* are the one who sailed across the ocean, leaving me alone to face the consequences."

His gasp made her cringe, and the beginning of a smile caused her stomach to churn sickeningly. "Are there consequences, my love?"

She hadn't been certain—perhaps she hadn't wanted to believe it could be true—but she could no longer deny the truth.

There was a flash of skirts at the threshold. "Silence," she hissed.

Lisette entered the drawing room with two servants. The maid carried Serafine's daisies in an opaque vase and headed toward a diminutive table on the far side of the room. How sad the common field flowers would appear tucked into a corner.

"Please, place the vase here." She swept a hand toward the low table in front of the settee, chiding herself for noting Isaac's relieved smile. His feelings meant nothing to her anymore.

Lisette took a seat adjacent to the settee and nodded to the footman. He rolled the tea cart beside her chair then took his leave. "Shall I pour?" She didn't wait for an answer.

Serafine accepted the cup of tea. "*Merci.*"

Isaac shook his head when she tried to pass a cup and saucer to him. "Madame Hillary, might I beg another word alone with Mademoiselle Vistoire?"

"No," Serafine blurted.

Lisette looked between them, a worried wrinkle appearing on her forehead. "Perhaps we should simply have some tea for now, monsieur."

❧

Daniel looked up as his wife swept into his study.

"I need you." The urgency in her tone made him set his correspondence aside at once and take to his feet.

"Is there trouble with Mr. Tucker?"

She beckoned to him. "Come now. We must stroll in the park."

"I beg your pardon?"

"You must come along and speak with Monsieur Tucker while I question Serafine. I cannot converse with her while the gentleman is present, and I dare not send him away."

What nonsense was this? "Tucker was to make his offer and be done with the matter." Daniel marched toward the doorway to put the situation to rights, but Lisette blocked his way, her hands on her hips.

"I don't need you to pound the poor man. Simply do as I ask and keep him distracted without allowing him to get away. I need to question Serafine. I think she may not wish for his offer of marriage."

Devil take it! Why did the fairer gender have to be so damned complicated? "The gentleman has ruined her. He's here to make amends. She will accept his offer and consider herself fortunate. End of conversation."

His wife drew back like a cat dropped in a bucket

of water: hissing mad and claws bared. "She will do whatever she damn well pleases."

"Watch your tongue," he warned, unable to keep a touch of amusement from his voice.

"I learned the word from you, so watch your own blasted tongue."

He chuckled and gathered her against him swiftly before she could argue further. He nuzzled her neck and nibbled her ear, silently celebrating when she melted in his arms. "What did I ever do to deserve you?"

"Probably something very wicked." She sounded much less surly.

He kissed her, reveling in the sweetness of her full lips and her willingness to abandon their argument. He took pleasure in living in harmony with his wife and the ease of loving her.

"I do enjoy wickedness," he teased, "but that will have to come later. I fear you will be cross if we don't accompany Serafine and Mr. Tucker on a stroll."

"*Oui*. Cross indeed."

Moments later, he and Mr. Tucker followed the ladies at a distance, close enough to keep watch over them, but too far away to overhear their conversation.

Sweat dripped down the younger man's face, and his eyes widened when the ladies' heads dipped together to share some secret.

"Damnation," Tucker mumbled.

"What are they saying?"

"How the hell would I know? I can't hear them any better than you can."

Irritation surged through Daniel. "You have no clues?"

What was the bloody trouble? He needed this

matter settled today. The *Cecily* departed in a few days. They would hit the Caribbean at the start of hurricane season if he delayed much longer. A swift pull in his gut served as a reminder of his own troubles. Lisette didn't yet know he intended to sail without her.

"Tell me what transpired in the drawing room," Daniel said through clenched teeth. "You were supposed to offer marriage and make things right."

"If you would tend your own affairs, maybe Sera would listen to me." Tucker skidded to a stop and Daniel turned to glare at him. "She believes you're *forcing* me to ask for her hand."

"And I am not?"

"Hell, no! I've been miserable since the moment we parted. As soon as I left New Orleans, I knew the horrendous mistake I had made."

"Then why didn't you go back for her?"

Tucker threw his arms wide. "If I had married Miss Vistoire, my father would have disinherited me. I had nothing without my father's fortune, no means of supporting her, so I decided to find work in England. I thought once I had saved enough, I would go back for her."

Daniel viewed the man with a reluctant measure of respect now. "What type of work?"

"I'm good at drafting. I've studied architecture for several years. Do you know the foundling hospital renovation project?"

"My sister-in-law's charity?"

Tucker nodded. "I drew up the designs, but no one knows it was me. I act as a liaison between members of the *ton* and Mr. Brown."

"And *you* are Mr. Brown."

"Yes, and I beg of you to keep my identity secret. If I am denied access to society, I have no means of earning my keep, much less supporting a wife. As it is, the Earl of Fairmill has commissioned Mr. Brown to draft an addition to his country home. And Mr. Collier is building a cottage for his mistress."

Tucker would remain in England, keeping Lisette's family in the vicinity. Daniel couldn't have asked for a better outcome.

He nailed Tucker with his most disapproving glare. "This doesn't excuse your behavior, you realize. She'll not easily forget you left her. Women possess long memories."

The man sighed, his shoulders drooping. "I know. I should have gone back at once or written, but I never dreamed she would find someone else so quickly. I can't compete with a nobleman."

"Westin? You have nothing to worry about from his direction." Daniel clapped Tucker on the shoulder and urged him forward on the path. "Rumor has it Westin's father is in negotiations with the Duke of Ashden, choosing Westin's bride. Poor sap likely knows nothing about it."

"The devil, you say!" A daft grin spread across Tucker's face.

Daniel wouldn't have pegged Tucker as a good match for Serafine, but it was obvious from the dolt's adoring gazes he was arsey varsey for the lady. Mr. Tucker simply required assistance to win her heart again.

"You'll join us for dinner this evening," Daniel said, "and begin your courtship in earnest."

Twenty-nine

SERAFINE STEPPED ONTO THE SIDEWALK, DREW IN A deep breath, and regretted it at once. The steamy stench of the summer morning made her stomach lurch. She gripped the iron gate of 17 Curzon to steady herself as a wave of nauseated dizziness washed over her.

Would this illness ever cease? Damn Isaac for leaving her in this state. Even as she cursed him, a secret smile appeared. Perhaps she wasn't prepared to forgive him for his shabby treatment yet, but his pitiable attempts to court her these last two days had softened her heart.

Oddly, Isaac's lack of *savoir faire* aided his attempts rather than hurt them as one might expect. Serafine had never cared for the cocksure dandies strutting around New Orleans, believing themselves a prize for any young woman. Isaac had been vastly different from the gentlemen courting her when she had met him months ago. He'd massacred his words when requesting her dance card, blushed throughout the entire minuet, then concluded the evening with spilling a glass of punch down his front. His hopelessly awkward act had deceived her. Isaac had seemed harmless and incapable of hurting her.

He wouldn't fool her again.

Serafine took a moment to get her bearings. A concentrated fog swallowed the grand town houses of Mayfair, making them appear as indistinct bulks. Cautiously, she moved along the walkway with her brother's last known address written on a piece of paper tucked into her reticule. With Lisette and Daniel still abed and Rafe breaking his fast with his governess, Serafine hoped to reach her brother's rented rooms and return before anyone discovered her absence.

Daniel's inquiries into Xavier's whereabouts had turned up no answers, but Serafine had to try. With any luck, he would have left something behind. Perhaps a clue could be discovered among his belongings.

The hack she had ordered waited at the corner. "Morning, miss." A note of wariness accompanied the driver's greeting. "Ye traveling wit' yer maid or chaperone today?"

She lifted her chin as she took his hand to climb inside the carriage. "I have no need of a chaperone, good sir." Once settled on the seat, she opened her reticule and extracted the address. "Number four Waverton Street. I will pay extra if you make our destination quickly. I haven't much time."

"Aye, miss."

The driver climbed to his spot and slapped the reins, urging the horse along at a plodding pace, much to Serafine's displeasure. Only a couple of turns later, the carriage rolled to a stop in front of a dark brick building. She could have walked if she'd known how close Xavier's rooms were and saved herself the cost of fare. Serafine perched on the edge of her seat, a sense of unease settling over her, and waited for the driver's assistance traversing the carriage steps.

Once the driver assisted her to the ground, she pulled coins from her reticule and handed them to him. "This should cover the fare."

"Do ye want me to wait, miss?"

"That isn't necessary. Thank you for your service."

He tipped his hat. "Aye, miss."

The lack of noise in the neighborhood was unsettling, but by society's standards, she was awake much too early. She had slowly come to accept most of the *ton* kept unhealthy hours, although she did not approve.

Serafine climbed the two front steps and checked the address on the paper. Her destination possessed nothing distinctive to differentiate it from the other two town houses butted up on either side, except for the number four attached to the peeling green door.

She rang the bell as the hack drove away. The jangle sent a shiver along her spine.

Someone is watching.

Whipping around to scan the streets, her gaze darted from side to side, but the dense fog obscured everything from view. A cloud of gray enclosed her in a secret world. Serafine twittered and rolled her neck. How asinine to think anyone could see her. Why, she could barely see the toes of her half boots.

She turned back to the door, prepared to ring the bell again, but halted as locks tumbled and the door screeched open. A diminutive lady with tousled silver hair and streaks of crimson rouge painted on her cheeks frowned through the crack in the door.

"What, pray tell, brings *you* to my door? I only rent to gentlemen." She opened the door farther, wrinkled her nose, and swept her gaze from Serafine's head to toes. "I run a respectable place, you know."

Serafine smiled, ignoring her insinuation. The woman clearly didn't have her wits about her, not when she had donned her gown backward and had her free hand shoved into a winter muff in this unbearable heat.

"I have it on good authority you cater to the most honorable of gentlemen," Serafine replied. "My brother once rented a room from you. Mr. Xavier Vistoire?"

The woman's frown deepened. "Him again? I already told the gentlemen before you that Mr. Vistoire disappeared." Deep lines appeared at the corners of her eyes as she narrowed them. Her pursed mouth formed a tight circle, giving her face the appearance of a dried-up apple core. The woman possessed either bad eyesight or a tendency toward suspicion. Maybe both.

"He kept late hours, you know." Her voice gurgled as if she swallowed water as she spoke. "He patronized the gaming hells, and he didn't pay his rent for the last two months before he vanished. He probably got himself into trouble."

Serafine suppressed a wince. Xavier had fallen in with a rough crowd in New Orleans before he left for the Continent, and he had gambled away most of his inheritance. She'd hoped a different locale would give him a new direction for his life. It appeared her hopes were for naught.

She opened her reticule. "This is precisely my reason for calling today, madame. I have come to settle my brother's debt and collect his belongings. How much does he owe?"

"Five pounds. I will only accept pounds, you know. No worthless foreign bills."

"Of course." Serafine forced a polite expression as she dug out the money and placed it in the woman's emaciated claw. "And two additional pounds for your trouble."

The woman snatched the money then flashed a gritted-teeth smile. "Peace and blessings," she hissed.

"Oh!" Serafine fell back a step. "Th—thank you."

"Come inside, my dear."

An eerie sensation shot through her, and she hesitated on the stoop.

The woman walked farther into the narrow corridor. Her bony shoulder blades jutted through the neckline of the backward gown. "I have your brother's items in a crate."

Serafine shook off her uneasiness and followed, but she left the front door open as a precaution.

The woman tugged the handle of a door off the foyer. She grunted as she pulled several times. The door surrendered with a crack and flew open, almost sending her to her backside.

Serafine peeked through the opening. "You store items in the water closet?" Crates filled the small space from floor to ceiling.

"Here it is."

"Allow me to assist."

The woman waved her off then stooped low and

lifted the crate with a guttural groan. Teetering from the weight of the crate, she pitched against the door frame.

Serafine jumped to take the burden from her arms. "Did you hurt yourself?"

The woman rubbed her elbow. "Pardon, dear?"

"Never mind." Serafine could see for herself the woman was uninjured, and she didn't wish to extend her time there unnecessarily. "Please accept my apologies for my brother's delay in paying his debts."

She spun on her heel and rushed out the open door without waiting for a reply. Bustling down the block, she didn't slow until she reached the corner. Was this the correct way? No landmarks stood out to her as she looked up and down each road, not that she could see much in the haze. She contemplated the best route back to Curzon Street. Should she stay on the current street or turn right?

She should have paid closer attention on the ride. She couldn't stand around like a ninny all morning. Lisette and Daniel would be awake and readying themselves for a ride in the park soon. Making a choice, she turned right.

Halfway up the block, hairs at the back of her neck stood on end. She threw a look over her shoulder. No one was there. Still, the sensation of someone watching her didn't go away.

She rushed forward, anxious to reach the next intersection where she recognized the outline of a milk wagon parked along the street. The sound of a boot fall echoed on the sidewalk several feet behind her. She whirled around. "Who's there?"

There were no movements in the gray, no flash of

color to reveal someone hiding in the fog. Perhaps the old woman's mental frailty was catching. Nevertheless, Serafine moved with haste toward the next block.

A carriage passed on the cross street, the horses' harness jingling, and then another. She would feel better once she reached a busier street with more people. Heavy footsteps echoed on the sidewalk behind her, running.

Serafine's heart leapt and she dashed for the street ahead, not daring to look back. The crate and her skirts slowed her down, but she was almost there.

Her heart pumped brutally and her chest heaved with labored gasps for air. She surged forward to reach the corner before her pursuer caught her and plowed into someone, the forceful blow disorienting her.

"What the devil?" a startled voice yelped.

The crate flew from her hands and Serafine tumbled forward too fast to catch herself. Bits of gravel ripped through her gloves as she landed in the lane. Her palms and knees screamed with pain.

"Watch out!" The panicked voice made her head pop up. A carriage barreled out of the fog toward her. She froze.

"Sera!" Strong hands gripped her shoulders and hauled her from the ground and out of the way. The wind of the carriage flying past lifted her hat brim. Breathing ceased and everything slowed. Isaac spun her around to face him. His lips moved, but she couldn't hear him.

She gulped in a lungful of air. The street sounds filtered back into her awareness. The warmth of Isaac's hands on her arms seeped into her skin.

"Blasted mad wench," an angry male voice said. "Watch where ye goin' next time. Would 'ave served ye right if ye was to get squashed."

"Go to the devil," Isaac snarled then reached up to brush her cheek with his thumb. "For the love of God, Sera, are you injured?"

She shook her head, too stunned to speak. Why was Isaac here? He had appeared as if he were her guardian angel.

"What happened?" he asked. "Why are you out alone?"

Her body quaked. "I—I thought someone was chasing me."

"Chasing you? From which direction?" She pointed. Isaac released her and ran a few paces down the block.

"I don't see anyone," he called before turning, stalking back to her, and enfolding her in his arms again. His embrace stirred her emotions. "Don't you realize it is dangerous to be out alone in London?"

Xavier's belongings littered the walkway.

"Oh!" She broke free of Isaac's arms and dropped to her knees to snatch the items before they became lost to her: a shaving brush, a comb, a mix of cuff links, and a letter. Her fingers brushed over Xavier's name on the missive. She opened the missive and scanned the contents. It was the letter her uncle's solicitor had sent long ago notifying Xavier of their uncle's death and urging him to return to New Orleans. She would read it later this evening.

"Let me help you." Isaac joined her on the ground. His hand touched hers as they gathered the items and returned them to the crate.

"It's Xavier's belongings." Her voice quivered.

"Is this all that's left?"

This is all I have left. Isaac's image blurred. Her brother was gone and all that was left of him was the sum of a few items that didn't fill a crate.

"Oh, Sera. Please, don't cry." Isaac pulled his handkerchief from his pocket and passed it to her. "Please, darling."

She refused his offering. "I'm not crying. Take it back." Even as she denied her emotions, salty tears rolled down her cheeks.

He touched the handkerchief to her cheeks. "Of course you aren't, darling."

Damn his tenderness. "I need help standing."

Gripping under her arm, Isaac helped her to her feet then picked up the crate.

"What are you doing here, Isaac?"

"I came to request an audience, but I can come back. I realize it's early to call, but I couldn't sleep." His face flushed a deep crimson. "I couldn't stop myself from seeking you out. You must think me foolish."

Serafine began to recognize her surroundings since the fog had dissipated some. They were three houses down from her cousin's town house.

Isaac shifted the crate to one arm and offered his elbow. "Sera, I'm sorry you didn't locate Xavier, but you mustn't give up hope." His eyes lit with love and compassion, washing over her and covering her fully. "I'll help you search."

His clumsy attempt at comfort brought fresh tears to her eyes. Did she dare to trust him now? She didn't have it in her to watch him walk away again.

She wiped her tears and sniffled. "You can never

again hurt me as you did, Isaac Tucker. I won't stand for it."

His eyes widened and his handsome face took on a somber expression. "On my honor, Serafine, I will treat you like the most precious of treasures if you allow me another chance."

He sounded so sincere, she couldn't help but to smile. "You need not wait until later to call on me. Come make your offer like a proper gentleman. I shan't deny you this time. Then I have something I must share with you."

❧

"Please take this crate to my chambers."

Lisette perked up hearing her cousin's voice outside the breakfast room. "Serafine is awake," she said to Daniel. "Perhaps she would like to join us in the park."

She slipped from the skirted dining room chair, swept into the corridor, and came up short. "Monsieur Tucker? What a surprise."

The man's face flamed, and he stepped in front of Serafine to shield her from view. Lisette leaned to the side and tried to peek around him. "Serafine, is there a problem?"

"It's all right, Isaac." Her cousin eased Monsieur Tucker aside.

"*Mon dieu.* What happened to your gown?" Serafine's pale yellow skirts sported vast streaks of dirt, a small tear, and possibly a spot of blood.

Daniel appeared at Lisette's side.

Serafine looked down, smoothing her soiled gloves over her dress. "I met with an accident."

"An accident?" With a threatening glare aimed at Monsieur Tucker, Daniel stepped forward. "Did you do this to her?"

Serafine inserted herself between the men with arms spread. "He saved me from being run down by a carriage. The gentleman deserves gratitude, not threats, Captain."

Lisette gripped Daniel's arm. "Run down by a carriage? But why did you leave the house?"

Daniel's muscles tensed beneath her touch. "The blackheart had her meet him. Isn't it obvious?"

"You're wrong, Captain. I took a hack to my brother's last address. I wished to retrieve his belongings. I crossed paths with Monsieur Tucker on Curzon Street when I fell into the road. He pulled me to safety." Serafine lifted herself up with dignity and peered down her nose at both Lisette and Daniel. "Now, if you will excuse us, I have granted Monsieur Tucker a private audience in the drawing room. I shall summon you when we are ready to announce our good tidings."

She whipped around with a swish of skirts, accepted Monsieur Tucker's escort, and headed for the drawing room.

Lisette and Daniel stared at one another.

"Did Serafine just indicate she has brought Mr. Tucker up to scratch?" he asked.

Happiness bubbled up inside Lisette and she giggled. "Oh, Daniel, she does still care for him." She threw her arms around his neck and kissed him soundly. "First you protected us from Reynaud. You are assisting Monsieur Baptiste. And now *this*."

He cradled her bottom and urged her closer, a pleased grin activating his dimple. "I had nothing to do with your cousin's circumstances."

Her finger dipped into the indent in his cheek. "You didn't maim or kill Monsieur Tucker when you found him on the terrace with Serafine."

Daniel turned his head to place a kiss on the tip of her finger. "You are easy to please, my love. Duly noted for the future: no maiming or killing of prospective spouses for our daughters. Unless they deserve it."

Her brows rose. "You wish to have daughters? I thought you would want a son."

"I'll be pleased with any issue you bear. Rafe has demonstrated how much joy can be found in fatherhood."

A warm tingle started in her chest. "You really are a father to Rafe, aren't you? You have no idea... You—" Her voice caught. Many generous thoughts rushed to mind, but she couldn't speak.

Daniel had become her everything.

"I know what you're trying to say, Lis." His fingers traced her jaw as he tilted her head upward. "I love him, too." When his lips touched hers, she tried to shove aside her disappointment. She had no cause to be jealous of Daniel's feelings for her brother. Hadn't she wished for a husband who could love and accept Rafe?

"Ahem."

Daniel sighed on a near growl and glanced toward the butler, not releasing Lisette. "Can you not see I'm otherwise engaged?"

"My apologies, sir, but you requested I inform you when Mr. Baptiste arrived."

Her husband's frown didn't fade. "Show him to my study. I'll join him in a moment."

"Yes, sir."

As soon as the butler disappeared, Daniel swept Lisette into another passionate kiss.

"Daniel." She laughed and halfheartedly pushed at his chest. "We have guests, not to mention a house teeming with servants. We can't make love in the corridor."

"It's my blasted house."

She kissed him once more. "And I shall await you in my chambers where we shall have privacy. Do not dawdle."

Thirty

DANIEL TOSSED BAPTISTE'S LETTER OF RECOMMENDA-
tion on his desk, his mind preoccupied with his
accommodating wife waiting for him upstairs. "This
should assist you with securing employment."

Baptiste picked up the foolscap, unfolded it,
and scanned the contents. Refolding the letter, he
looked up at Daniel with glimmering eyes. "I cannot
thank you enough, Captain Hillary. You and Mrs.
Hillary have been most generous. I don't deserve
such kindness."

"No need for thanks." Daniel was already moving
toward the exit.

"Might I request an audience with Mrs. Hillary?
Perhaps she and Master Rafe would like to go for
an ice later this afternoon while you visit the docks.
I could properly thank the lady for her kindness and
wish her continued good health."

The man grated on Daniel's every nerve. His
nasal voice offended his ears to be certain, but his
simpering nature made Daniel want to toss his breakfast. Nonetheless, his wife was fond of the gentleman,

which was the only reason he extended any kindness
to Baptiste.

"Mrs. Hillary is not available this afternoon." Daniel
wished to spend his last day in London with her doing
all kinds of wicked things she would not soon forget.

The *Cecily* would depart on the morrow. The
Certificate of Clearance had been obtained a week
ago, and his crew was prepared for their departure, but
he had yet to inform Lisette. He didn't look forward
to revealing his plans, not after their last discussion on
the topic, although it had ended pleasantly with her
underneath him. Surely, he would not be as fortunate
this time since she had sought to change his mind.

He halted at the threshold. "Mr. Baptiste, may I
request a favor?"

"Please, ask anything of me. I'm your humble servant."

"You can't mention anything to my wife until I've
had a chance to speak with her, but I set sail for New
Orleans on the morrow, without her and Rafe."

Baptiste sat up straighter. "And you haven't spoken
with madame about your departure? I fear she'll not
be pleased."

"I'm aware of the fact." Did the man think him
daft? "It's for her protection. There are too many
dangers associated with sea travel. I intend to deal with
Reynaud and settle the matter of Rafe's guardianship
then I shall give up sailing forever."

"Indeed." Baptiste tugged on his ear, appearing to
mull over this information. "Perhaps you are wise to
handle Reynaud before he manipulates the situation to
suit himself. How is it I may be of service?"

"I have made arrangements for my family to stay in

the country while I'm gone, but Lisette will require a distraction until my brother collects her at the end of the week. This is all I ask of you. Keep my wife entertained until the end of the week." Daniel's fingers curled into fists at his sides. "And keep the scoundrels at bay."

"She'll not be pleased in the least, but I will endeavor to help her accept your edict."

"You have my gratitude. Ned will show you out."

Daniel crossed the foyer and dashed up the stairs two at a time. He couldn't avoid the conversation any longer. Better to have everything out in the open with Lisette so they could enjoy their last moments together.

When he reached his wife's bedchamber, he opened the door without knocking. Lisette lounged on the bed on her side with her hand cradling her head. Her gleaming black hair fell behind her bare shoulders.

Daniel halted; his blood pounded in his veins. "How did you manage to lose your clothing?"

She offered a smug smile. "I called for assistance, of course. This is the reason you employ a lady's maid, is it not?"

He sauntered to the bed. "Good to know the girl is worth her wages."

"Come." Lisette rolled to her back and extended her arms. "I have grown tired of waiting for you."

His body ached for her. Unable to resist, he reached out to touch her. She stretched on the bed with a beguiling sigh as he glided his hands over her thighs. Her luxurious bronzed skin was akin to a light sea breeze, and her curves beckoned to him like the ocean waves. A pang wrenched his stomach. *Would* she grow tired of waiting for him to return home? He would be gone for almost three months if everything went as planned, longer if he encountered complications.

The need to hold on to her surged through him, and he climbed on the bed, rolling her into his embrace. She fit against him with perfect precision. Never had anyone felt as if she'd always belonged with him, not like Lisette. He buried his face into her fragrant hair. The scent of jasmine filled his nose.

As he kissed her neck, his hands followed the rounded contours of her perfect arse. "I'll miss you, darling," he whispered.

"Pardon?" Lisette pulled back into his view, her brows arched together and her green eyes clouded with wariness. "Did you just say you will miss me?"

Had he spoken his thoughts? Daniel released her from his hold; he licked his lips. "There's something I must tell you."

A tiny gasp reached his ears. "You're planning to leave on the *Cecily*."

"Lis, this is the only time, I swear it."

She shoved away from him and sat up cross-legged on the bed. "You will not leave me here. When are you traveling? I'll begin preparations to accompany you."

"Tomorrow." He captured her arm as she tried to climb from the bed. "There are matters in New Orleans I must see to in person."

"Very well. You haven't given me much time, but I can pack quickly."

He pulled her close, demanding her attention. "You're staying. A ship is no place for a lady."

She yanked free. "I had no troubles on the voyage to England. I'll have no troubles returning to New Orleans."

Daniel pushed up to his elbows as she scrambled off the bed and hurried to her wardrobe. "I can't believe you did not give me fair warning." She flung the doors wide, jerked a gown from inside, and draped it over her arm, followed by two more. "What demands your attention in New Orleans?"

"I intend to petition the court for guardianship of Rafe."

Lisette stopped snatching garments and gaped at him. "Without first discussing the matter with me?"

He moved to sit on the side of the bed. "What is there to discuss? He requires a protector, seeing as how your irresponsible cousin has either run off or gotten himself killed."

She marched to the bed, tossed the gowns on the counterpane, and faced him with arms akimbo. "If I didn't know your worth, I might think you are as crooked as Reynaud."

Daniel caught her around the waist. "I'm nothing like that blackguard, and you know it. I would never hurt you or Rafe. You are my life."

The sharp sound of her gasp hung between them in the quiet room.

"My *wife*," he corrected, then regretted he had spoken again when she winced.

"Your wife." Lisette's spark dimmed and she looked away. "*Oui.* I am your wife only."

"Not only." He released her and rubbed his forehead. What a complete arse he was. "That wasn't my meaning. You must know I care for you, Lisette. Why else would I go to such pains to keep you safe? Leaving you behind brings me no pleasure."

"I see." She returned to the wardrobe, all fire gone from her step, and retrieved a wrapper. She didn't turn back toward him as she slipped her arms into the sleeves. "If you harbored the same feelings I have for you, you couldn't stand parting from me."

This was going badly. They were supposed to talk things out. She was supposed to understand he wanted the best for her. Seeking guardianship of Rafe was meant to ease her worries, but maybe the thought of his absence increased her anxiety. "I won't be gone forever, Lis." He tried to inject light-ness into his tone. "But long enough to suffer greatly if you don't allow me the pleasure of your touch. Now, come back to bed."

She made a disgusted sound and peered at him over her shoulder. "You are a pig, Daniel Hillary."

"A pig?"

"*Oui.*" She ran into the dressing room and turned the lock. Her sobs penetrated the crack between the solid wood doors.

"Devil take it." He walked to the dressing room entrance and knocked. "Lisette, open the door." Her sobs continued and that horrible guilt he had felt for so many years following Cecily's death crashed onto his shoulders.

"Damnation, open this door at once."

He listened for evidence that she intended to obey, but he heard nothing aside from her crying.

He banged his fist against the surface. "Lisette,

open this door. I won't allow you to make me feel guilty. I'm doing this for *you*, for Rafe. I expect some understanding and gratitude."

She didn't respond. A memory of Cecily's tear-soaked face and her pouting stoked his temper. She had toyed with him, manipulated him like a marionette with her emotions. "To hell with you," he mumbled to her blurry image in his mind.

Turning on his heel, he stalked from his wife's chambers. Perhaps Lisette would see reason by evening. Until she came to her senses, he would oversee preparations on the *Cecily*. He wouldn't sit around listening to her cry and feeling like a failure.

❧

Reynaud hovered in the darkened street, keeping watch on number 17 Curzon, as stealthily as the king of beasts hunting in the night. The almighty lion possessed brawn, agility, speed, and a nice head of hair. Reynaud swept a hand over his own slicked-back locks and smiled.

Very nice, indeed.

The lion's prey stood little chance of survival once he set his sights on them. His domination was unavoidable.

The flickering lights from the upstairs windows extinguished. Tonight Lisette and Serafine burrowed under their covers, believing themselves to be safe. On the morrow, they would lose their protector. Captain Hillary hadn't planned to take the women with him as Reynaud had feared when he'd learned the *Cecily* was preparing to set sail.

The ladies would be at the lion's mercy.

A bolt of exhilaration flew through his limbs and left him trembling with agitated anticipation. Another known fact about the lion: he boasted superior sexual prowess, sometimes copulating as many as one hundred times in twenty-four hours. The dominant male got his fill of the females in his pride.

But first, he must seize his letters. After all, the threat of swinging from the gallows tended to interfere with one's lustful urges.

Thirty-one

AFTER A FITFUL NIGHT, HALF OF WHICH LISETTE SPENT staring up into the darkness and listening for sounds from Daniel's room, she couldn't stay abed any longer. She flung the covers aside and rang for her lady's maid. The bright morning sun slashed through the opening between her silk curtains and illuminated a swath of the Turkish carpet under her bare feet.

She couldn't submit to Daniel's wishes without one more attempt to change his mind. Whether he wanted to admit it or not, he loved her. She refused to believe otherwise. His soft expressions and gentle touch spoke of his regard. And once she convinced him of the truth, he wouldn't leave her.

Her maid bustled into her chambers. "Good morning, madame."

"I need to change."

"I have the perfect outfit." Henrietta, young, energetic, and always eager to please, hurried to the wardrobe and selected a gown. The girl made the same pronouncement each day, and she never disappointed.

But this morning, Lisette didn't care what she wore as long as the task was completed with efficiency.

"I need you to hurry."

"Yes, ma'am."

Lisette strained to hear if Daniel was readying himself to depart for the docks, but his adjoining chambers remained silent. The tension in her shoulders dropped away. Perhaps she shouldn't have worried about dressing first since he remained in bed, but if he retreated to the breakfast room, she wanted the option of following him.

Henrietta rushed through Lisette's toilette then bit her lip as she studied Lisette's image in the looking glass. "Are you satisfied, ma'am?"

Lisette offered a reassuring smile. "Indeed. *Merci.*"

She hopped up from the cushioned bench and approached Daniel's door. Tossing formality aside, she let herself inside his rooms and froze at the threshold.

Sunlight flooded the room, and his counterpane lay smooth, not a single wrinkle or indentation to suggest he had slept in his bed. Her gaze darted around the empty room for any hints he'd come home last night. There was nothing. Everything remained in its place.

A light mist of perspiration dampened her skin as panic welled up inside her. Papa hadn't come home from the mill all those months ago either. At dawn, two of his workmen had discovered Papa lying behind the Lavigne warehouses. A shiver shook her from head to toe and nausea swirled in her belly.

Daniel isn't Papa.

Her husband was strong and wise to the dangers

of the world. He would not fall victim to a cutthroat waiting to pounce from the darkness. Her hand covered her chest, and she felt the hammering of her heart beneath her palm.

Taking a deep breath, she tried to push her fatalistic imaginings aside. She had no cause for worry. Daniel had likely left early for the docks, even though she hadn't heard him.

She moved to the bellpull and yanked. Daniel's valet presented himself for duty moments later but came up short when he spotted her.

"Good morning, ma'am." The servant looked around the space. "Is Captain Hillary in need of my services?"

"It appears he may have returned to the docks already. Did he not request your assistance?"

The valet blinked several times. "No, ma'am. It has been customary for Captain Hillary to sleep onboard ship the night before a voyage, but I expected he would spend his last night at home."

Goddard glanced down at his shiny, black boots, red coloring his cheeks. Obviously, the valet had expected Daniel to share her bed as he had every night since their occupation of the town house.

"I see." Although this knowledge of his habits eased her worries for his safety, she was not comforted. Daniel had already dismissed her, not even bothering to say farewell. "Thank you. I have no further inquiries."

The servant left as unobtrusively as he had entered.

Perhaps she should travel to the docks to speak with her husband before the *Cecily* set sail. Or perhaps she could be an obedient wife and accept his edicts. Daniel had saved her life by marrying her. He provided shelter, food, and safety for her and her family. He desired her. Perhaps that should be enough.

Lisette crossed her arms and sighed. Must a wife accept her husband's wishes when she knew he was wrong?

She turned her back on his chambers. Bumps came from Rafe's chambers above.

Henrietta hung the last of Lisette's laundered petticoats on the pegs in the wardrobe then closed the mahogany doors. "Will there be anything else, ma'am?"

"Send word to the governess I would like my brother to breakfast with me this morning."

"Yes, ma'am."

Lisette might best be served by accepting her circumstances with grace and dignity as most well-bred ladies were required to do. The days would be long without Daniel, but she would find a way to fill them. Perhaps if she devoted herself to Rafe's studies and the running of Daniel's home, the separation wouldn't be as agonizing as she was anticipating. Her first task would be to meet with Rafe's governess to ascertain his progress with his sums.

She arrived to the breakfast room before Rafe and Miss Channing, and requested the footman pour her a cup of tea. "Is Mademoiselle Vistoire still abed?"

"No, madame. Mr. Tucker collected Miss Vistoire this morning. Almost an hour ago."

She held back a sigh. Lisette shouldn't feel jealous of Serafine's renewed love affair, but the timing of it highlighted her loneliness.

"Good morning, Lisette." Her brother recited his greeting as if he had been practicing before joining her.

She smiled at Rafe as he slipped into an empty chair

at the dining table and placed his napkin in his lap. He continued to improve in small ways each day under Miss Channing's tutelage and daily trips to the docks with Daniel.

A slight grin graced Rafe's face. "I will finish the model galleon today."

"How marvelous." Lisette tried to inject cheer into her response. Rafe would not take Daniel's absence well, and she didn't have the heart to tell him yet. "I should like to see it once you have completed the task. Please, join us, Miss Channing."

The governess sat on the vacant seat beside Rafe. "Your brother has done fine work, ma'am. I believe you will be impressed."

Lisette smiled. "I have no doubts."

At her urging, Miss Channing provided a detailed account of Rafe's learning while they consumed their breakfast. Lisette and Daniel had made a good choice in hiring the governess. The young woman exuded kindness, patience, and a gift for engaging Rafe.

"What other activities have you planned for the day?" Lisette asked.

"I would like to take Master Rafe on a stroll through the park, with your permission, of course."

Lisette inclined her head. "That sounds like an excellent idea. The fresh air will do him good."

Rafe bounded up from his chair and dashed for the door. "I want a boat for the lake."

"Wait," Lisette called, but he had already disappeared through the doorway. "He is single-minded when it comes to ships."

The governess smiled politely and ate her breakfast.

Rafe returned a few moments later with a stack of foolscap.

"You mustn't run inside the house," Lisette scolded. "Have a seat and finish your breakfast. Then you may make your paper boat."

Her brother frowned, but placed the stack on the table and resumed his seat. Lowering his head, he concentrated on pushing the eggs around his plate with his fork without taking another bite. Miss Channing tried to coax him into eating more, but her attempts were made in vain.

When Rafe began to wiggle on the seat, Lisette recognized the futility in keeping him at the table.

"You may be excused, Rafe. But you may not waste Daniel's paper. Two sheets only."

He lifted his chin, and for a moment she thought he would argue with her. She exhaled slowly when he complied with her command. He counted out two sheets, lining up the edges, and climbed from the chair with the pages clutched in his thin fingers.

After Rafe and his governess retired upstairs to ready themselves for the park, Lisette wilted against the seat back. The weight of her responsibilities settled over her. Rafe was under her care alone now. She wouldn't have Daniel's assistance for several months, and soon Serafine would marry and leave with her husband. The thought left her weary.

She touched the napkin to her mouth then placed it beside her plate. There was nothing else to do except keep her mind off her loneliness. Standing, she rounded the table and retrieved the extra sheets of foolscap to return to Daniel's study.

The room was too quiet, his vacant desk appearing as lost without him behind it as she felt. Shaking off her self-pity, Lisette skirted the massive piece of furniture, her fingers skimming the polished mahogany surface before lowering to the seat.

She opened the top right drawer to return his property and spotted a letter from New Orleans. Thinking the missive pertained to Rafe, she pulled it from the drawer, but the feminine scrawl gave her pause.

"Miss Paulina Fanchon." The letter came from a residential area of New Orleans. What business could Daniel have with this woman?

With the seal partially lifted, Lisette attempted to peek through the crack with no success. Even holding the letter to the light only revealed an alphabet jumble that made no sense.

To hell with grace and dignity. She broke the seal and devoured the words, her heart slamming against her ribs.

> *Dearest Daniel, my love.*
>
> *My heart pines for you. Memories of your touch and kiss do not sustain me as I await your return. I am tormented by my days without you. Yet, each moment spent lying in your arms is worth a thousand lifetimes of sorrow. I know ecstasy in your embrace.*
>
> *I have readied the house in anticipation of your arrival, and I have filled each room with everything you love. The only thing missing is you. Please, return home to me soon.*
>
> Forever yours,
Paulina

This was the true reason her husband had refused to take her to New Orleans. Daniel kept a lover, and she was waiting for him the same as he expected Lisette to wait.

Fury raced through her veins, scalding hot and blinding. She pushed from the chair and stalked from the study with the letter in hand. Bursting into the corridor, she nearly invoked a reaction from the butler, but he recovered in an instant. His calm demeanor only served to provoke her further.

He stepped forward with his ridiculous silver tray. "You have a caller, madame."

"I have no time for visitors." She whisked by him to walk toward the foyer. "I wish to see my husband before his ship departs. Who calls at this improper hour?"

She came up short. Monsieur Baptiste was loitering in the foyer, shuffling his feet. "It is I, madame. Please, forgive my intrusion."

Lisette shot an exasperated look over her shoulder at the butler but tempered her tone of voice. "You did not show Monsieur Baptiste to the drawing room?"

"My apologies, madame, but the gentleman has only now arrived."

"Indeed." She frowned, not at all pleased with the interruption, but she couldn't fault the servant. Had she not barreled from the study in a fit of pique, he would have approached her in private. Then she could have denied Monsieur Baptiste an audience without insult. "You may return to your other duties."

The butler offered a terse bow and escaped from the foyer.

"Monsieur Baptiste, please forgive my rudeness, but this is an inconvenient time."

"Yes, I couldn't help overhearing. I apologize for calling at such an early hour."

Lisette rubbed her forehead. Her racing thoughts brought a pain to her head. "You are like family, monsieur. You may call at any hour."

"I had anticipated your upset once you learned of Captain Hillary's plans. Is there anything I might do to provide solace? Perhaps a walk in the park would be of benefit."

Daniel had spoken with Monsieur Baptiste about his departure but kept it a secret from her. Her eye twitched with the effort of controlling her temper. It wouldn't do to lash out at the older gentleman, who offered her nothing but kindness. "How thoughtful, sir, but I fear the only solace I'll find will come from speaking with my husband. Now, if you'll excuse me, I wish to reach the docks before the *Cecily* sails."

Monsieur Baptiste stepped in front of her to block her retreat upstairs. "I gave my word to Captain Hillary I would watch out for you in his absence. Please allow me to escort you to the docks. The wharf is no place for a lady."

Rafe had wandered down the stairs with his paper boat and stood on the third step. "I want to go to the docks, too."

"This is not a good time, Rafe. Continue to the park with Miss Channing. You may visit the docks another day."

He walked down the remaining stairs and rounded

Monsieur Baptiste to stand before Lisette. "I want to see the *real* ships."

"You will stay here," Lisette snapped.

Her brother's face darkened and a low wail sounded deep within his chest. The noise rose, signaling the beginnings of one of his spells.

"Oh, dear." She hadn't meant to set him off. She really hadn't been thinking of him at all. "Forgive me for raising my voice. Another day we will visit the docks."

He began rocking back and forth from his waist. His hands fluttered as they often did before he launched into a full-blown fit of hysteria. The paper boat fell to the ground.

Miss Channing placed her hands on his shoulders. "Master Rafe, what is it?"

He jerked from her touch with a high-pitched scream. The governess's eyes rounded and she froze. Her gaze darted toward Lisette, questioning.

"Everything will be all right. Leave him be." Lisette lowered to one knee so she was on his level. Monsieur Baptiste quietly slipped outside. "There, there, Rafe. Shh. We must calm ourselves."

"I want to go. I want to go." To an outsider like Miss Channing, Rafe might appear to be nothing more than a spoiled child, but Lisette had ignited something in her brother he would be unable to stop once he reached a certain point.

She should have been calm, not allowed her anger with Daniel to seep out.

"I'll escort you to the docks," Monsieur Baptiste said from behind her. She startled, whipping her head toward his voice. He had slipped back inside undetected. "I will watch after Master Rafe while you speak with Captain Hillary."

Lisette looked up at Miss Channing. The governess hugged herself, a tremor shaking her slight frame. She wasn't equipped to handle one of Rafe's fits, and would have no idea how to provide him comfort.

"I think it's best if I take Rafe along," Lisette said over her brother's whimpering. "Miss Channing, would you retrieve my reticule from my chambers? It is resting on my writing desk."

"Yes, ma'am." The governess hopped to the task as if grateful to be charged with doing something productive.

Lisette spoke soothingly to Rafe. "We shall travel to the docks now. We will see the black waters of the Thames, and the frigates, barques, and the schooners…"

Rafe assumed recitation of all the ships he knew, mumbling them as he continued to rock.

Monsieur Baptiste stepped forward. "The hack waited out front to see if I would be received. I have asked the driver to carry us to the docks."

Lisette turned to the gentleman with a grateful smile. "You are too kind, monsieur. Your assistance is appreciated."

He bowed. "I am your humble servant, Madame Hillary."

The governess returned with the reticule, Lisette placed Miss Fanchon's letter inside, and grasped Rafe's hand. "To the docks to see the *Cecily*." She sounded much more cheerful than she felt.

❧

Serafine held back as Isaac banged his fist against Monsieur Baptiste's door again. There was still no response. Where could he be at this hour?

She held Isaac's handkerchief over her nose and tried to breathe through her mouth. "What is that stench?" The piece of cloth muffled her voice.

"That is the smell of debauchery, sweetheart. Spirits, cigars, and—" His face flushed pink, and he tried the handle instead of finishing his thought. "Excellent. It appears to be unlocked."

"We cannot enter uninvited." Serafine breached the threshold rather than remain in the corridor despite her protest. The landlord hadn't exhibited any qualms about allowing them entrance to the lodging house, and likely wouldn't sound the alarm if they slipped into Monsieur Baptiste's rooms. From all appearances, the man turned a blind eye to many things.

"It does seem less disgusting inside," she said.

Isaac propelled her farther inside and closed the door behind them.

The space housed few pieces of furniture, and those items were functional at best. There was none of the luxury enjoyed at number 17 Curzon.

"I'm fully convinced after seeing these lodgings," she mused, "Captain Hillary holds no fondness for Monsieur Baptiste."

"I wonder where the gentleman has hied off to this early."

"Good question." She sighed. "I was anxious to speak with him at once this morning."

After reading the letter from Uncle Robert's solicitor last night, she had hoped Monsieur Baptiste might be able to provide her with additional clues to her brother's whereabouts. "If Xavier sent instructions to Monsieur Baptiste regarding the disbursement of Rafe's funds as the solicitor suggested, the missive might indicate where Xavier has gone. We would at least know where to search if he sent something from a different locale."

She meandered through the room, uncertain of the reason she felt the need to linger when no one was home. "Uncle Robert must have been out of his mind to entrust Xavier with Rafe's fortune."

Isaac's gaze followed her. "But your uncle left Monsieur Baptiste in charge of running the mill. He was wise in that instance. Any man with a twenty percent share of the profits will be invested in making it a successful venture."

"True." She continued her circle of the room. "Uncle Robert thought a lot of Monsieur Baptiste. The solicitor's letter said Uncle had even arranged for his estate to go to Monsieur Baptiste if anything happened to Rafe or Lisette and neither left any issue."

Isaac frowned. "Doesn't that strike you as odd?"

"I think it was a gesture of kindness on Uncle's part. Monsieur Baptiste is advanced in age. He'll never outlive Lisette or Rafe. Besides, my cousin will have issue."

The hairs on her arms stood on end and she hugged herself. "Isaac, have you ever had a strange feeling you couldn't shake?"

"Like what?"

"Like something isn't quite right. I can't explain it."

"If you mean there's something not right about Mr.

Baptiste, then I agree. I've never fully trusted him. Let's see what secrets he keeps in his bedchamber."

Isaac's boots knocked against the wood floor as he stalked toward the back room.

"Wait! What are you looking for? You've never said anything about distrusting Monsieur Baptiste."

"There was never cause to speak up."

She paused outside the bedchamber door and watched as he moved to the wardrobe. "Monsieur Baptiste would stand to gain much if your cousins died without issue," he said.

"He doesn't know the contents of the will. Otherwise, he would have had no reason to worry about Reynaud stealing Rafe's estate. As long as it remains in a trust, it's untouchable."

Serafine wandered to the wardrobe also and peered inside. "Monsieur Baptiste appears to own nothing more than the clothes on his back."

"He was taken from his home by force. I doubt Reynaud left him the option of packing for the journey."

"He was allowed a satchel, I believe, but point taken. There's nothing here."

Isaac went to the bed next and pulled down the covers to search between the folds.

Really, what did Isaac hope to find? A suspicious bed bug? "Perhaps under the mattress," she teased.

"Good idea."

She moved to the foot of the bed to allow Isaac access when he tossed the coverlet aside.

Stooping, he snaked a hand underneath before sweeping his arm side to side. "I feel something."

He pulled a bundle of papers from underneath the

mattress with a triumphant smile lighting his handsome face, but Serafine's heart had stopped beating. With his back to the door, Isaac couldn't see they were no longer alone.

Reynaud filled the doorway. "Greetings, Mademoiselle Vistoire."

"Monsieur Reynaud."

Isaac whipped around. "What are you doing here?"

Reynaud lunged for him, a flash of metal catching her eye, and she screamed. The sickening sound of Isaac's grunt resounded in her ears. Reynaud jerked the weapon from Isaac's middle and shoved him backwards. He landed on the floor at Serafine's feet. A crimson tide soaked through his waistcoat.

"Isaac!" Serafine crouched beside him and pressed his handkerchief against the wound.

"I'm all right, Sera."

By the saints, he wasn't all right. "We have to get you to a doctor." A sharp pain exploded in her skull as Reynaud yanked her to her feet by her hair and pressed the knife against her neck. The cold seeped through her skin and into her bones. A violent tremor shuddered through her.

"Tell me, mademoiselle," he whispered in her ear. "Is Baptiste in on your blackmailing scheme, or are you using his rooms to hide my letters?"

"Blackmail? I know nothing about blackmail."

Reynaud twisted her around to face him and gripped her shoulders. The glimpse of his knife from the corner of her eye made her legs tremble. "Don't lie to me, mademoiselle. It is early and I fear I'm not a morning person."

She had never known him to be an evening person either. Nor was he pleasant midday or afternoon, for that matter. "I—I'm not lying."

Isaac attempted to push up from the floor, but collapsed. "Release her." His voice was raspy and weak.

Dear Lord, she couldn't die like this, not with Isaac helpless to do anything. She drew in a deep breath, willing herself to stay calm.

"I'll tell you whatever you want to know, but please, allow Monsieur Tucker to seek aid for himself. He is bleeding."

Reynaud's gaze flicked in Isaac's direction and he paled. Closing his eyes, his throat worked convulsively and his grip on her shoulders loosened. Whatever was the matter with him?

His dark eyes flew open and fixed on her. "Forget about him. He can't stand. How is he to seek out aid?"

"Please."

Reynaud's lip curled. "You're in no position to barter."

The monster enjoyed his domination. Hatred rolled off him, and exhilaration.

Show him respect. Serafine cleared her throat, praying her instincts were correct. "Monsieur Reynaud, I would never have the courage to cross you. Only a fool would try to manipulate a man of exceptional intellect such as you."

She hoped his ability to ferret out insincerity was overshadowed by his raging arrogance.

His brows rose slightly. A sign of interest or skepticism? She couldn't tell.

"I—I have too much respect for you, sir. You are much too powerful."

He grinned, baring most of his teeth. "You would be a reckless young woman, to be certain, but Lisette doesn't have it in her. I questioned her many times. Subtly, of course. She knew nothing of my letters."

"Truly, monsieur, our wits are no match for yours. You would see through both of us if we dared to lie."

"Indeed." He nodded slowly as if considering the logic of her statement. "And you claim no knowledge of blackmail or my letters?"

Isaac panted, wincing as he held his side and tried to lift to his knees. He sank back to the floor with a pained groan.

Stay put, please.

Serafine forced her attention back to Reynaud. She needed to act quickly if there was any hope of helping Isaac. "Monsieur Tucker unearthed a packet the moment you arrived. You witnessed his discovery. We have no idea what it is he has found."

Reynaud's jaw hardened. "How did you know to search Baptiste's rooms?"

Her heart tripped. Would he believe her if she spoke the truth? "I had an uneasy feeling… about Monsieur Baptiste. I cannot explain it. I thought he might know something about my brother." She met Reynaud's cold gaze, pleading with him to believe her. "When we didn't find him at home, we sought clues to help me understand this feeling I have. There's something untoward about the gentleman."

"Tell me what made you suspicious of Monsieur Baptiste."

She swallowed hard and held tight to her belief she couldn't lose everything now that she had received everything she'd ever wanted. "I learned of the details contained in Uncle Lavigne's will this morning. Monsieur Baptiste inherits everything if Rafe and Lisette die. I'm uncertain what any of this has to do with you being blackmailed or the packet Isaac found."

"Intelligent, Mademoiselle Vistoire, a woman who doesn't ignore her animal instincts." Reynaud released her and she stumbled against the wall before catching herself. He strolled to Isaac's crumpled body, averting his eyes as he bent down to pick up the packet from the floor.

"The sight of blood bothers you?"

He shook his head slowly, looking green around the gills.

Oh, for heaven's sake! Serafine could have argued the point with him, but she didn't care. If he fainted from the sight, all the better.

She nodded toward Isaac. "How very red it is."

Reynaud didn't look in Isaac's direction again. Instead, he approached her slowly. "You've answered my questions remarkably well *and* discovered my letters, Mademoiselle Vistoire."

She steeled herself for the plunge of his knife, and jumped when he captured her by the shoulders again and kissed her left cheek then her right.

"My apologies for Mr. Tucker's injuries," he whispered in her ear. His hot breath on her skin chilled her to the bone. "You should seek help for him at once." Releasing her, Reynaud tucked the bundle under his arm. "I have a rendezvous I'm loath to miss, or I would offer my assistance."

He spun on his heel and stalked from the

bedchamber. Serafine's body quaked, and she would have collapsed to the floor except she didn't have time to swoon. Isaac needed her.

Thirty-two

"THE VOYAGE WON'T BE THE SAME WITHOUT YOU, Captain." Even though Patch sounded sincere, he grinned like a lad presented with a new toy.

Daniel assumed a severe frown as he handed his former first mate the logbook. "I expect you to bring her back in one piece, Captain Emerson."

"Yes, sir." Patch accepted the book and Daniel's congratulatory handshake. "You won't be disappointed."

The man had proven his competency many times over the years. It was a wise decision to turn the *Cecily* and her crew over to Patch.

Daniel would still need to travel to New Orleans at some point to complete the guardianship proceedings, but not now. And not without Lisette.

Last night, he had unintentionally fallen asleep onboard, and when he woke slumped over in his chair this morning, he had understood the true meaning of loss. He'd thought he had known grief when Cecily died, and he *had* mourned her. She was a young and capricious lady struck down before gaining the wisdom of adulthood.

But Daniel felt the loss of Lisette deep in his heart. She had become a part of him that gave him purpose and lent meaning to his existence. She had taught him to live. And how to love.

Now, when he looked around his quarters, he saw Lisette singly softly as she tidied his office. The balcony held sweet memories of shared kisses as the sun sank into the sea. Even Amelia's forgotten copy of Byron sitting on his shelves reminded him of nights with Lisette. She had read to him in their bed, and he'd changed the poems to nonsense just to hear her bewitching laughter.

Mad as a March hare. That was the only explanation he had to explain how he had thought he could sail away from her. Lisette *was* his life, and he must tell her at once.

"Excuse my abrupt exit, Captain Emerson, but I have a rendezvous I don't wish to miss."

"Aye, Captain. Until we meet again."

Daniel hurried from the great cabin and down the gangplank to the waiting carriage. How fortuitous it would be to discover his wife still in bed.

❧

Rafe's rocking ceased as the carriage rolled away from the town house, but he still recited the class of every ship in his repertoire.

Lisette glanced at the brooch watch pinned to her gown. She had no way of knowing the schedule of the tides, so it was pointless to consult the time, but her action was compulsive. Withdrawing into herself, she prepared for the coming confrontation with her husband.

She had no recourse, obviously, but Daniel would

be well acquainted with her opinions on the subject of adultery before she left ship. Her limbs trembled with unspoken indignation. He had lied to her, pretending to fear for her safety when all along he sought to keep her ignorant of his mistress.

"Wrong way," Rafe murmured. "Wrong way."

She patted his knee and tried to exude serenity she didn't feel. "Shh, we are going to the docks now. You shall see the *Cecily*."

Scooting closer and draping her arm around his shoulders, Lisette stared out the carriage window. She didn't wish to ruminate on Daniel's betrayal. There would be many months to come to torture herself without wearing herself down now.

"Wrong way." Rafe slowly began to rock again. "Wrong way. Wrong way."

Lisette glanced at the landscape outside and sat up straighter. She glanced across the carriage toward Monsieur Baptiste. "Why, I believe Rafe is correct. The driver appears to be going the wrong direction."

Monsieur Baptiste looked out the window and shrugged. "Surely, you're mistaken. We must be on course."

The sun was to their backs. There was no doubt the carriage was driving away from the docks. "We must travel east to reach the docks. Notify the driver to turn back, monsieur."

Rafe whimpered, his rocking becoming more pronounced.

Monsieur Baptiste smiled in a placating manner. "I'm certain the driver will turn in a moment, and you will see we are following the correct course."

As he predicted, the driver turned left at the next intersection and another turn corrected their direction. Lisette sank against the cushion with a sigh. Her husband's betrayal soon invaded her mind again. Immersed in her anger, she almost missed the carriage's change in course, but Rafe's high-pitched squeal alerted her.

"Monsieur Baptiste, something is amiss. The driver possesses no sense of direction. He seems to be taking us in circles."

"Nothing to be concerned about, dear girl."

His dismissal stoked her already ill-temper. "Monsieur, we must stop this carriage at once." She reached across the carriage to knock on the roof to signal the driver to stop.

Monsieur Baptiste shoved her back against the seat. "Do stop carrying on, Lisette. I don't know which of you is more trying, you or your idiot sibling."

"How dare you?"

Monsieur Baptiste rolled his eyes as he reached inside his jacket and withdrew a small firearm, pointing it at her and her brother.

Lisette gasped and drew Rafe against her bosom, wrapping her arms around him to shield him from harm. "I am not amused by your antics, sir. Put that away before you accidentally discharge it."

"I'm skilled with pistols, madame. You needn't worry my firearm would go off by *accident*." He yanked the curtains closed on his side of the carriage then motioned her to follow suit, but she refused to relinquish her brother. "I can only shoot one of you, Lisette. You decide which of you it shall be."

She pulled Rafe closer. "What are you about, monsieur? It is I, the daughter of your dearest friend."

He scoffed. "Very well. If you will not choose…" He aimed the gun at Rafe.

"No, please!" She threw herself in front of her brother, her arms out to the side.

Rafe's whimpers escalated into shrieks, and he pushed against her back.

Monsieur Baptiste leaned across the carriage and snatched her arm. "Close the curtains, or you will take a ball to the head. Then I shall strike Rafe with the smoking barrel."

Mon dieu. Who was this man? She had known him all her life, but he was a stranger. A sob caught in her throat. "Please, don't hurt Rafe. I will do whatever you ask of me."

"Then quiet the little bastard and close the damned curtains."

His insult slammed against her gut. "He is not a bastard," she snapped, unable to let the comment slide. He had a father who had loved and protected him once. Now it was Lisette's calling to keep him safe.

She snatched the curtains and jerked them closed then cradled Rafe against her side. She attempted to focus his attention on reciting ships again. "Baltimore flyer, galleon, frigate. You say them now, Rafe." His cries grew louder.

Please, please be silent. "Andromeda, Antila, Apus, Aquarius." Lisette murmured the constellations as best as she could recall in alphabetical order. "Come on, Rafe. Help me recite the constellations. Aquila, Ara, Aries, Auriga…"

Rafe's rocking slowed incrementally as she progressed through the constellations. Eventually, he took over, whispering the names to himself. "Delphinus, Dorado, Draco."

"Very good, Lisette." Monsieur Baptiste flashed a pleasant smile. "Now, pass me your reticule."

"You have kidnapped us to lift my reticule?"

He pointed the barrel at Rafe again. "Your questioning makes me weary."

"Fine. You may have it, but it clashes with your waistcoat." Lisette suppressed the urge to hurl her purse at him. She would not risk having the pistol fire in the confines of the carriage. At this range, he would not miss. "If it is money you seek, I can provide more if you allow us to go unharmed. Daniel has plenty. He will pay for Rafe's safety."

Monsieur Baptiste sneered. "You always were naive, Lisette, but your father preferred you that way. I judged him a dolt for believing naïveté was an asset. But I must say, it has worked to my advantage these past months."

Monsieur Baptiste placed the gun beside him on the bench and unclasped her reticule. Reaching into his jacket pocket, he extracted folded sheets of paper and stuffed them inside.

"What are you doing?"

"More questions. Perhaps you have never heard hell was fashioned for the inquisitive, madame." He threw her reticule across the carriage. It smacked against her chest, and she scrambled to keep it from tumbling to the floor.

Monsieur Baptiste shoved the pistol back inside his jacket as the carriage slowed to a crawl then stopped.

The door flung open.

"Greetings, my dear."

Her vision narrowed on the new arrival and a whirlpool of dizziness tried to suck her under.

"Reynaud." Lisette tucked Rafe tighter against her side, grasping at something to keep herself afloat. There was solace in togetherness, but her brother squirmed from her embrace with a small grunt of protest and retreated into himself. His vacant eyes stared through her. She wanted to shake him, demand he stay present.

Reynaud clambered inside the carriage and slammed the door. "I liked when you referred to me as Louis. No warm greeting, my dear? Perhaps a kiss upon my cheek?"

She would sooner kiss a toad. Lisette shrank away from him, and he laughed before assuming the seat across from her.

Monsieur Baptiste glowered. "Where have you been? We've been circling the block."

Reynaud waved off his concerns. "My jacket was soiled, and I required a fresh one for Mademoiselle Lavigne."

The carriage jerked forward to continue their journey.

Reynaud smiled as if this encounter was a social call. "You look as lovely as ever, my dear."

Her spine felt forged of metal. "It is Mrs. Hillary now. I am married, monsieur."

"*Oui.* How could I have forgotten?" His blue eyes darkened as he reached across the carriage to stroke her cheek with his finger.

She froze. Her breath, heartbeat, the blood in her veins paused.

"It was poor form running away in the middle of the night, Lisette. Your antics have vexed me a great deal." Reynaud's finger lingered against her skin. "So exquisite. I deeply regret having played the gentleman with you. I suspect your captain plowed you like a whore as soon as the opportunity presented. Pity. I would have treated you with a gentle hand."

Hatred writhed within her belly, but common sense stopped her from striking back. Instead, she appealed to Monsieur Baptiste, her father figure. "Monsieur, you helped us escape New Orleans. Please, tell me he has threatened your well-being. You cannot be his accomplice." She would latch on to any reason to explain his treachery. "What did he do to you on ship?"

"Nothing he didn't agree to undergo for the sake of appearances," Reynaud said. "The good captain wouldn't have allowed just anyone to board his ship, but a battered, helpless victim stood a chance at earning his trust. Add to the equation your fondness for monsieur and the odds were improved."

Reynaud dropped against his seat with a weary sigh. "Lisette, my dear, you have stumbled upon an important life lesson. One you shall never forget."

The smug gleam in Monsieur Baptiste's eyes startled her. Reynaud had not coerced him into assisting. The man she had grown to respect, the one who'd been her confidant, had willingly betrayed her.

"Why, monsieur?" she whispered.

"Profit, my dear," Reynaud said.

She had always believed Monsieur Baptiste was honorable. "You are both despicable. How did I not see your true natures from the start?"

Reynaud formed a peak with his fingers, his posture relaxed. "Allow me to enlighten you on the ways of men."

Oh, sweet Mary above! She'd had enough of his enlightening speeches during their betrothal.

"Men are not so different from the beasts of the land, Lisette. We are all predators of some sort, not in the same class, but all very dangerous. The biggest distinction is in how we are identified."

Her mouth filled with derisive words she wished to heap on him, and would have if not for Rafe's small frame curled against her side.

Reynaud's eyebrow lifted as if he knew she was insulting him in her mind. "When you stand in the presence of a lion, you prepare yourself for the deadly pounce. You know it's coming. The mighty cat knows it too. There are no pretenses between hunter and prey. You have no doubts you face an adversary, and you have the choice of fight or flight."

Lisette's gaze focused on Reynaud; her breath grew shallow in agitated anticipation. His hands dropped to his lap and she flinched.

"You comprehend my meaning, do you not?" He smiled as if pleased by her jumpiness. "Now, consider the duck-billed platypus. Such an odd creature, appearing to be half duck, half beaver. It waddles on short legs with webbed feet, so comical and disarming. A harmless appearing creature. Yet in reality, the male of the species is venomous. He has hidden spurs on his legs that release a substance that can incapacitate a human."

Monsieur Baptiste's mouth puckered as if he'd licked a lemon. "Please, spare us your inane mutterings of the animal kingdom."

Reynaud chuckled, but a fierce gleam sparked in his eye. "Monsieur does not like being compared to the platypus, but he is no lion. *He* uses deception to confuse his prey. His success depends on his ability to maintain his pretense long enough to strike. I, on the other hand, have might on my side."

"Enough of your blathering." Monsieur Baptiste swiped her reticule from the seat and shook it in Reynaud's direction. "She has your letters."

"He lies. Monsieur put them in my reticule moments before you joined us."

Reynaud opened the bag, reached inside, and extracted the folded sheets of foolscap. He frowned as he leafed through the letters. Holding one up, his lips quirked. "Miss Paulina Fanchon. My dear, why are you in possession of correspondence from a known paramour? Or did Monsieur Baptiste place this one in your reticule, too?"

She swallowed hard, shame forcing her eyes down. She and Rafe were in danger, but Lisette still experienced deep humiliation over her husband's activities. Daniel cavorted with a paramour. He set up house with her a world away.

"It's none of your concern. And I have no knowledge of the other letters."

"I see." Reynaud lifted the curtain to peer outside. "We have left the city, and we are clear to settle this matter as I should have done months ago."

He signaled the driver to stop the carriage.

Fear sliced through her heart. "What are you going to do? Please, Rafe needn't be involved."

"I intend to dispatch with my blackmailer once and for all," Reynaud said.

Monsieur Baptiste grinned, baring his teeth. "Splendid. You should deal with her brother at the same time."

"I believe Monsieur Baptiste wishes you dead, madame." Reynaud's eyes widened with surprise, but the hard glint there betrayed him. He was not amused nor caught unaware.

Thirty-three

ISAAC'S COMPLEXION HAD LOST COLOR, LEAVING HIM cold and pale as marble.

"Sera, go for help." His voice came out hoarse and gravelly.

When he had attempted to stand with Serafine's help a moment ago, his knees had buckled. She pushed from the floor, and with one more glance over her shoulder at Isaac, she dashed from the room.

In the corridor, she searched for someone, anyone who might offer assistance, but the area was deserted. She grasped the balustrade to steady her descent and galloped down the stairs. The morning light blinded her when she burst outside, and she stopped on the walkway to allow her eyes to adjust.

Down the block, a gentleman hobbled along the walkway, supporting his weight on his cane. He would be no help. Serafine intended to rush past him, but he stepped into her path.

"Egads! You are bleeding, miss. Allow me to assist you."

"My betrothed is injured above stairs. I must find a doctor."

The gentleman sucked in a sharp breath and took off in a half-hop walk toward the street away from her. Just as she had anticipated. He would not be any assistance.

Serafine spotted another gentleman preparing to climb into a carriage. Lifting her skirts, she ran to intercept him. "Monsieur! Monsieur, please wait."

The man turned to her with wide eyes then scrambled inside and slammed the door. The liveried footman barred her from approaching the carriage door. "Stand down, miss."

"Monsieur, please. My betrothed requires assistance. He needs a surgeon."

The gentleman peered out the window. "It's a ploy. Be watchful for her accomplices."

The servant placed a large hand in the middle of her chest and shoved. Serafine stumbled backward and lost her footing, but a pair of firm arms caught her from behind. She banged against an even firmer chest.

"Now, see here, Chester Newbury," an angry voice at her ear commanded. "I won't allow you to disrespect a lady. What is the meaning of this outrage?"

The gentleman in the carriage poked his head out the window. "Lord Ellis. The lady is with you?" Monsieur Newbury looked like a slap-cheeked boy, duly chastised for unbecoming behavior. "I thought she meant to distract me whilst a pickpocket liberated my blunt."

"For shame, Newbury. The lady is finely attired and obviously no threat."

Serafine struggled from the gentleman's hold and turned to face him. "Please, I need assistance, sir."

"Upon my honor!" Another gentleman approached from the coffeehouse at the far corner. It was Lord Westin. "Mademoiselle Vistoire, you're covered in blood. What has happened?"

"My lord!" She nearly leapt into his arms, she was so relieved to see a familiar face. "It's Monsieur Tucker. He has been stabbed. Please, I need your help."

"Where is he?" Lord Westin allowed Serafine to drag him along the walkway toward the building where Isaac lay injured. The elderly gentleman with the cane hobbled toward them, his cane clicking against the cobblestone street. "I have sent for a doctor. Where is your betrothed?"

Serafine pointed. "Above stairs."

Lords Westin and Ellis dashed inside and up the flight of stairs ahead of her. By the time she reached the back room, the gentlemen had moved Isaac to the bed. Lord Ellis pressed against his wound.

Isaac turned his head toward her and offered a weak smile. "Sera."

She rushed to his side to hold his hand. "The doctor is coming. You'll be fine." She didn't know if she spoke the truth, but if her sheer will could determine one's fate, Isaac would live to be a centenarian.

He squeezed her hand in response, but he was weak. "Madame Hillary should be warned."

"Good heavens, yes." Serafine had forgotten about her cousin with Isaac slipping through her fingers, but Lisette could be in danger.

Lord Westin knelt at her side. His intense blue eyes met hers. "Tell me what is wrong."

She briefly retold the story of Monsieur Baptiste's

interests and gains if Lisette and Rafe were dead, as
well as his hand in blackmailing Reynaud. "I don't
understand it all, but I know Monsieur Baptiste is a
threat to my family's well-being. And Captain Hillary
set sail this morning."

Lord Westin bolted from the floor and started
toward the door. "I'll carry word to her at once."

❧

Daniel trotted up the staircase leading to his wife's
chambers. He anticipated doing a fair amount of grov-
eling before Lisette forgave him. He would expect
nothing less of his proud wife, nor would he wish her
to be any different. It was her strength of conviction
that had appealed to him from the moment of their
first encounter in New Orleans. Fortunately, she
possessed a generosity of spirit as well, and he hoped
she would have compassion for him.

He knocked once on her chamber door before
barreling inside. The newest chambermaid squealed
in fright, clutching the counterpane to her chest and
upsetting the bed she had just made.

"Captain Hillary." The young girl curtsied like a new
filly adjusting to her gangly legs. "Sir, greetings, sir."

He grinned in an attempt to ease her discomfort. "I'm
seeking Mrs. Hillary. Do you know of her whereabouts?"

"No, sir. She had breakfast with Master Rafe this
morning. Perhaps she is upstairs."

Daniel left the maid to her work. A moment
later, he barged into the schoolroom and startled
Miss Channing. The space was empty aside from the
governess and her book.

"Pardon the intrusion. I'm looking for my wife. Have you seen her?"

Miss Channing stared at him, her eyes bulging. "They have gone to the docks to see you, sir. Mr. Baptiste accompanied them."

His grin widened. Lisette was on her way to convince him to stay. She should be pleased he made the decision without her applying pressure.

"Our carriages probably passed one another on the street. Thank you."

Bidding Miss Channing good day, he sauntered downstairs to his study to wait for Lisette's return. No sooner did he pour himself a brandy than there was a knock at his door.

"Enter." He took a swig from his snifter.

His butler opened the door a crack, and Daniel waved him inside. Ned approached him to speak discreetly. He didn't know why the man bothered with protocol after years under his employ, but it was for the best. Now that Daniel was becoming a respectable gent with a wife and family, he required respectable servants.

"'Tis Lord Westin requesting an audience with Mrs. Hillary. He says it is a matter of urgency."

Devil take it. Daniel hadn't been gone from home for a day and the dandies were already calling on Lisette. He hadn't expected it of Westin, though, the bloody scoundrel.

"Show him in."

A moment later, the marquess stalked into Daniel's study with a somber expression. "Hillary, I heard you'd left London."

"So I gathered." He flexed his fingers.

"Thank God Mademoiselle Vistoire was mistaken. I just left her."

Daniel's fist loosened. "Has something happened to Serafine?"

"She's unharmed, but I'm to warn your wife to steer clear of Mr. Baptiste. Miss Vistoire and Mr. Tucker had an encounter with a blackguard named Reynaud today. She believes he and Baptiste are conspiring together and wish to bring harm to your family."

All the air whooshed from Daniel's lungs. He couldn't breathe.

"Mr. Tucker is gravely wounded." Westin sounded far away, as if speaking from the opposite end of a tunnel. "Hillary, did you hear me? Good God, man. Are you going to faint like a chit?"

The marquess rushed forward to help support Daniel's weight.

A chit? Daniel pushed him away. "Don't be ridiculous. Let me be."

Westin stepped back.

"Southampton," Daniel mumbled. Reynaud would have docked in the closest port. If the *Mihos* had docked in London, Daniel would have known. He must go after her.

"What about Southampton?" Westin asked.

"Reynaud may have my wife and her brother. He'll try to leave England, but his ship will be in Southampton." With his bearings straight, he hurried from the study with Westin on his heels.

"Send for a horse from the mews immediately," Daniel commanded his butler and continued to the staircase.

"I'll accompany you," Westin said.

He rounded on the marquess. "This isn't your concern."

"Allow me to assist for Mademoiselle Vistoire's sake, if not your own." Westin opened one side of his jacket to reveal a holstered pistol. "I'm an excellent marksman."

What manner of man carried a firearm about Town? One who found danger invigorating. Westin would have been well suited for the life of a military man if not for the unfortunate condition of his birth.

"This isn't a fox hunt or raucous adventure. My family's life may be in jeopardy."

"I comprehend the gravity of the situation. Did I mention I am exceptionally skilled with firearms?"

Daniel sighed. He would be a fool to turn away the man's assistance. "Send for two horses," he called to his servant as he started up the stairs. "I must arm myself as well. Try to avoid shooting any of my staff while I'm gone, Westin."

The marquess chuckled. "As you wish."

Thirty-four

LISETTE'S MOUTH WAS AS DRY AS COTTON, AND HER thoughts weaved together into a jumbled mess. An unnatural calm had descended over Rafe, so that he sat beside her in silence, his unblinking eyes trained to the countryside out the window. There would be no escaping from Reynaud this time, no assistance from anyone. Could she reason with a lunatic?

She reached a hand toward him, forcing herself to use his given name. "I swear to you, Louis. I've never seen those letters before today."

Reynaud grasped her fingers and lifted them to his lips. Her skin crawled and she struggled with the urge to snatch her hand from his.

"Save your lies, Lisette," Monsieur Baptiste snapped. "Exit the carriage as you have been ordered to do."

Reynaud frowned at Monsieur Baptiste. "*Please*, exit the carriage. Have you abandoned all pretenses at civilization, sir? She remains a lady. Treat her as one."

Reynaud released her hand then bent forward to withdraw a knife from his boot. When he flicked his wrist in the direction of the door, a shaft of light glinted off the knife's blade. "Go on, my dear. I'm anxious to have this behind me so I may leave this godforsaken country."

Her immediate inclination was to stall, but their only possible route of escape would be outside the carriage. She nudged her brother. "Climb out, Rafe. It's all right. I will be behind you."

He did as she requested without protest. The dried grass under Lisette's boots crunched as she joined him on the side of the road. Rafe cuddled against her, hiding his face against the bodice of her gown. Her gaze darted around for a place to hide if they broke free.

The sound of water in the distance alerted her that the river was close. Rafe wasn't a strong swimmer, and Lisette wasn't strong enough to assist him, but the wooded area between the road and water might provide shelter.

The driver climbed from the box. "Whas the trouble? We ain't close ta the coachin' inn yet."

Reynaud had sheathed his knife, and he aimed a warning look at Lisette before offering a disarming smile to the driver. "My wife insists we are on the brink of losing a wheel. Apparently, her backside is more sensitive to shimmies than the average lady."

"Ye don't say." The driver leered at her, cackling at her expense. No telling what lewd thoughts crossed his mind at the mention of her backside.

You fool. She clamped her lips together and narrowed her eyes.

"It's the left front wheel," Reynaud said. "Perhaps we could check it to offer her peace of mind."

What trick was this? "Wait," she blurted. "I'm fine, really. Just a case of female hysteria. Silly of me."

Reynaud winked as if sharing a joke with the driver. "And she will have another fit of hysteria not a mile down the road if we don't check now." He guided the driver around the back of the carriage and out of sight.

"Nothin' 'pears amiss," the driver said.

The sounds of a scuffle carried on the air, followed by a low grunt. The driver landed in the lane with a loud thud.

Sweet Mary. Reynaud truly planned to kill them. Lisette eased Rafe farther away from the road.

"*Merde*," Monsieur Baptiste muttered and raked his fingers through his thin hair, his eyes bulging.

Reynaud rounded the carriage.

"What the hell are you thinking?" Monsieur Baptiste nearly screeched. "We can't leave a trail of bodies across England."

"The driver was a witness. I could either chase him down, risking injury to myself and frightening the man, or handle him as I did." Reynaud's lip curled as he advanced. "You knew I was a killer when you set everything into motion, Baptiste. I daresay you raised no protest when I rid you of Robert Lavigne."

Lisette gasped. Surely, she had misheard. "You had Papa killed?"

"No!" Monsieur Baptiste tugged his earlobe and backed up a step. "I—I had no hand in Robert's death."

Reynaud continued his advance. "So you say."

"For the love of God, I was in Boston."

Reynaud bared his teeth in a mockery of a smile.

"Quite right. Lavigne was the one with the audacity to blackmail me, nearly drained my coffers. *His* actions led to his demise."

A fierce protectiveness reared inside Lisette, giving her courage to speak out. "Papa would never do such a thing. He was a gentle and kind man, not a cowardly thief. Papa had no cause to extort money from anyone. The farm and mill are prosperous."

"Madame poses an excellent point," Reynaud said. "When I made inquiries into Lavigne's profits, his earnings were respectable, even at eighty percent ownership."

Monsieur Baptiste's gaze locked on Reynaud, and he retreated another step. "She's lying to cover up her involvement. You saw she had possession of your letters."

"Yes," he hissed, advancing on Baptiste. "And your task was to locate my property. You had ample time to search the ship and Captain Hillary's town house, and yet you brought me nothing until today. She must be a clever wench to have hidden them so well."

Lisette nudged Rafe toward the trees while the men were focused on each other. Reynaud brandished his knife, crouching low as if to pounce. "My letters were under your nose, Baptiste, or more aptly, under your arse. I found them hidden beneath your mattress."

Reynaud launched at him with a feral growl. Monsieur Baptiste fumbled with his coat.

Lisette shoved her brother. "Run!"

A loud crack rent the air, the sound of a gunshot echoing off the rolling hills.

Lifting her skirts, Lisette ran after Rafe. "Head for the trees."

Her brother entered the thicket at a full run and disappeared for a moment. Monsieur Baptiste had discharged his one shot, which meant she had a chance of mounting a defense if he had survived the encounter. But if Reynaud had survived…

She shuddered. She must find a safe place for Rafe to hide.

Inside the dense copse, she caught up to Rafe and spotted a tree lying on its side. Vines wove through the dead branches as if devouring the fallen giant, their copious teardrop leaves creating an additional visual barrier. She captured Rafe's hand and pulled him behind the brush.

"Get down," she whispered then crouched beside him. "You must stay hidden, no matter what happens."

His amber eyes turned up to her. "But I have to take care of you. The captain said."

Daniel. His name alone made her throat ache with unshed tears. The *Cecily* would be at sea. Lisette may never see her husband again. Hugging Rafe close, she placed a kiss on his dark hair. She couldn't think of Daniel now, not when her brother's life was in danger.

"You must stay hidden." The stubborn tightening of his jaw made her belly twist. "Rafe, please. Stay down. You cannot leave your hiding spot. That's the only way I'll be safe."

The tight lines around his mouth relaxed and he nodded slowly. "I will help you."

Lisette released a relieved breath. "Yes, stay put and help me."

She stood and searched the area for a weapon. Fallen limbs covered the ground of the wooded sanctuary, and she lifted one to test its weight. Rotted on the inside, it crumbled when she knocked it against the tree trunk.

"Lisette," Baptiste yelled out. "Rafe. Come out of hiding, children."

She discarded the useless club and snatched another. The bark fell away, exposing smooth, hard wood underneath. Her fingers gripped it firmly.

"Stay here no matter what." She dashed through the trees to lead their pursuer away from her brother.

Branches snapped as she tromped on them, giving away her location.

"Damnation!" Baptiste shouted and ran her direction. He was old and moved clumsily. Lisette had a substantial lead, and she felt certain he hadn't seen her yet.

Locating a fat tree, she took up post behind it and lifted the branch above her head in preparation for attack. Every sound was amplified as she awaited his approach: the rush of water behind her, the call of a raven, the sharp snap of a twig.

"There are few places to hide, children." He was still several paces away. "I shan't hurt you."

Ha! She would hardly consider him a reliable bet.

"Reynaud will no longer hurt you. I've taken care of him. Now, please come out of hiding." Every time he spoke, he gave up his position.

Lisette's arms ached and burned with the effort of holding the limb aloft, but she couldn't lower it. Not now. Not without gaining his notice. The crack of a stick sounded close. Streams of sweat flowed down her face and stung her eyes. Her chest rose and fell in jerky starts and stops, her breathing surely loud enough to announce her location.

"Where are you, Lisette?" Baptiste's elongated shadow projected on the leafy floor.

She waited, trying to judge when he was close enough to strike. Each footfall contained an eternity in between before the tip of the knife surged into view.

Followed by the blade.

Then the hilt.

His wrist.

Lisette swung the limb downward with a guttural cry and with every ounce of hate inside her for her father's murderer. Baptiste's agonized wail filled the air. The knife dropped to the ground and slid along the hard-packed earth.

Lisette drew the club back and whipped it through the air to bang into his chest. Baptiste toppled backward and landed with a grunt. She scrambled to reach the knife, but he kicked out a leg and entangled her. She stumbled, falling forward. When she connected with the ground, a searing pain shot through her belly and all the breath rushed from her lungs. She gulped several times, struggling to draw a decent breath.

His hand clamped onto her leg. He dragged her toward him. Lisette clawed at the dirt, but she had nothing with which to gain purchase. Her fingers left paths in the debris. Grabbing her shoulder, he forced her onto her back.

"No!" She drew her knee up and shot out her heel, smashing into his chin. The blow snapped his head back. Another wild kick connected with his cheek and knocked him to his back. She rolled out of his reach and pushed to her feet.

Horses' hooves sounded in the distance, too far away to assist her. She cried out anyway. "Help! Help us!"

Her foot slid in the leaves when she bent to snag the knife. Regaining her balance, she ran toward the river. Baptiste was slower, but his strength could overpower her. She must get rid of the weapon before he used it on her.

The riders were closer. "Someone, please! Help!"

The grass grew tall closer to the water and slowed her strides. Her skirts tangled in branches. Burrs coated the fabric, scratching her legs.

"Get back here, you bitch." Baptiste barreled through the undergrowth, bearing down on her. She pulled back her arm and hurled the knife into the midnight waters. A force slammed her from behind and knocked her to the ground.

Baptiste sat his full weight on her back, crushing her against the earth.

Lisette pushed with her arms and struggled. A length of cloth went around her neck. He twisted and tugged. Throwing her head back, she connected with his nose.

"Damn you!"

He loosened his grip and she clawed at the sash, looping her fingers inside to purchase breathing space.

Thwack!

The dreadful squeezing released, and Baptiste's weight shifted off her. Lisette gasped, each inhalation a sharp stab.

"Lisette?" Rafe knelt beside her. "I took care of you like the captain said."

Panicked, she turned her head to find Baptiste lying in a heap next to her.

Lisette crawled away, trying to regain her breath. She looked once more at Baptiste. His chest rose and fell with steady regularity. "We have to go quickly before he wakes." Her voice was no louder than a whisper.

She struggled to her feet.

Rafe took her hand and pulled her away from the river. "Do you think Captain Hillary will buy me a cricket bat?"

"To—to play cricket?"

He wrinkled his brow as if she'd grown noddy.

"Lisette!" a voice called from the distance.

Her heart leapt.

"Lisette! Rafe! Where are you?" The urgent call came from the direction of the road as they moved out of the tall grass.

"Daniel." Her voice was too soft.

"Over here, Captain," Rafe bellowed. "We are here."

Her husband appeared inside the tree line, breaking into a run when he saw them. "Lisette!" Upon reaching them, Daniel swept her against him. She cried out in pain.

"Darling, you're hurt." He held her at arm's length, his expression a twisted mask of horror and fury. "Did Baptiste do this to you? Where is he?"

Another gentleman came up behind Daniel. It was Lord Westin.

"He is sleeping by the river," Rafe said and pointed.

"Please, allow me." Lord Westin took off for the water's edge.

Rafe tugged Daniel's hand to gain his attention. "I took care of Lisette just like you told me to."

Daniel patted his head, his blue eyes misty. "You did a fine job, son." Gently touching Lisette's forehead, he grimaced. "I never should have left, Lis. I failed you."

Hurt welled up in her chest as Paulina's letter came back to mind. "You failed me greatly."

His stricken expression should have given her satisfaction, but instead she felt more alone than ever.

Thirty-five

Daniel's shoulders heaved with a defeated sigh when Lisette turned away from his embrace.

She held her head high as she limped to the carriage, but a shudder passed through her when she glanced to where Reynaud lay in the lane.

"You need to be seen by a doctor," Daniel called after her. She climbed into the carriage without responding. He had let her down, broken his vow to protect her. His loving wife could have died because of his failure.

She could have died. The realization hit him like a fist to the gut. Daniel bent at the waist, his hands braced against his knees as he gulped in a great lungful of air.

But she's safe. Lisette is safe. The dizziness began to recede and Daniel straightened. He couldn't allow himself to be crippled by the "what if." Lisette was safe.

Rafe's small fingers wrapped around Daniel's larger hand and held tight, providing comfort but also driving home the fact of how fragile his family was. He would never leave them again.

"We should go home so you can see my galleon," Rafe said.

Daniel looked down into his innocent eyes. "First-rate suggestion. I look forward to it."

They walked hand in hand to the carriage then Daniel lifted him inside. Rafe stretched out on the bench across from Lisette with a yawn. He had been exceptionally brave today, but bravery appeared to have taken its toll.

Bruises were already forming beneath Lisette's skin. Daniel reached out to brush his fingers over the hollow of her delicate collarbone, but she scooted out of his reach and looked away.

The crunch of dried grass made him turn. Westin returned, supporting Baptiste's weight as he wobbled. White-hot hatred surged through Daniel as he closed the carriage door and stalked toward Baptiste, ready to beat him bloody.

Westin caught the bugger as he pitched to the left and kept him on his feet. "Whoa, steady there. We don't want anything happening to you before the hangman gets his noose around your neck."

Baptiste turned blurry eyes on Westin. "Does *he* have my umbrella?"

Daniel came up short. *Umbrella?*

"I told you twice already you have no need for an umbrella today."

Baptiste frowned. "Very well then. I *will* have a cup of tea, thank you."

The marquess shrugged as they neared Daniel. "A blow to the head has addled his brain. Time should clear his mind. He should know what he has done when he receives punishment, wouldn't you agree?"

Daniel's fists loosened and he dropped his hands at his sides. Westin was right of course. The courts would have to dole out vengeance on Daniel's behalf. It was time to take his family home.

"I think I can escort this piece of refuse to the authorities with no trouble," Westin said. "Do you have any rope?"

"Are you suggesting you don't carry any on your person? Shocking, considering you carry a concealed firearm."

Westin grinned. "I left the town house in a hurry this morning."

"Perhaps your cravat will work."

Baptiste weaved when the marquess released him to remove his cravat, but he showed no inclination toward fleeing. Westin secured his hands and, with Daniel's assistance, draped him head first over the back of Daniel's horse.

"Move and you will fall and break your neck," Daniel growled, not that he would mind, but Westin was correct. Baptiste should be aware of the consequences of his actions.

Westin secured Daniel's stallion to his own horse then mounted. "I'm certain you will want to summon a doctor to tend your wife, so I'll deliver this blackguard to the authorities then collect the undertaker."

"Your assistance is much appreciated, Westin."

"My pleasure. Please give my regards to Mademoiselle Vistoire." His expression hardened. "If you had seen what she witnessed today… Tell her if her betrothed has need of anything, I am at her disposal."

Daniel offered a sharp nod out of politeness. Never again would he leave his family's well-being up to another man, and he considered Serafine to be as much a part of his kin as his wife and Rafe.

"I should be off then." Westin flashed a mischievous grin before urging the horses into a trot. Baptiste groaned with each bounce. Served him right. Daniel wished as much distress and pain on him as he had brought to Lisette and Rafe today.

Devil take it! More pain.

Daniel walked back to the carriage, checked on Lisette and Rafe once more then climbed onto the box to drive back to London. Every moment on the rutted lane, he thought of Lisette's battered body and spirits. He couldn't stand how far away she was. He needed to see her to reassure himself.

He veered the carriage off the lane, pulled firmly on the reins to stop the team, and set the brake. Hurrying from the driver's seat, he jerked the door open. Lisette recoiled with a soft squeak. Her hand covered her heart.

"Gads, I didn't mean to frighten you. Forgive me, darling."

Rafe lay curled in a ball on the opposite seat, deep in slumber already.

Lisette eyed Daniel with wariness, waiting.

"You were right yesterday, Lis. Separation from the one you love is unbearable."

She gawked as if he had sprouted roses from his arse. "And just who is it you love, Daniel?"

His smile was instantaneous, a result of surprise and amusement. "Why you, you dotty girl. Who else?" He held his hand out. "Come sit beside me on the box. I do so enjoy your company, and I can't bear another minute apart."

She nailed him with a scathing glare. "Better than the company of a certain paramour?"

His smile faded. Good God, had one of his past indiscretions presented at the town house? It was hard to comprehend anyone doing so, but his wife's lips quivered and her eyes were watery. She wasn't engaging in unbridled speculation.

His gaze traveled to Rafe then back to Lisette. "I'll tell you whatever you wish to know, but not in here."

She studied him, her eyes narrowed and mouth pinched. It seemed at first she wouldn't accommodate his request, but she scooted her bottom on the bench and curled her fingers around the door frame to climb from the carriage without his assistance. She wouldn't even deign to touch him.

"I would have helped you."

She brushed by him without a word, stalked to the side of the lane, and spun to face him. Her arms crossed under her breasts, plumping them to the point of distraction. Daniel shook himself mentally. She already judged him a lecher, not that he faulted her.

For the last five years, he had lived the life of a rake, caring for no one, seeking solace in pleasures of the flesh. He had finally found peace with Lisette, but even that seemed tenuous now. Would she hold his past indulgences against him just when he had found his way?

"Lisette, I warned you of my history when we

arrived in London. I feared you would hear tales and not understand, but you promised you wouldn't pay attention to gossip."

"This is not idle gossip, and you know it."

No, he didn't know. He had no idea what had been said to her or by whom, nor did he wish to speculate.

"I never meant for my actions to encroach upon our marriage. I apologize."

Her face flushed a deep red. "What the bloody hell"—her hands jabbed the air for emphasis—"does that *mean*?"

He flinched. Egads, he had taught her some unbecoming language for a lady.

She marched to him, stood toe to toe, and glared up. "So, you never wished me to know of your depraved activities. Does that make everything better?"

"Of course not, and yes, I would have liked to have kept that part of my life a secret. It doesn't do me proud."

"Then why?" Pain clouded her green eyes, but she didn't look away. "Why debase yourself in such a manner? Do you love her so very much?"

Love her? Surely, his wife wasn't that naive. "Love has nothing to do with it. Surely, you understand the difference."

"You speak of lust."

He nodded. Lust was as good as any word.

Lisette's hands landed on her hips. "And does she know you do not return her love, or is she as foolish as I am?"

Daniel blinked. "Return her love—Who, in God's name, are you referring to?"

Her chin jutted forward. "Paulina Fanchon, you *imbécile*. How many more women are you bedding?"

"No one else."

"Just her. Oh, well. Pardon me. What a world of difference that makes." Lisette stormed for the carriage.

"Wait! That wasn't my meaning." She didn't slow her step. "Come back here. We're not finished talking. How do you know of Paulina?"

She climbed inside the carriage but then nearly tumbled to the ground scurrying back down the steps. She waved a piece of foolscap in her hands. "I found her letter."

Devil take it. He had forgotten about Paulina's correspondence. She meant nothing to him so he'd assigned her letter to the bottom of his priorities. "I see you found her letter in *my* desk."

Lisette neared him and shook the paper in his face. "Yes, I read all about your plans to reunite in New Orleans, and the house. How she has created a home for you. She is like your wife on the other side of the world. How many more of us are there?"

Daniel shook his head. Good Lord, if he ever survived this scolding he would never do anything to deserve another. "You're the only wife I have, Lisette, and you're the only woman in my life."

She shook the letter in his face again and he snatched it from her. "I had no idea what Paulina had written. I never read it. Perhaps you noticed when you were pilfering through my desk her correspondence remained unopened. Did you ever stop to consider the reason?"

She opened her mouth as if to speak but halted.

"You didn't, did you?" He took a step closer and she backed away. "Let me ask you one more thing, luv. If I wanted to be with her, why am I here? The *Cecily* sailed without me this morning."

A flicker of emotions played upon his wife's face. Her gaze shot to the carriage then back at him.

"Oh, no you don't." He captured her around the waist before she ran again. "I tossed her letter aside without any thought, because I care nothing for her. Even before you and I met in the tavern, I had ended our association and never desired to see her again. The house was severance. I felt I owed her that at least. And I did not leave this morning because I couldn't abide being away from you. So if you think I could ever love anyone besides you... Well, then you are the *imbécile*."

"Oh!" Her breath quickened and a rosy flush colored her cheeks.

"I love *you*," he murmured, pulling her tighter into his embrace and burying his face against the soft skin of her neck. "No one else, Lis. You are my life, sweetheart."

She softened in his arms.

Daniel smiled, pleased to have derailed her rant, but even happier to have spoken his heart. "I should have told you yesterday. Hell, I should have told you before we ever arrived in London. I love you."

"Oh, Daniel." She tilted her face up, her eyes shiny with tears. "I love you, too."

He leaned down to kiss her. Her soft lips contained forgiveness, certainty, and promise.

She wrapped her arms around his waist and

snuggled into his embrace. Daniel rested his cheek against her luxurious hair. "I have only ever loved you. I was foolish to think I had known what love was before I met you."

Lisette turned her head and placed a kiss over his heart, nearly launching it from his chest.

"You should take me home now, Daniel."

"With pleasure."

Thirty-six

LISETTE LOUNGED AGAINST THE SMOOTH COPPER TUB and closed her eyes. The warm, scented bathwater enveloped her sore muscles. In two days' time, her body had begun to heal, but the memory of Monsieur Baptiste's betrayal might never go away completely.

Another runner had come by the town house to ask her a few final questions this morning and returned later in the afternoon to report the conclusion of the inquiry. After reviewing the packet of letters on Reynaud and conducting multiple interviews, the authorities had pieced together what they believed occurred.

Monsieur Baptiste was a murderer.

The man her father had trusted and given so much over the years had arranged for her father's death. He had been blackmailing Reynaud and made Papa appear responsible as Reynaud drew close to discovering his blackmailer's identity. Baptiste had made certain Reynaud received the name of his blackmailer while he was away in Boston. The New Orleans authorities had never considered Monsieur Baptiste a suspect in Papa's murder, but he was as guilty in Lisette's eyes as if he had drawn her father's blood instead of Reynaud.

Monsieur Baptiste had stolen money from a vicious killer, a traitor to his country who had amassed a fortune selling secrets to the British during the war. According to Daniel, who had read Reynaud's letters, the pages were filled with information about secret meetings, information sought, and the monetary reward for Reynaud's success.

How Baptiste had come to be in possession of Reynaud's correspondence remained a mystery, but it didn't matter to Lisette. His treachery had killed her father, and then he had sought to kill her and Rafe. Baptiste was as evil as Reynaud, maybe even more so, because he had hidden his true intentions while pretending to care.

The door to Lisette's bedchamber softly clicked beyond the dressing room, bringing her lady's maid to attention. Henrietta moved to intercept the interloper, but Daniel appeared in the doorway. Lisette's maid froze in place.

"You may go, Henrietta," Daniel said with a soft smile for Lisette. "I will assist my wife with her bath."

"Yes, sir." The poor girl twittered and bumped into the tub in her haste to escape, almost toppling into the water with Lisette. Henrietta closed the door on her way out.

Lisette couldn't suppress her smile. "You embarrassed her, but I'm glad you are here. What word do you have of Isaac Tucker's condition this evening?"

Daniel removed his jacket and waistcoat, tossed

them over the ivory tufted chair in front of her dressing table, and crouched beside the tub.

"There's still no sign of infection. He's a lucky gent." Grabbing the cloth draped over the tub, he stretched for the bar of jasmine soap sitting in a dainty mother-of-pearl dish on a side table. Daniel dipped the soap into the bathwater and rubbed it into the cloth to create a lather.

He had arranged for two of his men to move Monsieur Tucker to Curzon Street as soon as the doctor had deemed him stable enough.

Daniel frowned. "Serafine remains by his bedside. I believe she's sleeping in his room."

"They are to be married. Besides, who am I to pass judgment? I slept in your bed when you required tending."

"Still, I should arrange for the crying of the banns this Sunday before anyone notices something is amiss. Lean forward, darling, and I shall tend *you*." She did as he requested, and Daniel smoothed the cloth over her back, his touch gentle and soothing. His loving caresses washed away her tension and cleansed her mind of distressing thoughts.

"Are you still sore?"

"Only slightly. I hardly notice." She understated her condition for fear of his reaction. He had sent for the doctor upon their return the other day then questioned the man relentlessly until Lisette began to pity the poor doctor. She wouldn't relish a repeat performance of *The Browbeating of Doctor Cassian*.

Daniel glided the cloth down her arm and back to her shoulder again before trailing up her neck. She rested with her eyes closed, reveling in his touch. He repeated the same action in reverse on her other side before moving to her chest. His breath came out in a low hiss as he skimmed the cotton square across the tips of her breasts and over her stomach. Tingles traveled through her body, feeding her desire for more.

She opened one eye and peeked at him. "Your sleeve will become wet. Perhaps you should remove your shirt."

A corner of his mouth lifted and his dimple dented his cheek. "I'm here to take care of you, luv, not to seduce you."

"Pity." She drew back her hand with a wicked grin and splashed him, saturating his linen shirt.

Daniel's smile widened. "Behave yourself, vixen."

"I don't wish to behave." She made to splash him again, but he captured her wrist.

"You are positively dreadful this evening, Mrs. Hillary. Whatever shall I do with you?"

Lisette grasped the front of his shirt and pulled him closer until his lips lingered a whisper away from hers. "You know very well what to do with me, Captain."

She kissed him as her fingers twisted into the wet fabric of his shirt. Slipping her tongue into the welcoming warmth of his brandy-tinted mouth, she sighed. This was what she had yearned for all day.

Daniel turned his head, breaking the kiss, and pushed to his feet. "I'll collect a towel."

Disappointment made her sink lower in the water. He hadn't touched her since their return home and exhibited no inclination to do so now either.

Snatching the folded towel from her dressing

room chair, he draped it over one arm and offered her a hand up. Lisette accepted his assistance, trying not to grimace as her stiff legs and back screamed their disapproval.

The worried crease between his brows returned. "You are more than a little tender, luv."

Daniel wrapped the towel around her body as if she might shatter from the slightest touch. Although his concern was sweet, his sensitivity was interfering with her desire. She wanted her husband to bed her, not treat her like a newborn babe.

She hugged the towel close to her body. "I'm as fit as ever."

"You're not as fit as ever." Daniel slipped a stray tendril of hair behind her ear. "Therefore, I shall have to take extra care when making love to you."

"Oh!"

Daniel chuckled. "Surely, you didn't think I had the wherewithal to resist you."

"But you haven't touched me in days."

"I thought it best to practice restraint until you had time to recover, but it has been killing me."

As gently as possible, Daniel scooped Lisette under her knees and lifted. The ease with which he held her in his arms sent a shiver down his spine. His wife felt so fragile, yet she had shown great strength of spirit in her encounter with Baptiste. Perhaps Lisette was fashioned of sterner elements than Daniel had imagined, but he would still treat her with care.

Carrying her to the bed, he placed her on the

counterpane and removed his shirt. Her eyes darkened to that of a lush forest as her gaze roved from chest to waistband then back to his face. She gave him an appreciative smile. Daniel groaned deep in his chest. Lisette's blatant admiration served as a potent aphrodisiac.

Her heavy eyelids lowered to half-mast, giving her an air of seduction. "Remove your trousers." Her voice was smoky with desire, and her confidence stoked the slow-burning fire in his lower belly.

He kicked off his boots and unfastened the front fall of his pants. Reaching for the towel wound around her, he unwrapped her like a gift and rained kisses on her bronzed skin—neck, shoulders, collarbone, breasts.

"*Oui.*" She twined her fingers in his hair and held him against her bosom.

Daniel chuckled then blew on her nipple, not giving her what she wanted yet. A tremor coursed through her body, and she released him.

"Please hurry."

He moved with speed to lose his trousers then climbed on the bed beside her. When she rolled toward him, he caught her under the arms and hauled her to perch atop him.

Her eyes flew open. "What are you about?"

"Shh." His fingers feathered over her breasts with nipples the color of ground ginger. Lisette sighed, wiggled until his shaft nestled against her bottom, and sighed again.

Daniel's chest rose and fell with each labored breath as he fought to gain control of his lust. He wished to take time making love to his wife, demonstrating his adoration, not devouring her in a matter of minutes. But she was making it damned hard to control his urges.

Caressing her back, Daniel coaxed her to lean forward and took her nipple into his mouth. Lisette dissolved against him, threading her fingers with his hair. She kneaded his scalp and arched her back like a contented feline as he lavished her breast with the attention she enjoyed. Grinding her hips against his lower belly, soft moans fell from her lips and shattered his control.

"Come here, Lis." He adjusted her position, sucking in a sharp breath when his shaft slid inside her. Lisette held still, her body hugging him tightly. Her mouth sought his, and she kissed him with such tenderness, he thought he might burst.

"I love you," she whispered, her sweet breath fanning across his lips.

His heart felt light. He grasped the back of her head to kiss her deeply, expressing his affection in ways words failed. When she finally broke the kiss, she didn't pull away. They lay there lip to lip, breathing life into one another. Everything that was Lisette, her essence, flowed into him. And all that composed him, he gave freely to her.

"I love you, sweetheart."

He kissed her again and rolled her beneath him, slowly sinking into her. Lisette welcomed him, held him securely. Rising above her, he delved deep again, luxuriating in the warm glow surrounding them. Her arms clutched at his back, urging him closer. He met her clear gaze and held it as he reveled in their partnership. She had been correct all along. He needed her as much as she needed him. With Lisette, he had become a whole person again.

A wave of passion flooded over them, leaving them quaking. Lisette grasped at his shoulders; her movements grew frenzied. Daniel rolled to bring her on top again, handing control over to her. Not only control of their lovemaking, but of his heart.

Lisette accepted his invitation and cried out two heartbeats before him. But then he too reached the pinnacle of ecstasy and hovered there a breathless moment before tipping over the edge to fall back to earth.

Back to his home.

Back to his wife's loving embrace.

Lisette melted against him, and he shifted her to his side to cuddle her. She lay entwined with his limbs a long time, her steady breaths flowing over his neck. He caressed her from rounded hip to her tapered waist, savoring her softness.

"Lis, how do you feel about me becoming Rafe's guardian? If you don't lend your support, I will withdraw the petition immediately."

Her fingers forged a lazy path over his chest. "I have no concerns about Rafe becoming your ward, but if you think you are leaving me alone in London, you're mistaken."

Daniel kissed her temple. "Never again."

She lifted to her elbow and eyed him with arched brows. "And what of your proclamation of no ladies onboard the *Cecily*?"

He shrugged one shoulder. "I'm afraid there's nothing to be done for it. I can't change the *Cecily*'s rules."

Fire ignited in her eyes. "And why not?"

"Captain Emerson makes the rules. Now, the *Rafaela* has an entirely different set of standards."

"The *Rafaela*?"

"Did I forget to inform you?" Daniel laughed when she scowled at him. "I've purchased another ship ripe for creating new memories."

"Daniel." She caressed his cheek, her expression softening and making her more beautiful than he had ever seen her. "You named the ship for Rafe?"

He smiled, pleased by her reaction. "Perhaps he will captain it someday."

"That is the kindest, most generous act." She placed a kiss on his cheek. "So tell me of these new standards? Will the *Rafaela* allow passengers of the fairer gender?"

"Only the ones willing to share my bed."

She pulled a mock frown. "I believe I made it clear I don't share my husband."

"How convenient for me." He hugged her close. "For I don't wish to be shared."

Miss Hillary SCHOOLS *a* SCOUNDREL

London, England
May 26, 1816

TWO TYPES OF MEN CROWDED THE ELDRIDGE BALLROOM this evening: the dashing gentlemen whose ardent, but proper, pursuit any debutante would welcome. And *then* there were the ones who pursued Lana Hillary.

While the pretty ladies, like the shy Miss Catherine Mitchell and her intimate circle of acquaintants, captured the hearts of the handsome Lord Gilfords of Town, Lana hid behind a potted fern, hoping the desperate Lord Carrington and those of his ilk didn't spot her without the protection of her brother.

How long did it take Jake to collect two glasses of punch?

Drat!

Carrington's black gaze locked on Lana. With a satisfied smirk accentuating the viscount's droopy jowls, he came straight toward her, jostling past the elegant guests awaiting the first dance. Lana's less than subtle discouragement last evening had obviously failed.

Where *was* her blasted brother when she needed him? A quick perusal of the crowded ballroom proved futile.

Carrington stalked in her direction, a destitute predator in expensive evening dress. Rumor had it duns circled the viscount's property like merry children around a Maypole, ready to seize the last of the small luxuries left to him. He was desperate. Determined. But then so was she. Lana would never consent to become the third Lady Carrington given marriage to the lout transformed the sweetest of debutantes into empty vessels with no will to live.

He shouldered his way through the crowd, coming closer. Dread washed over her. If word of his interest reached her mother… Lana shuddered. Why, Mama would wrap her in gilded paper with bows and have her delivered to the viscount's doorstep posthaste. Nothing would thrill Mama more than hoisting her off on *any* gent. A title would simply be the icing on the wedding cake.

Dashing into the crush to evade the gentleman, Lana threw a hurried glance over her shoulder. Carrington followed, proving as skilled at tracking as the bloodhound he resembled. She reached the perimeter of the room only to realize she had nowhere to go.

Carrington flashed his rotting teeth in a triumphant leer. He had her where he wished, trapped between a wall of French doors opening to the terrace, a completely unacceptable alternative, and a doorway leading to the inner maze of the house.

Heaven help her. On impulse, Lana darted into the deserted corridor moments before Carrington reached her. She would hide in the retiring room.

The first bars of a country dance floated from the ballroom and faded as she made her escape. Lamps mounted on the damask walls spilled pools of light on the polished wood floor. Staying to the shadows as best she could, she glided down the wide passage past gilt-framed landscapes she had no time to admire. She didn't slow her pace until she rounded the first corner.

Lana released an elated breath. She had done it, thought quickly, and orchestrated her own rescue. She smiled as she continued to the retiring room, a newly acquired bounce to her step. Who needed Jake, or any of her older brothers for that matter? She could handle the odious viscount without their assistance, thank you very much.

"Miss Hillary?" Carrington's voice rang out in the empty corridor.

She wheeled around with a gasp. *Oh, blast it all!* He followed?

"Miss Hillary, did you come this way? I desire an audience." He sounded closer and winded, as if he hurried after her.

Lana would rather die than be discovered alone with him. Abandoning all regard for etiquette, she ran. The whisk of her slippers grew silent as she reached the thick Turkish carpets lining the corridor.

"Miss Hillary." He sounded exasperated and much too close. She would never reach the retiring room in time.

Would the blackguard truly ruin her reputation to acquire what he wanted?

"Miss Hillary, I *demand* you wait."

What had she been thinking to leave the ballroom?

If caught in his presence without a chaperone, Carrington could demand anything once her parents forced them to marry. A shiver of revulsion shook her frame. Well, she'd not let that happen.

Lana tried the next door she came to and, finding it unlocked, slipped inside before closing it again with an almost imperceptible click. Leaning her ear against the solid oak surface, she listened for evidence of the blackguard dashing past. Minutes ticked on a clock from somewhere in the darkened room, but there was only silence from the corridor. No imperious demands, heavy footfalls, or arduous wheezing. Where was the pudding head? He should have passed the room by now.

She pressed her ear closer to the door and strained to hear any little sound. Only the thundering of her heart filled the silence. Had he abandoned his pursuit? Lana wilted against the door with a relieved sigh.

What a narrow escape. She would never do anything so foolish again. And this time she meant it. Lana brushed a hand over her skirts to set herself to rights. She really should return to the ballroom before she stumbled upon more trouble. Lana reached for the handle as a bump shook the door. She scurried backwards, banged her hip on a corner of a sturdy chest, and uttered a soft cry of surprise.

Carrington was still out there.

If any member of the *ton* discovered her and the viscount in a darkened room, her mama would *kill* her first and then force her marriage to the man.

Frantic, Lana searched for an alternate exit. *The window.*

She ran across the room, lifted the lower sash, and poked her head outside. A glow from the lanterns lining the garden pathway provided enough light to assess her situation. The second story definitely presented an obstacle, but not an impossible one. Lana eyed the rose-laden trellis, looking for footholds.

Double drat!

The thorns would rip her to shreds.

Dismissing the trellis, she contemplated a maple tree growing close to the house. If she sat on the ledge and stretched, she could reach one of the sturdier branches. Climbing trees proved easy for Lana, a lesson she'd learned as a girl with four older brothers happy to teach her. Scaling a tree in a ball gown, however, was a feat she'd never undertaken.

She glanced between the door and window. For a long time, nothing but the constant whirring of crickets on the balmy evening air filled the silence and diminished her fears.

Now who's the pudding head?

She studied the long drop to the ground. Had she really considered such a foolhardy plan? Her parents would have her carted to Bedlam if they knew, which sounded surprisingly more appealing than marriage to the bloodhound.

Lana twittered nervously. She really should return to the ball before her brother organized a search.

The door handle squeaked.

Oh, drat, drat, drat!

Lifting her skirts, Lana scrambled to sit on the window ledge before stretching one arm toward a lower branch.

"Miss Hillary, come out, come out, my sweet." Carrington's hushed voice invaded the space. "I know you're in here. I heard your laughter, you naughty temptress. I grow weary of these childish games. Allow me to claim my prize."

Of all the—

Lana whipped her head around to deliver a sharp retort and knocked herself off balance. She pitched forward, barely grabbing the branch with both hands before slipping from the window ledge. One second she swung through the air and the next she came up short.

Oh, heavens above. Something caught her skirt, causing it to bunch up around her waist and expose her drawers for all God's tiny garden creatures to see.

Lana tightened her grip and suppressed a whimper. Why did she leave the ballroom? Giving the miserable lout a cut direct in front of the *ton* at large would have been wiser. Now, certain death might be the reward for her hasty decision. Nevertheless, one thing remained absolute; Lana would risk breaking her neck before she would call out for Carrington's assistance.

∽

Andrew Forest, the Duke of Foxhaven's youngest son, tossed his cheroot to the ground and sprang forward to rescue the young lady dangling from the tree. He had been watching her with curiosity ever since she poked her head through the open window. Only a fool would have bet on her rash action. What were ladies about these days, throwing themselves from windows? She'd barely saved herself from a nasty fall, and she remained in a precarious predicament.

"Miss Hillary?" A perplexed male voice drifted out the window.

Drew froze in place, not wishing to draw the man's attention outside. Any young lady desperate enough to escape the gent's company by means of a second-story window wouldn't wish her effort for naught.

"Are you in here, dearest?" A loud bang, like the barking of a shin against a solid piece of furniture, sounded in the room. "Bloody hell. It's too bloody dark to see a bloody thing in this damned room. Bloody, no-good chit."

Drew raised his eyebrows. Quite inappropriate language if the lady were in the room, but as luck would have it, the no-good chit swung from a tree branch with her skirts up around her middle. Drew glanced between the lady and window, debating on whether he should give away her location to save her foolish neck or trust her to hang on a smidge longer.

The room brightened a brief moment followed by the slamming of a door. The foul-mouthed gentleman gave up his search without ever checking the open window, but who would have imagined any woman so bold as to climb out a window? Drew's interest was piqued.

He hastened to the dangling debutante. "This must be my lucky night," he drawled. "It's raining ladies."

The chit kicked her legs. "Oh, get me down at once, sir. Can't you see I'm in a compromised position?"

The lady's *position* revealed a great deal of shapely ankle and long leg, a poor motivator to rush to assist the damsel under normal circumstances. "It appears your skirts are caught on the trellis. I'll climb up and release it."

"Oh, please hurry. I—" Her voice caught on a sob.

He hurried up the trellis, ignoring the pricks and pokes of thorns through his gloves. Having had his share of narrow escapes through windows, Drew held some sympathy for the young woman, but damned if he'd ever gotten himself into a pickle like this one.

"Almost there. Just a moment longer and you may let go." Drew spoke to her as he would a spooked filly while he worked the hem of her gown loose. He climbed halfway down the trellis then jumped to land with a thud. "Looks like a trip to the retiring room will be in order, but otherwise, you'll go unscathed, Miss Hillary, is it?"

The lady must be related to the Hillary men, a younger sister. What had Langford been moaning about at the club as of late? Something in the way of doubting his admiration for the miss could overcome his aversion to her mother.

Reaching up, Drew grasped her thighs in a hug. "You may let go, Miss Hillary. If you don't mind my asking, what manner of gentleman drives a lady to flee out a window?"

"Only the most despicable curs, I suppose." A violent tremor raced through her limbs despite her bravado.

Miss Hillary released the branch and even though they tottered, Drew held tight, unwilling to let her fall at this juncture. Once he had steadied them, he loosened his hold. She slid down his front, his hands brushing her delectable backside. It was a fleeting reward for his gallant act. He'd certainly received greater rewards from the fairer gender for less heroic acts.

When her feet touched the ground, his arms encircled her slim waist. She felt quite nice in his embrace and smelled like lily of the valley, sparking visions of a wild romp in a field. Perhaps he would keep her.

Her delicate hands rested against his chest. "You may release me, sir."

A flicker from the lanterns behind him illuminated her plump lips. Damn, she had fine kissable lips. Did she feel it too, this heat between them? He urged her closer and sensed the quickening of her breath. "They say if a gentleman snags a debutante, he's allowed to take her home."

Her fingers curled softly against his waistcoat and sent blood rushing to his groin. Inclining his head, he grazed his lips over hers, testing her receptivity.

She gasped and shoved her fists against his chest, twisting her face away. "Oh! Release me at once, you scoundrel."

Her commands brought a lazy smile to his face. How he'd love to hear her sultry voice issuing orders in the bedchamber. But alas, he wouldn't drag her there without consent.

"As you wish." Drew dropped his hands from her waist, but he didn't step away and neither did she. Her heat and perfume enveloped him, urging him to abandon all semblances of manners and kiss her anyway.

"I have a good mind—"

A twig snapped, causing him and the temptress to startle and knock heads.

"Ouch," she hissed and held a hand to her forehead.

"Drew?" Lady Amelia Audley called out in a hushed voice. "Did you come out here?"

Bloody nuisance. This was the last time he'd play hero to a lady in distress.

He had hoped to avoid a scene when he had spotted the widow in attendance this evening. With a tiny push, he directed the alluring Miss Hillary toward the house.

"Run along before we're discovered," he whispered.

Acknowledgments

I would like to thank Suzie Grant for sharing her abiding love of the sea, and for her patience in answering numerous nautical questions, or pointing me in the right direction. To all the lovely people at Sourcebooks, especially my editor, Deb Werksman, I offer my heartfelt thanks for their hard work. It's a pleasure working with everyone. And last but not least, I am grateful to my agent, Nephele Tempest, for generously lending her wisdom and keeping me grounded without discouraging my dreams.

About the Author

Samantha Grace is the author of *Miss Hillary Schools a Scoundrel* and *Lady Amelia's Mess and a Half*. It is her belief that everyone has a story worth remembering, and she cherishes her work with aging adults, immersing herself in their tales of eras gone by. She is happily writing her next book and loves blogging with fellow authors at Lady Scribes. Samantha is married to her best friend, strives to stay one step ahead of their two precocious offspring, and lives in Onalaska, Wisconsin.

Discover a new LOVE

Are You In Love With Love Stories?

Here's an online romance readers club that's just for YOU!

Where you can:

- **Meet** great *authors*
- **Party** with new *friends*
- **Get** new *books* before everyone else
- **Discover** great *new reads*

All at incredibly BIG savings!

**Join the party at
DiscoveraNewLove.com!**

Lady Amelia's Mess and a Half

by Samantha Grace

— ❧ —

Jake broke her heart by leaving for the country after sharing a passionate kiss.

Lady Amelia broke his by marrying his best friend.

When she returns to town a widow—pursued by an infamous rake, Jake's debauched brother, and just maybe by Jake himself—Lady Amelia will have a mess and a half on her hands.

A sparkling romp through the ton, Lady Amelia's Mess and a Half *delivers a witty Regency romance in which misunderstandings abound, reputations are put on the line, and the only thing more exciting than a scandal is true love.*

— ❧ —

"Clever, spicy, and fresh from beginning to end."—Amelia Grey, award-winning author of *A Gentleman Never Tells*

"A delightfully witty romp seasoned with an irresistible dash of intrigue and passion. Samantha Grace is an author to watch!"—Shana Galen, award-winning author of *Lord and Lady Spy*

For more Samantha Grace, visit:

www.sourcebooks.com

A Little Mischief

by Amelia Grey

— ❧ —

How can a lady avoid a scandal…

Just as Miss Isabella Winslowe is finally achieving comfortable respectability, the fascinating and decidedly unrespectable Earl of Colebrooke inconveniently appears…

When a gentleman is so determined to flirt…

The darkly handsome Daniel Colebrooke is intrigued and alarmed when an alluring young lady arrives at his door in need of assistance. In a moment of impetuosity, Daniel decides he must keep a close watch on Isabella, and what better way than to strike up a not-so-innocent flirtation…

Together they'll cook up more than a little mischief when a disappearing dead body and a lascivious scandal spins their reckless game entirely out of control.

— ❧ —

"If you like Amanda Quick, you will absolutely LOVE Amelia Grey."—A Romance Review

For more Amelia Grey, visit:

www.sourcebooks.com

When You Give a Duke a Diamond

by Shana Galen

He had a perfectly orderly life...

William, the sixth Duke of Pelham, enjoys his punctual, securely structured life. Orderly and predictable—that's the way he likes it. But he's in the public eye, and the scandal sheets will make up anything to sell papers. When the gossips link him to Juliette, one of the most beautiful and celebrated courtesans in London, chaos doesn't begin to describe what happens next...

Until she came along...

Juliette is nicknamed the Duchess of Dalliance, and has the cream of the nobility at her beck and call. It's seriously disruptive to have the duke who's the biggest catch on the Marriage Mart scaring her other suitors away. Then she discovers William's darkest secret and decides what he needs in his life is the kind of excitement only she can provide...

For more Shana Galen, visit:

www.sourcebooks.com

New York Times Bestselling Author

Lessons in French

by Laura Kinsale

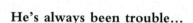

He's always been trouble...

Trevelyan and Callie are childhood sweethearts with a taste for adventure. Until the fateful day her father discovers them embracing in the carriage house and in a furious frenzy drives Trevelyan away in disgrace...

Exactly the kind of trouble she's never been able to resist...

Nine long, lonely years later, Trevelyan returns. Callie is shocked to discover that he can still make her blood race and fill her life with mischief, excitement, and scandal. He would give her the world, but he can't give her the one thing she wants more than anything—himself...

For Trevelyan, Callie is a spark of light in a world of darkness and deceit. Before he can bear to say his last good-byes, he's determined to sweep her into one last, fateful adventure, just for the two of them...

For more Laura Kinsale, visit:

www.sourcebooks.com

Fortune's Son

by Emery Lee

She is the ultimate gamble...

Beautiful young widow Susannah, Lady Messingham, refuses to belong to any man again. Until she inadvertently draws handsome Lord Philip Drake into an exhilarating game of terrifying stakes and unimaginable rewards...

And he'll risk everything on a toss of the dice...

Philip is a seasoned gambler who knows all the tricks and isn't afraid to use them. He'd do anything for Susannah, including sacrificing his honor and his freedom...

For more Emery Lee, visit:

www.sourcebooks.com

The Most Improper Miss Sophie Valentine

by Jayne Fresina

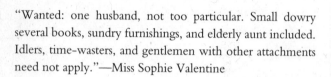

"Wanted: one husband, not too particular. Small dowry, several books, sundry furnishings, and elderly aunt included. Idlers, time-wasters, and gentlemen with other attachments need not apply."—Miss Sophie Valentine

A Scandalous Lady

Sophie Valentine knew placing an ad for a husband in the Farmer's Gazette would bring her trouble—and she was right. When the darkly handsome, arrogantly charming Lazarus Kane shows up on her doorstep, the nosy residents of Sydney Dovedale are thrown into a gossiping tizzy. After all, it's common knowledge that Sophie is a young lady In Need of Firmer Direction. But even Sophie isn't so scandalous as to marry a complete stranger...is she?

Seeks Handsome Stranger

Lazarus Kane has been searching for Sophie half of his life. She may not remember him, but he could never forget her. But the past is a dangerous thing, and it's best if his remains secret if he wants to tempt Sophie with...

A Most Improper Proposal